Neil Tidmarsh lives in central London. *Crackle* is his second novel. His first novel was *Fear of the Dog*:

'A clever, sophisticated crime novel with more twists than a mastiff's tail.' *The Sunday Times*

'Neil Tidmarsh's blackly ingenious thriller... displays an impressive knowledge... The skill with which he keeps us guessing... makes this a gripping read.' *Cosmopolitan*

'It's British, brutal and clever, set in London's art world, a brilliant and frightening study of a psychotic mind. Very good indeed... could not put it down.' *The Bookseller*

'Tidmarsh's strength in this book is the clarity and simplicity of his writing. He knows when to leave a sentence well alone, when you do and do not need adverbs, how much description is just enough... The deaths in the book are original and suitably gory and the set-up is admirably meticulous.' *The Times*

GU00382096

CRACKLE

Neil Tidmarsh

Copyright © Neil Tidmarsh 2014, 2017

Neil Tidmarsh asserts the moral right to be identified as
the author of this work

ISBN 9781521339008

All rights reserved. No part of this publication may be
reproduced, stored in a retrieval system, or transmitted, in
any form or by any means, electronic, mechanical,
photocopying, recording or otherwise, without the prior
written permission of the author.

For Jan
with love and thanks

PART I

'That motley drama – oh, be sure
It shall not be forgot…'

Edgar Allan Poe, *The Conqueror Worm*

'At Clare… we brake down 1000 pictures superstitious…
and the sun and the moon in the east window, by the
King's arms, to be taken down…'

William Dowsing, January 1543

Chapter One

I gripped the scaffolding pole with both hands and swung it as hard as I could. Boom! A sound like a bellow of pain and fear echoed around the deserted street. But the big window didn't break - the heavy pole just bounced off it.

I tightened my grip. I took a deep breath. I swung the pole again. Harder. Again it bounced off the thick glass. But this time a sharp 'crack!' like a gunshot rang out through the darkness. I peered at the window. Now it was frosted with a spider's web of fractures, spreading out from a puncture-hole at its centre.

I gritted my teeth, closed my eyes, and swung the pole yet again. The window exploded. A shower of crystals and shards flew through the air, crashing and tinkling all around me, clattering and tapping on my crash-helmet and visor. A burglar alarm began to scream inside the gallery.

I climbed in through the smashed window. It was dark out in the Mayfair street, but it was even darker inside. I stumbled against a big canvas in a heavy frame. The legs of its easel tried to trip me up as it toppled over. I angrily kicked it aside. I was shaking and trembling. My heart was pounding. The alarm was shrieking at me, hurting my ears, freezing my thoughts. But I didn't hesitate. I knew what I had to do and I was determined to do it. The police would be here in minutes but I only needed seconds.

There it was, in the far corner of the gallery, crouching where the shadows were at their thickest. I made straight for it, ignoring the canvases crowding the walls on either side. It emerged from the darkness; inane, obscene, flippant, just as I remembered it. A life-sized statue of a naked man, moulded in clear Perspex, filled like a pill-bottle with thousands and thousands of little blue tablets. He had a big grin and a massive erection. We stared at

1

each other for a moment, face to face. In the shadows, he seemed to glow with a strange purple light. I could see the reflection of my own crash-helmeted head in the Perspex of his brow.

'Adam'. By Harry Jutting. Sculpture. Life-sized. Modelled on Michaelangelo's 'David'. Perspex, hollow, moulded. Filling: Viagra tablets.

I was still clutching the scaffolding pole in my gauntleted hands. I swung it with a roar of anger and hatred. The statue shattered. Fragments of broken Perspex flew through the air, smashed against the wall, skidded across the floor. A torrent of little pills rained down on the polished wooden boards, flooded the Persian rugs. Suddenly Adam was no longer standing there. He had disappeared. There was just a carpeting of broken Perspex and purple pills across the gallery from wall to wall. I attacked the scattered scraps of torso and arm and leg and head, smashing them with the pole, stamping on them, kicking them, grinding the pills to powder under my feet. I was gasping, grunting, shouting with triumph and exertion and rage.

It was done. I dropped the scaffolding pole. I turned and walked away, my biker-boots crunching on the debris. I stepped out through the broken window onto the pavement. The street was still deserted, the alarm was still screaming. In the distance I could hear the wail of a police siren. It was coming closer. It was coming from my right, from Piccadilly. I turned left. I wanted to run. I forced myself to walk. Stay calm. I came to a corner and turned left down a side-street, hearing the police-car come screeching into the high-street and pull up outside the gallery. Now I ran. I ran past dustbins and back doors and blank walls. Then the alleyway turned to the right and suddenly I was back on another Mayfair high street, wide and bright and glitzy, even in the early hours.

I stopped running and turned left, walking west towards Park Lane. I could still hear the alarm and the police siren, but they were fading into the background noises of a city at night. There was traffic in this street, groaning taxis and the occasional car, and even pedestrians. Where were they going at this time of the morning? Where had they come from? I walked on past art galleries, designer shops, fashion houses, eager to get away, not just from the police but from the oppressive luxury and restless glitter of the whole area.

I listened hard for more sirens, for the screeching tyres of speeding police cars. For the sound of running feet behind me, for shouts ordering me stop. The crash-helmet muffled my hearing, but I wasn't taking it off. The whole area was thick with security cameras and I wasn't about to show my face to any of them. I walked faster, in spite of myself. Every instinct screaming for cover. How conspicuous was I, a figure in full motorcycle gear – helmet, boots, gauntlets and leathers – walking down a street built for millionaire shoppers, at two o'clock in the morning? Hyde Park seemed a long way away, my bike even further still, home and safety unimaginably distant, another planet.

Then suddenly Park Lane was in front of me, a deafening, brightly-lit, ever-flowing river of traffic. And beyond it was the beckoning darkness and emptiness of Hyde Park. I ran across the south-bound carriageway, paused under the trees in the central reservation, then ran across the north-bound carriageway. Nearly there. I crossed the pavement and was up and over the railings in a few second's mad scramble. I crouched among the bushes at the base of a big plane tree. Had anyone seen me? No. I stood up and strode off into the darkness.

I was pretty sure there'd be no security cameras covering the perimeter of the park. But even if there were,

I doubted that anyone would connect a figure entering the park from Park Lane with a figure leaving half-a-mile away at Bayswater, let alone tracking me from there to Notting Hill where I'd left my bike. In half-an-hour's time I'd be back on the road, heading out of London. In less than three hours I'd be home. Safe and sound.

It was very dark and still and quiet in the park. I breathed slowly and deeply as I walked. I realised I was grinning. Then suddenly I was laughing. It sounded strange in the silence and darkness of the park. It was the sound of relief and triumph.

I had done it. I had destroyed 'Adam' by Harry Jutting. It no longer existed. I'd done it and I'd got away with it.

Harry Jutting. I hated that bastard. I was going to wipe every last trace of him off the face of the earth.

*

I turned off the main road at the top of the hill. It was already light.

I didn't want to wake anyone up so I stopped the bike in the Farm Shop's car-park. I cut the engine and dismounted. I took my helmet off and stood there beneath the Scots pines, blinking in the sea-reflected light of a new day. The fresh air on my face felt wonderful. It was clear and clean and smelt of the ocean. A few gulls cried overhead. The oaks on the side of the hill swayed in a light breeze, sighing and creaking. The hell of central London was a million miles away. A bad dream I'd left far behind.

I walked down the hill. The lane was rutted and overgrown. It dipped and turned, and there - at the bottom of the hill, on the edge of the pastureland – was the house. It was small and plain, just an ordinary farm-labourer's cottage. A rather ugly square block of red brick and grey slate, facing south and east across the marsh.

Exposed to the sun and the sea-wind, and standing just below sea-level. It was baking in the summer, and very damp and chilly in the winter, and the salty air ate away at its woodwork all year round. But it was home. Our home. Safe. Hidden. A perfect refuge. I looked down at it, feeling the usual strange mixture of relief and gratitude and incredulity. Sometimes I couldn't believe my luck. Sometimes, when I was away, I didn't believe it, and the terrible idea that it wasn't real, that I had imagined it, would torment me.

Beyond the house, the flat green pastureland spread out towards the horizon. It was criss-crossed with dikes and sluices and separated from the sea by the big sea-wall a few miles away. The wall was so high and so distant that I couldn't see the pebble-beach or the cold, heaving, grey-green ocean on the other side of it. If the sea-wall ever broke, the pastureland would be flooded and the cottage would be inundated or simply swept away. I often had nightmares about that. Terrifying visions of a huge tidal-wave bearing down on us. The cottage reduced to a muddy ruin sticking up out of a salt-marsh. Or submerged beneath the waters of a tidal lagoon.

I let myself in as quietly as I could. I dumped my helmet and boots and gauntlets in the kitchen and crept upstairs. The door to the children's room was closed. I listened hard. Silence. The door to our room was open. I peered inside.

Helen was still asleep, sprawled across the double bed. Bare feet and ankles stuck out from the bottom of the duvet, bare arms and a glimpse of black t-shirt from the top. A tangled mass of copper hair all over the pillow. Her eyes were closed, her mouth slightly open. She was breathing slowly and deeply. She turned in her sleep and threw her left arm out across the empty half of the bed. I could see the white scar there, long and thick, running up from her elbow towards her shoulder.

It was strange to see her lying so still. To see how small and skinny she really was. Frail, even. You didn't notice it when she was awake, when she was on the move, she was always so full of life and energy.

I went down to the kitchen and took a bottle of formula from the fridge and put it in the warmer. Then I went back upstairs and listened at the children's door. I could hear Richard rummaging and rustling around in his cot now. He was ready for a feed. Any minute now he'd start crying and that would be the end of Helen's lie-in. I opened the door softly and went into the room.

Liz was still asleep, just a motionless heap under her duvet on the bed against the wall. But Richard was lying on his back thrusting his arms and legs into the air. His head turned and his eyes widened as soon as I came into the room. I leaned over his cot and he grinned and chuckled. He was four months old. 'Good morning, sir,' I whispered. 'Were you kind to your mother last night? No midnight feasts?'

He was like his mother – short and thin and pale and red-haired, full of fun and, I was sure, good sense. His sister was more like me – always serious, and often anxious, and... But I didn't like to think about that. It made me worry about her.

I got him out of his cot and changed his nappy. Then I carried him down to the kitchen and washed my hands and grabbed the bottle. As soon as he saw it, his grin stretched itself into a grimace of impatience and excitement. But I got him back upstairs before he could start screaming and shouting, got ourselves settled in the armchair beside his cot, and soon enough he was happily gulping away.

Liz stirred and sat up in bed and rubbed her eyes.

'Hello, sweetie,' I said 'Sleep well?' I wanted to get up and kiss her, but Richard was in my lap, his hands clamped tight round the bottle, sucking hard. I hoped she'd get up and come over and kiss me and put her arms around me, but she just sat there gazing at me with blank eyes.

'Do hedgehogs have tails?' she asked.

I almost laughed, but I managed to stop myself. It would have upset her, insulted her. She'd asked me a serious question, she deserved a serious answer. 'Well,' I said. Do they? Do they have tails? 'Remember when we saw a couple of them out by the shed, last week? It was a bit dark, but…'

She peered at me, frowning, still half-asleep.

'Of course they have tails!' Helen was standing in the doorway, leaning against the frame. Bare legs thin and pale under her short t-shirt, bare arms crossed, hair tumbled around her face. She was laughing. 'Just like you!'

Liz looked up at her. She blinked once, twice. She frowned. Then she shrieked with laughter. 'I do not have a tail!' She was still sitting on the bed, but she was bouncing up and down on it now, outraged and happy and amused. 'I don't!'

'You do! You have a tail just like a hedgehog!'

'I don't! Where is it? I can't see it!'

'Just because you can't see it, doesn't mean it isn't there. Can you see the bottom of your back, just above your bum? No, you can't. Well, there you are then. That's where it is, just where the hedgehogs have their tails!'

Liz was on her feet now, laughing madly, twisting to and fro, trying to look over her shoulder and round her side, running her hands over the small of her back.

'I can see it!' Helen exclaimed. 'Under your pyjamas! There it is! There!'

'It's not! It's not! I don't have a tail! I don't!'

'Go and look in the mirror in the bathroom, then, if you don't believe me!'

'You've got a tail! You've got one! You're the one with the tail!' Liz rushed out of the room and across the landing.

'I know! But mine's a cat's tail!' Helen called after her. 'And Daddy's got a fox's tail! And Richard's is a mouse's!' She looked down at me feeding Richard. He was still drinking but he was waving his arms and legs around and grunting, excited by the laughter and action all around him. 'I can put my boobs away, then,' she said. She uncrossed her arms and I saw the damp patches on her t-shirt over her small breasts.

'I thought I'd give him a feed. Save you getting up.' I could hear Liz laughing in the bathroom. As usual, the sound of it made me feel both happy and strangely sad. Happy that Helen could make our serious daughter laugh so easily. Sad that I couldn't. 'How was he in the night?'

'He slept right through.' She put both hands up to her face and pushed her hair out of her eyes. 'I slept like a log. Feel like I've already had the longest lie-in ever.' She sat down on Liz's bed. 'Did your mistress give you a good time last night?'

I looked up at her, shocked. She was laughing, joking, but I was still shocked. I looked down at Richard. I looked up, out of the door, across the landing. We could hear Liz in the bathroom, jumping up and down in front of the mirror. 'You shouldn't talk like that. The children…'

'Oh, Richard can't understand, Liz can't hear.' She got up from the bed and came and sat on the arm of the chair beside me. She kissed me. 'I'm only joking, Will. You're so serious.' She stroked Richard's sucking cheek. 'I don't know where you go at night and I don't care. You've told me you'd never do anything to hurt us or upset us, and I believe you. You don't have to tell me where you go, what you do. I trust you. I know you love me, Will. And Liz, and Richard. That's all we need to know. That's all that matters.'

I couldn't speak. I couldn't look at her, even. I watched Richard emptying the bottle.

'And thanks for feeding Richard.'

'Do you want to take over? He's nearly done, anyway, but if you take him for a moment I can go and get breakfast ready.' I stood up, and when she'd settled herself in the chair I handed the baby over, teat still in mouth.

'Thanks. I thought I'd take them out for a walk this morning. Across the marsh to the sea. If you've been up all night, you'll need a kip, a bit of peace and quiet.' She put Richard up on her shoulder and patted his back. He belched and a trickle of milk ran down his chin. 'Oh, and Fred was wondering if you could give him a hand this afternoon, with the calving.'

Fred Barrett was the farmer we rented the cottage from. His place was half a mile further along the lane. Helen worked part-time in his Farm Shop up by the main road. They were his cows grazing the pastureland between the hill and the sea-wall. 'Sure. I'll go down there after lunch.'

Liz came back into the bedroom. 'I knew I didn't have a tail. I knew it.' She gave her mother a playful swipe on the left arm, giggling, but she looked disappointed. She took Helen's left hand in both of hers and snuggled against her, rubbing her head against the long white scar.

A security guard had been clumsy with his bolt-cutters when Helen had handcuffed herself to a mechanical digger, trying to save ten acres of ancient woodland from development. It had happened years ago, before I'd known her. The stitches had only just come out when I'd first met her, and the idiot who'd been her boyfriend at the time wouldn't stop going on about it. 'He was a right fascist bastard, that guard, a real animal! You should have seen it! There was blood everywhere! I thought he'd cut her bloody arm off! He did it deliberately, the bastard, he thought it was funny!'

Helen had laughed. 'No, he didn't. He was scared and panicking. There was a battle raging all around us. Everyone was pushing and pulling and shoving, me included. He slipped, it was an accident. He was even more upset about it than I was. He was in tears, poor sod!'

She had tried to laugh it off, but I was sure that she'd fought fiercely and passionately for what she'd loved and believed in then. What she loved and believed in now was our children, Richard and Liz. And seeing her looking even more tigerish than ever with her red hair falling all over the shoulders of her black t-shirt, I was sure that she'd fight even more fiercely and passionately against any danger that threatened them.

Even if, God forbid, that danger ever happened to be me.

*

After breakfast Helen and Liz pulled on their wellies and put Richard into the baby sling and set off across the fields to the sea. But I didn't go to bed. I cleaned out the wood-burning stove in the sitting room. I bagged up the cold ashes and laid paper and fire-lighter and kindling. But didn't light it. It was warm for early April. We wouldn't need a fire until the afternoon. In another month or two we wouldn't need a fire at all.

I took the ashes out to the shed behind the house. I'd extended the shed myself when we'd moved in, building out the wooden walls and tiled roof until it was big enough to work in. Now it was a good-sized studio. I put the bag of ashes on a shelf with other ingredients for glazes – felspar, china clay, oxides – and looked around. Everything was in good order. A pottery workshop has to be kept neat and tidy, especially if there are children about. It can be a dangerous place. Some materials are harmful. Powdered flint can damage the lungs if you breathe it in. Many of the oxides used to colour glazes are toxic. A working kiln is terrifically hot and can give off noxious fumes. Years ago I'd been messy and careless in my work, but ever since Liz and Richard had been born I'd been careful enough.

Not that the children often came into the studio. Nor Helen. But it wasn't as if I discouraged them. I suppose they just sort of felt it was my personal space.

I pulled a cardboard box out from the back of a cupboard. There was a pile of newspapers in the box. I'd hidden the catalogue under the newspapers. I took it out and sat down at the table and opened it. 'Harry Jutting: the Complete Works'. A catalogue raisonné. Compiled a year after his death. The what and the where and the how much. Published by Scott Feathers, the Pyramid Gallery. I turned to the list at the back. The first five items had been crossed off. The sixth item was 'Adam. Sculpture. Life-sized. Modelled on Michaelangelo's 'David'…'

I took a marker pen and crossed it off the list.

I looked at the next item on the list. 'Eve. Sculpture. Life-sized. Modelled on the Venus de Milo. Perspex, hollow, moulded. Filling: silicone implant sacks… Companion-piece to Adam (see above)… Pallant House collection, Chichester, W.Sussex…' I sat and thought about that for a while.

Chichester. Not so very far away. On the bike, I could be there and back in half a day. I knew Pallant House. A beautiful eighteenth-century townhouse converted into a museum of fine art. Modern British art. A public art gallery - it would have to be a daylight job. I didn't like the idea of that. Dangerous. Was I frightened? Yes, for a moment, thinking about it. Then I thought about Eve, the sculpture, and I wanted to destroy it, I couldn't wait to destroy it. I remembered smashing Adam, the satisfaction of it, the savage joy. I would do the same to Eve. I had to do it. I had no choice in the matter.

When could I do it? Friday. Three day's time. Could I wait that long? Yes, I'd have to. Friday was soon enough.

I put the catalogue back under the pile of newspapers and put the cardboard box back in the cupboard.

I stood up and stretched and walked slowly round the place. I always felt relaxed yet excited in there. Eager to get down to work, to disappear into it. Work is always a good hiding-place. I felt safe in the studio. It was so private, so familiar. There, in the big plastic dustbin, was prepared clay, wrapped in polythene bags, all ready for use. And there was my power-wheel, the turning tools - scrapers, palette knives, sponges, leathers, ribs, cutting-wire, callipers - all laid out beside it. There was my faithful, hard-working kiln, an electric top-loader; bats and props were stacked against the wall, rows of pyrometric cones stood ready on a shelf.

But I was too tired to do any real work. Not that there was much I could do at that moment anyway. I checked a batch of greenware I'd thrown over the last couple of days. A tea-pot, tea cups, a couple of vases. They'd all dried out nicely. No shrinkage or cracking. Now they were ready for biscuit-firing. But I wouldn't load up the kiln and get it going until that evening. Then it would have all night to build up heat slowly and evenly. And tomorrow I could take it up to the higher temperatures to complete the firing.

I'd already mixed the glaze for it. It had been standing overnight in a big ten-litre bucket. I stirred it and sieved it through a hundred-mesh lawn and then left it to stand again. It would be good and ready when I needed it in a couple of day's time. I looked around for something else to do. I took that morning's bag of ash from the shelf and emptied it into another bucket. I filled it with water, gave it a good stir and then sieved it through an eighty-mesh lawn into another bucket. Right... give that a while to settle before pouring off the water... What shall I do while I'm waiting..? Let's see what's in that bin of reclaimed scraps... No, I'll just sit down for a moment... a bit of a rest...

I came round with a start, my head resting on the table. I'd been fast asleep. The crunching sound of a car pulling up outside the house had woken me. A car. That was rare. There was hardly ever any traffic in the lane. Tractors and vans only, coming and going to Fred's place further along. I stood up, feeling dizzy and weak-kneed. Still half-asleep, I left the shed and walked unsteadily across the yard and back into the house. I could hear knocking at the front door. I froze, suddenly wide awake. Knocking at our door? I wanted to ignore it. I didn't want visitors. I didn't like visitors.

I'd been in hiding for ten years. And time hadn't blunted the dread of being found out. It had sharpened it. I had so much more to lose now. There was no forgetting why I was hiding, what I was hiding from. It was always there, bubbling away in the darkness, like a dangerous and unstable chemical in an abandoned laboratory. And now I could smell its fumes, caustic and toxic. I could taste it. I was afraid.

I peered out through the kitchen window. A fair-haired young woman, hand raised to knock again. Behind her, a bored and impatient looking young man. A shiny Mercedes stood in the lane, blocking it. They'll have trouble turning that round, I thought. My mind was still groggy from sleep. Even more trouble reversing all the

13

way back to the main road. I shook my head to try and clear it.

Who were they? What did they want?

I opened the door. The young woman looked up and smiled, eyebrows raised, an apologetic smile acknowledging the intrusion. Her right hand, coming down from the knocker, turned towards me in greeting. Her left hand held a coffee-pot. I recognised the coffee-pot.

'Hiya!' she said. Her smile broadened nervously. Her voice was bright, ingratiating, uncertain. 'Listen, I'm really, really sorry to bother you and everything… but are you… are you… William Brin?' She said my name as if it was new to her, wasn't too sure how to pronounce it or something.

'Yes?'

'Ah!' She laughed, pleased but still hesitant. 'Look, er, I brought this, this pot of yours – it is yours, isn't it? You made it? – over at Burmarsh, Burmark – is that the name of the village, John?' She turned round to her companion and he gave the slightest of nods, saturnine and impassive behind his wispy beard and dark glasses – he was wearing skinny jeans rolled-up at the ankle, which made him look like a fifteen-year old. 'Yes, Burmark, a shop called Anna's, lovely shop, I suppose you know it of course, they have lots of your pieces there, cups and tea-pots and mugs and coffee-pots and… you know… and I thought they were wonderful, really, really exquisite, beautiful, unique, I asked who made them, asked about you, looked you up, found out where you lived, and here I am. I just wanted to meet you, ask about your work, tell you how much I like it. I'm really sorry, I really hope you don't mind…'

I looked at her. I was confused. She had a nice face, an attractive figure, she seemed to be a nice girl, pleasant, polite. But she was dressed… well, she wasn't dressed for

14

our rural backwater. She was so polished and burnished and gilded that she glowed with a sort of unnatural, artificial beauty. Her hair was metallically bright and fluffy and so blonde it was almost white. Her skin was tanned a deep gold. She was wearing what looked like tights – black, thick, skin-tight - but no skirt. Knee length suede boots with high heels and lots of metal buckles. A short black leather jacket flared around the waist. A pale-blue t-shirt. Low-cut. A necklace of silver wire dumped a big cluster of amber beads in her deep cleavage. I felt shy. Embarrassed. I didn't know where to look. 'Thank you,' I said. 'No, I don't mind at all…'

'Oh good!' She laughed, relieved. She held out her hand. 'I'm Becky, by the way. And this is John…'

I shook her hand. John nodded at me impassively, his hands in the pockets of his vintage tweed jacket. I eyed the coffee pot. 'Look, why don't you both come in and I'll put the kettle on and we can get that pot working for us?'

'That would be wonderful, thank you, yes!' She looked very grateful. Her hand had felt cold, and she was shivering. The weather wasn't quite warm enough yet for her kind of outfit.

'Would you mind pulling your car off the lane a bit, please? Just into this gateway here. My neighbour needs to get his tractor past every now and then. Thanks.'

I led the way through to the kitchen. She talked all the time, looking all around, taking it all in. Our house, our home. 'We're just down here for a couple of days, a little break, we've never been down this way before. Isn't it beautiful? So out of the way, peaceful, but not so very far from London, really…'

I took the pot off her and rinsed it under the tap. I dried it and spooned ground coffee in and put the kettle on. All the while she was looking at all the other crockery in the kitchen, gasping and nodding as she picked up mugs and cups and plates and saucers. 'All your work? Unusual. Unique.' Her manner had changed. She was no longer nervous and uncertain. She was calm and focused. 'The shapes – very novel, and very pleasing, to hold, and to look at – but I can see they're highly functional as well – not merely decorative, or even primarily decorative… Why hasn't someone made a tea-pot this shape before? It seems obvious, looking at it now, but it really is unusual…' I looked at her, looking at the pieces. She wasn't smiling any more, but frowning in concentration. A more serious, intelligent, authentic Becky was emerging. She opened her bag and took out a camera. 'May I?'

'No!' I hadn't meant to shout. But that's how it came out. It startled the girl. She jumped, almost dropping the camera. 'No photos. Please. If you don't mind.' She gave me an odd look, frowning and puzzled, but put the camera away. The kettle boiled. I filled the pot, stirred it, put the lid on and took three coffee cups from the shelf beside the sink. I put out a milk jug and a sugar bowl and filled the three mugs.

'Thanks.' The girl took her coffee. I could see that she was wearing a lot of make-up. It was very carefully applied, you didn't really notice it until you were close up. And I could smell her perfume – something sweet and floral, as clean and new and antiseptic as an air-freshener. 'Porcelain. All porcelain. No stoneware? No earthenware?'

'No. Only porcelain.'

'Why is that? Isn't porcelain difficult? I mean, stiff to work with? And don't you need really high temperatures in the kiln?'

I shrugged. 'It's hard-wearing. Practical. Impermeable. Safe to eat out of.'

'Not because it's beautiful? I mean, look at this. It's so delicate, so light. Translucent. It really is beautiful, isn't it?'

Beautiful? I felt a stab of irritation. But I didn't say anything.

'And the wonderful colours - pale green, pale blue, pale yellow. White, cream. So subtle, and yet so rich… How do you do that? Do you use reduction firing? Is that how you get such depth to them?'

She knew her stuff, all right. I sighed and nodded. 'Yes. I always reduction fire.' I paused. 'The colours… I don't like them to distract from the pot itself, its form and function, what it does, what it's for. High temperature glazes are quieter, less shiny. And I use ash in the glazes. Tends to produce subtle colours. Less distracting, as I said. These pots are to be used, they're not ornaments.'

'Why so practical? Why shouldn't they be ornaments as well? Because they are, you know. Aren't they?'

'No. They are not.' Ornaments? Now irritation had become annoyance. It was threatening to burst into a hot anger. I could feel it beginning to bubble and swirl around in my guts. Careful. You're tired. You're half asleep. Don't lose control. 'They are not ornaments. Where's the decoration? There isn't any. I never decorate.' I could hear my voice getting louder. 'Where's the incising? The impressing? The relief, the inlay, the marbling? Show me. Where is it? The sgraffitto? The slip-trailing? The slip-painting? The wax-resist? The stencil-resist? The underglaze painting?'

'Ok, ok.' She laughed, but it was nervous laughter, and I saw the look she exchanged with her companion. 'I hear what you say. But some people – people who knew what they were talking about – would say that your work was more than merely functional. They would say it was art.'

Art? I breathed in sharply. The anger inside my head was about to explode. Get a grip, I told myself. For heaven's sake control yourself. Don't start. Don't.

She looked around the room, still puzzled and frowning. 'You know, I would expect the house of the man who made these to be full of art. Paintings, drawings, pictures all over the walls. But the walls here are bare. And nothing in the hall, or in the corridor....'

'Don't use that word in here.'

She looked at me, blinking. 'What word?'

'Art.' I was beginning to tremble. I couldn't stop myself. I tried, but I could feel my self-control slipping through my fingers. 'There's no art in this house. And no television, no computer.'

'Why not? Everybody likes to have nice pictures on their walls. We don't all agree on what makes a nice picture, of course, but something pleasing, refreshing, inspiring...'

'No picture can do that. Look out of the window. There's beauty for you. The only beauty. Nature. There's nothing more pleasing, refreshing or inspiring than that. God's work. The real thing.' I wasn't speaking slowly or quietly any more. The words were tumbling out, hot and angry, and my voice was rising again. 'Anything man makes, it's artificial, it's fantasy, it's second rate! And it's dangerous, arrogant, presumptive! The painter, the sculptor, the film-maker, they're pretending to be gods, they're usurping God's position as creator! They're competing with God! How dare they?'

'But you are an artist! This is art!' She held out the coffee cup, indicating the pot. She seemed puzzled, hurt.

'Take that back!' I demanded. 'I am not an artist! This is not art! I am just a technician! I make things which work, things which people need! Humble things! Useful, practical things!'

She laughed incredulously, threw back her hair and put her mug down. She wasn't going to back down from this argument, not even for the sake of politeness. 'Either

18

you're blind, or you're fooling yourself. I've never seen work like this before. You're not doing yourself justice. Your work deserves more than that. Listen, I'm a journalist. I write for 'Forwards Backwards'. Do you know it? It's a style magazine. I'd love to do a piece on you. And there are galleries in London which would love to see some of this, to show it. To sell it. I could make introductions for you. Your prices... you're really under-selling yourself... people would pay ten times as much...'

She was pulling a business card out of a wallet. 'Believe me, this is art. You are an artist. I should know.'

'Get out!' I was no longer wrestling with my anger. It had leapt free, something too hot and strong to hold on to. Its seething red mist clouded my sight. It was like looking through the spy-hole into my hot kiln and seeing the dull red glow grow into something fierce and roaring and frightening, something too painful to watch with the naked eye. I snatched her coffee cup from her and emptied it into the sink. 'Get out of my house!'

'But...' The girl flushed. She was upset and confused, but determined. 'I don't understand. You're a creator, you're creative, you need...'

'Creator? Creative?' I was shouting now. 'I'll tell you what's creative! There are cows in a barn down the road which are giving birth even as we speak! Have you ever seen that? That's creation for you, and the only artist with a hand in that is God!'

'Right. I'm going. I'm only trying to help. There's no need...'

'Birth! It's a miracle! The miracle of creation! But what do we worship these days? Pictures and sculptures and movies. Idle fantasies, make-believe, evil imitations of reality! We waste all our money on them, all our time, when we should be paying attention to the real world, to its miraculous beauties and challenges, and worshipping the power that made it for us!'

'There's no need to shout. We're going.' She was shaking. She looked very frightened. She wasn't flushed now, but very pale beneath her make-up. She turned to the door, then stopped. 'But I'll take my coffee pot with me. Please.'

'You won't! It's my pot! I'm not having you showing it around to magazine editors and gallery owners and art critics!'

'I've paid for it. A lot less than it's worth, I grant you. But I bought it.'

'I'll buy it back, then! How much?'

'It's not for sale. My pot, please.'

In my rage I almost smashed it over her head, almost poured hot coffee and dirty grounds all over her unnaturally-bright blonde hair. But somehow I restrained myself. I thrust it at her, half full and still warm as it was, and she took it from me and stalked from the house. Her boyfriend followed her. 'Nutter' he muttered, sneering at me. 'Bloody nutter.' He checked the rear of the car to make sure it hadn't been scraped by passing farm vehicles, then got in. They reversed noisily back up the lane. Angry though I was, I felt a stab of guilt that I'd forgotten to suggest they drove on to turn round in Fred's yard.

I should have broken that bloody pot, I thought as I turned back into the house. Given it back to her in pieces. I sat in the kitchen until I'd stopped shaking and my breathing and heart-beat slowed down and my anger ebbed away. Then I regretted losing my temper. I regretted my rudeness. She hadn't meant any harm. She'd been pleasant. She was a nice person, I could tell. Even if she did dress like… well, that was her business. She was only trying to help. Well, too late now. I shook my head. I was too tired for company. Perhaps I should have gone to bed after breakfast after all.

But there was a valuable lesson here, and I'd do well to learn from it; losing my temper wasn't just rude, it was dangerous. I must not lose control, I must not let myself go, I must not give anything away.

*

I helped Fred with the calving that afternoon. It was what it always is. Exciting. Frightening. Humbling. Ugly. Beautiful. We worked hard and it went well. There were no complications, no emergency calls to the vet, no deaths.

Afterwards we went into the farmhouse to clean ourselves up and Fred's wife Mary made a pot of tea and cut us some cake. Fred made himself a ham sandwich and poured a glass of whisky. 'Fancy some?' he asked, then laughed before I could reply so I'd know he was joking. He shook his head. 'I don't know. Vegetarian. T-total. Perhaps I'll try it myself one day. Might save me from a heart-attack. Might put me out of business, though.'

We went into their sitting-room, to chat in competition with the television blaring centre-stage half-watched by their two children. 'Oh, hello, Mr Brin,' Kylie said brightly. Skinny and freckled and eleven years old. She was busy painting her finger-nails and toe-nails bright purple. Her mouth was vivid with garish lipstick. 'Like the shade?' She wiggled her fingers at me. 'Midnight Beauty, it's called.'

'Oh Kylie.' Her mother chided her gently, flushing, embarrassed by her daughter's precociousness, her flirtatiousness. 'I don't suppose it'll do her any harm. I dare say I shouldn't allow it, but it stops her from nagging on about getting a tattoo.'

'Can I have a tattoo?' Kylie sprang up, eager and demanding. 'When can I have a tattoo? I want a butterfly right here, and - '

'Andy, say hello to Mr Brin.' Fred spoke sternly. He was tired. He wanted a bit of peace and quiet, but the sound of the television was drilling into his nerves.

Andy turned from the television and tried to focus dull, empty eyes on me. He frowned silently, conscious thought just evading him. He grunted, and turned back to the television. He was fifteen years old. I'd known him for quite a while, but I don't think I'd ever heard him say a single coherent sentence.

Here were country children, born in the midst of God's plenty, and where were they this fine spring evening? Out in the fresh air, enjoying the glory and beauty of it all? No, here they were, plugged into a machine feeding them an empty fantasy of big city life. And from the glimpses I caught of it, the lives of its characters were ugly and unhappy ones at that.

'You don't have a telly at home, do you, Mr Brin?' Kylie saw me watching the screen. 'What's the matter, don't you like it or something? Don't you believe in it?'

'Now don't be cheeky, Kylie. Mr Brin's been helping your dad all afternoon.'

We drank tea and ate cake in silence for some minutes, surrendering to the television, our own lives in suspended animation. The soap-opera finished. A chat-show started. The first guest was one of the actors from the soap-opera, a heavy-set young man, big and handsome but thuggish and semi-articulate. I finished my tea and cake without really watching or listening. It was hot and stuffy in there, I was tired, I was fighting to stay awake, I wanted to say thank you and goodbye. Then a snatch of conversation hit me from the screen, jerking me awake like a slap round the face. My heart stopped for a second and then raced on at twice its normal speed.

'Tell us about the movie you're shooting at the moment,' the attractive and flirtatious hostess urged her guest.

'Yeah, it's great, it's about this geezer who died ages ago, ten years or so, it's well proper.'

'Harry Jutting, the artist?'

'Yeah, that's his name. It's a true story, real life and all that, but it's a proper movie, you know, not a what's it, documentary.'

'And you play Jutting? The leading role?'

'Yeah, he was a real diamond, a right player, know what I mean?' His eyes lit up, and he laughed, sniggering. 'Pissed in the Queen's pond and all that, off his head all the time, girls killing themselves over him. Like a rock star.'

'But he was a brilliant and successful artist, a critically-acclaimed and widely-collected painter and sculptor?'

'Oh yeah, he was well-famous, made a packet and all that.'

'I knew him,' I said. Harry Jutting. Yes. I'd known him all right. And I'd hated him. He'd been the biggest bastard the world had ever seen. My heart was really pounding, my hands were shaking.

'What, you know James Hobson!' Kylie's voice was loud with amazement and admiration.

I shook my head, puzzled. 'James Hobson? Who's he?'

'James Hobson! Him! Him! You must know who he is!'

Her mother laughed. 'It's the name of the actor there. Him, Nina's guest. He's the star of First Orders, what we've just been watching. Kylie really fancies him. She's got pictures of him all over her wall.'

'Mum! Ow, Mum!' Kylie screamed. Andy sniggered. Kylie threw a cushion at him.

23

'No, not the actor,' I said. 'The artist. The man the actor's playing in the film.' I peered closer. 'But he does look like Harry, I'll give him that.'

'Oh.' Disappointed, Kylie turned back to the screen.

'Sounds like your kind of role,' the hostess simpered.

'Dead right. I wouldn't mind a bit of what he had. We'd have got on, if he was still around. Shared a pint or two, swapped notes, know what I mean?'

'But it's quite a dark and tragic story, isn't it? The wealth and the success, wasn't it all too much for him in the end?'

'Yeah, well, he killed himself, didn't he?' He shook his head stupidly, frowning. 'What was that about? I mean, he had everything, and he threw it all away. I don't understand it, suicide. It's the coward's way out, isn't it? Know what I mean?'

There was a low gasp of surprise and embarrassment from the audience, followed by an uneasy silence. Even the glib interviewer was lost for words. The camera caught a flash of panic in the young man's eyes as he realised he'd said something indelicate.

'I mean, all right, it gets us all down from time to time, doesn't it, like, life and all that?' He shifted awkwardly in his seat. 'But never give in, that's what I say. Know what I mean? Never give in. You've got to fight back, haven't you? Got to keep fighting. Right?'

The audience eagerly grasped at this philosophical gem and began to cheer and clap with relief. Hobson nodded at them, trying to look serious and compassionate and humble, acknowledging this tribute to his wisdom. The interviewer gave the camera her brightest smile. She was back on track.

Hobson frowned. 'Yeah, but was his death really suicide, anyway?' He sat forwards. 'He could have been done in. There were rumours, you know. Perhaps someone had a grudge against him. Well, he was no saint, was he? No angel.' He chuckled. 'More like the devil himself, I reckon.'

'Oooh!' A close-up of Nina, her big beautiful eyes even bigger and wider with exaggerated surprise and amazement and delight. 'He's hinting at dark deeds and murky mysteries! And we love those, don't we? So, are you going to let us in on a giant secret, then? Are you saying he was murdered?'

'You'll just have to watch the movie.' Hobson's smug grin filled the screen. 'All will be revealed when it comes out.'

'Oh, you're such a tease!' She pulled a sulky face at the camera, then glanced down at her notes. 'But it isn't all glamour, is it, working in films? There's danger as well, isn't there? Or at least there is in this film, from what we've heard? There's been something in the papers...'

'Oh, what, you mean that nutter, whoever he is? Writing those threatening letters? Nah, I'm not frightened of that. Takes more than that to get my wind up.'

'That's right. Anonymous letters. Threatening arson and sabotage if shooting continues. Burn down the set, destroy the cameras. And worse. I think the police have been informed about death threats? Threats to your life?'

The TV audience gasped.

'Yeah.' He snorted with laughter again. 'But it takes more than that to put me off my job, and I don't care if he knows it, whoever he is.'

The TV audience cheered.

'And the police have no idea who this character is? Or why he's doing it?'

'Nah. He's just some sort of religious nutter, reckons it's blasphemous or sacrilegious or something for me to pretend to be someone who's actually existed, a real person, know what I mean, not a whatsit, a fictional character. Mad sod thinks make-believe is a crime against God or something. Says we should live in God's real world, not in an artificial one of art and movies and stuff. Reckons art is evil or something. You know, graven images and all that. A right load of boll... I mean, nonsense. Yeah?'

'It sounds like you're not taking it too seriously.'

'Nah. Well, the show must go on, know what I mean?'

Cheering and loud applause from the TV audience.

'Well, we wish you a safe and successful movie. When will we be able to see it?'

'It'll be out next year, in the summer. Not this summer, the summer after.'

'Can't wait. Ladies and gentlemen, James Hobson, star of next year's must-see summer movie, Art Crash Express, the wild life of the artist Harry Jutting...'

A phone rang. It was Andy's mobile. 'Yo, blud. Was apnin'? You wiv the homies?' He laughed. 'Oh yeah? Respec, or what?'

Kirsty gave a theatrical sigh. 'My brother thinks he's a Jamaican gangster,' she explained witheringly, jeeringly. 'He's not really a farmer's son, living in the middle of the countryside, up to his knees in mud and cow-pats, oh no.'

Andy dropped the phone, suddenly and frighteningly angry. 'Yeah? And you? Wannabe wag, eh?' he shouted. 'Glamour model, porno, prossie? Marry a wop football star? Minger!'

'Mum! Mum! Listen to what he's calling me! Can you hear what he's saying? Can you hear? Mum!'

The woman on the television was still talking to us. 'And if you'd like to know more about Harry Jutting, watch the Culture Show on BBC2 at ten o'clock tonight, when Andrew Graham-Dixon will be talking about Montezuma's Revenge, a posthumous work by Jutting to be unveiled at Tate Modern next week, and described as "one of the strangest and most original works of art ever made…" '

I walked home through the evening darkness, pausing by the farm gate to listen to the sounds coming from the cows in the barn. A soft lowing, and the rustle of slow and gentle movements in the straw. Why had I admitted that I'd known Harry Jutting? Why hadn't I just kept my mouth shut? An unguarded moment, a moment of shock and anger, and out it had come. What a foolish, dangerous thing to say. My hands were still shaking, my heart was pounding. I waited, breathing the fresh air deeply. I felt myself calming down. An owl hooted overhead, and a fox barked up on the hill. The real world, the natural world. True and beautiful. Lights shone from the window of our cottage further along the lane. Helen and Liz and Richard and home.

I walked up the unlit lane, and I thought about Kylie and Andy besieged by violent and harmful fantasies, and I thought about Liz and Richard. Would my own children be like that in ten year's time? Would Liz be precociously flirtatious? Would Richard be truculent and hostile? Would they hate each other? Would they hate Helen and me? Is that what the modern world did to children these days? I'd do whatever I could to protect them from it. Fred and Mary were good people, they were good parents; if their children weren't safe, was there any hope for mine?

I shook my head as I came to the front door. I could hear Helen and Liz laughing inside. Ten year's time. Why worry about ten year's time? We have today. That's enough for anyone, isn't it?

Chapter Two

I rode over to Chichester on Friday morning. I was outside Pallant House by mid-day.

I went in, through the doors and across the clean, gleaming, well-lit entrance hall to the front desk. Keeping my head down. I paid for my ticket and set off into the galleries. I pulled a baseball cap out of my pocket and put it on, jerking the peak down over my eyes. My heart was thumping. I could hardly breathe. I moved fast. I knew where I wanted to go. Room five, on the first floor.

And there it was. I didn't want to look at it at first. But when I raised my eyes, when I saw it, I was filled with such a rage that there was no question of changing my mind, of backing down. I wanted to destroy it, I was going to destroy it, I was going to smash it into a thousand pieces and grind its dust underfoot.

The sculpture was a hollow copy of the Venus de Milo in pink transparent Perspex. It was twice the size of the original. The breasts were grotesquely enlarged. The piece was filled, vase-like, with hundreds or perhaps thousands of sacks of silica gel, the type used in breast-enhancement implants.

'Eve' by Harry Jutting. Sculpture. Life-sized. Modelled on the Venus de Milo. Perspex, hollow, moulded. Filling: silicone implant sacks... Companion-piece to Adam (see above)...

I glanced around the room. Two girls – schoolchildren, very young – were giggling at Eve's monstrous breasts. They saw me enter and moved away, stifling their giggles, to examine a painting on the far wall. That was all. No attendant. A security camera on the ceiling at each end of the room. I went up to Eve and stood as close to her as I could, waiting for the two girls to leave. I struggled to control my breathing. I couldn't get enough air into my lungs. My chest felt as if it was full of a steamy mist, hot and damp and heavy. Sweat ran down my face with the effort of pumping the air in and out.

The two girls drifted into the next room.

I struck out almost blindly, lunging with both arms, trying to hit the monster, throw it to the floor, dash it against the walls. It teetered and wobbled, its smooth surfaces escaping my grasp. I kicked out with my right foot. A direct, goal-scoring punt. Over it toppled – smash onto the floor - ringing and chiming and crashing like a falling bell-tower. Sacks of silica gel thumped dully as they spilt out across the polished wooden boards. Skittering shards of broken Perspex flew and scattered across the room.

There was a deep silence. I saw two horrified faces peering round a doorway – the two school-girls, struck dumb as they surveyed the debris in the room they'd just left, the room which had been dominated by a massive sculpture but which now seemed mysteriously empty. One of them gasped. The other one started to scream.

I turned and walked out of the room. Don't run until you have to. Walk quickly and calmly and you won't attract any attention. A uniformed attendant rushed past me. Other visitors to the gallery, curious, followed him. A family with young children, frightened, was hurrying in the other direction, ahead of me, eager to get out and away from whatever had happened. I passed through two more small galleries, across a landing, down some stairs. Along a corridor, the entrance hall visible through a fire door at the far end. Still walking. There was a shout from behind, and footsteps running towards me, then I was running too. I burst through the fire-doors into the entrance hall. More uniformed attendants, shocked faces, angry faces, screaming and shouting, some stepping towards me with outstretched arms, others shrinking back, others frozen motionless. I ran towards the exit, dodging grasping hands, tearing myself away from gripping fingers, pushing blocking bodies aside, bowling them over. Had they locked the glass doors?

'Got you! Bastard! Got - !' Strong hands seized my arms, grabbed handfuls of sleeve. Someone else was trying to get me in a head-lock, trying to trip me up. 'Police! Call the police!'

I was fighting my way forwards, inch by inch. I was struggling wildly, thrashing and wriggling, hitting out blindly. I could hear the gasping and swearing of the guards wrestling with me. I could smell them, I could feel their breath on my face. One of them was growling through gritted teeth, growling like an angry dog. The other one was shouting. 'Got you! Got you! Bastard!'

They wrestled me to a standstill. They were pushing and shoving at me, trying to get me on the floor. I gave a last convulsive heave, got an arm free, swung it wildly. My elbow hit something hard and one of the guards gasped and fell away, clutching his nose. I got my hands on the other guard, gripping his shirt, and tried to throw him off. There was a loud tearing noise. Buttons popped and his shirt gaped open – a glimpse of a flabby white chest. The zip on my jacket broke and I felt one sleeve splitting a seam round the shoulder. The guard was off balance and I shoved him away with both hands and suddenly I was free, stumbling towards the exit.

The exit – had they locked those glass doors? I staggered forwards. I could see the steps down to the pavement, the street outside. My arms were out, my flat palms hit the heavy glass – and the door swung open.

Down the steps I ran, almost tumbling head over heels. My feet hit the pavement and I was off down the street, running as fast as I could. There were shouts and sounds of pursuit behind me, but not close, not getting closer. I came out into a shopping street, a busy street. Some shoppers stopped and stared uncertainly at me, stared back at my shouting pursuers, but I was past them before they could even decide to do anything about it. Seconds later I was inside a massive store, crowded with shoppers flicking through racks of CDs and DVDs. I passed furtively through them, a needle burying itself in a haystack, making my way to the back of the store. A moment later I was out of the rear entrance, in another busy shopping street, and there was no sight or sound of pursuit.

Then I started shaking. It was the delayed fear and relief and shock. By the time I got back to the bike I was trembling so much I wasn't sure I could ride the thing safely. But I knew I had to get out of there as fast as I could. I forced myself onto the machine and away I went.

*

I was back home by mid-afternoon. Helen and the children weren't in – they must have gone for a walk across the marsh or over the hill. It was very quiet in the house. I sat down at the kitchen table and began to unwind. To relax. There was Richard's high chair, a patch of sunlight showing up some lunchtime crumbs on its blue and white striped fabric. There were Liz's little green slippers on the floor. A claret-coloured sweater of Helen's was draped over the back of a chair. A long, stray golden thread hung from it. I picked it up. A strand of her hair, glowing in the sunlight.

Helen and I had been together for seven years. When we first met, I'd been living on my own in a battered caravan on a farm below the Downs just outside Canterbury. The caravan was in a yard outside a decaying oast-house. The old building was used for storing wooden pallets and rolls of chicken wire and bundles of wooden posts. I'd set up a kiln in one corner and was trying to master the potter's craft. The caravan was cold and draughty, and had no power or water in it, but the tiny rent I paid to the farmer was all I could afford. One corner inside the oast-house had been screened off and equipped as a farm office; there was electricity and a toilet and hot and cold water there and the farmer let me use them.

The oast-house was surrounded by apple-orchards. There were caravans in those fields, too; they were for the workers who came every late summer to pick the crop over the autumn and winter. Almost all of those labourers came over from eastern Europe every year for the work. I kept myself to myself, and that seemed to suit them; I had my work to do, and they had theirs. But one year a group of half-a-dozen youngsters arrived from London and took over one of the caravans and joined the Poles and Latvians and Estonians at work in the orchards, and they weren't going to keep their distance. They were willing to break off work whenever they felt like it, to lean over fences and hedges for a chat, to drop by the oast-house at odd moments, shouting and banging on the door of my caravan on the way to the pub, inviting me to join them. I resented their intrusion at first, then I came to welcome it. They were entertaining enough – drop-outs and squatters and protesters, masking laziness or muddle-headedness or bitter failure with idealism. I knew the type and got on well with them. They drank as much as the Poles and the Latvians, made twice as much noise and worked half as hard.

They were three couples – three boys and three girls. One of them – one of the girls – was much more conscientious than the others. She was never late out into the orchards of a morning, even though her companions always started work hours later than everyone else, stumbling out of their caravan bleary-eyed and hung-over with half the day already wasted. She worked hard, refusing to be distracted, never wandering off for an unofficial break as her companions did at every opportunity. She was quieter, too, and was no more muddle-headed or bitter than she was lazy, and from what little she said she was the only true idealist among them. Her name was Helen, and she was the reason why I found myself welcoming the intrusions I'd initially resented.

But as the season wore on, the growing coldness and the isolation and claustrophobia took its toll on their group. Two of the boys had a fight. Two of the girls had a screaming match. One of the couples split up. Some of them stopped working altogether. Eventually, on a November day of freezing fog, the farmer kicked them off his land. There was a lot of shouting. Parasites and free-loaders, the farmer called them. Fascist bastard, capitalist bully, they called the farmer. Five of them left in their battered van. Helen stayed behind.

She worked through all the rest of the back-breaking season, side-by-side with the Slavs among the fruit-laden trees. Of an evening, she came over to my caravan to talk, or I went over to hers. And when the season was over, and the other labourers departed for Poland and Latvia and Estonia, she stayed behind and moved into my caravan with me.

Then and now, I couldn't believe my luck. I couldn't believe that Helen – so unlike the rest of her group, hard-working, intelligent, sensible, cheerful, funny, genuinely idealistic - should stay with me. But she was fed up with that chapter of her life. She was disillusioned with squatting and protesting, with movements and big communal endeavours. Whatever the cause, she said, someone would let it down or betray it or simply not care enough about it. So she'd concluded that the only way you could hope to improve the world was to be pure and committed and radical in your personal relationships, in your private life; and she gave me credit for that conclusion, for the opportunity to put it into practice. As for me, I'd been kind of broken when she'd found me. She'd put me back together again, whether deliberately or accidentally I don't know, but she did a pretty good job of it.

I'd been drinking heavily, for one thing. She never drank, not so much as the odd can of beer. Soon after she'd moved in, she'd asked me why I drank so much. I'd shrugged, and said that it kept me warm, which was true in a way, because it'd been bloody cold in that caravan. She'd simply said, 'Don't we keep each other warm?' I'd looked at her, but there'd been no criticism in her expression, no disapproval. Only honest curiosity. 'Yes,' I'd said. 'We do. You're right.' And I hadn't touched alcohol since that moment. There was no decision taken, no effort involved, I simply hadn't bothered with it ever again. She was a vegetarian, as well, and in that also I had followed her example. Again, I hadn't made any kind of decision or resolution, it was just that she'd done all the cooking at first and I'd been more than happy with what she'd put on the table for me, then later when I began to do my fair share in the kitchen I'd simply followed her instructions and recipes.

She'd worked around the farm, and behind the bar at the local pub, and at a local garden centre. I'd thrown pots on my wheel and fired them in the kiln and we sold them at stalls in markets around the local villages. They sold well. Gift shops and craft shops began to stock them, and soon they were selling faster than I could make them. We moved out of the caravan and rented a room in an annexe of a Bed and Breakfast place down the road from the oast-house. Then Helen became pregnant, and we found the cottage below the hill on the edge of the marsh and we moved there and became a family.

We'd never talked much about our pasts. She told me that she'd been a student – political sciences - but she'd dropped out of university after little more than a year, finding the studies just too abstract and sterile. I told her even less about my own past, and she didn't dig, didn't insist on knowing more. There were many things which I didn't tell her, things which I thought I didn't need to tell her, things which perhaps I should have told her, nevertheless. Things which I hoped, even as I watched that stray strand of golden hair turning and glowing in the early April sunlight, that I would never have to tell her.

I stood up, feeling suddenly restless and unsettled. I went out to the studio.

*

I pulled the cardboard box out from the cupboard and took the catalogue out from under the pile of newspapers. I turned to the list at the back and crossed the sixth item off it. Eve no longer existed. Then I looked at the seventh item.

'Dirty Flirt. Oil on canvas. Private collection…'

Dirty Flirt. I nodded. I knew where to find it. Or at least, I knew where to start looking for it. I'd done my homework.

I knew all about Dirty Flirt. It was a big canvas, four feet by six. Nine years ago, it had been sold in an auction at Christie's in New York. It had been put up for sale by an American collector who'd bought the piece from the Pyramid stand at the Basel Art Fair in Switzerland only two years earlier. That auction had destroyed that collector's reputation and status with dealers around the world - serious collectors aren't supposed to re-sell pieces on the secondary market, especially not so soon after buying them, and not for such a huge profit (he'd bought the piece for over a million euros at Basel, but sold it for almost four million dollars in New York). Which was unfair, because he really did collect art for the love of it, not as speculative stock to be played on the market - he'd built an art gallery for his collection, opened it to the public three days a week and employed an art-historian full-time to curate it. He'd sold the canvas only because he was getting divorced and he knew his wife wanted it and he was determined she'd never get her hands on it. As it happened, it was the beginning of the end for him anyway – soon after that, his business collapsed and he had to sell all the rest of his collection.

'Dirty Flirt' had been bought by a Mrs Irina Rashnikov, daughter of one of Russia's most powerful oligarchs, wife of one of Russia's richest bankers.

I knew where Mrs Irina Rashnikov lived. A big house in Chelsea. A beautiful nineteenth-century villa, detached, sash-windowed, flat-fronted, three-storied (not counting basement and attic), big garden, in a wide, quiet, clean, tree-lined street a stone's throw from the King's Road. She and her husband, Mr Sergei Rashnikov, a president of the Moscow Vasily Bank, had bought it sixteen years ago when he'd come to London to head up the bank's City offices. He'd moved back to work in Russia seven years ago, but his wife and children and their nanny had stayed put. His children got an English public school education and his wife enjoyed the West End shopping. She was too frightened to go back to Russia anyway – her father had just been imprisoned, a political falling-out between him and the other robber-barons who ran the country. Her husband flew back and forth between that house in SW1 and his mansion in Moscow as often as he could.

Nevertheless, the house was often empty. The children were at boarding school and Mrs Rashnikov flew around the world from one fashion show or charity gala or opening night to another. Right now there was no one in the house. It was the school Easter holidays. The whole family had decamped to the Caribbean for some early sun or to Switzerland for some late skiing.

But it wouldn't be easy. I'd have to be careful. Very careful indeed. Sergei Rashnikov had a lot to lose and a lot to fear. Kidnappers, burglars, Russian mafia, Chechen terrorists, business rivals, political enemies. He had to be obsessed with security. Even an empty house had to be protected.

I checked a calendar pinned up on the wall. New moon in six day's time. No moon, dark night. Perfect. That's when I'd do it.

No moon… a dark night… I shivered. I had a bad feeling about Dirty Flirt. It was a sinister-looking picture in itself. Why would anyone want it hanging on their wall? Why would anyone pay a penny for it, let alone millions of dollars? And I couldn't help associating it with the misfortunes which had befallen its owners as soon as they'd acquired it – the American collector's divorce and ruin, the arrest and imprisonment of Irina Rashnikov's father on politically-motivated tax-evasion charges. Ridiculous, I told myself. Just coincidence. But the bad feeling persisted. It was an unlucky piece, I was sure. It brought bad luck to anyone who had anything to do with it. Well, all the more reason to destroy it. But if the piece really was malevolent, wouldn't it fight back? Wouldn't it do all it could to defend itself?

Nonsense. What sort of mad superstition was that? It was just an over-hyped painting in an empty house. I would strike under cover of darkness in six days time and that would be the end of it. I put the catalogue back in its hiding place.

*

I worked hard over the next few days, to try and keep my mind off Dirty Flirt and that big house in Chelsea and what I'd have to do there. Nevertheless, it cast a shadow over everything I did and thought, a shadow which grew darker and darker as the days went by. I worked things out so the current firing-cycle was completed on the sixth day, the day before the night of the new moon. I was hoping the excitement and anticipation of opening the kiln would eclipse the fear and dread and apprehension of what I had to do that night.

I opened and unloaded the kiln after breakfast. The glaze firing had finished the previous afternoon, and I'd left it to cool down overnight. And yes, I was as excited as ever, rushing my porridge and coffee, eager to get to the workshop and see how the pieces had turned out. You never know exactly what you're going to find. Firing isn't predictable. No one glaze is ever exactly like another. Strange transformations and chemical reactions take place under the stress of the intense heat inside the kiln.

But everything had turned out well. No cracks or faults. No dunting, crazing, shivering, peeling. No scaling, crawling, pitting, pin-holing, blistering or blebbing. I'd been lucky. I breathed a sigh of relief and wrote down the results in the firing-log.

I cleaned the kiln out, focused and concentrating, refusing to think about what I was going to do that night. What I had to do that night. I carefully vacuumed dust and debris from the element grooves. I chiselled blobs of dripped glaze from the base and walls. I checked for fresh cracks or holes in the brickwork. I checked the elements, reaching down inside the kiln with a hand-mirror to look right into the grooves. I didn't find any new damage. But I did notice that many of the elements were losing their protective oxide layer. That's the problem with reduction-firing in an electric kiln. It's all very well dropping combustible material into your kiln to burn off the oxygen in the atmosphere, so the combustion then has to grab oxygen from the glaze on your pots; but the combustion will also grab oxygen from anywhere else it can, including the protective layer built up on the elements. I closed the lid, opened the spy hole, and turned the kiln on. Firing it empty for seven or eight hours would help to re-build the protective layer on the elements. With a bit of luck.

I was worried about the kiln. I'd had it for quite a few years now, and I'd worked it hard from the very start. It served me well, but it had been showing signs of wear and tear for some time now. I was having to replace failed elements and repair cracked brickwork and fire on empty more and more often. I knew I couldn't go on using it for reduction firing or high-temperature porcelain glazes for much longer. Sooner or later it was going to break down completely. I needed a new kiln. Could I afford one? I pulled out the accounts and bank statements filed away with the firing logs and charts and glaze-recipe note-books, and started going through the figures.

Then some sort of defensive barrier in my mind burst and I couldn't keep the thoughts about Dirty Flirt out any longer. In they flooded, boiling up from my subconscious like the storm waves that swept in over the broken sea-wall of so many of my nightmares. Dirty Flirt. I relished the idea of destroying it, of crossing it off the list. But the more I thought about it and how I would do it – the more my plans and preparations ran and re-ran themselves through my mind – the more uneasy and anxious I became. I tried to stop thinking about it. But it wouldn't go away. I had a really bad feeling about it. I tried to concentrate on the figures in the accounts and statements, but I couldn't.

I was still thinking about it an hour or two later when I heard Helen at work in the garden. I went to the door and looked out. There she was, busy digging over the vegetable patch. She was wearing jeans and wellington boots and a big green woollen sweater. Her mass of copper curls had been tied up loosely at the back of her neck. She looked up, saw me watching her, and waved. But she didn't stop digging. I guessed that both Richard and Liz were having a nap and she wanted to make the most of her free time before they woke up.

It was a bright April day. The spring sunlight had just enough warmth in it to take the chill out of the breeze blowing across the pastureland from the sea. The trees in the lane were budding green and would soon be in leaf. The daffodils and primroses up against the cottage were vivid with colour. It felt warm enough to sit outside, for the first time that year. I left the studio and went and sprawled on the grass in the sunlight, watching Helen at work.

At last the dark shadow which had been oppressing me for the last few days – the shadow of my impending encounter with Dirty Flirt – faded and dispersed.

Helen grew most of our vegetables – potatoes, beans, carrots, cabbages, onions. She worked hard. And the soil here was very rich. For thousands of years, before the marshes were drained, the fast-flowing rivers of the hills around us had flowed into the marsh. They'd carried fertile silt down from those hills and dumped it as they wound their slow way across these flat lands to the sea. It was that silt which fed us now. Vegetables did well in it, but fruit not so well. Helen had tried fruit trees and bushes, but they hadn't thrived; they'd struggled against the chill, salty air that blew in off the sea day after day. Two apple trees survived, withered and stunted. A stubborn raspberry bush flourished on the sheltered side of the studio, but its fruit never came to much as it was always in the shade; the winds came from the south and the east, so any shelter from them was inevitably out of the sunlight as well.

Helen stopped to pull off her heavy sweater. Her cheeks were flushed. The sunlight was bringing the freckles back into her face. She threw the sweater aside and returned to her work. She dug fiercely, stamping on the spade, working the soil loose, turning it over. Although she was small and skinny, she was tough and strong. She had a round face, a small nose and big green eyes; but her colouring – pale skin, red hair – her sharp bone-structure and her physical toughness made me joke about her Viking ancestors. I'd never known her to wear make-up, but she didn't need it, she always looked so bright and healthy.

She loved fresh air and exercise, loved being out of doors. Before we'd had children, we used to spend hours together, whole days, hiking over the hills and through the woods, something I'd never done before I met her. She loved swimming in the sea, and in the rivers, no matter how cold the water, particularly if there was no one else around. She rarely bothered with a swimming costume. She didn't give a damn about other people's approval or disapproval. I'd been more cautious at first, and she'd laughed at me. But I'd soon lost my inhibitions.

She stopped digging for a moment and leaned heavily on her spade. Long strands of her hair had come loose. She tried to brush them aside with the back of one muddy hand, smearing her cheek. She was wearing an old shirt of mine, a big cotton one in red and yellow tartan. It looked huge on her. It had come untucked from her jeans and

41

hung open, all but one or two buttons undone. I could see the white vest she was wearing underneath. She saw me looking at her and grinned. 'In Russia, we say, man who watch woman dig potato, is big potato.'

Russia. Mrs Irina Rashnikov. Her father the oligarch. Her husband the banker. Dirty Flirt. That dark cloud of dread began to gather again, threatening to blot out the light.

Then she crossed her eyes and stuck her tongue out at me. 'We say, only crazy woman dig potato for lazy man.'

I laughed. She was a great mimic, good with accents. 'Fancy a cup of tea?'

'Is the rich young master trying to seduce the poor innocent peasant girl?' She put one hand on her hip and the other on the handle of the spade, eye-brows raised, a wanton west-country wench. The voice was straight out of Hardy's Wessex. 'Tempting her with wicked and irresistible pleasures?'

I made to get up, but she said 'No, don't go in. You'll wake them up. Thanks, I can wait.' She came over and sat down beside me. I put my arm round her. She smelt of fresh earth and cut grass, of the spring. She was hot and breathing heavily from her exertions, and I could feel her heart beating rapidly. She put her head on my shoulder. 'Why aren't you rich? Or young? Or a master?'

'Not young? Don't let this beard fool you, I'm only a couple of years older than you.'

'So you say. But have I seen your birth certificate?'

'Listen, we might not be rich, but we're not doing badly. We have money to spend, which is just as well, because there are things we need to buy.'

'Oh, yes?' She looked at me warily.

'That's what I came out here to talk about.' I lay back on the grass and looked up at the sky. A flock of jackdaws tumbled by overhead, squawking and squabbling. For some reason they reminded me of the security guards at Pallant House. I'd only just got away with it that time. They nearly had me. Was that why I was feeling anxious and uneasy about Dirty Flirt, why I was dreading getting to grips with it? I felt sick in the pit of my stomach about it. All this, I thought, I could lose all this. It could all be taken away from me. 'I could really do with another kiln.'

'What's wrong with old faithful?'

'He's getting a bit knackered. He'll pack in altogether if I don't give him a rest. He's not the best sort of kiln for the way I work.'

She lay down beside me. 'What sort do you want?'

I sighed. 'A bigger one, a front-loader. And gas-fired, not electric.'

'But we don't have gas here.' She sat up. 'Are you saying we might have to move?'

'No!' I looked at her, and was reassured by the alarm on her face.

'I don't ever want to move. Do you?'

'Never. But we wouldn't have to. We could get one which burns propane, and use LPG canisters or a storage tank. Save us money in the long-run – much cheaper to run than old faithful. And make us money. With two kilns – old faithful's still good for biscuit-firing – I'd be twice as productive. I could get two cycles running at the same time. No more hanging around, waiting for stuff to dry out and that.'

'So what's the catch?'

'Well. As it is, we're doing pretty well. Well enough for you to give up working at the farm-shop, if you wanted to.'

'But not if we splash out on a new kiln?'

I nodded.

'Do you want me to give up the job?'

'No. It's completely up to you.'

She shrugged. 'Well, I don't mind the job. I quite like it, really. I'll stick with it.'

'Thank you!' I sat up and kissed her. 'Listen, Helen, I reckon, with two kilns, in a year's time we'll be even better off than we are now. Then you could pack it in if you wanted to.'

'What would I do with myself?'

'You could help me in the workshop. Yes, with two kilns, I'd be really busy, I'd need an assistant, someone to prepare the clay and mix up the glazes, and load the kilns, and...'

Helen was laughing. 'Oh yes? Bossing me about? So you do fancy being a master, after all?'

'Well, OK, not an assistant, but more like an apprentice, I could teach you the real stuff, you know, throwing and turning, we could be partners...'

'No, no. I'd be no good. It's your work. I'd be happy to help you, though I don't think either of us would get much done if we were working side by side, do you?' She laughed. 'But the children, Richard and Liz, when they're old enough, they could help, couldn't they? You could teach them.'

I nodded. That was a dream of mine. Passing everything on to Richard and Liz. The three of us working together. Teaching them, seeing them learn, nurturing their talent, being surprised and amazed by it, the pupils outgrowing the teacher. Happy for them to surpass me, knowing that I had helped them to secure a living for themselves... I sighed. 'Yes. That would be great. But I mustn't expect... I mean, they might not want... We have to let them find their own way in life, don't we?'

'They adore you, Will. They'll want to follow in your footsteps.'

'Anyway. Enough about kilns. Is there anything else we should be thinking about? Anything else we should be splashing out on? Anything for you?'

'Ooh. Let's think.' She lay back and closed her eyes, thinking hard. 'What about... jewellery? Gold and diamonds? And... and a boob job?' After a while, when I didn't reply, she opened her eyes again and looked at me. 'You do realise I was joking, don't you?'

'If you wanted jewellery...gold and diamonds... if you really wanted it...'

'I married the village idiot.' She shook her head and laughed. 'My friends are so jealous.'

'Well, I was thinking, could we do with a van or a car of some sort?'

'Why? Isn't Fred letting you borrow his any more?'

Fred was kind enough to let me borrow the farm van when I needed to deliver pots to gift-shops and craft fairs, as long as he wasn't using it himself and as long as I returned it with a full tank. 'Fred's still fine with it. But I can't go on relying on his kindness for ever. It doesn't seem right. And sooner or later...' I paused.

'Sooner or later?'

'Richard and Liz... they'll need to go to school, down in the village, and then in town... They'll need driving about, they'll have school kit...'

'School?' Helen was looking at me. She was surprised, but I could see that she was pleased as well. 'I always thought... you'd want them to be home-schooled...'

'Home-schooling would be great... but on top of the way we live... it would be too much for them... it would be selfish of us... we can live without the world, but we shouldn't force them to. As much as we might want to protect them from it...'

'They'll be fine out there, Will. They'll be OK.'

45

'But I can't help thinking... when they make friends, see how other people live... they might think, why don't we have a television at home, and a computer, and... all kinds of things...'

Helen laughed. 'Yes. They'll suddenly realise how weird we are.'

'Do you think we're weird?'

'I think the world's weird. I think the way other people live is weird.'

We lay side by side on the grass, staring up at the white clouds scudding across the blue sky.

Helen laughed. 'Mary, bless her, do you know what she said about you the other day? "They can say what they like about your Will, Helen, I mean, he's... he's... he's not... not... he's not like the rest of us, exactly..." 'It sounded just like Mary, her tongue running away with her, flustered and embarrassed, but well-meaning. ' "But that's all to the good, I say, because I've never met a kinder man. You're very lucky to have him..." '

'Good old Mary. Do you think she'd put that in writing for me?'

Helen turned onto her side and kissed me. 'Listen. We don't have to worry about the children growing up just yet. Let's buy that kiln. Let's carry on using Fred's van, if he's happy with that. I'll leave work when we can afford it. We'll buy our own van when we can afford it. And it sounds like the sooner we get that kiln the sooner we will be able to afford it.' Then she put her mouth to my ear and murmured 'And when the children do go off to school, we can look forward to going off on our own again, can't we? I do miss having roots and stalks and insects scratching and stinging my bum.'

In the days before Liz and Richard had been born, we'd often made love outdoors in the seclusion of the woods, or hidden among the dunes, or in sheltered valleys between the hills. I remembered the first time she'd taken off her clothes outdoors, laughing, pulling me down onto the carpet of bluebells in the middle of a wood. I'd been stunned by the dappled sunlight on her pale naked skin, surprised by the fierce eagerness of her passion. But the shock hadn't lasted for long. Curled up together in the undergrowth like a pair of foxes, or entwined in a patch of sunlight like a pair of grass-snakes, or rolling about on a river-bank like a pair of otters, we'd be oblivious of any discomfort, of the cold and wet, and it was only when we'd undress indoors for the night that we'd notice the mud and the scratches and the stings covering us. Richard and Liz had both been conceived out of doors, I was sure of it. And I was glad of it. What happier or more glorious start in life could a human soul hope for?

I turned to her and our lips met. I closed my eyes and saw again her thin white body naked against the bluebells, remembered the feel of the breeze on my bare back, the sound of it sighing happily through the foliage... 'I love you, Helen. I love you...'

Helen pulled away laughing. 'But that's a few years away yet. And in the meantime, I can hear Richard shouting. Which means Liz must be awake as well.'

We stood up and I followed her inside. 'I'll put the kettle on,' I said. 'You've waited long enough for that cup of tea.'

I loved Helen and Liz and Richard, and I hated Harry Jutting. Those two equal and opposing forces governed my life, they defined me. And they were very powerful forces. I could feel them tearing me apart. Well, what if they did tear me apart? It would be my own fault. I'd only have myself to blame. But what if they tore my family apart? That would be my fault, too. There'd be no one else to blame. And it would be terrible, unforgivable. Help me, Helen, help me. What should I do?

*

Over the back wall, across the garden and in through a ground-floor window. A dark night. Good cloud-cover, no moon.

It was too simple. It shouldn't have worked. But it did work. More or less. Security lights flooded the garden and CCTV cameras stared down from the back of the house, but I ignored them. All the ground-floor windows were barred, but I scrambled up onto the extension to break in through a tiny first-floor bathroom window. I was expecting a burglar alarm to go off as soon as I put my gauntleted fist through the glass, but it didn't, not even when I tumbled through into the dark interior. I should have known that something was wrong.

The small bathroom gave onto a large bed-sitting room; the nanny's room, I guessed. It was dark and I didn't put the lights on. I took my helmet off so I could hear more clearly. The door out of the room was closed. I stood against it for some moments, listening hard, but hearing nothing other than my own frantic heart-beat. I opened it slowly and peered out. A short passage, leading to a hallway. I stepped out. A door opposite, open, leading into a spacious kitchen. Into the hallway; the front-door of the house was ahead of me, faint traffic noises coming in from the street outside; this was in fact the ground floor, not the first floor; from the back, the ground-floor was actually the basement. Stairs up to the first floor, down to the basement. Doors into a dining room on the right, a sitting room on the left.

I didn't know for sure that Dirty Flirt was still in the house. But there was no reason to suspect that it had been moved. It was a big picture; it somehow belonged there. But it was a big house – how many rooms? I was worried that it would take a long time to find it. There was no alarm ringing, so I had more time than I'd anticipated, but I still knew that the longer I was in there, the more likely I was not to get out and away again.

The sitting room was big and grand. Enough light from the streetlamps outside squeezed in through the heavy satin curtains to dimly show marble and glass tables, a piano, cream leather sofas, stripped wooden floor spread with rich rugs from Central Asia. Facing me, against the wall on the far side of the room, a marble fire-place, and above it – yes, it was too easy – that painting, a big, dark canvas. Dirty Flirt, by Harry Jutting. I felt for a switch and turned on the light. I stared at the picture. I laughed, suddenly flooded with a hunter's triumph and excitement. There was the prey, it was cornered, there was no way it could escape.

I went back to the kitchen and found a big, sharp carving knife. But as I crossed the entrance hall again something pulled me up short. A sound from upstairs – a creak of floorboards or furniture, then what I thought was a human voice, wordless but moaning or muttering. I stood stock still and listened hard. Nothing. Nothing at all. I must have imagined it. An empty house at night is full of noises. I was on edge and over-wrought.

I went on into the sitting room. I dragged a chair from the table across to the fireplace. I stood on it. The picture was so close I could see individual brush-strokes, smell the oil of its paints. I felt a kind of dizziness, faintness. I wanted to stab the blade through the canvas, again and again, plunge it in right up to the handle, slash and cut and thrust until it was hanging in shreds. I could feel an uncontrollable frenzy building up inside me. I fought it down. Careful, careful. Do this properly, do it safely. I slid the blade through the canvas just inside the frame. Then I cut round the edge, sawing the sharp blade to and fro. The canvas gradually came free, a flapping, heavy, hanging sheet, and finally slid to the floor with a rustling, scraping thud. I jumped down off the chair and seized it in both hands and tore it in half. And half again. And again. Ripping and tearing with my bare hands, slashing and stabbing with the knife. Burn it, I thought savagely. Take the shreds into the kitchen, dump them in a sink, drop a lighted match onto them. Leave nothing but a heap of ashes behind.

'Stop! You!'

I started, the shock leaping through me like a giant electric current. My heart missed a beat. My knees almost gave way. I realised I'd stopped breathing, and took a big, ragged lungful of air. I turned to the door, and froze with horror.

A man stood in the doorway. He was facing me, glaring through the shadows, heavy brows knitted with anger and concentration. He was naked. His body was pale and solid. He wasn't tall, but he was broad and muscular. He stood square-on, feet spread wide, both arms thrust forwards, hands together gripping a gun. The gun was pointing straight at me.

He gave another harsh bark of command. His voice was deep and threatening, but I couldn't understand what he said. It wasn't English. It sounded Slavic, the words rolled out from the back of his throat or squeezed from the roof of his mouth. Russian…

I was crouching by the fireplace. I raised my hands and stood up slowly. Fear squeezed my bladder, tightened my bowels. I was trembling. I thought I was going to piss myself. Shit myself. Run for it, I thought, run! But the gun was steady in its aim, and the man's eyes were grim and unblinking as he stared at me, frowning and sneering.

'What you doing? Thief? Huh?'

I couldn't speak. My mouth was too dry. I shook my head.

'Thief? In this house? You mad, eh? You crazy bastard?' He came slowly into the room. He was a tough-looking character, mean and hard and primitive. There were tattoos on his arms and stomach, black hair matting his chest. His hair was dark and cropped short. He was not a banker, he wasn't Mr Vassily Rashnikov, that much was clear. He was military, security... Soldier? Gangster? Bodyguard? There was a pale welt of a scar on his left shoulder, a couple of inches long, and another across his ribs, just below his right nipple. He wasn't young. There was grey in his hair. The muscles of his belly and thighs were beginning to sag, but they still looked solid enough. His eyes went up to the empty frame above the mantelpiece, then down to the shredded canvas at my feet. He frowned, puzzled, angrier than ever. 'You tear picture! You bastard! You break in and tear picture? You mad bastard!' He stepped forwards and lashed out so quickly and suddenly that I didn't see it happen. He must have clubbed me on the back of the head with the gun. There was an explosion of lights and colours inside my skull. Then I was sprawling on the floor, my cheek against the finely-knotted silk of a Persian rug, my eyes dazzled by its bright red-and-black patterning. 'I kill you.' The muzzle of the gun was thrust hard and cold against my temple. I could hear the man's breath, deep and harsh, feel him crouching over me, tense and poised.

'Anton!'

Another voice. Female, shrill, almost hysterical. A torrent of words I couldn't understand. Another Russian, a woman... The man grunted in response. He took the gun away from my head and stood up. 'No move,' he said. 'We have fun first, then I kill you.'

51

I turned my head to look towards the door. A young woman stood there, bare-footed, bare-shouldered, wrapped in a white sheet. Not Mrs Rashnikov. A tangled heap of peroxide hair, lots of make-up – thick mascara, dark eye-shadow, bright lip-stick – all smudged. She was looking down at me with a mixture of alarm and disgust. I searched for concern or pity or sympathy in her face, as I had listened for it in her voice, but saw none, as I'd heard none. She looked as hard and tough as the man. She came and stood at the man's side, and they peered down at me with disdain, speaking to each other quickly and quietly. The man spoke to her at length, and she nodded, laughing unpleasantly.

'I give you to her as slave,' he said to me. 'My present to her. You her slave now. She do what she like to you, you do what she tell you. I watch. Then I kill you.'

'Why?' I coughed and spluttered. I could taste blood in my mouth. 'The police…'

The man laughed. 'No police. We are Russian. I Russian policeman, once upon a time. I deal with Russian mafia. I learn from Russian mafia, do business with them. I Russian army, once upon a time. Special Forces. I deal with bastard Chechen terrorists. I cut their balls off. I deal with you easy. You nothing.'

'Mr Rashnikov… Vasily Rashnikov…'

'I work for Mr Rashnikov. Security. But when Mr Rashnikov not here, I use his house. Party, girls. Friends bring cocaine, vodka, champagne. A little business, sometimes. Mr Rashnikov not know. Mr Rashnikov angry if he knew security screwing pole-dancing Ukrainian whore in his bed. Security lose job. So I kill you, so Mr Rashnikov not know. Also, I like to kill. I want to kill you. Show off to Ukrainian whore lap-dancer. She never see man killed before. Me, many times. See many men killed. Killed many men. Women, too, some. Easy.'

The woman spoke again, fast and angry, gesturing impatiently at me with one fist, clutching the sheet to her naked body with the other.

'She say she always wanted man-slave,' the man continued. 'She hate men. She hate Englishmen. Fat, drunk, they go to club where she dance. They shout at her, grab her. They mean with money. They treat her like pig. They – how you say – abuse her. Now she get her own back. Now she shout at you, grab at you. Now she abuse you, she treat you like pig. She get her revenge.'

She laughed. She pointed at me again and made a swaying motion with her body. She spoke to the man, then leant forwards and spat on me.

'She say you do sexy dance for her. She say why not man dance for her, for woman, for change? You do sexy dance for her. She shout at you, she grab you. You any good, she shove ten pound notes down your knickers. You take clothes off. She treat you like pig. You get naked, then she kick you in balls. She piss on you. She cut your cock off. She shove gun up your arse. See how man like that, eh?' He laughed. 'Then I kill you.'

I was still lying on the floor. Pain was hammering away at the back of my head, terror was thrashing my heart, bubbling vomit into my throat. I couldn't move.

'You do sexy dance!' he shouted. He stepped forwards and hit me across the head with something I didn't see, something long and heavy and blunt. 'Now! Move! Get up!' He hit me again. I passed out for a moment. I was lying on my back when I came round, only seconds later. I opened my eyes. He was standing over me with what looked like a poker in his left hand, the gun still in his right. 'You do sexy dance for girl! Take clothes off! What you waiting for? Fucking music?'

I rolled over. I put my hands out to push myself up onto all fours. I groaned with pain. My right hand went under a pile of shredded canvas – the remains of Harry's painting – and felt something cold and hard and metallic. The blade of the kitchen knife. I'd forgotten all about it. There it was, on the floor where I'd dropped it before I knew I had company. Hidden from sight. No one else knew it was there. I felt for its handle, found it, gripped it tight. Concealed by the heap of torn rags which had been Dirty Flirt.

'You have a small cock,' I said quietly.

There was silence. Then a sharp and angry intake of breath. 'What you say?' The man's voice was low and threatening and ugly. I couldn't see him – my eyes were on the heap of rags covering my right hand – but I felt him leaning over me, coming closer. Not quite close enough. Not yet.

'You have a very small cock,' I said.

There was a yell of anger, a clanging clatter which was the dropped poker, and then he was right over me, reaching out to grab a handful of my hair and shove the gun into my face. I turned quickly, bringing my right hand up and round, swinging the knife in a big slashing arc, wild and blind. Putting all my strength into it, all the tension of my twisted, prone body. I felt the blade hit something, slice through, swing on. I heard a yell, another clatter – the gun falling! – and I was on my feet. The man was facing me, crouching, hissing with pain and anger, his left hand clasped to his right upper arm, blood oozing between his fingers. The gun was on the rug between us. He made a lunge for it and I swung the knife again, wild and blind with panic and terror. It caught him in the face. His head whipped back, spraying blood into the air. He staggered away from me, groaning. The woman was screaming. I grabbed the gun. Both my hands were shaking, the knife in my right, the gun in my left. I pointed the weapon at the man.

'Lie down!' I shouted. The man didn't seem to hear me. He was swearing, a long string of oaths in his own language which I didn't need to understand. He had both his hands up to his face. They were covered in blood. The wound on his right arm gaped and bled horribly. 'Lie down!' I shouted again. I stepped towards him, waving the knife, and he backed away and then went down on both knees, and then lay on the floor, on his left side. The woman was still screaming. Her hands were balled up into fists, raised to her temples, her face was contorted with horror. The sheet had slipped to the floor. Her naked body tensed and bowed in rhythm with each scream. Her skin was a strange bright orange colour all over. 'Tell her to lie down beside you!' I shouted. 'Tell her!'

She did as she was told. Her screams subsided to frightened, gulping sobs. She curled up on her side like a terrified child, trying to cuddle up against the man. He pushed her away with an angry curse. He glared at me, at the gun in my hand. He was calculating his chances, waiting for his moment. The weapon was unsteady but it was pointing straight at him. My finger was on the trigger. My fear was ebbing away. Anger and pain were taking its place, throbbing, overwhelming. Kill him. Kill him now. You've beaten him, finish him off, teach him a lesson. Get your own back. Pull the trigger! Kill him now!

They must have seen it in the look on my face, in the tension of my body. The man shrank away from the gun, trying to push himself away across the floor, his lips curling back in a grimace, Slavic curses spilling from his mouth. The woman started to scream again, curling herself up into an even tighter ball, clawing and grabbing at the man's chest and arms.

I laughed. I couldn't help it. Their abject reactions were somehow funny. I backed away, still covering him, until I could see my crash-helmet just in front of my feet. I bent down quickly and picked it up. He twitched, but didn't try anything on. I edged across the room to the door without taking my eyes or the gun off them. Then I was through the door and out into the hallway. I slammed the sitting-room door closed and ran across the hallway to the front door. I thrust my head into my crash-helmet, tugged at the latch, turned the handle, and the front door opened. I stepped out into the fresh air. There was the porch, the doorstep, the front garden, the pavement, road and street-lamps. I was out. I was free. I slammed the door behind me and ran down the front steps and out through the gate into the street.

When I got back to the motor-bike I realised I was still clutching the gun in my right hand. I had no idea what I'd done with the knife. The gun was hard and heavy and warm. It felt good to hold. Comforting, reassuring, empowering. I felt good. My terror had gone. Euphoria was masking the pain of the blows I'd received. Absently I realised I was bleeding from some minor wound I hadn't noticed, but I didn't care. I was triumphant, invincible, all-powerful. And it wasn't yet two o'clock. I could return home now, be back well before daybreak. Or I could do more work. There was time enough for it. And there was indeed work to be done. I felt eager, ready for more. The night had gone well, was going well, there was no point in stopping now. I weighed the gun in my hand. Yes, I thought. Let's get on with it.

Chapter Three

I washed the blood from my face as soon as I got home and went straight to bed. Everyone was fast asleep. I was careful not to wake anyone up.

I came to with a start a few hours later. Daylight. Helen was standing by the bed, looking down at me. She was dressed and ready for work in a dark blue skirt and a grey sweater. Thin and pale. Her hair was still wet from a shower; damp, it looked darker and heavier than usual, dark gold. Her face, as she regarded me, was troubled. Anxious. I knew I looked a mess. Even though I'd washed before going to bed, there was no disguising the cuts and bruises. I smiled at her, painfully, but she didn't return the smile. She reached down and put a hand on my cheek, gently. 'Are you all right?' she asked.

'Sure.' I suppressed a groan. My head throbbed, my shoulders ached. 'Nothing to worry about.'

'But I am worried. I see you like this… I'm more than worried. I'm frightened…'

'You have to trust me, Helen.'

'I do. I…' She hesitated, biting her lip. 'I'll tell the children you came off the bike.'

She wasn't going to ask me what happened. I wasn't going to have to lie to her. The relief was overwhelming. I took her hand and kissed it. I couldn't tell her what had happened. That was bad enough. But lying to her… That was impossible. I never wanted to lie to her. There were many things I couldn't tell her. Not yet. But I would never lie to her. I loved her so much, I was afraid to tell her, and I was so grateful for her faith in me, for not interrogating me, not insisting on knowing everything. It made me love her all the more. Her trust and faith in me were amazing, astonishing, humbling.

'I'll get you some aspirin.'

The bedroom was full of sunlight. It was so peaceful. I could hear birdsong. Seagulls overhead and starlings in the garden. It was as if everything that had happened last night was a dream, a bad dream. I'd woken up now, and the nightmare had gone. It had never existed. None of it had ever happened… No. There was no fooling myself. It had happened. My head still hurt. There was a cut behind my ear which was still bleeding. I put my hand to it and it came away wet and red. There were blood-stains on the pillow. I've got to give this up, I thought. It's madness. I was lucky last night. Next time I won't be lucky. Or the time after that… Sooner or later it will end badly. I could lose everything… Helen and Liz and Richard, they could all suffer. It wasn't fair on them. It was insane. Stop it now, before it's too late.

Then I remembered the satisfaction, the joy, the righteous joy I'd felt when I'd shredded Dirty Flirt, and smashed Adam, and… No, I wasn't going to stop. I couldn't stop. It was my duty, my responsibility. I had to carry on until every last work of Harry Jutting had been destroyed. I had to make sure every last trace of him was wiped off the face of the earth. It was a question of justice, of right and wrong. I couldn't back down from it, even if I wanted to.

Helen returned with a glass of water and some aspirin. I struggled to sit up. 'I'd better get moving,' I said. 'Get Liz and Richard up… let you get off to work…'

'You stay in bed,' she said firmly. 'Liz and Richard are up. I'll take them to the shop with me. They can amuse themselves there, pretend they're helping me. Morning's are never busy.'

'You're a saint,' I said quietly. It hurt when I spoke. 'I love you. I worship you.'

'I knew.' She put her hand to my face again, gently stroking the cuts and bruises. She still looked worried and upset. 'William…'

'Yes?'

She hesitated for a moment. Then she straightened up, as if changing her mind. 'Come and get them in the afternoon, OK?' she said briskly. 'I'm not sure I can look after them and mind the shop all day.'

I heard them bustling out, then the house was suddenly very quiet. I was very tired, I tried to get back to sleep, but I couldn't. My mind wouldn't relax. For some reason, it kept on fretting about that woman's visit, that journalist with the coffee pot. It troubled me. I wondered if she was making more enquiries about me, the kind of questions she might be asking, the people she was asking, the answers she might be getting. Who was she showing my work to? I shook my head. She'd learn nothing from that. I was sure there was nothing in that pot, nothing in any of my work, to give anything away. Was there? She could buy every plate, cup, mug, dish, tea-pot and coffee-jug of mine, show it to every gallery and critic and collector in the world and she still wouldn't learn anything about me. But her curiosity, her interest, what if it spread, if she sparked something off? I shook my head again, laughing at myself. Don't be stupid. They're just pots. Just ordinary tools for the ordinary kitchen. What interest could they have for anybody? What was I expecting, a mad stampede of metropolitan collectors down the lane? Ridiculous.

Strangely, I wasn't worried about what had happened last night. I wasn't worried about the Russian and his woman telling the police anything about the intruder. I guessed they'd clear out sharpish, leave the mess for someone else to find, pretend they knew nothing about any of it. They weren't going to hang around as witnesses. It was more than his job was worth, and she'd want as

59

little to do with the forces of law and order as possible. The Rashnikovs would get the cleaners and decorators in, the cost of getting everything straight wouldn't bother them for a second, they'd be grateful nothing had been stolen, they'd claim insurance on the picture ('I never could understand what you saw in it, Irina, ugly monstrosity, I'm glad it's gone') and that would be that. They might not even get the police involved. And what if they did? Fingerprints? Blood stains? DNA samples? What did I have to fear about any of that? The CCTV footage from the cameras at the front and the back of the house – an intruder, anonymous in biker leathers and crash-helmet – what could that tell anyone about me? No, I wasn't worried about any of that. Perhaps I should have been.

I got up and took a shower and pulled on some clothes. I avoided the bathroom mirror. The pain of the cuts and bruises on my head was enough, without seeing them as well. I went into the kitchen to make coffee and toast. While the kettle was boiling, I looked around for the journalist's business card. I found it on the windowsill where she'd left it. Becky Short. Forwards Backwards. An office address in east London. I tore it in half and threw it in the rubbish bin.

After breakfast I pulled on wellingtons and a coat and strode out towards the sea across the lush, flat fields of pasture behind the house. The grass was a rich, dazzling bright green. The cows were knee-deep in it. Happy and incurious, they looked up from their grazing as I passed along the dykes and hedges. The fresh air cleared my head. I climbed up onto the sea wall and the wind from the south west hit me, tugging and buffeting, trying to send me bowling back across the fields. I crunched down across the pebbles to the sea's edge. The tide was in, and the wind was thrashing white-capped waves towards the shore, and the water itself looked bruised and muddy. The sky was cloudy, but still shed a silvery light down on the glittering sea all the way out to the bright horizon. At my feet, the shingle rattled and the water hissed as the waves came in and out, in and out. It was like the earth breathing, the earth and the sea and the sky, a single living being, huge, magnificent. It was very beautiful. It was always very beautiful, this world. Until man started shitting all over it. Created by God, spoiled by man. And worse than the vandals who shit all over it are the spivs and con-men like Harry Jutting who say 'So God gave you a beautiful world and you spoilt it? Never mind! Here's another one, made by me, just as good, no, even better! Forgotten how to worship, what to worship? Well, worship this, worship me!'

Men like Harry Jutting had to be stopped. Their work had to be destroyed. All trace of them had to be wiped off the face of this beautiful world. Stop? Give it up? No. I had to carry on. It was my duty, my mission, my purpose. The evil bastard might be dead, but an artist always lives on in his work. He'll never be truly dead while any of it survives. There was still a lot to do before I could say 'rest in peace' over his grave.

*

I fell asleep just before mid-day, and when I woke up there wasn't much of the afternoon left. I came awake suddenly, with a jolt of guilt and fear. Helen had asked me to take the kids off her hands. I'd let her down. I was hungry but there was no time for lunch. I hurried out of the house and up the lane. I had a bad feeling, a sense of apprehension, of dread even. I don't know why. Perhaps it was just the weather. The clouds had thickened and darkened overhead. The wind was rising and it was cold. It was going to rain.

61

It started pouring down just before I reached the shop. I ran the last hundred yards, and pushed open the door, laughing with relief, ready to apologise. But the laughter froze and the apology died on my lips.

Mary, Fred's wife was in there. That wasn't unusual. She often walked up the lane at this time of day, to meet her children off the school bus and walk back to the farm with them. And if she was early, she waited in the shop. She was talking to Helen, talking quietly, but I could hear the anxiety in her voice even if I couldn't hear her words. I could see the worry in her face, in the way she stood. Helen was listening, sympathetic and attentive, and shot me a brief glance of warning as I came in. I looked round quickly for Liz and Richard. Liz was standing on an upturned wooden box behind the counter, playing shop with an old-fashioned set of scales and a queue of invisible customers. Richard was asleep in his fleece-lined basket, on the floor beside her. They both seemed fine, though Liz kept shooting inquisitive and concerned glances at the two grown-ups.

'Ah! There it is!' Mary exclaimed, and looking up we saw the school bus pulling off the main road and into the shop's car-park. She hurried past me, turning up the hood of her coat, out of the shop and into the rain.

'What's the matter?'

Helen sighed and shook her head. 'She's got some bad news for Kylie.'

'What is it?'

Helen smiled wryly. 'It shouldn't matter, but, well, I can remember being eleven years old... Mary's worried she might have heard already, at school...'

'Heard what?'

'Some actor's died. Some actor off the television, stars in some programme they watch. Some sort of heart-throb,

Kylie's got a big thing about him, pictures all over her bedroom, you know…'

'Who? Who is it? What's his name?'

'I don't know. Some actor. Can't remember his name. Found dead some time this morning. Mary thinks Kylie'll take it really badly…'

'Found dead? How? Where?'

'Don't know. He was young, in his twenties, sad really…'

'How was he killed?'

She looked at me, frowning, puzzled. 'Killed? Was he killed? I don't think they've said…'

The door burst open and a storm swept into the shop. Kylie was wailing and crying and shouting, Mary was trying to sooth her but was too agitated to do anything but wind up her daughter's hysteria, Andy was alternatively groaning in disgust and gleefully teasing his sister with cruel laughter. 'But you didn't even know him, you stupid cow,' he was shouting. 'You'd never met him! It wasn't as if you were bloody married to him!'

Kylie shrieked and sobbed, kicking out at her brother and trying to scratch his face. Her mother held her back and her brother taunted her, grinning. 'I was going to marry him!' she screamed. 'I loved him! We would have met, would have… but not now! Not ever! He was going to marry me! He was! He was!'

Richard suddenly woke up and started crying. I picked him up and rocked him in my arms. Liz was standing very still and stiff, staring silently at the human maelstrom. Her eyes were wide and filling with tears. I took her hand and squeezed it. It was shaking, but she looked up at me and blinked back the tears when she saw my smile.

'Kylie! Now, Kylie! Kylie!' Mary was trying to restrain her and comfort her at the same time, but her daughter just writhed and wailed and screamed in her grip.

Helen stepped forwards and suddenly Kylie was in her arms. The girl clung to her, burying her face in her chest, sobbing her heart out, her body limp but her arms tight round Helen's waist. Helen hugged her and bent her head to her ear and made quiet hushing sounds. Kylie was no longer screaming and wailing, and her muffled sobs grew quieter and slower.

Mary stood back, gasping for breath, fanning herself with one hand, the other hand pressed to her heart. She seemed dazed, but relieved that some sort of calm had been restored. Andy withdrew grumbling and moaning to inspect the shelf of chocolate bars below the counter. Richard stopped crying, and I sat him on the counter and Liz passed him his plastic teething ring to chew on. It was quiet enough to hear the rain drumming on the roof of the shop, and the traffic speeding by along the main road outside.

Who was dead? Who? I had to know. I could guess, but I had to know for sure.

Andy was humming to himself and singing softly under his breath, as he rummaged through the shelf of fair-trade organic chocolate. '...'s dead and done for, la-la-la-la-la, la-la-la-la,' he sang to the tune of 'Deck the Hall with Boughs of Holy', the ditty he'd no doubt been tormenting his sister with for the last half-hour. Some words were drowned by the traffic and the rain and Kylie's intermittent sobs. '...'s dead and ... for, la-la-la-la-la, la-la-la-la. Dead and done for, dead and done for, la-la-la, la-la-la, la-la-la. Jimmy Hobson's...'

Jimmy Hobson. James Hobson. The actor we'd seen interviewed on the television last week. The actor who had been playing the lead role in the film about Harry Jutting...

'Andy! Stop that!' his mother snapped. Andy fell silent, grinning with secret and malicious satisfaction, his back to the women. 'William, would you mind walking Andrew home? We'll be along in a while, once Kylie's...'

I exchanged glances with the Neanderthal child. He seemed bored and eager enough to move on. I could see the sense of separating him and his sister. He was, of course, old enough to make his own way down the lane, but mothers often don't see such things. I didn't suggest it – my heart leapt at the chance to question Andy on his own. I glanced at Helen. Her arms were still round Kylie. The girl's thin, pale, freckled face was still half buried in her shoulder. Would she be OK if I left her with Liz and Richard again? She nodded. Just get that little devil out of here.

It had stopped raining. But the sky was still heavy and dark, and the lane was a flood of running water. Andy splashed his way downhill, swearing at the puddles. 'I bloody hate this place. Bloody mud and shit and stupid, boring stuff. Bloody hate it.'

'What happened to James Hobson?' I asked bluntly. I couldn't help myself. I should have been more subtle, indirect, but I couldn't wait.

Andy made his right hand into a gun and pointed it at me, sniggering. 'Bang bang!'

'He was shot?'

Andy shrugged. 'Dunno.' He shoved his hands back in his pockets and trudged morosely on.

'How did he die? Was he killed?'

'What do you think I am? News at Ten?'

I wanted to grab the little troll and throttle and beat the news out of him. When his sister didn't want to hear about it, he wouldn't shut up; but now I wanted to hear about it, he wouldn't open his mouth. He squinted sideways at me. 'Here, what happened to your face? All those cuts and bruises and stuff?'

'I'll tell you, if you tell me about James Hobson.'

He shrugged. 'Fair enough. But why are you so interested in a prat like him, anyway?'

'How did you hear about his death?'

'The kids at school were talking about it. I wasn't bothered. Good riddance, I say. Can't stand First Orders. Can't stand him. Always right up his own arse, know what I mean? Reckoned he was the geezer, the man, always banging about his dodgy dad, his gangsta background. Made it all up, I bet, just to be the Bad Boy. Yeah, the girls all loved it, they swallowed it whole. Pathetic. Makes me want to puke.'

'So what happened?'

'Dunno. You know what it's like. Someone says he had a heart-attack. No, someone else says, it was an over-dose. Don't be bloody stupid, he was so drunk he puked up in his sleep and drowned on it. No, he was shot, he was knifed, he killed himself, whole bottle of sleeping-pills, slit his wrists. Who knows? Take your pick.'

We were at the bottom of the hill now. We walked past the cottage and on towards the farm. It was starting to rain again.

'Shit.' He hunched his shoulders and pulled his hood down over his eyes and quickened his pace. 'Didn't believe any of it, at first. There's always some mad, made-up story going around at school. Last week, some nutter started the rumour that Prince Harry had been done for flashing. So perhaps it's all lies about James Hobson. Perhaps he's alive and well, after all.' He sniggered. 'I hope not, though. He deserves to die after that record he made with the Zap Crew last year. Did you hear it? What a piece of shit. Why did the Crew do it? He made even those well-hard ass-kicking geezers sound like a bunch of wet pussies. What were they thinking of? The money, probably. Number one for five weeks. Still charting in the States. Every dumb girl in the world must have downloaded ten copies each. Makes you sick.'

He pulled a pair of ear-phones out of his pocket and plugged them into his head. A tinny rattle rose in a monotonous beat over the whisper of the rain in the trees around us. Andy trudged on, head down, nodding and grunting and looking more like a troglodyte than ever. He seemed to forget all about me. We came to the open gate at the end of the lane and he was inside the farmyard before he suddenly remembered. He tugged the earphones out. 'Here, what about your face, then?'

'I had a fight with a naked Russian body-guard and a Ukranian pole-dancer.'

He looked at me and grinned. 'Yeah. Heh heh heh. Cool. As if.' He sniggered. He liked the idea but couldn't quite bring himself to believe it. 'Yeah. Heh heh heh. If only.' For some reason he raised his right hand like a gun and pointed it at me again. 'Bang bang!' Then he slouched off across the farmyard, stuffing the earphones back into his head.

I turned and retraced my steps back up the lane. It was growing dark. The rain was falling heavily again. I was shivering feverishly. I was still shivering when Helen and the children returned to the cottage a little later.

'No wonder,' Helen said, bringing me a towel. 'What do you expect, sitting around soaked to the skin? Why don't you go and put on something warm and dry?'

I grunted in pretend agreement. I was cold and wet, but that wasn't it. That wasn't it at all. I went and got changed, but that didn't stop me shivering.

*

It was still raining two days later when I rode over to Folkestone on the bike. A gift-shop there had taken some

67

samples of my work on trial. They'd all sold, and they now wanted to place a big order, so I told Helen I wanted to go over and chat about it. But I really wanted a library where I could search newspapers for reports of Hobson's death. I had to know how he had died. Had he been shot? I had to know everything. I couldn't sleep, I couldn't think about my work. I had to know.

My work routine had gone to pieces over the last few days. I'd fired a batch of glazed pots the day before. They had cooled overnight, and I could have unloaded them that morning, but I left without opening the kiln. Which just goes to show how eager I was to know more about Hobson's death.

But I went to the shop first (was I frightened of what I might find in the library?). It was in the old town, on one of the pedestrianised streets winding down towards the sea-front, every shop an art gallery or craft centre. The owners – a gay couple who had moved down from Manchester only a few months ago – made tea in a pot of mine and we sat around drinking it from my cups and chatting about the order.

'We'll take whatever you've got,' Tom said. He was middle-aged, wore tweed suits and a tie and smoked a pipe. He was the business half. 'Those samples shifted so quickly, we could have sold them five times over.'

'We were surprised, to be honest,' Tim said. He was in his twenties but looked like a teenager. Beautiful. Fashionably dressed. He was the art half. 'You know, no decoration, subtle colouring, we thought we might have trouble shifting them, but... well, there's something about them, the shape, they're lovely to look at, and a pleasure to use...'

'There was a lot of interest as well,' Tom cut in. 'Some journalist was in here a week or two ago, heard we had some of your pieces, she was really disappointed they'd gone. She was asking all about you. Said she'd looked you up. Seemed puzzled, excited by the encounter…'

Tim chuckled. 'Hmmm, what did you do to her, Will? She was really turned on, wanted to know everything about you. But don't worry, we didn't give away any of your secrets. Not that we know any. Care to tell us some?'

'Who was she? What did she look like?'

'What was her name, Tim? Becky something? Betty? She left a card, didn't she?'

'Yes. Here it is. What did she look like? What, I believe, your lot would call 'hot'. Wasted on us, of course, but she did her best to charm us, poor thing.'

I looked at the card, and saw again that girl knocking at my front door. Becky Short. What did she want? Why was she so interested in me?

'She wants to make you rich and famous, Will. You'll still remember us when dealers and agents are pouring champagne down your throat in London, won't you? You'll still let us have stock for our humble concern, won't you?'

The library was on a busy road outside the old town. It was a shabby Victorian building huddled between a multistory car-park and a shopping centre, the red-brick filling in a concrete sandwich. I stood outside for some moments, hesitating, even though it was still raining and my ears were full of the roar of the traffic and my lungs were choking on its acrid fumes.

You don't have to go in there, I told myself. You don't have to know about James Hobson. What do you care about a minor TV actor? You can just walk away, forget about the whole thing, just carry on and nothing will change. But if you go in there… if you find out for sure…

I opened the door and stepped into the dingy entrance hall, out of the rain and away from the traffic.

The newspapers were in the reference section at the back of the building. I gathered as many as I could find from the day before and the day before that and sat down among the students and the tramps and the unemployed and the harmless mad. My hands were shaking. I skimmed through the tabloids first. Their headlines screamed at me. They were making the most of Hobson's death. A heart-throb TV star and chart-topping singer, about to break into the movies - it was gift for them. Actual facts about his death were few and far between. It had happened on location in London during the filming of Art Crash Express. He had retired to his caravan after working half the night, and his body had been discovered there the next morning when runners had tried to rouse him for breakfast at eight o'clock. The cause of death had not been made public. Foul play had not been ruled out. There was a huge amount of speculation, most of it wild and contradictory.

The tabloids concentrated on the sensational sides of his showbiz career, his love-life (masses of grieving girlfriends), punch-ups with fellow actors and paparazzi, and his picaresque background. Born and brought up in Essex, family well known to the police, parents divorced, father in prison for tax-evasion, re-married to an ex-glamour model, mother living in Florida re-married to a night-club owner. There were plenty of photos. Once again I was struck by the resemblance to Harry Jutting. The same thuggish good-looks. Thick-set, fair-haired. Aggressive jaw, arrogant mouth, give-a-shit sparkle to the eyes. A right pair of bastard, selfish egomaniacs. They'd have got on together like a house on fire. Or tried to beat the hell out of each other, two stags locking horns over one herd of deer.

The broadsheets concentrated on his acting achievements, trying to assess his abilities, suggesting tragic lost potential. There was a lot about Art Crash Express and what would become of the project. Filming was only half-complete. Would there be funding to re-cast and re-shoot? Or would the whole thing have to be abandoned, written-off? There were interviews with the director, screen-writer, co-stars. There was background information about Harry Jutting, the usual wild-boy stories, bright-comet-burnt-out-too-early stuff, parallels drawn between Hobson's death and Jutting's death.

There was much discussion of the death-threats Hobson had received through the post. The police wouldn't comment on them, but it was presumed that the anonymous letters were playing a large part in their enquiries. One journalist claimed there was a curse linking Hobson's death with that of Jutting ten years ago.

I found myself reading very carefully everything that was written about Harry Jutting. A lot of it was rubbish. Ill-informed, misunderstood, or just plain made-up. It was amazing how facts and events could be distorted over a mere ten or fifteen years. But they'd got the broad and basic outline of his short career well enough. Art-school drop-out. Brit Art success based on canny marketing, audacious ideas, novel techniques and materials, tongue-in-cheek humour, irreverent and outrageous imagery. And bad behaviour, of course. His life as scandalous, insulting and offensive as his art. There was a lot of discussion about whether his behaviour was a calculated marketing ploy, or just the way he was. A consensus emerged that it was both. A lucky coincidence. Lucky? It lead to fame and fortune, sure, but shortly and sharply to a lonely and sordid death. Suicide. All the old theories about why he killed himself were given predictable treatment. As was all the old speculation about what he might have achieved had he lived: the Turner prize (rumour had it that they'd short-listed him for the prize just before his death, and that there'd been a furious row among its trustees and judges because some of them had thought its rules should be changed to allow a posthumous nomination), the Venice Biennale, etc, etc.

One paper even raised the old question about whether his death really had been suicide. My head span as I read about it. I shivered, remembering Hobson's words: 'He could have been done in. Perhaps someone had a grudge against him...'

There was a lot about the forthcoming exhibition of Montezuma's Revenge, the posthumous and previously unseen work of Jutting's which was about to be revealed at Tate Modern. The Tate was being very mysterious about it, they'd been having a hard time marketing something they wanted to keep a secret, so this was all a blessing in disguise for them. There were lots of photos of Jutting and his work. One of them pulled me up short, and I spent a long time just staring at it. It was a black and white shot of a crowded gallery. In the foreground was a group of youngsters, Harry and his mates, they were all grinning or laughing, waving bottles of beer, blowing kisses or making obscene gestures at the camera. They looked more like a punk band and hangers-on than artists. Little more than teenagers. The caption explained that the shot had been taken at the infamous Brick Shit-House exhibition at Canning Town, which of course had launched Harry's name and work (Shit-A-Brick!) on a strangely grateful and credulous world.

I stared at it for so long that it seemed to come alive in front of me. I shut my eyes. Memory took over. I could see the flashing of the cameras lighting up the semi-dark gallery. Gallery? It was hardly that. Just a half-derelict warehouse, work standing around on the bare concrete floor or hanging from bare brick walls. But hot and crowded that night. Packed and sweaty and noisy. I could hear the roar of laughter and shouted conversation drowning out even the rock music in the background, smell the cigarette smoke and the fumes of beer and wine. Taste it.

I opened my eyes again. I glanced around the library. My fellow students were all either concentrating hard on their own work or fast asleep or muttering blankly as their minds wandered harmlessly in their own private worlds. No one was paying me any attention whatsoever. I folded the page once, twice, flattened the folds into sharp creases, then coughed twice as I tore the photo from the paper. I quickly and furtively folded it up and stuffed it in my pocket.

It was time to go. On the way out, I stopped in the main part of the library to check today's papers. The tabloids were still interviewing tearful ex-girlfriends, but the broadsheets were already losing interest. Not a single journalist seemed aware of a campaign of destruction against the works of Harry Jutting in recent months, let alone tried to put two and two together over it. Each single attack probably wasn't enough to make the news, but put them all together… Sooner or later someone was going to join up the dots and realise something was going on.

The cause of death had still not been announced. But the police had declared that foul play was now suspected.

So how had he died? Were we ever to know? And did it matter? I shook my head, trying to clear my thoughts. He was dead, did it matter how or why? What a fool he must have been. He'd been warned, hadn't he? What did he think he was doing, trying to re-create another's man's life? What did he think he was, a god? Challenging God's reality with man's fantasy. What kind of a job was that, anyway? What kind of a work for a respectable, responsible adult is acting, anyway? Why turn your back on God's world and immerse yourself in artifice, fantasy, make-believe? And then sell that artifice to hundreds, thousands, millions around the world? Isn't God's world good enough, that you have to invent a rival one? And what kind of a life, what kind of a world, what kind of a man had he been trying to recreate? An evil one, an irresponsible one, a selfish one. Just the kind of life and man to be left in the past, in the grave, buried and forgotten. James Hobson had tried to dig Harry Jutting up, and look what had happened. It was difficult for me to feel sorry for him. He had been warned not to defy reality, he had ignored the warnings, and reality had caught up with him. Inevitably.

It was time to forget about James Hobson, I told myself as I left the library. But that was easier said than done. I remembered Andy raising his right hand, saw him aiming it at me again, but this time aiming a gun at me, the gun I'd taken off the Russian security man. 'Bang bang!' Andy said, grinning, and pulled the trigger.

Chapter Four

It was late afternoon when I saw the farm shop appear at the top of the hill ahead of me, the leafy entrance to the lane off to the left beside it. I slowed down to turn off the road, and then I saw it, in the shop's car-park. A police-car, parked and empty. An ordinary-enough sight, but it made my stomach turn over with alarm. I steered into the car-park, and made a slow circuit of it without stopping. There were no other vehicles there. I peered through the shop windows. It was closed and dark. Where were the policemen from the car? There was only one answer to that. They had left the car here and walked down the lane.

I turned back onto the main road and drove on for another five minutes. There was another car-park and a picnic area where the road came down level with the sea and ran along behind the sea-wall for a mile or so. I parked the bike and climbed up to the path on top of the sea wall. I followed it back to where the pasture-land of the drained marsh began to spread out to my left, away from the sea. Then I turned onto the foot-path which left the sea-wall and followed the bottom of the hill, joining up with the lane as it came down the hill to our cottage.

It was beginning to get dark by now. The lights were on in the cottage but the curtains were not yet drawn. I didn't go over the style to enter the lane, but kept on the pastureland and skirted the low wall which separated it from our back garden. Stealthily, I climbed over the wall into our yard and crept up to the back of the house. I could see into the sitting room. There were at least three policemen in there, two talking to each other, a third on his phone. I couldn't see Helen or the children.

I backed away, slipping past the shed and climbing back over the wall out of the yard. I walked away from the house. The flat darkness and emptiness of the marsh was ahead of me. My mind was numb. A door in my brain seemed to have closed to all thought and feeling, a panic reaction to keep panic at bay. I found myself on the track to the sea, away from the hill. My feet and legs were wet, I must have stumbled into a drainage ditch on the pasture. I climbed up the sea wall and down onto the beach. There wasn't much light left in the sky, and the tide was so far out I couldn't even see the sea in the darkness or hear the sound of the waves on the muddy sand beyond the shingle.

I sat down in the lee of the sea wall. I was hiding and waiting. Hiding from the police, waiting for them to go away. I couldn't think further than that. My brain was paralysed by fear and shame. I felt ashamed because I'd brought the police down on Helen and the children, I was hiding out here in the darkness and emptiness while they were having to face whatever questions and shocks were being dumped on them by the police. I was afraid because the sanctuary of the cottage, protected by the hill and the sea and the marsh and the lane, had been penetrated. It was the safe haven I'd found and fortified for Helen and the children, but it was no longer safe. I was afraid of what the police might want with me, of course, but I was more afraid that Helen and the children were no longer protected from that by where we lived, this separate world which was separate no longer. While it was separate, I'd been sure nothing could come between me and Helen, between me and my family. But if it was not separate I could no longer feel safe from what I feared more than anything else – losing Helen, and losing our children.

I sat in the thickening darkness and thought about my life with Helen. Ever since I'd met her, I'd been afraid of losing her. I'd been so lucky. Helen, and then Liz, and then Richard. But luck is fragile, unreliable. There were things I should have told her which I hadn't told her because I was afraid I might lose her if I did. Well, I hadn't told her, and it had come to this, so I was going to have to tell her now, that was for sure. And I had a feeling that it was going to be so much worse than it might have been had I told her earlier, that nothing was ever going to be the same again.

I found myself thinking about the children's births. They hadn't been easy, either of them. Liz's had been particularly difficult. Her birth... it was something I didn't like to dwell on, something my memory usually shied away from. But it came back to me now. The abrupt change in the monitoring machine's beeps and silences, the alarm of the midwife, the medical team suddenly appearing in the ward from nowhere, their rapid and well-drilled disposition, the rush to the theatre, Helen lying back with her eyes closed and her mouth open, rocking and juddering with the speed her bed was being wheeled along the corridor. And the sick feeling in the pit of my stomach, the feeling that everything was slipping through my fingers, the fear that Helen and the baby... The helplessness. The guilt that I was causing her all this suffering, the dread that her suffering wasn't going to stop, or that it would only stop if...

I waited hours. I waited until I was sure the police must have gone. Then I waited some more, just to make sure, I told myself. But I knew I was fooling myself. I was delaying my return because I was frightened to go back and face Helen with the truth. Eventually I screwed up my courage and made my way back across the marsh.

It was fully dark now – the cottage was visible only as window lights against the black mass of the hill behind it. I let myself into the kitchen through the back door. Helen was standing at the sink. She turned a face pale with fear and anxiety to meet me. At first she looked hesitant and bewildered. Then anger and relief flashed in her eyes as she saw me. She crossed her arms and the gesture somehow stopped me dead as I stepped towards her. She made no move towards me. 'The police,' she said. She sounded dazed. 'They were here… they…'

'I know.' I glanced out into the hallway, at the foot of the stairs. It was very quiet in there. 'Elizabeth and Richard – are they OK?'

Helen nodded. 'They're in bed.'

I sat down to take off my wet shoes and socks. I was frozen, shivering with the cold.

'William, what's going on?' She didn't sound dazed any more. Her voice was hushed – she didn't want to wake the children – but it was urgent and demanding. 'The police were here. They were asking about you. They were asking all kinds of questions. It's about that actor – the one who died the other day – they're investigating his murder!'

I sighed and closed my eyes. So it was murder, after all. A murder investigation. 'How did he die? Did they say?'

'No! William, what is this? What do you know about it? Were you involved? William!'

I was still sitting down at the kitchen table, one foot bare, the other still clad in wet sock and wet shoe. 'I'm sorry,' I said. 'I'm so sorry.' My eyes were still closed, my forehead in my hand.

'William, you must tell me! They were asking me where you were, the night he was killed. I told them you were here with us. But you weren't. Were you?'

I sighed again and opened my eyes. I leaned back and found myself looking at the ceiling. Somehow I couldn't bring myself to meet her eyes. 'Thank you,' I said. 'But you should tell the police the truth. I don't want you getting into trouble, trying to protect me.'

'The truth.' She laughed sharply. 'How can I tell them the truth, when I don't even know what it is?'

I took off the other wet shoe and sock. I stood up. I went over to the other side of the kitchen and put the kettle on. 'I'll tell you,' I said. 'Sit down. I'll make some tea. Then I'll tell you everything.' I reached for the tea-pot, getting my thoughts together, preparing my words. I glanced at Helen. She was sitting at the table, her hands together on the cloth in front her, waiting, a frown of anxiety and impatience on her face. She was no longer pale, but flushed. But she seemed calm. I knew she wasn't the type to shout and scream and throw things, and I was grateful for it. But I wondered if even she was strong enough, self-contained enough, to remain calm and sensible after what I was about to tell her.

'There was a man called Harry Jutting – an artist – he was quite famous ten or fifteen years ago – remember?'

Helen frowned, concentrating, trying to remember. 'Vaguely. Something about pissing in the Queen's pond? Some kind of wild genius… And a bird-cage someone in Hong Kong bought for millions of quid? Didn't he kill himself or something?'

'A bad man. Cruel and insensitive. A bad life.' The kettle boiled. I filled the pot, stirred it. 'Part of it was his own nature. Part of it was success – it corrupted and spoilt him.' I opened the fridge, reached in for the milk. 'And part of it was the way he lived. Always drunk or drugged, never fully conscious of the world around him, never fully in control of himself.'

I put the tea things on the table and sat down opposite Helen. I poured her a cup of tea, added milk, put the cup down in front of her. She ignored it. She was staring at me, waiting for me to continue.

'Well, a number of bad things happened all at once. Bad things he did to other people. And at last, somehow, some awareness of the evil he'd done suddenly broke through to him. In a sudden flash of enlightenment, a vision, he saw himself for what he was – a monster, a freak. He'd always seen himself as a creator – and yet now he saw that in his life, in the real world, he was in fact a destroyer. His influence on everyone and everything around him was destructive.'

I paused and took a drink of tea. It was far too hot and scalded the roof of my mouth, but I hardly noticed.

'And what's more, he suddenly saw why he was such a monster. He began to see clearly the world around him, the real world, the objective world, the world which he - self-centred and self-obsessed - had never really noticed before, had ignored, had always taken for granted. He saw it all as if for the first time and it seemed wonderful to him, miraculous. The miracle of physical creation.'

The words were coming easily now, smoothly. It was as if I had been preparing them for years, rehearsing them. As indeed I probably had.

'And most of all he saw, or rather felt, a creator behind it all. And he saw that this creation was complete and perfect. So what was he doing, trying to create an alternate world, the virtual world of art? He saw that all artistic pursuit was wrong. It was futile and indeed evil, a challenge to the creator, an attempt to set himself up as god, a rejection of the world created for us, for our use and nourishment and delight. Such arrogance, such presumption. No wonder his life was so disastrous; what he was doing was unnatural, literally against nature.'

I was looking at my hands, on the table, on either side of my cup, but I wasn't really seeing them. They could have been someone else's hands. It was as if I wasn't there, or rather as if I had become just a voice in this room, and the body left behind wasn't mine any longer.

'He felt a sudden and overwhelming love for the creator. Gratitude for the beautiful world given to us all. He felt shame and guilt that he had been rejecting this gift, abusing it, competing with it. And he felt a dreadful and terrible sorrow for the damage he had done to the people around him. He was completely repentant.'

The words were like heavy weights falling off me. Difficult and painful to move at first, inert and resisting, but then shed effortlessly, gravity doing all the work, relieving me of a heavy burden.

'So what was he going to do? Only one thing was possible – a total rejection of the life he had been leading. He thought about suicide, but of course that would be the ultimate crime against nature, against the creator. What he wanted was a fresh start, the chance to leave his old life behind and start a new life, a humble and useful life he could live in full harmony with the creator and in gratitude for his gifts.'

I paused. I was suddenly very thirsty. I knew what I had to say next, but my mouth and tongue were too dry. They were protesting, they were mutinying on me. I emptied my cup, refilled it, drank again. With the words queued up like a traffic jam in my brain, waiting. And then released.

'So he staged his own death. Harry Jutting had to die. And he did die, in the eyes of the world. A body was found, which was identified as his. It underwent a post-mortem, a death certificate was written out, a funeral was arranged, the body was buried. But it wasn't Harry Jutting. Harry Jutting changed his name, changed his life, changed everything. He's still alive, though transformed in every way.'

Helen was staring at me, the cup of tea cold and untouched on the table in front of her. She was staring at me with shock and disbelief.

'I changed my name to William Brin ten years ago,' I said. 'Before that I was Harry Jutting.'

She gave a short, sharp laugh, a dazed and incredulous laugh. 'But this is incredible! This is crazy! You're making it up!'

I shook my head. 'No, Helen. It's all true. And I rejoice in it, I celebrate it. You can't imagine what it was like, that sudden moment of complete enlightenment, suddenly realising why everything was wrong, seeing how everything could be right. And managing to put all that darkness behind me, to move on into the light. The last ten years, it's been wonderful. The last seven years, my life with you, it's like a miracle, I've been so lucky…'

She put her face in her hands and sat there, shaking. I thought she was crying at first, and then I realised she was laughing.

'Look.' I reached into a pocket and pulled out the sheet of newspaper I'd torn out at the library. I unfolded it and spread it on the table in front of her. 'Look at that photo. There's Harry Jutting and his mates, fifteen years ago. There. Do you recognise me?'

She looked down at the cutting, then she looked up at me. It was as if she was seeing me for the very first time. 'You look so young. And even better looking. No beard. Shorter hair…'

'I hate what I was. I hate that bastard Harry Jutting. Looking back, it's as if he was another person, someone I've always hated.' I looked down at the photo, at the grinning, arrogant face, at the obscene gesture and the brandished beer-bottle, and felt just that. Sheer hatred. Violent, blind hatred. I took the cutting from her, folded it up again, and put it back in my pocket. 'Helen, I'm sorry, the shock of all this… I should have told you before, perhaps… I'm so sorry…'

She looked at me strangely, as if everything was changing, as if everything she had ever thought and felt

82

about me was under review. 'You were rich…' she said accusingly. She sounded amazed. 'You were famous…'

'Yes. Rich, famous and evil. Helen, I've changed. I am what you've always thought I am. I am the man you know. The man you didn't know really is dead, he doesn't exist.'

'Why didn't you tell me..? All this time… you didn't tell me… years and years..!'

'I was frightened. I was terrified I'd lose you if you knew the truth, if you knew the kind of bastard I was…'

'Didn't you trust me? I trusted you. I always trusted you. Why didn't you trust me?'

'I was frightened it would change everything. But it doesn't, does it? I am Will Brin, I am the man you've always known.' I stared at Helen, but she wasn't looking at me. She was looking at the table in front of her. 'Please tell me nothing has changed. Helen, please, tell me…'

A fox barked and yelled outside in the darkness, a vixen, screaming as if in torment. But Helen was silent. She shook her head, puzzled, bewildered. 'But the police… this actor… his murder…'

I sighed. Yes, there was more. I hadn't finished yet. 'I hate Harry Jutting so much that it isn't enough to get rid of him and then leave the memory of him behind. I want to erase him completely, all trace of him, every last memory. His works still exist – each one is a crime that has to be destroyed. A crime against the creator, against nature, against the real world. And I am destroying them, one by one. That's what I do when I go away at night. I have to do it. I'm responsible for them. It's my duty to rid the world of them. And I won't stop until I've succeeded, until every last one has been destroyed. Then perhaps the world will be able to forget that Harry Jutting ever existed.'

Helen was staring at me again, frowning.

Get it all out. Tell her everything. 'So when I heard, months ago, that a film was going to be made about Harry

Jutting's life, I knew I had to stop it,' I continued. 'I wrote to the lead actor, as soon as he was cast. I warned him of the danger he was putting himself in, I explained why it was wrong, what he was doing, why it was wrong to make the film. Why Harry Jutting's life shouldn't be preserved in any way.' I closed my eyes, rubbed my hands over my forehead. 'What did they think they were doing, anyway? Creating a fantasy world, a copy of reality? Isn't reality good enough? Is the natural world inadequate? Do they think they can make a better one? Film-makers, they're like counterfeiters, they're cheats, making money by selling us fake worlds, fake lives for us to live in!'

'Hush, William.' Helen sounded alarmed. She was looking at me strangely. 'Not so loud, you'll wake the children. No need to shout.'

'Did he take any notice of my warnings? No. The idiot. The fool. And look what happened to him. He was like a man insisting on driving the wrong way down a one-way street. Blind-folded. What did he expect?'

'William.' Helen leaned forwards. She reached out and took my hands in hers. She looked into my eyes. I could see fear there, and alarm, and anxiety. 'Did you kill him? Did you kill that actor?'

I held her hands. They felt warm, and small and delicate, but strong. I looked away and closed my eyes. I had never lied to Helen. There were things I had chosen not to tell her, but I couldn't lie to her. I mustn't lie to her. No, I thought, I didn't kill him. But I could remember the feel of the Russian's gun in my hand, its hardness, its heaviness, its coldness, in the hands that now held Helen's. And I could see the row of lorries and trailers and caravans in the dark backstreet, night-time, the whole world asleep. The film-makers' gypsy encampment, parked under the moon and the street-lights. Did I see it in my memory, or my imagination? 'No! I didn't kill him!' And there was another image. A body sprawled on the floor. The body of a young man. Blood in his hair, blood pooling on the floor around his head. The smell of cordite, the echo of a gunshot. Brightly lit inside, darkness outside. Was that memory? No! No! It was imagination! I was imagining it! 'I didn't!'

I opened my eyes, and found myself staring into Helen's again. They were still full of fear and alarm and anxiety. When I spoke again, my voice was very quiet. 'But there are these… images… visions…' I licked my lips. 'And to be honest they… I don't quite… it's…'

She shook her head, bewildered. 'This isn't you, Will. All this anger and hatred and violence. It can't be. You're kind, and gentle, and loving…'

'I was warning him, Helen. Not threatening him.' I sighed. 'If you saw someone doing something stupid and dangerous, like… like… walking too close to a crumbling cliff-edge, wouldn't you want to warn them? And would you be to blame if they ignored you and the ground gave way under their feet and they fell to their death? No! You'd be praised for trying to save them, surely!'

'But the police… how… how did they find you?'

'Yes. That's the question.' I got up and began to pace around the kitchen. 'I don't know how they got onto me. I can't work it out. Those letters, of course. But how did they connect them with me? How did they find out who sent them, how did they find me? Someone must have put them onto me, someone must have set me up with all this.' I turned to Helen. 'Do the police know who I really am? Did they give any sign that they know about my past?'

'No, they didn't say, there was no suggestion…' Helen frowned and shrugged. 'But that doesn't mean they don't know… William, they said you've got to go and see them, at the station, first thing tomorrow… they left their details, they're written down over there on top of the fridge…

perhaps you should phone them right now… they threatened to come back with a search warrant, an arrest warrant…'

'No.' I shook my head. 'Someone's discovered my secret. Someone's setting me up with James Hobson's murder. I've got to find out who, and why. And I won't be able to do that if I give myself up to the police.'

'What are you going to do?' Her voice was unsteady. There were tears in her eyes and she was breathing hard. She was strong and sensible, but there was a limit to even her strength and common sense, and she had had one shock after another that evening.

'I've got to go away for a while.' I put my arms round her, and she didn't resist, though I could feel her shaking as if she was still afraid. 'I'll have to leave you and the children here, while I go off and find out who betrayed me.'

'I'm frightened, William. I'm really frightened. Everything you've told me… Shouldn't we just go to the police?'

'I can sort this out. I've got to.'

'But where will you go? Where will you stay?'

I shook my head. 'If I told you, you'd have to tell the police. I don't want to make you lie to them, I don't want you to get into trouble for that.' I was beginning to feel angry. Angry with whoever it was that had done this, who was driving me away from my home, from Helen and Elizabeth and Richard, from everyone I loved. Yes, I would find them…

The sound of crying came from upstairs. Richard. Our voices must have woken him up. I felt Helen stiffen in my arms. 'I'll go,' I said, and released her and headed for the stairs.

The sound of crying had stopped even before I reached the landing. I went into the children's room. Some light from downstairs came into the dark room through the open door behind me. Richard was asleep; he must have woken up for a moment, then gone back to sleep. It often happened. I leant over into his cot and kissed him on the forehead. 'Bye, Richard. Sleep tight, little chap. See you soon.'

I turned away from the cot and saw that Elizabeth was awake. She was lying quite still in bed, her head on her pillow, but her eyes were open and she was watching me silently. I sat down on the edge of her bed and stroked her hair. 'All right, sweetie?'

She nodded. 'Richard woke up,' she said. 'He had a little cry.'

'He's fine now. Fast asleep. Are you going to go back to sleep?'

She nodded again and closed her eyes, but she reached out from under her quilt and took one of my hands.

'Lizzy,' I said, 'I've got to go away for a little bit, away from you and Mummy and Richard.'

She opened her eyes again. 'Why?'

'Just to sort a few things out. But I won't be long. A few days, a few weeks. You'll be good for Mummy while I'm away, won't you?'

'Yes.' She looked at me and I could see that she was barely awake. She'll probably think this is all a dream in the morning, I thought.

'You go to sleep now, Lizzy.' I bent over and kissed her cheek. 'Love you lots, Lizzy.'

Her eyes were closed and she was breathing slowly and deeply. She was already asleep. I tucked her hand back under her quilt and left the room.

Helen hardly spoke while I packed. It didn't take long. She seemed to be in a state of shock when we said goodbye. I didn't know what to say to her. There was so much I wanted to say, but I didn't know how to say it, and

I had said more than enough that night anyway. If I had said any of it earlier, years earlier, would it have made any difference? Who knows?

I walked through the darkness back to where I'd left my bike. I felt like I was being expelled from Eden. I was being driven into a cruel and solitary exile. Even Adam had Eve with him, but I was on my own. If I had turned round, I wouldn't have been surprised to see a fierce angel towering over the cottage, brandishing a fiery sword at me and warning me never to return. I found my bike parked by the sea wall and the deserted picnic area, unlocked its right-hand pannier and stuffed my bag inside. The sound of its engine roaring into life cruelly tore the silence of the night apart. I steered it round to the gate, its headlamps probing the darkness out at sea, and then I was on the main road and accelerating up the hill. At the top I passed the turning down to the cottage and the farm, passed the dark and shuttered shop and its empty car-park, and became just one more of the scattered sets of lights speeding away into the night.

*

I stopped at a motorway service station to fill up with petrol. I'd covered many miles already that day, and it was now the middle of the night and I was half-way to London. It wasn't until I'd left the speeding darkness and come to rest in the floodlit forecourt with the pump in my hand that I realised how cold and tired and hungry I was feeling. I went into the café and sat down with a mug of tea and a baked potato and tried to think about where I was going and what I was doing.

Who had betrayed me to the police? Who had told them that Harry Jutting was still alive? Who might want to do that?

I took out the page I'd torn from the newspaper and spread it on the table in front of me. I peered at the grainy photo, at the wild young faces leering out of it. They were all there, all five of them. Harry had his left arm round the shoulders of a fat little kid with dyed blond hair, and his right arm around a tall slim girl with masses of dyed black hair and black eye-shadow. The fat kid was sneering and gurning comically at the camera, flicking v-signs at it with both hands. The girl had a bottle of beer and a cigarette in one hand, the other was raised to give the camera the middle finger; her tongue was sticking out. Just to one side stood another lad, very thin, an intelligent face and a nervous smile, beer bottle in right hand, left hand raised in a salute which could be either a welcome or a warning. And behind them, somewhat detached, another youth, not smiling, not gesturing, staring at the camera with a hard, minimal cool, as sober and wary as a bouncer at a riotous nightclub.

Harry Jutting, Gary Hughes, Stella McNye, Patrick Joyce and Steve Smith. There they were, all together at this party where it had all begun. Gary Hughes, the funny little fat kid, always good for a laugh, who hero-worshipped Harry. Harry's dog, Harry's slave. Yes, Harry, no, Harry, of course, Harry, no problem. Stella McNye, who did her best to keep Harry on the straight and narrow but failed miserably, Stella the unattainable, the constant challenge, Harry's conscience. And Patrick Joyce, intelligent, highly-strung, painfully thin but looking Ok for once, yes, looking fine, surprisingly relaxed... And Steve Smith; fit and tough and well-groomed, you'd think he was a soldier or a policeman, if it wasn't for his good gear, his expensive threads, his bling – jeans, t-shirt and leather jacket immaculate, clean, ironed, looking brand-new, designer-labelled. Expensive watch round his right wrist, chunky gold bracelet round his left. What's he doing here, smart and cool and casual, among these wild and scruffy art-school punks? He seems to be asking himself the same question.

One of them was the only person in the whole world who had known my secret. Each one of the other three had reason enough to punish me, to want revenge, to hate me enough to betray that secret to the police. One of those three had discovered my secret, tracked me down, and turned the police onto me. But which one? And how had they done it?

I sighed and shook my head. I drained the mug of tea and let my eyes wander over the photo. Whoever it is, I thought, James Hobson's death has given them the perfect opportunity for revenge. One word to the police, spilling the truth about Harry Jutting's death, putting two and two together about those written death threats, and I'm the prime suspect. How long had they been waiting for that chance? Or perhaps… could it be… whoever it was, could he or she have killed James Hobson so they could fit me up with his murder? Was that possible? Were any of these three capable of going to such lengths? All three of them must hate me, but could any one of them hate me that much?

That's what I had to find out. I was going back to where it had all started, to where it had all happened, and somehow I'd track them down and uncover the truth. Back there. I shivered, thinking about that patch of East London, remembering the crumbling terraces and the grey tower blocks, the bare concrete expanses, wind-swept and rain-washed. The smell of dog-shit, chip-wrappers, diesel fumes. The coughing roar of taxi-cabs and the whine of buses, the hoarse jeers of bike-pedalling hoodies winding each other up, the snort of padding and harnessed Staffies tugging at the lead as fag-smoking, shaven-headed hard-men walked them in the park among vandalised trees and across mud-patched grass. Down and outs drinking in the stinking darkness under the canal bridge, abandoned supermarket trolleys half-submerged in the stagnant water beside them. Back there. That's where I was going.

I went out to the toilets for a piss, and caught sight of myself in the mirror above the basins as I washed my hands. I looked hard at myself, remembering the fifteen-year old photo. How much had I changed? It was hard to tell. I'd had short-cropped hair and scruffy stubble in those days. Now I had long hair and a thick beard. If I shaved it all off, had a ruthless hair-cut, how easily would I be recognised? Did I want to be recognised? Would it make my task easier or harder?

And would I be able to recognise those four – Gary and Stella and Patrick and Steve? Would I even be able to find them? Ten years ago – who knows where they were now. They could be anywhere. Except Patrick Joyce, of course. I knew where he was, I knew how to find him, even if I didn't want to think about it and could never imagine going there. But the others… Well, the search had to begin somewhere.

There was a motel next to the filling station. I booked in for the night, too exhausted to travel on. I lay down on the bed with relief, but odd memories and strange flash-backs seemed to fly out of the darkness at me, keeping me awake. They were hallucinatory and disconnected and very disturbing. I tried to fight them off, to avoid them, ignore them. At first they were persistent and vivid, but after a while they became less frequent and demanding and I began to drift off to sleep. Eventually they began to fade and then ceased altogether.

But even asleep, I was conscious that they were still there, beyond the darkness and the night, those memories and flash-backs. It was as if I could hear them whispering and murmuring and rustling somewhere outside sleep's field of vision. They mixed themselves into my dreams, dreams of what had happened that day, frightening and distorted dreams of empty police-cars and policemen in the cottage and Helen and the children lost on the dark marshes. And they kept on dragging me awake, time and again, until eventually I was wide awake, and I knew there'd be no more sleep that night. You'll have to face up to them sooner or later, I told myself, or you'll never get another moment's sleep for the rest of your life.

I got out of bed and turned the light on. I reached into my bag and pulled out a bulky A4 envelope. It was one of the few things I'd packed. Inside it was a thick, dog-eared manuscript. I slid it out, and began to read it. 'Number forty-seven, Navarino Row. End of terrace…' The sound of cars coming and going to the filling station and speeding by on the dark motorway outside faded as I read. I sat there on the bed, in that pool of hard, dim, crappy light chucked down by the low-energy bulb, and read it from beginning to end. It took almost all night. Over a hundred creased and crumpled pages. Over thirty-thousand faded, photocopied, hand-written words. It was hard, painful, even agonising, forcing myself to revive memories I'd been suppressing for years. It was all there, everything that had happened, everything I should have told Helen years ago. She has to read it even now, I thought. I owe it to her. She has to know everything. I must send it to her. Yes. That's what I'll do. I'll buy a jiffy bag for it first thing in the morning at one of the shops out there in the motorway services. I'll find a post-office as soon as I get to London. Yes. I'll post it to her from there.

I took up a pen and paper and began to write a letter to go with it.

'Dear Helen,

I'm sorry. Truly, deeply sorry. I know that what you read here will hurt and upset you. But I've been hiding these pages and the story they tell for far too long. You have every right to read it. I should never have hidden it from you.

I wrote this manuscript eight or nine years ago, soon after the events it narrates, in an attempt to get to grips with them. I wrote it in that strange limbo period, that strange pitch-black time of suspended animation between the twilight of everything that happened and the miraculous, magical dawn of meeting you. And it's been on my mind ever since that bright and brilliant meeting, because I've been meaning to give it to you to read, I really have, I've known that sooner or later you would have to read it, that I couldn't keep all this from you forever, that you deserved to know everything.

But the time never seemed right. At first I thought, wait until she knows you well, knows you for who you are now. And then Liz was born… and then Richard… and then… with every year there was so much more to lose, I became more and more scared to show these pages to you. Yes, I was scared. I still am. I'm terrified that once you know everything, every last detail, you'll regret ever meeting me, you'll leave me and take Liz and Richard with you. That would destroy me. Which is no more than I deserve, you might say after reading these pages.

But you must believe me, I'm ashamed of what I was, of what I did. Bitterly ashamed. I'm overwhelmed by guilt and regret and self-hatred. You must believe that I am no longer that man. That man is dead. I killed him and buried him and now I am someone else entirely…'

PART II

'…With its Phantom chased for evermore
By a crowd that seize it not…'

Edgar Allan Poe, *The Conqueror Worm*

'God is really only another artist. He invented the giraffe, the elephant and the cat. He has no real style. He just goes on trying other things.'

Pablo Picasso

Chapter Five

Number forty-seven, Navarino Row. End of terrace, council-owned, condemned for demolition years before, to make way for a new roundabout, or for road-widening, or for a car-park, no one was quite sure why. It had stood empty for some time before the first squatters had found it and moved in and somehow persuaded the council to turn the power and water back on. The outside paintwork was cracked and peeling, the wooden window-frames were rotting away, the roof leaked where fallen slates hadn't been replaced. There were no carpets, curtains, lamp-shades, hot water or central heating.

'It's a shit-hole,' I said, looking out of the window of that second-floor room, down at the tiny back garden. It was a cold, grey, rainy October day. The garden was on the north side of the house and deep in shadow. It was overgrown with brambles and long pale grass which barely covered rusty pieces of machinery and a scatter of bottles, cans, plastic bags, tin-foil take-away containers and other rubbish.

'But there's a great pub on the corner,' Gary Hughes countered. He'd found the place for me, through some grape-vine at the art college. I'd needed a room but hadn't been bothered to do anything about it, leaving Gary to do the work for me as usual. And now Gary was doing his best to sell it, as if he was an estate agent with a good commission in the balance. 'And that girl downstairs,' he chuckled. 'What about her? Wouldn't mind thrashing her guitar, eh?'

I grunted. I turned back to the room. Bare boards, bare walls, bare bulb, dirty mattress. Freezing cold. It would do. It was a shit-hole, but that didn't bother me. I couldn't care less. But I wasn't going to show Gary any gratitude.

Didn't want the little creep thinking I was under any kind of debt to him. I dumped my back-pack in a corner. 'Give us a beer,' I said. Gary pulled a can out of the plastic bag full of four-packs I'd persuaded him to buy from the off-licence outside the tube station. I cracked it open and sucked out a frothy mouthful.

A string of slow and resonant notes came bouncing up the stairs from the first floor. The girl in the front room down there was practising on a bass guitar. Yes, I'd noticed her. Not exactly pretty. But quite striking. Tall. Very tall. Slim. Long legs. Masses of long black hair. Must be dyed. Very white face. Black leggings, black sweater, leather jacket. What had she said her name was? Ella? Bella? I'd seen her around the work-spaces at college from time to time, but somehow I'd never actually met her before. What was she studying? Fabrics? 'Welcome to the Navarino Row igloo,' she'd said. 'Hope you've brought your thermal underwear with you.' She'd actually smiled, and she'd looked quite sweet for a moment, at odds with the heavy 'back off, dick-head' vibe of her gothic biker chick appearance. Her room was thick with cigarette smoke and seemed crowded – there were two other guys in there, one zipping a rhythm guitar back into its case and the other fidgeting with a pair of drumsticks, though there was no sign of an actual drum-kit.

There was another art school student in the other first floor room. A fine art student, like me, but I'd never seen him around the college. Skinny, shy, shivering with the cold. Wrapped in an ancient tweed coat, much too big for him, buttoned right up to the throat. Sneezing and snuffling and dabbing at his streaming nose with a disintegrating tissue. He'd looked up from the book he'd been reading, taken off his glasses, and raised one hand in an enigmatic wave of welcome, a nervous grin replacing the frown of concentration on his thin, intelligent face. He was surrounded by piles of books. Hundreds, thousands of them. No book cases. They were just piled, one of top of another, in great columns up against the wall or standing precariously on the floor. There were sketch-books open on the rickety desk by the window. Pencils, sticks of charcoal, water-colours and brushes. The old wicker chair he was sitting in looked like it had been rescued from a tip. He was leaning back in it, his feet up on the window-sill.

'Hi. I'm P-Patrick.' He sneezed violently. 'Patrick J-Joyce.'

I'd never seen the character in the room on the other side of the second-floor landing before, either, but I was sure he wasn't an art student. He'd been about our age, but he was too clean and well-fed. Too fit and healthy. Expensive casual clothes, proper hair-cut. And his face – there'd been something dull and hard and unimaginative about it. All bone. A face which suggested that destruction rather than creation was his way of doing business. He'd been lying on his mattress playing a computer-game on a hand-held consul when Gary had put his head round the door and tried to introduce us in his typical be-my-friend way. The geezer had given him the middle-finger and kicked the door shut without even looking up from his game.

Four rooms. Two on the first floor, two on the second. Bathroom on the first floor. Looked surprisingly clean and well-used, in spite of the lack of hot water. Was that the girl's touch? Some sort of kitchen, not clean, on the ground floor, leading out to the back garden. The front room on the ground floor had looked like a cross between a vintage junk shop, a council tip, and the DJ's cock-pit at a rave venue. The whole house was freezing cold. Portable electric heaters whirred away in each room, but when anyone spoke, their breaths clouded in the icy air.

'What do you reckon, Harry?' Gary was still hoping for a thank you.

'I reckon it's time to hit that pub.' I crossed the landing and opened the door to the other room. The geezer was still lying on his mattress, playing his computer game. Tinny noises trickled out of it and echoed faintly around the bare unfurnished room. 'Coming down the pub?' I said. 'Gary's buying.'

The geezer didn't look up from his game. 'Fuck off,' he said.

I felt a rush of something hot and red, as if my guts were a kettle and it was coming to the boil and sending steam up my spine to my head. Then Gary was pulling and pushing at me and I was walking down the stairs, the stained boards creaking underfoot. 'Coming to the pub?' Gary called out, trotting at my heels. 'Pub, anyone? Pub?' He bustled across the first floor landing, knocking on doors. I could tell he wanted to keep me moving, down the road to the pub, might calm me down. He knew my moods, could sense it when something was brewing. The tall girl followed us downstairs, winding a thick woollen scarf round her long neck. The skinny guy came after her, shivering and pulling on a beanie hat. 'Bloke at the top isn't much of a laugh, is he?' Gary said as we came down to the hallway. He was trying to make a joke of it. 'What's his name?'

Patrick and Stella didn't answer. They exchanged pale glances. They looked really frightened.

'No name?' Gary laughed. 'Man of mystery?'

'Just pretend he isn't there,' Stella whispered. 'And don't say anything to anyone else about him.'

'You what?' Gary said. He laughed uncertainly. He looked a bit frightened himself. It was catching, like a disease. The three of them were beginning to look as if they were sick or something.

'Stay well clear of him,' the girl warned, her voice hushed and serious. 'He's only here for a week or two. The landlord of the Ellerby Arms dumped him on us. Some sort of cousin of his. The family... they're local. Well, were local. Most of them moved out to Essex a while ago. Still well-known round here, though. Get my drift? Our guy made some sort of balls-up, and the family want him out of the way for a while.'

Patrick was nodding in worried agreement. Gary was staring at them, opening and closing his mouth in disbelief. 'Hiding out..? Lying low..?'

'Shhhh!' Stella put her finger to her lips. She sighed and shook her head. 'I feel a bit sorry for him really,' she whispered. 'I mean, he's been here for almost a week now, and he hasn't left the house. Not once. The family have ordered him to stay out of sight. No wonder he's pissed off. He must be going mad up there.'

I laughed. 'What did he do? Forget to fill the getaway car up with petrol?'

Patrick and Stella went even paler and joined in a chorus of urgent 'hush!' noises. 'Please!' Stella hissed. She looked genuinely terrified. 'Don't cause trouble! You should see his cousins, they're really, really scary! They're seriously heavy guys!'

'Give us another beer,' I said. Gary nervously handed me another can. I went back upstairs and kicked the mystery guest's door open. He looked up. His eyes narrowed and his lips pulled tight. 'Too scared to come down to the pub, mate?' I said. 'What are you frightened of, the landlord's daughter?'

He gave a grunt of anger and tried to spring to his feet. But the mattress was very low, right on the floor itself, and I pushed him over again before he could get his feet under himself. 'Don't worry, mate, here's a beer for you. Enjoy it while we're down at the pub.' I cracked the can open and poured the yeasty, foamy cascade all over him as he bounced back onto the mattress and struggled to get up again.

He tried to grab me before he was back on his feet, which was a mistake. I kneed him in the face and over he went again. 'That's for telling me to fuck off.' I lashed out with my right foot, missed, and then he was up and swinging his fists. Something hard and heavy cracked against the side of my head. My ears rang and my sight misted over. I reached out blindly and caught an arm, a handful of jacket, and we were heaving and twisting against each other, shouting and swearing as we wrestled.

I could hear Stella screaming at us to break it up but it was coming from a long way away. Then there was a loud crack and a louder hiss and a powerful jet of something wet and white hit us. The force of it knocked us sideways, the shock of it broke us apart. We were covered in white foam, and the girl was still spraying it at us, the heavy canister of a fire-extinguisher cradled in both arms.

When I got to know Stella, I recognised this as typical Stella behaviour. Typical that she would be sensible enough to keep a fire extinguisher even in a squat, clever enough to improvise with it, and brave enough to wield it in a just cause.

She didn't stop spraying until the canister was empty. 'I warned you!' She dropped it on the floor and put her hands on her hips. She looked angry. Gary and Patrick were white-faced and frightened. Then all three of them started laughing.

We were too wet and shocked to say anything. We were shivering, the foam soaking through our clothes and freezing our skin. 'Sod it,' the guest said at last. 'I'm too cold and wet to hang around here any more. I'm off to the pub with you lot.'

The Ellerby Arms was small and dark and stank of cigarettes and spilt beer, but it was warm and snug. We sat down at a plastic table by a pin-machine and I sent Gary off to get a round in. The bar-maid stared through the smoke at us. As soon as she'd served Gary she disappeared through a door behind the bar. She came back seconds later with a trim, tough-looking middle-aged man at her side. She pointed at us. They stared across the bar at us, frowning and serious. The man came over. He stood opposite the guest, his arms folded, glaring at him. He wore a crisp white shirt with the sleeves rolled up to the elbows, tattoos all over his sinewy forearms. He had cropped hair and a moustache. He looked worried and angry. He wasn't a big man, but he was a hard one, that was obvious. He looked like a welter-weight boxer whose ring-days were over but who kept himself fit and would still be up for a scrap.

The guest looked up at him. He lowered his pint and grinned. "'Lo, Uncle Jeff.'

'Steve. Stupid sod. You mental or something?'

'Calm down, mate.'

'I'm phoning your mum. I am. I'm going to phone her.'

Steve's grin disappeared. 'You bloody won't!'

'Piss off or I call her.' Jeff unfolded his arms and pointed an angry finger at his nephew. Then he looked at his watch. 'Thirty seconds.'

Steve stood up. 'You do that and I'll smash the place up!'

'Oh yeah? You and this bunch of art-school fairies?'

'I'll do it on my bloody own!'

'I'll give you a hand.' I drained my glass and stood up. 'Sounds like fun.'

Jeff turned to me. His hard blue eyes narrowed as he sized me up. 'Jenny,' he said to the barmaid. 'Give Carl a poke.' He turned back to Steve. 'I'm counting.'

'Come on, Jeff. Just a half hour in the boozer. Just a jar or two. I tell you, I'm going mad up there. Bloody freezing, on my own all day, bored out of my skull…'

'Twenty seconds.'

Jenny the bar-maid was coming back and she wasn't on her own. The sight of the man with her made me grope for Gary's barely-touched pint and down it. The man was a giant. Younger than Jeff, older than me, bigger than the two of us put together. He was wearing jeans and a t-shirt with the name of the pub on it. His gut bulged beneath the t-shirt, but so did everything else – shoulder-muscles, chest muscles, back-muscles. His arms and his neck were thick with bunched muscle. His head was huge and round and shaved. He looked as big and solid as a beer barrel. He gripped a baseball bat in each massive fist. He gave one of them to Jeff. He pointed the other one at me and grinned.

A surge of beer-fuelled excitement washed the fear out of my veins. I laughed. 'All right, Carl?' I held the empty pint glass out to him at arm's length. 'Ready?'

A hush had fallen over the whole pub. Everyone was watching and waiting in a tense, expectant silence. I could hear the dripping of one of the taps behind the bar, the rumble of traffic passing by outside.

'Gentlemen!' Patrick stood up suddenly. He was white-faced with fear and his hands were trembling. He looked like he was going to puke with terror. 'Surely… surely the harm is already done, and… and… any further action will only make it worse? This… your… your nephew… has unwisely shown his face in p-public, true, but… so far his appearance can have had only limited p-publicity. However…' Patrick swallowed. His mouth was dry. His voice was thin and shaky. But everybody was listening to him. 'However… if this confrontation develops to its logical and spectacular conclusion, news of it will spread far and wide, and its cause – your nephew's p-presence –

is sure to reach the ears of those who you are eager should not be aware of it.' Patrick's voice was steadying. His eyes flickered from one to another of us. 'But if confrontation can be avoided, and all sides can come to a p-peaceful compromise – say, he is allowed to enjoy one swift drink before returning to the obscurity he should never have left – news of his p-presence may never reach those p-parties who must not know about it.'

Jeff wasn't stupid. He didn't want trouble. He'd face it if he had to, but he didn't want it, especially if it was only going to make the situation worse. I could see him thinking hard, weighing up Patrick's argument. Carl and I were still grinning at each other. I was hot and sweating. I was hoping the glass wouldn't slip in my grip when the time came to use it.

'Just one drink?' Stella begged sweetly. She was smiling, but it was strained, and her hands were shaking too. 'Then we'll all go, I promise.'

'One drink.' Jeff pointed the baseball bat at Steve. 'And make it quick.' He turned swiftly and disappeared behind the bar.

I lowered the glass and Carl lowered the bat. 'Carl, mate,' I said. 'Fancy a pint? Gary, go and get the man a drink.'

Steve looked at me. 'You're a mad bastard.' He laughed. 'A right nutter.'

'Gary?' I looked around. 'Where's he gone?' Gary had disappeared. It was a minute or two before he reappeared. He'd gone to hide out in the gents until the trouble had passed and it was safe to come out. He came out looking sick with fear. We all laughed. Shame and embarrassment wiped the fear from his face. Then he laughed too, and relief wiped away the shame and embarrassment. He got a drink for Carl, and for everyone else as well. He was in no position to protest.

It was a good evening. We had a quick drink, relief fuelling our laughter, and then another. And another. Jeff and Carl didn't try to move us on. Jeff turned a blind eye to us, and Carl was happy enough to drink with us. He arm-wrestled with us, flushing with pride and beer and exertion as he ground all our fists onto the sodden table-top (except Stella's – he graciously allowed her to beat him). We were there till gone closing time. I flirted with Stella, relentlessly, even though she made it clear from the very first that she wasn't interested in that kind of frivolity. And when I transferred my attentions to Jenny the bar-maid, who had no qualms about laughing at my jokes and my mock-obscene and half-serious suggestions, I could feel Stella's disapproval radiating off her in waves.

Gary redeemed the time he'd spent hiding in the gents by amusing us with the graffiti he'd discovered there. There were some choice jewels of wit on display and we all laughed. We laughed even more when Patrick subjected them to a barrage of critical theory. Bull-shit for the shit-house, a piss-take for the pissoir. Patrick disingenuously insisted that he intended no parody. Serve the graffiti up to the art-market, he said, and the art-market would lap it up. It was exactly the kind of product that the critics could exercise their theories on, that the dealers could slot into the selling-machines, that could make the collectors feel avant-garde and edgy, punky and youthful.

I borrowed Gary's camera – he always had one with him – and staggered out to the gents and took photos of all the graffiti I could find. I did the same in the ladies, too. The jokes in there were even funnier, even more obscene.

Steve Smith drank more than any of us. It was as if he was trying to make up for his two weeks of abstinence in two hours. At first he wouldn't tell us why he was in hiding. He was a too-cool-to-talk tough guy, a man of few words. But drink and indignation made him loquacious, it all came out after a drink or two. His family had pulled off some job with another family, and he'd been detailed to help work out the split in proceedings between them. He'd made a simple and innocent mathematical mistake. The other family had seen red when they realised they'd been short-changed, even though the mistake had been put right straight away. They'd threatened all kinds of dire revenge – physical punishment, fitting him up with the police – so the Smiths had thought it best if Steve disappeared for a while.

'I'm not a bloody accountant, am I?' he complained. 'I mean, it isn't as if I shot anybody, or shopped anyone to the law, or betrayed the family, is it? I mean, it's not as if I've spent years studying financial management. That's not the career I chose. If I'd have known a maths degree was required, I might have gone in for something else! I might have worked harder at school!'

I was the only one who laughed. No one else was sure whether he was joking or not. They sat around nodding, serious and sympathetic.

'And why did they send me to this shit-hole?' His dull, blank face creased with resentment and incomprehension. 'My brother was sent to the Costa del Sol when he cocked up – he had six months on the beach, six bloody months of sun and sand, sangria and senoritas. Lucky bastard. And a cousin of mine cleared off to Columbia when he had to be out of the way for a few months, as a guest of some business associates out there. He ended up setting up his own business, marrying into the associate's family, now he's stinking rich, honoured and respected, beautiful wife, lovely kids, big house in Bogota, huge ranch in the country, horses, swimming pools, Ferraris, private jet, the lot. So where do they send me? A bloody squat in bloody Shoreditch!'

'But the company, Steve, the company!' Gary insisted. 'Future stars of the art world, every one of us a genius waiting to be discovered!'

'I reckon they're punishing me, my mum and dad. They're ashamed, they think their youngest kid's too much of an idiot to get his sums right. They're punishing me because they lost a lot of face, admitting to those tossers from Elephant and Castle that we'd made a mistake, having to give money back to them. Well, they're still tossers. We should never have done business with them. They're all tossers south of the river.'

'Here, you watch what you're saying about your mum and dad,' Uncle Jeff warned, leaning over the table to collect the empties. 'They're doing their best for you, like they've always done. Now it's time you all pissed off down the road back to that palace you call home. And Steve, I don't want to see you again until we're having Sunday lunch together at your mum and dad's out at Chelmsford. Or I'll be the one in trouble. And if I have to go off and hide in some shitty hole somewhere, I'll make sure you suffer for it. All right?'

We staggered home, laughing and singing, too drunk to feel the cold wind cutting down the scruffy back-street or the drizzle falling in the darkness, too young to have to worry about the leaking roof or the draughty windows or the lack of central heating or the absence of hot water waiting for us back at number forty-seven.

*

Steve Smith moved out about three weeks after my arrival. By that time he was looking like one of us. Scruffy, dirty, unshaven. We were almost sorry to see him go. We missed his cash. He always had plenty of it and was happy enough to spread it around if we took his bets down to the

108

bookies and got him the DVDs and computer-games and other poisons he was addicted to. So he didn't have such a bad time. Nevertheless he was delighted when his reprieve came through from his family and he was a free man once again.

Gary Hughes took his place in the house, the room next door to mine. 'You're an idiot,' I said, winding him up. 'You don't need to squat. What are you putting up with this shit for? What was wrong with that flat in Herne Hill?'

'Boring. It was boring.' Gary looked upset and embarrassed. He wasn't going to admit that a room next to mine was a dream come true – even he had some dignity – and he didn't like being teased about it.

'You're pathetic,' I laughed. 'You fat little hobbit.'

That was a cold winter, but a good one. We kept ourselves warm in Navarino Row with fags and booze and worse. I got to know Stella and Patrick. Stella was supposed to be studying Textiles, but she spent more time playing with her band, CapsLock, than she did at her work-place in college. Her room was always full of musicians and musical kit, she was always coming and going with her fellow band-members. But there was no sign of a boyfriend. Or girlfriend. And there were no casual over-nighters, either. I couldn't work her out. I was always trying to flirt with her, but she never responded with anything other than disapproval. She disapproved of the string of girls I brought home as well. She was civil enough with any of them she met on the staircase the next morning, but was relentless in questioning the rightness of my behaviour and trying to talk me out of it whenever she could. In the end it was like a kind of game we played with each other, me trying to flirt with her and her trying to convert me into better habits, both of us knowing our efforts were futile.

Patrick Joyce was studying Fine Art, like me. Like Stella, he hardly went into college. But he worked hard. His room was his studio, small and cramped, but tidy and well-organised. He was completely dedicated to his work, and he was good at it. Good? No, he was brilliant. I saw that straight away. He must have been one of the most gifted students the college had ever had. And he was bright, too. He'd already gained a degree from some Northern university – he was a couple of years older than most of the other art students – a degree in Philosophy. Which meant that he knew bullshit when he heard or read it. One of the many things I liked about him was his dislike of Critical Theory. He loathed and despised it intellectually. I loathed and despised it because it made my brain hurt. He blamed the collapse of aesthetic standards and the lowering of technical skills on the rise of Critical Theory; I just thought it was boring and baffling. He was shy and quiet, and kept himself to himself most of the time, but he wasn't anti-social, and he could be generous and quick-witted and open enough in company.

Gary Hughes was studying Photography. He always had a camera to hand, but his only ambition in life seemed to be getting drunk with me. When we weren't getting drunk on cans in the house, we were drinking in pubs all around East London. I couldn't remember the names of more than half-a-dozen of them now, and I certainly couldn't find my way back to them, but we saw a good few of them. And it wasn't all play; in every one, I borrowed Gary's camera and photographed the graffiti in the Gents and the Ladies. You can imagine the rows and fights and altercations that caused, taking a camera into the toilets of East End pubs. Gary found it terrifying. He never understood the fun of it, seeing only the black eyes and bleeding noses. But Gary was a born hanger-on, a hero-worshipper, and stuck to me like dog-shit on crepe-soles. He was short and fat and unattractive. Frightened of being ignored, he dyed his hair outrageous colours and sprayed the world with jokes and ready cash to keep it sweet.

He made me laugh, all right. His jokes were always bitchy. He couldn't resist taking the piss out of people. Especially women. Good-looking women in particular. No matter how good-looking they were, he could always find something in their appearance to take the micky out of, sniggering at them behind their backs. Something about their hair, or their shoes, or their make-up. Which was funny, because he was no beauty himself. But he always went very quiet and pissed off and sulky whenever I pointed that out to him, and that made me laugh even more, this joke that Gary the joker didn't find funny.

His cash came from his dad, who was some kind of ducker and diver, juggling a string of motor-trade businesses somewhere in Wales. Garages, dealerships, petrol stations. He'd divorced Gary's mum many years ago and remarried twice since then. Gary said he and his dad couldn't stand each other, hardly ever saw each other. He said the old man was always generous with the funds to make up for being such a crap father.

Those photos – the graffiti from pub toilets – I ended up with quite a collection. I got Gary to blow them up, and then I started to copy them onto huge canvases. It became quite an obsession that winter. Before I knew it, I was working really hard at it. I didn't try to edit the content, just treated it all as found object. I reproduced them all as accurately and as big as I could. It didn't matter whether the jokes were hilarious or pathetic, the graphics well-executed or primitive, the comments obscene or banal or clever or stupid. I treated them all the same. My task was to communicate my material, not to comment on it or to analyse it. I'd leave all that wanky bollocks to the critics and dealers, if any of them could be persuaded to look at it.

We began to talk about showing our work, the four of us in the house, in the vague, wishful way of all art-students. Wouldn't it be great if we could set up an exhibition, the four of us, do it properly, invite dealers and journalists and critics, everybody who mattered, get some sort of catalogue together…make some money… get recognised… get a contract with a Cork Street gallery… But where? In the house? Too small, too cramped. What we wanted was a big open space. Could we rent a gallery? No way. How much would that cost? Impossible.

One night that February, a fall of snow covered Navarino Row and sent the temperature in the squat plummeting to levels that no amount of fags or booze or coffee could fight. So we cleared off to the warmth of the Ellerby Arms. And there was Steve Smith, standing at the bar with a couple of characters in dark blue suits who could have been City types if it wasn't for the tattoos and the muscle. It was the first time we'd seen him since his departure from the house, and we didn't recognise him at first. He was looking neat and clean again, his short brown hair recently trimmed and his jeans and shirt and leather jacket, famous logos prominent, apparently brand-new. 'No problem,' he was saying. 'Been done before. Dozens of times. New name, new passport, new National Insurance number. All kosher, no fakes. And the death certificate, funeral, all in order, doctor's signature, undertaker, vicar and everything. Life after death, know what I mean? Not cheap, naturally, but we're talking about expert help here, aren't we, and that's always something you have pay over the odds for, isn't it?'

He came over to talk to us a few moments later. 'Hello, you wasters. How's life at the old palace?'

We asked him what he'd been up to since he'd left us, but he was evasive. He wouldn't go into details. He did let slip, however, that he or an associate had an empty warehouse on their hands. Some business they had interests in had gone bust, so he said, and they'd taken the remaining lease on the building as part of the debts owing to them. An empty warehouse. A big open space.

We spent the rest of the day talking him into letting us use it for a week. He tried to negotiate with us at first, as if it was a piece of regular business. But we just laughed at him; what were we going to pay him with – empty beer bottles? We were begging it as a favour, as charity, for looking after him when he was our guest at number forty-seven. He gave in eventually, shaking his head with disgust at his own soft-heartedness.

The warehouse was miles away, in the middle of an industrial estate beside the river out east towards the Thames Barrier. It was surrounded by derelict factories and rusting machinery. But it was perfect. A big open space with walls and a roof. A few windows were broken, and there were puddles of rainwater on the concrete floor. There was a scattering of rubbish everywhere – broken packing cases, torn plastic sheeting, chunks of polystyrene, old newspapers. And it was bitterly cold. But we could tidy it up if we put our backs into it, and if we packed it full of bodies it would be warm enough.

We worked hard throughout March getting it all together. We produced posters and flyers, printed invitations and even a catalogue. I have no idea where we found the money. I guess Stella must have thrown something into the pot from her band's takings – they had a lot of gigs that winter – and Gary must have tapped his old man. It was such a big space, we got a number of other art students to join us, and they contributed towards the costs as well. We publicised it around the college, at

Stella's gigs, at every gallery, commercial and public, in London. We hung our works on the big bare walls and sent our smart invitations out to every critic and dealer in town.

The show lasted for a full week in April, and it was a huge success. It was one big party from beginning to end. It was a twenty-four hour a day event; in the morning and afternoon it was a gallery, in the evening it was a rock venue with Stella's band playing, and then it was an all-night club, with a different DJ each night. It was all free, and open to anyone. There was a bar – Steve organised that, and he must have made a fortune out of it. For the first day or two, hardly anyone came. Then the word got round and by the end of the week we were having to turn people away at the doors. We'd thought the location would be a liability – and it was at first, nobody wanted to trek so far east and then get lost in the middle of a post-industrial waste-land. But then the news spread and it became an adventure, a challenge, a quest, a source of curiosity and excitement. And we didn't have to worry about the noise or disturbing the neighbourhood – our only neighbours were rats and tramps. Steve had first described the place to us as a brick shit-house, and that's what we called the show. The Brick Shit-House. It lasted a week, but it became an instant legend, and that legend is still alive.

I did well out of it. It was where it all took off for me. Roberta Fielding bought all my big toilet-graffiti canvases and offered me a contract with the Compass gallery. A deal I grabbed with both hands, obviously. I couldn't have hoped for more if I'd sacrificed virgins for it at the full moon. Everyone did well out of it. Stella's band got some sort of record deal, and was signed up to support Fire Drake's UK tour that summer. Gary took hundreds, thousands, of shots of the crowds at the show, and they got to be quite famous. All the outrageous behaviour, on the floor and behind the scenes, all the celebrities – by the end of the week, the place was thick with super-models and TV personalities and movie actors – documented for ever. He'd put the catalogue together, as well, and that became a collectors' item in itself. The other art students who came with us sold plenty of work.

Only Patrick did badly out of it. His work was clearly the best on show, but for some reason it didn't move. It was almost as if it got lost there, in that big, noisy, crowded, badly-lit space. Trying to appreciate his work there was like trying to listen to a late Beethoven string quartet on the car stereo of a beaten-up old banger driving at top speed along a bumpy, twisty road. Fast punk or heavy metal played at full volume would sound great under those circumstances, but anything else just wouldn't be heard. I think the only pieces of his that were sold were some sketches I'd nicked from his waste-paper basket, mounted on a big sheet of card, and covered in obscene cartoons drawn in brightly-coloured felt-tip pen. Just for the fun of it. For a joke, a laugh. And it sold. For thousands of quid. The work had my name on it, so the money came to me. But Stella reckoned I should have shared it with Patrick. She got quite worked up about it, cornering me in the squat one day when Patrick wasn't about.

'Have you no decency?' she shouted. Her Scottish accent really came out when she was angry. Have ye nae decency? Her great mass of long black hair trembled. Her grey eyes flashed from the middle of their absurd pools of black make-up. Her cheeks flared scarlet, bars of angry war-paint across her chalk-white face. 'No sense of justice?'

'No,' I laughed. 'But I tell you what. If you sleep with me tonight, Patrick can have the lot.'

'You bastard!' She screamed. 'You greedy, selfish shit!'

I enjoyed winding her up. It was too easy, really. She was so upright and humourless. Ok, she was kind and honest and conscientious, but the Edinburgh granite was so close to the surface you couldn't resist striking sparks off it. She was so well brought up, came from a close and loving family, mum and dad were both teachers up in the Athens of the north, that she somehow brought out the worst in me. I was a yob by nature, but being around Stella nurtured the yob in me too.

I offered Patrick half the cash, but he just shook his head and waved the offer away with a dismissive gesture. He wasn't interested. 'That work, it was scrap. I'd chucked it away. I'd done with it. But you took it, worked on it, sold it. The money's yours.'

'You don't want it?' I was amazed, confused. 'Any of it? Money, fame, success?'

'I could have worked the toilet graffiti myself, couldn't I? It was my idea, remember? But I'm glad it's got you into Compass. I knew Roberta Fielding would go for it. She could sell that kind of stuff with her eyes shut. Proved me right, didn't it?'

That was Patrick for you. He got nothing out of the Brick Shit-House, but he just shrugged his shoulders and laughed. He wasn't surprised. He'd enjoyed the party, but hadn't expected anything from it. Buying and selling were an irrelevance for him anyway. All that mattered was creation, the private pursuit of a private perfection. So he went back to his room and his work as if nothing had happened. As calm and quiet as ever. But it must have bothered him. The three of us, Stella, Gary and me, we all knew he'd deserved better. Some sort of recognition, at the very least. And he must have known it, too.

Chapter Six

I dropped out of art school there and then. There was no point in continuing with the course. The whole point of art school is getting a contract with a gallery like the Compass. I knew I'd been incredibly, fantastically lucky. The best students get contracts from their graduation show; others have to work for years before they get contracts; others never get contracts at all. But I hadn't even had to graduate.

Of course, it was all a matter of business. Roberta Fielding knew what she was up to. Her publicity machine went into overdrive, feeding me and Shit-A-Brick to the contemporary art world's opinion-formers and market-makers, and they gobbled it up. Within a few months her wealthiest clients were falling over themselves to own one of those big, obscene, lavatorial canvases. There weren't enough to go round. She was soon urging me to make more. 'You paint them, darling, and I'll find lovely homes for them. All these world-conquerors from America and Russia and China, that's why they're here in London. Because you live and work here, darling, and they love you. Their wives love you. Their children love you. They all want to own a piece of you. And you're not going to disappoint them, are you?'

The prices she asked for them, it was beyond shock and amazement. They won't go for that, I thought, aghast. And they won't go for that once her clients meet me. And they did meet me – unwashed and unshaved as I usually was, frequently drunk, often sporting black eyes and bruised knuckles, always in torn jeans and scruffy leather jacket – in the gallery, at other people's first nights. She insisted on my attendance, and relished introducing me to collectors. I have no idea what I said or how I behaved –

my memory is blank and I fear the worse – but it amused Roberta and delighted her PR people. Yet neither her prices nor my appearance seemed to discourage sales.

'The great thing about you, Harry,' she said, 'I can always rely on you to misbehave. A big, handsome young brute like you, no fear, no morals, I can sell you easily. You're a gift, a dream come true.'

'And you're a pimp,' I laughed. 'A madame.'

'Yes, darling, and you're damned lucky I'm your pimp.'

She let me into her bed quickly enough. Business, pleasure, it was all one to her. There were no lines drawn between her personal life and her professional life. She was good at her job and she enjoyed herself. It was all very uncomplicated and I admired her for it.

The money came my way quickly. A lot of money. I could afford to move out of the squat. I wondered about moving to Islington, renting a flat, but I couldn't be bothered to look. It was summer and the squat wasn't so cold and damp any more. It wasn't so bad. And there was more space there – Stella was on tour with her band. And it was more relaxed – though more of a slum – with her out of the way. She was the one who kept the place clean and tidy, and tried to push and bully us into following her example. She looked like a scary rock chick and played in a band but she was really the least rock-and-roll person I'd ever met. She really was very well-behaved indeed. We called her 'Matron' – it was the nick-name I'd come up with soon after meeting her, and it stuck. But she wasn't around that summer to keep us in order and make us behave so it was a lot more fun living there.

But I did get myself some studio space. I had to, as I couldn't use the college's any more. Steve Smith got me the lease of the top floor of one of the disused factories down by the canal. Some associates of his used the ground floor as some sort of warehouse; the windows were boarded up and barred and steel doors had been fitted and always seemed to be locked, no one ever came and went during the day, so I never got to see what was stored there or who used it. Access to the top floor was via an outside fire-escape. But the light was great. It was nice and bright; there were big windows all along one side, facing north as it happened, looking out onto the canal. The other wall was blank, which cut out the noise from outside: the rap and the dub-step playing at full blast from the neighbouring tower-blocks day and night, each one a cliff-face of windows wide open to the summer; the barking and growling of angry young white men, hard and tattooed and shaven-headed, yelling at the pit-bulls they exercised on the parched playing-field; the jeering laughter of young hoodies winding each other up as they kicked a football across the thin and patchy grass or rode their bikes around concrete courtyards strewn with dog-turds and broken glass.

And it was about this time that I started to get a bit fed up with Gary following me around like a shadow. Just the sight of him, short and fat with his stupid 'look at me' hair... I avoided him as much as I could, going up to the studio to get away from him. He often dropped by, but I never let him in. Most of the time I didn't even go to the door, hoping he'd think I wasn't there. He'd always been an irritating little twat. I was sick of his continual sniggering and giggling and his bitchy wise-cracks. And now I didn't need his money there was little point in putting up with him. And strangely enough he'd started to bum cash off me, the odd fiver or tenner now and then, which was a right weird pain in the arse.

But I found it difficult getting down to work up there. It was a big space, and I was all on my own, and I easily got bored and just ended up drinking and idling around. So I persuaded Patrick to work up there with me. He jumped at the chance. He was delighted with the light and the big open space and the view down onto the canal. We still did plenty of drinking and idling around in there, but I was no longer bored or on my own, and we did do some work and we talked a lot about work. I talked to him about Roberta Fielding and the Compass gallery. She didn't want new work from me – she just wanted more of the same. Shit-A-Brick was my thing, she said, my brand, that was what the world wanted from me, stick to it. But I wasn't sure how much more I could produce without simply repeating myself over and over again. After all, there had to be a finite number of public toilets with graffiti in them.

'Variety,' Patrick said. He sneezed. Hay-fever. He'd had a streaming cold all winter, and now it was summer his eyes and nose were streaming with the pollen. He was wearing shorts and a vest. Now the winter coat and sweaters had been discarded I could see just how fragile and skinny and pale he really was. It was almost shocking. His skin looked so white and sensitive and vulnerable. It never seemed to tan, but just go an angry mottled red with sun-burn and insect bites and hay fever. 'Variety. Not of content, but of form. You've given it to them on canvas, now give it to them on something else. Another medium. Something which will give you an excuse for raising your prices. Roberta would love you for that. Really go for that high-end market. Metal. Casting, sculpting.' He laughed. 'I know! Gold! Silver! Massive gold- or silver-plated slabs, as if you've taken castings of the urinals themselves! A full-size trough and tiled-wall pissoir which some collector with more dollars or yen or renminbi than sense can stand in his front room! Hugely expensive, and intellectually compelling, too – you know, the dramatic contrast between pissing and gold, the exciting tension between the high and the low, the cheap and the expensive, the organic

120

and the inorganic, the humour of it, the irony, so clever, so funny, so camp, so post-modern. On the one hand, daring and dirty and cutting edge, and on the other – perfect bling! Yes, Roberta could sell that to the critics, and that would sell it to the punters!'

'Gold and silver? Don't be crazy! Too bloody expensive! And metal – how am I going to do that? Technically? I don't know anything about it. The equipment, the facilities...'

Patrick shook his head and pointed a finger at me. 'Listen, Harry, you're in the game now, and if you want to play it, you might as well play it hard, for everything you can get. If you haven't got what you need, Roberta will get it for you. That's what she's for. She'll know foundries, she'll know her way around gold and silver vaults. If she thinks your ideas are going to make her money, she'll make them happen. You're the artist, she finds the materials and craftsmen you need to get your work done. Believe me. She has access to some of the richest men and women in the world – what she wants from you is something she can sell to them.'

'I'll talk to her about it.' I shrugged. But I knew he was right. Absolutely bang on target. He always was. 'You're a bloody genius, Patrick. Why aren't you in the game as well? You'd be on top of the world by now, you'd make a fortune, you'd be in every gallery and every private collection between here and Mars!'

He laughed again. 'No,' he said. 'I've got other work to do.' Then he shook his head, and sighed, and turned over the pages of the sketchbook he had on the table in front of him. 'Though I sometimes wonder if it's worth it.' He hesitated. 'This... this...'

'What?'

'This pursuit... this exploration... I'm not sure I know what I'm looking for. I don't know whether I'll find it...'

'Course you will.' I opened a bottle of beer and passed it to him. 'You're going further and faster than anyone I know.'

'Art. Creativity. Making things. Does it sometimes feel like a curse to you?'

'It's a game, Patrick. Enjoy it.'

He shook his head again. 'Not what I'm doing. Oh no. It's no game.' He turned to look at me, his face thinner and whiter than ever. 'Sometimes I feel I'm being punished for what I'm trying to do. Punished by something, some power, for daring to… for presuming to…' He shook his head again, and he was suddenly smiling, though his grin was strained and feverish. 'And do you know what? That's what keeps me going. That's what tells me I might be onto something. There must be something in what I'm doing, if I'm being warned off it…'

'Beer, mate, have a drink.' I was still holding the bottle out to him. He hadn't noticed it. 'Go on, you'll feel better for it.' It always made me a touch uneasy, Patrick going all weird on me.

He took the bottle. His hand was shaking. 'I try so hard… I work so hard… and yet nothing happens… I'm in a vacuum… I could be the only human being alive…' He put the bottle to his lips at last and drank eagerly. 'Applause, recognition, I tell myself they mean nothing, and yet, from time to time, I think it would help, it would be encouraging, reassuring, if someone noticed, if someone understood…'

'They will, Pat. They will. Sooner or later they'll catch up with you. Until then there's beer and there's women. Let me set you up with a nice girl. That'll cheer you up, take you out of yourself a bit.'

His bottle was empty. He took another one and drained it quickly. His pale face was flushed now, and his voice less than steady. Patrick never could take much in the way of booze. 'Oh no. That will only make it worse. There's only one girl who…' He stopped suddenly, and laughed uneasily.

'Oh yes?' This was more like it. This could be fun. 'Anyone I know?'

He put his elbows on the table and his head in his hands. 'I really miss her, Harry. It really hurts. I know she'll be back after the summer, but I can't stand it. Her away, out of sight, among other people, I try not to think about it but I can't help it. The blokes in the band, Micky, and the Switch, and…'

'Hang on,' I said. 'Hang on. Are you talking about Stella? Stella?'

He nodded, staring at the table. Then he started to cry.

'Stella? You and Stella? You mean the two of you..?' I hadn't seen that. I hadn't seen that at all. How could I have been so blind? This was amazing.

He laughed through his tears, a wry and bitter snort, and shook his head. 'If only. I wish.'

'So you're not..?'

He shook his head, still crying.

'But does she know? How you feel?'

'Oh yes. She knows.' He looked up, sniffing and wiping his eyes, trying to control himself. 'We've talked about it. We've talked about it a lot.'

'Nothing doing?'

'Nothing doing.'

'But Stella… there's never anything doing with her, anyway, is there? I mean, I've never seen her with anyone, never heard anything…'

'Stella – she has problems – a problem – terrible things –'

I was all ears. 'Oh yes?' I prompted him. This I had to know. How could I prise it out of him?

'I can't tell you. I'm sworn to secrecy. But it's as well you know that... that there's something... some reason for you, Harry Jutting, the Shagmeister, the Fuckfiend, to keep your hands of Stella McNye.'

'Come on, Pat. I'll beat it out of you if I have to...'

But then the doorbell rang. The sound of it buzzed and clattered around inside the studio like a trapped bird, and we froze. Then a voice called from outside. 'Harry? Harry!' It was Gary.

'Shit,' I said.

The bell rang again.

'Shall I get it?' Patrick asked.

'Nah. I don't want to see the little twat. Pretend we're not here.'

'Harry! Harry! I know you're in there!'

We didn't move. We stared at each other silently. There was something like shame in Patrick's eyes, and no doubt irritation in my own. The doorbell rang again, three long blasts, and then we heard footsteps going back down the iron steps of the fire-escape.

'He worships you, you know. It's not right to ignore him.'

'Little twat. Bores me.'

Patrick looked at me. He'd stopped crying. 'You're a bit of a bastard, aren't you?'

'Only a bit of a bastard?' I laughed. 'Thanks! Everyone else reckons I'm a complete bastard!'

'Are you my friend, Harry?'

'Yes, Patrick. We're mates.'

'Because if we're friends, Harry, I've got a favour to ask of you. I want you to promise me something. Because, you see, I know what you're like with girls, I've seen the never-ending line of the poor fools trailing through the house up to your room. I'm worried about you and Stella, about what you might try on with Stella...'

124

I laughed. I stood up and walked away from him towards the other end of the room. 'Me and Stella? Come on, Patrick, is she my type? The Matron? Come on...'

'I want you to promise me, Harry. If you're my friend, I want you to promise me that you'll leave her alone. OK? It's not for me. Yes, I'm the jealous type, but that's my problem. No. It's for her. She's... It would be wrong. You'd hurt her, Harry. She wouldn't be able to cope. It would be wrong.'

'Patrick, mate!' I laughed.

'Promise, Harry. Please. If you're my friend, if you're Stella's friend. Promise me you'll leave her alone. Promise me that you'll never hurt her.'

'OK, Patrick, OK. I promise. I'll never lay a hand on Stella McNye. I'll never do anything to hurt her. OK?'

Harry stared at me. He smiled, a great smile of happiness and relief. He stood up and put his arms round me and hugged me. 'Thanks, Harry. We're mates. I love you.'

'But I like flirting with her, I like the way it winds her up. I'm not going to stop that.'

Patrick laughed and shook his head. 'You're a bastard, Harry. But I still love you.'

I was thinking about Stella, on stage, in performance. We'd been to see the band play more than once that summer, the three of us – Gary, Patrick and myself – heading out of town in Gary's car on a Friday or Saturday afternoon for an evening's gig in some university or midlands town. They were hot, sweaty, crowded, manic events – the music was surprisingly heavy and aggressive, considering Stella co-wrote all the songs – music and lyrics – with other band members. And Stella herself, on stage, was someone else. She might live the life of a virgin queen, but in performance she was a violent and erotic presence. Long legs in black leather, long black hair a thick cloud around her head and shoulders, eyes flashing from great dark pools of mascara and eye-shadow. The guitar in her hand a weapon. Prowling around the stage like a great hungry black panther. Her voice strong and throaty, singing from the chest, harsh and musical at the same time. Challenging, defying, threatening. Like it, bastard? Come on, then. See what you get. Bastard.

'Back off! Look what you've done!
I'm gonna bust your smoking gun!
Shove your bullets, shove 'em,
One by one..!'

It was more than just a performance. It was Stella liberated, releasing a part of herself she kept locked away all the rest of the time. Stella free to scream at the keys and locks and prison door, to attack the jailer. What was that about? Problems, Patrick had mentioned. Secrets. I looked at him. He'd never tell me. I knew that for sure. I could get him drunk, beat him up, but he'd never betray the sacred mysteries of this religion. He might be sensitive and unstable and neurotic and highly-strung, but he was also strong-willed and principled.

Under the stage lighting, her face had been very white, her lips very red, her tight leather gear smooth and shiny and wet-looking. The gasps and groans of her singing had been a warning, but also an invitation. Fancy a go? Yeah? Just you try. Come on. I'm ready for you…

*

Patrick was right. Roberta more or less wet herself with excitement when I floated the idea of Gold Editions and Silver Editions of Shit-A-Brick with her. We sat down together and I drew up some plans on a scrap of paper and she took care of all the rest – sourcing the precious metal, finding the foundries and craftsmen, managing their work – just as Patrick said she would.

And the finished pieces looked fantastic – literally dazzling – fine sheets of shiny metal, rich and flashing and beautiful, etched with curious but satisfying patterns. And when you stepped close to examine the patterns – so close that your breath steamed up the shiny surface – only then did you see that they were made up of toilet-wall graffiti – cartoons and jokes and odd words and illustrations – some funny, some weird, some sick, all of them obscene. The shock of it – the surprise, the amusement, the disgust, the contrast between the gold and the shit – gave the work real punch.

We made half-a-dozen different sheets – three in gold, three in silver – and ran limited editions off them. That was the beauty of it – the work could be reproduced, like an etching or a bronze sculpture. Each run was over-subscribed within a week or so of exhibiting the six original sheets. And the prices, the money – well, I was beyond surprise at this stage.

Then of course Roberta wanted yet another new angle on Shit-A-Brick. She wouldn't consider anything else. She wasn't interested in new work – Shit-A-Brick was a successful brand, my brand, and she didn't want her clients to be troubled or distracted by anything else. A change of direction would be too much of a gamble, too risky. But I was bored stiff with Shit-A-Brick by then. And I was annoyed by her flat refusal to consider even the idea of new work. Not that I had any ideas or new work to show her, but I was pissed off nevertheless. I began to think about moving on, finding myself another contract with another gallery.

I began to think about moving on from the squat, as well. It was beginning to get me down, with autumn setting in. The cold and the damp returned. I was determined not to spend another winter there. And once Stella came back, the place seemed cramped again, and less relaxed. Over the summer I'd forgotten what a bossy, fussy pain-in-the-arse she could be. She threw a fit when she saw the state of the place – it was a squat, for shit's sake! – and was soon throwing her weight around getting the place clean and tidy enough for a royal visit once again.

And the area was beginning to get me down, too. The drab high-street, where half the shops were boarded up and the other half were kebab-joints or off-licences or charity shops. The rattle of the train as it passed over the back-gardens of the next street every half-hour, shuttling zombies between the offices in town where they worked and the boxes in Essex where they lived. The rumble of traffic heading east out of town along the motorway which swept over the canal a few blocks away. The Victorian terraces shedding plaster from their brick-work and paint from their wood-work and tiles from their roofs like elderly invalids shedding teeth and skin and hair. The concrete tower blocks, looking as big and ugly and aggressive and unnatural as giant, steroid-bloated body-builders. The constant scream of police-sirens.

And the crime, ever-present as a threat or an actuality. Muggings were common – Gary had his pockets emptied at knife-point once that summer, Patrick twice – though neither of them was carrying much more than loose-change. And, funnily enough, we were broken into just after Stella had got the place clean and tidy again. They took most of her gear – guitars, amps, microphones – and left the place in an even worse state than we had over the summer. I thought it was hilarious – so did Gary. Patrick was scared they'd come back while he was there. Stella was in tears. We went down the pub to try and get her to drown her sorrow. Steve was there, and he wanted to know why she was so upset. We told him, and he went quiet and thoughtful, and left soon after. The next day a gang of kids knocked on our door, returned all the gear, did a bit of tidying up, apologised, and scarpered. They were a tough-looking bunch of hoodies, black, white, brown, male and female, but they were terrified.

I was spending a lot of time in the West End, around the gallery in Cork Street, where everything and everyone was clean and bright and affluent, and that only made things worse. I decided to move out. I found a flat to rent in Islington, just off the Liverpool Road, a stone's throw from the bars and pubs and restaurants of Upper Street. They threw a farewell party for me at the squat. It was a strange sort of bash. Gary was sulking, as usual – he'd got the message at last, and stayed out of my way most of the time; whenever we happened to find ourselves in the same place, he was sullen and resentful. Stella almost seemed relieved to be getting rid of me. Only Patrick, in his twitchy, neurotic sort of way, seemed to be his normal self, perhaps because we'd still be seeing each other most days in the studio. He and I were chatting about whether I should leave Roberta Fielding. A couple of other dealers had been hinting that they'd be willing to take me on, including Scott Feathers, who was just taking off at that time. Patrick reckoned he'd be a good bet.

'I'm bored with Shit-A-Brick,' I was saying. 'Sick of it. But what the hell would Feathers want from me?'

'Oh, his type of stuff is predictable enough. You know, bang-on contemporary, witty, sexy. Extreme. Irreverant. Something which gives us a laugh about the mad way we live, and takes the piss out of the past, and looks good at the same time. Glamorous and tacky, in an acceptably knowing and ironic post-modern way. Something like... I don't know, what about a copy of Michaelangelo's David with a massive boner?'

Gary sniggered and giggled like his old self, Stella looked disapproving.

'Yeah,' Patrick laughed, warming to his idea. 'Life-size, cast in plastic, you know, Perspex, transparent, and hollow, like a vase, but filled… yes, how about this… filled right up to the top with Viagra pills, like a massive, man-sized pill-bottle? They're purple, aren't they? Pretty… Yeah, a bright purple Perspex David with a massive hard-on and a big grin…'

We were all laughing, even Stella.

'Yeah, and a copy of the Venus de Milo as his girlfriend,' Patrick went on. 'With enlarged breasts, as if she's had a massive boob job. And we could fill her with silica gel, you know, the bags of the stuff they use as implants…'

We ended up down the pub, of course. After a few drinks I realised Gary was trying to catch my eye, he wanted a quiet word with me, but I was busy – there was a new barmaid there and I had to make hay while the sun shone, as it were – after all, it was the last night that pub was going to be my local. In the end, ten minutes before closing time, just as she was about to hand over her phone number, Gary barged right in and grabbed my arm. 'Harry,' he said. 'I need a favour. I'm in trouble.' He looked angry and scared and embarrassed all at the same time, as if he knew he was pushing in where he wasn't wanted but couldn't help himself. 'Could you lend us some cash? A few hundred quid? A grand, perhaps?'

'Piss off, Gary.' I tugged my arm free and glared at him. 'What do you want my money for? Go and count your own – you're loaded, aren't you?'

'No, Harry,' he said quietly. 'It's all gone. I'm skint. Worse than skint.'

'Well, that's your business, mate.' I turned back to the bar but there was no sign of the barmaid. Shit. Had she signed off for the night? What was her name again? Mary? Kelly? 'You shouldn't be so bloody careless.'

'Harry, please,' he said. His voice went up a note and shook a bit and I thought he was going to start crying. His fat little face was all flushed and wobbly, like a pink jelly. 'I really need it, and you've got so much coming in now, and I've always helped you out in the past…'

I wasn't listening to him. There she was, in the back room. The frosted glass door was ajar and I could just see her, fixing her lipstick or something. She turned round and saw me looking at her and grinned, teasing. I waved at her to come out to the bar again, and she shook her head and stuck her tongue out. Right. I lifted up the hinged section of the bar and stepped through.

'Harry..!' Gary was pleading now.

'Another time, mate.' I was in the back room now. I closed the door behind me. She was on her own in there. Her hair was too blonde and her lips were too red, but she had a neat figure and looked as if she knew how to enjoy herself.

'Here,' she said. She flushed, as if she really was a bit concerned. 'You ain't supposed to come back here.'

'And you're supposed to be out there, calling last orders. But I won't let you out until you give me that phone number.'

*

The place in Islington was OK. It was a neat and tidy flat in a neat and tidy building, with a communal garden out at the back. There were five other flats, occupied by young lawyers and bankers, quiet and well-behaved City types. I didn't really fit in. The first night, one of my neighbours was knocking on my door at two o'clock in the morning, in his dressing gown, asking me to keep the noise down as his girlfriend, a solicitor, had to go to work in the morning. I got my own back by nicking a book off him the next day. When I came home from the off-licence at lunchtime, I noticed that his front door was ajar. I stepped across the hall and listened hard. I could hear him tapping away at his lap-top somewhere inside. I learnt later that he was trying to write a novel, poor bastard, taking time out from his job writing software manuals. I could see a pile of books on the floor just inside the door. I reached in and grabbed the top one and carried it into my flat with the cans of beer and dumped it on a windowsill in the kitchen without looking at it or even thinking about it.

A few days later, Patrick, Stella and Gary came round for a housewarming. It wasn't much more of a success than the farewell bash they'd given me the week before at the squat. It was a grey autumn day, cold and wet, and the neat back-garden with the rain and the leaves falling was somehow more depressing to look at than the squat's bomb-site back-yard had ever been. Patrick sat in a corner with his nose in a book for the first half-hour. Gary was surly and sullen and hardly spoke. Stella was trying to be nice and polite and complimentary – she gushed about the domestic comforts, the light and space and hot-water and central heating - but you could tell she was just smiling and gritting her teeth while a storm of bitter and violent envy raged inside her. She knew the nice flat was wasted on me – that was the irony, the injustice, she found so hard to swallow. It was very amusing.

'But Stella, it could all be yours, too,' I said. 'You're welcome to move in, anytime. There's room for both of us in here.'

She looked at me doubtfully. She was tempted. She wanted to believe that I was being straight and serious with her for once. 'But there's only one bedroom...'

'Well, we'd share. Bed, bath, everything. I'm generous like that.'

Patrick looked up from his book. He caught my eye. He was glaring at me with suspicion and alarm. I pulled a face at him. What? I'm only winding her up.

The penny dropped. Stella's gracious façade crumbled. 'You arsehole,' she laughed scornfully. 'Not in a million years.'

'Don't be bitter, Stella,' I said. 'After all, the place will be a complete tip by the time I've been here a fortnight.'

'I know. That's the tragedy of it.'

'Well, at least drop by any time you fancy a hot bath. I'll hold the towel for you.'

'I'd rather be dirty.'

'Dirty girl. Even better.'

Patrick waved the book at me. No doubt he wanted to break up the flirtation. I realised it was the paperback I'd taken from next door. I squinted at the title. The Conquest of New Spain. By Bernal Diaz. 'This is tremendous,' he said. 'Not your usual kind of thing, is it, Harry?'

'Oh, it was lying around in here when I moved in. What's it about?'

'The conquest of Mexico by Cortez. A first-hand account by one of the Spanish soldiers. Written nearly five hundred years ago but it's so fresh. It's like a science-fiction adventure, you know, spacemen crash-landing on a strange planet inhabited by a sophisticated but cruel civilization. Vivid descriptions of the Aztec way of life, their cities and dress and religion. Listen to this.' He read out an account of the Conquistadors' first sight of Mexico City floating in the middle of its lake, of the way its beauty and riches and vast size left them breathless and amazed and wondering if they were awake or dreaming. 'And what about this?' He read out a passage describing their terrifying rituals. Human sacrifice, torture, cannibalism, sodomy. Blood-soaked temples, blood-soaked priests, blood-soaked idols. 'And listen. One of their idols was actually made of blood. They mixed the blood of their victims into a porridge with all kinds of seeds - flower seeds mainly – moulded it into the shape of a man, dried it out and hung it up in the temple, and then in the spring they'd bring it out and water it and all the seeds would germinate and grow and bloom and the idol would be all covered in flowers. And then rot away, of course. Clearly some sort of fertility ritual. Strange mixture of beauty and horror, though.' He laughed. 'Imagine that in some gallery in Cork Street.' Then he was silent for a moment. 'Yes. Why not? Imagine it. It would be brilliant. Life and death, the beauty of nature, the horror of its transience. Yes. We could do it, couldn't we?' He looked around at us, serious and eager.

I laughed. 'Who are we going to sacrifice, then? Gary? Or Stella? Or both of them?'

Gary seemed to come out of himself, sniggering and giggling like the Gary of old. 'No, no, we'll grab some geezers off the street. Wait till it's dark, and then get them in here and do away with them in the bath. After the correct rituals, of course. What is it? Cut their chests open while they're still alive, pull out the hearts and eat it raw? While it's still beating?'

'Ugh, you're disgusting. All of you.' Stella shivered with disapproval, and wrapped her arms round herself. 'Horrible. Make a statue out of blood? Disgusting.'

'No, I don't think we'd have to kill anyone.' Patrick was still eager and determined and serious. It just made us laugh all the more, even Stella. 'Oh come on. Listen. We could do it. Haven't any of you given blood before? You know, blood doning, blood banks. They take it out of you, it goes into a bag, no harm done.'

'But we'd need gallons of the stuff.' How would you work it out? The calculations – even a way of calculating it - escaped me. 'Gallons and gallons.'

'Well, what is the volume of the human body? Think about Archimedes, the original 'eureka' moment. You're in the bath, you duck down under the water, total immersion. The water level rises. Imagine the amount of water displaced. That's how much we'd need.'

'Impossible.'

'No, no. How much do they take when a donor gives blood? A pint? Half a pint? The body replaces it in days, probably hours. If each one of us gave a pint each month for a year, we'd have forty-eight pints. More than enough, surely.'

There was silence. We looked at each other, thinking about it, beginning to take the whole thing seriously.

'A year? Does blood keep that long? Wouldn't the first lot be going off by then?'

Patrick shrugged. 'They must have some way of keeping it. Freezing, for instance; why not?'

We looked at each other again. I could see Gary and Stella nodding thoughtfully. 'We'd all give blood, and our blood would all be mixed up together to make this work of art, this object of beauty and terror,' Stella said. 'A monument to our friendship, the four of us. It would be like blood brotherhood, sisterhood. It would bind us all together, forever.'

Nobody laughed at her. We glanced at each other in silence. This was big, this was serious. Then we started grinning at each other, excited and eager. We could do it. Shit, yes, we were going to do it!

'More to the point, there might be some money in it for us,' Gary said. 'Some sick collector's bound to pay a fortune for it!'

'I'm not so sure about that,' Patrick said. 'After all, it would be a transient piece. Flowers growing, blooming, dying away. The blood would go off, sooner or later. Not something you could hang in a gallery forever. More like a performance piece, I suppose.'

'Well, we could get someone to commission it, perhaps? Some arts legacy – what about the Jerwood? – or a public gallery. Or even a rich patron. Or there might be some way it could be preserved at its height, you know, when all the flowers are in bloom? Freeze-dried or something?'

'Sure, sure,' I said. 'That's just technical stuff. Ask the right people, we'll get the right answers. Only one question matters now – are we going to do it? The four of us?'

We were. We laughed and cheered. We toasted each other in beer, and when that ran out I went out to the off-licence round the corner in Upper Street for champagne. Stella insisted on coming with me. She wanted to get me on my own, that much was clear, but she remained hesitant and silent as we walked down the road, and I didn't try to help her out, amused as I was by her awkwardness. I paid cash for the booze, and the sight of the wad I took from my wallet must have loosened her up because she started the moment we left the offie.

'You're doing all right now, aren't you?' she began. 'I mean, money-wise?'

I grinned at her. 'Don't tell me you want to bum some of it off me, just like Gary?'

'No, I don't, but I do want to talk to you about Gary.'

I groaned.

'No, listen, Harry. He's in trouble, I don't know what it is, but I do know it's about money. He needs help, Harry, he needs money. Can't you lend him some? Can't you find him some sort of job, you know, paid work? Don't you need an assistant or something? '

136

I groaned again. 'Oh, he's such a dick-head. He always had loads of cash. What's happened to it? Has he blown it all?'

'Harry, he spent a lot of it on you. You know that. Can't you return the favour? He needs your help, Harry. Aren't you friends, you and him?'

'What about his dad?'

'He disappeared months ago. Went bust. Did a runner on all his debts.'

'Is that my fault?'

'Harry!'

I stopped walking. I put the bottles down and turned to Stella. She was looking at me, clearly making an effort to be patient and reasonable, but I could see a frown forming, the beginnings of irritation. She was on the verge of unleashing her righteous anger on me. She stood there and stared back, her arms folded. Her long slim legs were in tight black trousers. The collar of her black leather jacket was turned up. She was tall – taller than Patrick or Garry – almost as tall as me in her high-heeled boots. Her face, round and white, not pretty, but – or was it? Her thick black hair was all over it, down over her shoulders. Her eyes were hidden behind great patches of dark eye-shadow, her mouth behind crimson lipstick. I'd shared a house with her for a year, but I'd never seen her without make-up. I suddenly wanted to see that face clearly. I wanted to reach out and sweep that hair out of her face, tug great handfuls of it back and away. I wanted to scrub away that eye-shadow, wipe off that lip-stick. I could imagine doing it, in my mind I was doing it, she was twisting in my grip and protesting, gasping and hissing because it hurt. I was pulling her hair and scrubbing her face, but it was for her own good, and for my pleasure, I wanted to see her face at it really was, see her as she really was, I wanted her to face the world as she was.

137

'Well? Are you going to do it?'

'Do what?'

'Help Gary!'

'Oh. Garry.' I stepped towards her and put my hand out. I touched her hair, over her temple. She didn't step back, and she hesitated before moving her head away. I tried to brush her hair back from her forehead but she looked down and it fell like a curtain over her face. I put my hand under her chin and lifted her face so she had to look at me.

'Harry....' She said, trying to look away. 'Harry, don't...'

I put an arm round her waist and pulled her closer.

'Don't... please...'

I had a hand on her cheek and she didn't move her face. Her eyes were closing. I bent down to kiss her... and a hand was on my mouth, pushing me backwards.

'Don't!' she gasped. She was breathing heavily. She looked frightened. She pushed harder. 'I told you!'

I let go of her waist. I took my hand from her cheek. I stepped away from her and forced a laugh. 'I'm only teasing, Stella. You know I like to wind you up.'

'Well don't!' She peered at me. She was still breathing heavily. She was blushing and she looked confused. She took one of the bottles from me – 'Let me carry something' – and we walked on. She was shaking and trembling – I could feel it as we walked along side by side – and she was keeping a fair distance between us so there was no danger of bumping against one another by accident. 'So are you going to help him? You owe him, Harry.'

I sighed. 'Ok. All right. I'll sort something out.'

'Great!' She beamed at me. 'But soon, please. I'm really worried about him.'

The party might have started badly but it finished well. There was the champagne, and the Chinese we ordered round from the local take-away, and then the other three of them took it in turns to have a bath. Stella insisted on going first, grabbing the water at its hottest and the towels at their driest and cleanest. She didn't let me hold the towels for her. And she was careful to put her make-up back on before she unlocked the door. We argued about the name we'd give the Aztec blood-statue. Patrick suggested 'El Sangrado' – like El Dorado, but the Man of Blood rather than the Man of Gold. Gary suggested 'Bloody Hell!', which made everyone laugh. I suggested 'Montezuma's Revenge' and everyone laughed even louder, so that won the day. Stella had a rough recording of some of her band's new songs on a disk in her bag, so we played it over and over until we could all sing along with her lyrics. My neighbour knocked on the door three times to complain about the noise and the late hour before my guests left.

And that must have been the last time the four of us were all together.

Chapter Seven

I broke with Roberta Fielding soon after that. It was messy, personally and professionally. But Scott Feathers welcomed me with open arms and shielded me from most of the flack. At that time, his Pyramid gallery was just a few doors down from hers on Cork Street, and he was adept at poaching artists from his fellow dealers.

I moved out of the Islington flat as well. The residents' association – the farts who lived in the other five flats – more or less had me evicted. They were young professionals – thrusting and focused and ambitious, but utterly boring and lifeless – and complained relentlessly about my loud and careless ways. I was glad to move out. By the time I handed back the keys, the place was depressing me even more than the squat ever had.

Scott Feathers' PA found me a loft in Docklands. The top floor of a Victorian warehouse beside the river. You know the kind of thing, a vast open space all on one level, bare brick walls and bare wooden boards, floor to ceiling windows looking down on the Thames. I didn't rent the place – I bought it. Scott arranged the mortgage and everything. I had little idea how much it cost or how I could possibly afford it, but Scott insisted that wasn't a problem – he was pouring money my way from the word go. He loved the idea of Michaelangelo's David on Viagra, of the Venus de Milo with a boob job, he loved the idea of Montezuma's Revenge. The loft, he said, was proof of his faith in me. I had no trouble with the neighbours there. I had no idea who my neighbours were or even if I had any. The lift took me up from the silent, always-empty, glass-fronted lobby straight up to the sixth floor, and once there I was all on my own right on top of the world.

I saw less and less of Stella and Patrick and Gary. In fact I saw hardly anything of them at all. I started mixing with Scott's crowd, with his stable of artists – Dan Woodhill, the Pedlar twins, Trudy Whitfur, Grey and Black, the Dot Foundation – all of them as loud and wild and carefree as myself, all of them recently blasted into the stratosphere from Scott's Pyramid launch-pad, all of them roaring on a hot, bright trajectory towards world fame. We hung out together at other galleries' private shows, in clubs and bars at all hours, back-stage at rock concerts and movie premieres. I spent so little time in the loft that the place remained unfamiliar, hardly mellowed into a home. I went there to sleep only, snatching a few hours at dawn or in the late afternoon, often waking up suddenly and still not quite sober, wondering where I was and what I was doing there. My own bed seemed no more familiar than the strangers' beds I more often woke up in.

I kept on my lease of the studio space beside the canal. As it turned out, however, I hardly needed it. Most of my work was done with Scott in his office, sketching out ideas for new pieces. The pieces themselves were to be made by craftsmen in factories and foundries; leave the nuts and bolts to the mechanicals, Scott urged, artistic creation is the idea forming in the artist's imagination, everything else is industrial drudgery to be left to the manual workers, the modern equivalent of a master's studio assistants. That was why his artists had the time and leisure to live fast, extreme lives in pursuit of the fast, extreme ideas Scott would turn into fame and fortune for them. Why did no critic or collector ever see that it was those fast, extreme lives which were the source of that fame, were the product he was selling, as much as any idea?

Scott took the Montezuma's Revenge project in hand. He arranged monthly appointments at a private clinic for the four of us to give blood. Somehow I never made those appointments. My life was so chaotic I rarely knew what the day of the week or month it was. And I didn't particularly want to meet up with the other three. Yes, I did my best to avoid them. Friends. I'd never been one for friends, much. Friends? What are they? Are they electric? What are they for? What do they do? I dropped into the clinic to give my monthly pint at odd moments, here and there, whenever I remembered, without bothering to make appointments in advance.

I did drop by the studio occasionally, to pick up with Patrick, to tell him about my triumphs. But not often, and after a while, hardly at all. Something put me off the place. Patrick was working hard, he was in great form creatively, but the lack of recognition and reward was beginning to get him down. He was either in a place all on his own, working feverishly on his canvases or in his sketch-books, and almost beyond communication, or he was sunk in dismay, despondent and sluggish. At those times he'd often break down in tears.

'Is it so bad, what we're trying to do?' he'd ask. 'Is it so evil? Art, artistic creation? Are we competing with a greater force than ourselves? With the Original Creator of the world? With God? Is that why we are so often punished?'

I'd laugh, and try to make a joke out of it, try to bring him round, but he wouldn't listen.

'Can you think of one true artist who didn't suffer, who wasn't punished, for what he was trying to do? Madness, illness, poverty, unhappiness? Is it all a coincidence?'

He was thinner than ever. He wasn't looking after himself. He wasn't washing, changing his clothes, getting his haircut, shaving. The studio stank. Was it any wonder I stopped going there? It was nothing to do with my conscience. It was nothing to do with the fact that his ideas had helped me on my way. They were ideas he didn't want, had thrown away, so why should I feel guilty? It was me who was making something of them, who was selling them, hustling them, making them work. And it was nothing to do with envy. I could see that Patrick was going places in his work I didn't even know existed, would never have imagined could ever have existed, that his work had a power and accomplishment I'd never seen in anyone else. But why envy that, when it left you all alone in a stinking studio beside a stinking, redundant canal?

And Gary… I'd meant to do something about him, after Stella spoke to me, but somehow I never got round to it. I kept forgetting. Sometimes I'd remember, but at moments when I was doing something else and couldn't do anything about it, then by the time my hands were free to do something about it I'd forgotten again. And eventually it just went out of my mind entirely. For weeks Stella tried phoning about it, leaving voice messages and texts, but I never answered the phone or got round to replying, let alone doing anything about it. She gave up after a while, and I thought that was that, until one day – I can't remember when or what time it was, early morning, late evening, afternoon, the middle of the night – I came back to that warehouse by the Thames after some party or other and found her waiting for me in the lobby.

I was on my own. She was on her own. She looked like she'd been waiting there a long time. I could tell she was angry – angry in her Matron's cold, controlled, grown-up way – but she was looking good. Same old long legs and cloud of long, thick, jet-black hair. Same old tight black jeans, black boots, leather jacket, round pale face, scarlet lip-stick, panda eye-shadow. I grinned at her as I came in through the big glass doors, but the face she turned on me as she rose from the leather and chrome arm-chair in which she'd been sprawling was serious and thoughtful and still angry. Then her eyes narrowed and her lips tightened with disapproval as she took in my condition. Same old Stella.

'Stella!' I held my hands out, reaching for her, but she stepped away from me and folded her arms.

'I was beginning to wonder if you really lived here,' she said coldly. 'I've been waiting ages. And not for the first time, either.'

'This is a lucky meeting, then,' I laughed. 'We'd better make the most of it!'

'Harry...' she began, and I recognised her tone. Let's get down to business. Let's be grown up and responsible.

'Not here, Stella,' I cut her short. 'I've the devil of a thirst, and there's cold beer upstairs, and I won't be able to concentrate until I've got one in my hand. I'm hungry, too, but I think I'm going to be disappointed... Nothing to eat up there, if I remember rightly...' I was in the lift by then, pressing the door-open button, gesturing Stella to come in. She hesitated, biting her lips, arms still crossed. 'Come on, Stell. Can't think, can't talk like this. Come and see my palace.'

She got in. Up we went, six floors, in almost total silence. The lift seemed to go very fast, and then very slow. Was it going up, or down? Stella, still serious, still disapproving, still angry, but now peering at me with curiosity and concern, was a long way away, then very close, then a long way away again. I wanted to touch her, see if she was really there, but when I put my hand out I was afraid I was going to fall over, and pulled it back again....

'Shit, Harry, what are you on?' she muttered, shaking her head. I heard the words echo around the tiny lift as though it was huge and cavernous.

The lift stopped – that was better – and the door opened and I stumbled out into the flat. I went straight to the fridge and found the beer and downed half a bottle.

That was much better. I handed one to Stella but she shook her head. She was looking around the place, and her frown of disapproval was deepening. I followed her gaze. It was a mess. How had it got to be such a mess? I was hardly ever there… Didn't I have a cleaner? I couldn't remember… Something about leaving her money out… or forgetting to leave her money out… a heated conversation… weeks ago…

Food… food… But there was no food, not so much as a hard crust or a soggy biscuit. Oh well. Plenty of beer… Stella walked over to the big window, looked down at the river, turned back. 'Why haven't you done anything about Gary?'

She was breathing heavily with suppressed anger. Her leather jacket was open and I could see her breasts pressing against the thin grey cotton of her t-shirt as they rose and fell. Stella's boobs. I'd never really focused on them before. Why ever not? They were good. Not too big, not too small. Went well with her trim waist, belt pulled tight through jean loops, big shiny silver buckle below her navel…

'Sit down, Stella. Take your jacket off. Make yourself at home. Relax.'

But she didn't sit down. She didn't relax. 'Gary needs money. He needs it now. Or he's going to do something stupid and dangerous…'

'Oh, Gary, Gary…' I shut my eyes and sighed. 'Do we have to talk about Garry?'

'Yes, Harry. We do.'

'Can't we talk about him later, then?'

'Later?' Stella frowned, puzzled. 'No, we have to talk about him now.' She shook her head. 'He's been trying to set up a business. A photo library or something. Hasn't gone well. Borrowed a lot of money. He's having trouble paying the interest. He's got a job pulling pints in the pub, but that just gives him enough to live on. He's talking about doing a job, or jobs, for the landlord. You know, Steve Smith's uncle. Working for Steve Smith's family, Harry! You know what that means! He won't tell me what it is they want him to do, but it's bound to be dangerous! Dangerous and stupid! He reckons they're going to pay him well, but the risk..! Imagine it! Can you imagine what he might be getting himself into? He's frightened. He won't talk about it, but I can tell he's terrified. But he's desperate, Harry, desperate enough to do anything!'

'Take your jacket off, Stella,' I urged again. Was she wearing a bra? I'd be able to tell if she took her jacket off. 'It's hot in here. You must be sweltering.'

'Listen, Harry. I reckon he's already in debt to the Smith family. I reckon that's where he borrowed the money from in the first place. And now he can't pay them back, I reckon they're going to make him pay for it by doing all sorts of dangerous things for them. I've tried to talk to him about it, he won't admit it, but he won't deny it. And he's really worried, Harry. He's more than worried, he's really frightened!'

'Gary's a grown-up,' I said, sighing, and got up and reached for another bottle. 'Are you his mum? Am I his dad?'

'No. But we are his friends. Aren't we?' She looked heated. She looked and sounded angry and imploring and passionate. 'You have the money to help him out, Harry. You must have. You're living in this billionaire's loft, you have a contract with Scott Feathers, we all know what the wives and daughters and mistresses of Russian oligarchs are paying for your work. You've got to help him, Harry. You owe him.'

I went over and stood very close to her. 'Is that why you're here? Because you want me to help Gary?'

She frowned, puzzled and irritated. 'Yes. Why else would I be here?'

I reached out and touched her cheek. She jerked her head away as if I'd given her an electric shock. She took a step backwards and glared at me, her eyes fierce and flashing. 'Harry..!' It was a warning, almost a growl. It reminded me of the prowling beast she'd been on stage, hot and challenging and defying.

I laughed and put an arm round her waist. She struggled, but I pulled her closer. I could hear her gasping, feel her breath on my cheek, smell her perfume. I tried to kiss her, my mouth searching blindly for hers, but she was twisting her face away. I got my other hand on the back of her neck, fingers deep in her thick hair, and forced her mouth against mine. At the same time I felt her hand on the side of my head. She grabbed a handful of hair and tugged hard. It hurt. I swore. The sharp pain of it jerked my head aside and away from hers. Then there was a terrific 'smack!' as a stinging blow caught me across the left cheek. The shock and the pain of it made me release her, instinctively freeing my hands for defence, but I wasn't quick enough to stop a second blow – 'smack!' – exploding across my right cheek. I stepped backwards, shaking my head, trying to get the ringing noise out of my ears, the red mist out of my eyes, the sharp, stinging pain out of my face.

'You arrogant, selfish bastard!' Stella was crouched in front of me, half turned away, hands up, ready to defend herself against further advances. She looked frightened and angry and determined. Her t-shirt was torn – how had that happened? – and her hair was messier than ever. Her lip-stick was smudged. 'You try that again and I'll bloody kill you!'

I could taste her lipstick on my lips. I could also taste blood. I put the back of my hand up to my mouth and wiped it and saw blood there. My hand was shaking with anger and surprise. There was almost enough anger to make me throw myself at her and teach her a lesson, punish her, but I held myself back. We glared at each other, both panting and gasping and holding our ground.

'I hate you!' she spat. 'You're the most self-centred, selfish shit I've ever met. Don't you have any feelings for other people? Gratitude? Affection? Compassion? Pity? Concern? No. Not a shred. You take what you want from whoever you want, and sod everyone else. Harry Jutting is the only human being in the whole world. No one else matters. How did you get this way, Harry? Were you born without feelings? Without a heart? Or did you just chuck it away somewhere?'

I wanted her more than ever. It wasn't just a game now. I wanted her because she was defying me, because she had to be punished, because I couldn't lose face. And because she was that prowling, challenging beast ready to spring out of its cage. 'Do you want me to help Gary?'

She peered at me, puzzled and already suspicious, but didn't say anything, waiting for what she might have guessed was to come.

'OK, I will help him. If you help me. And help yourself. Spend the night here, Stella. Stay with me tonight, and I'll do whatever I can for Gary.'

She frowned at me, as if she couldn't believe what she was hearing. Then her eyes flickered away to the far end of the loft where my big double bed lay in wait, sprawled wide and low under its soft lighting. Then she laughed. It was an ugly laugh, humourless and taunting, unlike Stella. She zipped her jacket up over her torn t-shirt, found her bag, and strode to the door. 'I despise you, Harry. I pity you.'

I didn't move for some time after Stella had left. I stood there, paralysed by fury, somehow bewildered,

148

swearing and cursing at her as if she was still there. Then the anger gave way to a kind of panic as I realised I was on my own, and the panic sent me scrabbling around the kitchen looking for my phone. I called someone I'd met the day before, some art-critic's girlfriend who'd given me a smile I understood when we'd been introduced, and whose phone-number I'd eased out of her when the boyfriend went out to the gent's. The sense of panic and loneliness slipped away as I heard her laughing and agreeing to meet me in half-an-hour's time in a bar just around the corner. Fuck Stella. Fuck her.

A month later I heard that Gary had been arrested. The police had picked him up off the street and found him in possession of a handgun and a pocketful of cocaine. The handgun had been used the day before in a shooting in south London which had left two men dead. Gary was charged with possession of an illegal weapon and with possession of an illegal drug, with conspiracy to murder and with obstructing the police in the course of their enquiries. He was found guilty on all charges and sentenced to three years imprisonment.

The gossip said that the shootings had been related to organised crime. A member of an east London family had killed two members of a rival south London gang. Gary had been given the gun to dispose of it, and he was following instructions when he was arrested. The police had been tipped off by members of the south London gang – somehow they'd got wind of Gary's part - and the drugs had been planted on him by an officer in south London's pocket. But that was gossip only. Gary had refused to answer any questions, either in the cells during police interrogation or in court during the trial.

Stupid bastard. So that was how he planned to pay off his debts, was it? Running a bloody stupid errand for stupid criminals. Stupid sod. Serves him right.

I didn't go to court for his trial. I didn't visit him in prison after his trial.

*

The days that followed were the mad days. Mad months, mad year. I remember little about them. But they're well documented. The press cuttings and TV footage about them would make quite an archive. Part of Scott Feathers' genius was his command of PR; he could always generate publicity about his artists; often wild, frequently hostile publicity, but always the kind to push up value and demand. Of course, he relied on us for the kind of behaviour which would generate publicity in the first place, and we never let him down.

Some of it I wouldn't believe now if it wasn't for the documentary proof. OK, a lot of it is credible enough – the paparazzi shots of me stumbling out of nightclubs in the early hours, my arms round a glamour model/TV actress/pop singer at the height of her brief fame, or the stories in the gossip columns about me and that politician's young wife. But others... I have absolutely no recollection of the Queen's garden party that summer, when I was supposed to have stripped off and gone skinny dipping in the lake in Buckingham Palace's back garden, and pissed into it from its rustic bridge into the bargain. Or those TV appearances – chat shows, late-night cultural discussions, red-carpet premieres – but there I am, captured on film, looking and sounding more like a pissed scaffolder, big and brawny and scruffy and aggressively determined to have a laugh, preferably at other people's expense, than 'one of the country's most gifted, exciting and daring young artists' as introduced by the presenter. There I am, relentlessly taking the piss out of some pompous, pretentious, po-faced young novelist until she bursts into tears. There I am, decking some art critic when he gets angrily to his feet to protest about something I've said or done. There I am, brawling with an up-and-coming (and up-his-own-arse) movie star who fancies himself as a hard man because he plays geezers and gangsters in second-rate derivative Brit flicks. There I am, at a charity dinner and auction, fast asleep and snoring in a borrowed and badly-fitting dinner jacket and black tie, my feet up on the table among the bottles and glasses and empty plates and silver-ware, as some academic guest-speaker drones on about tradition and innovation or something. There I am, on the Guy Bolton show, drunkenly staggering across the stage to join Nicky Jaws at the microphone as he's singing his latest come-back attempt. See the look on poor Guy's face – horror and alarm and fear of the unscripted and unrehearsed giving way to satisfied realisation that his chat-show is about to give birth to great TV – one of those immortal, water-cooler, car-crash moments which will do his prospects no harm whatsoever when his agent comes to renegotiate his contract with the TV company at the end of the series. Followed by sheer relish and amusement. See the look on Nicky's face – outrage and disgust, then a game determination to see the thing through, trooper that he is, forcing himself to sing ever louder than my own bellows, his aging, over-worked vocal chords be damned, finally delight that the audience clearly loves this weird, outrageous, hilarious, impromptu duet. He could have flounced off-stage, but he stayed put and I'd like to think that it was this one performance rather than the song itself – bland and boring as it was - which gave him that number one hit he'd been chasing for so long.

I do remember the first time I exhibited at the Pyramid gallery. I remember the opening party, the private view, for very specific reasons. It was there that Patrick showed the first symptoms of his impending break-down.

Scott had put together an exhibition of work by three or four of his new recruits. 'Bang!', it was called. My work included 'Adam and Eve' - the well-hung post-modern David and his big-busted Venus de Milo girlfriend. I hadn't seen or heard from Stella or Patrick for months. I didn't particularly want to see or hear from them. I hadn't sent them invitations to the private view. So I was very surprised to see Patrick that night, to catch a glimpse of his short, skinny, nervous figure across the crowd of critics, collectors, artists and hangers-on packing the gallery. He looked cheerful enough, which itself struck me as strange and untypical, laughing and chatting and drinking as he crossed the room, but something in the faces of those he talked to in passing – uneasy smiles, puzzled frowns, uncertainty, hesitation, shaken heads – rang alarm bells for me. Eventually he made his way over to where I was standing with a couple of Scott's big boys – Dan Woodhill and one half of the Pedlar twins.

'Well hello there!' he said to me. His manner was bright and loud. He had a big grin on his face. He had an empty wine glass in one hand; he waved the other hand around expansively as he talked. 'We know each other, don't we? How's it going?'

I looked at him. I didn't say anything. I had a strange feeling that things were about to slip out of control and I wasn't sure whether good-natured banter or aggressive insults or outright violence would be my most suitable weapon.

'Aren't you going to introduce me?' he laughed. He turned to Dan and held out a hand. 'I'm Harry Jutting,' he said. 'Of course, you might know that already.' He giggled. 'I certainly know who you are.'

Dan looked stunned. He ignored the outstretched hand. If this was some kind of joke, he didn't want to be the butt of it. The Pedlar twin giggled. Patrick turned to him. 'Harry Jutting,' he said cheerily. 'How do you do?'

They both looked at me. Dan was frowning. The twin was still giggling. I looked at Patrick. He grinned at me, eyebrows raised, as if all was fine and hunky dory and now some amusing and bonding banter was in order.

'You're pissed,' I said. 'You twat.'

'Yes,' he laughed. He held his empty glass to a passing waiter and the red wine glug-glugged into it. 'Isn't that the idea, Patrick?'

'I'm Harry!' I said stupidly, my anger rising. 'And you're Patrick! And you're gate-crashing, so piss off!'

Patrick took a deep swig from his glass, more or less emptying it in one go. 'Well, did you make those two pieces, the perspex pair with my name on them? And Shit-A-Brick, you know, the bog-wall graffiti stuff which kick-started Harry Jutting's career? And the work-in-progress, the bloody Aztec statue, which will no doubt crown it?' He laughed again. 'Well, I don't mean 'make' in the old-fashioned way, we all know none of us actually makes our work any more, do we? What I mean is, is it your work? Did you make it as in conceive it? Come up with the idea? Originate the concept? No, you didn't. I did. Me, myself, I. It's all my work. Harry Jutting's work is my work. Thus, I must be Harry Jutting. Not you. QED.'

I grabbed his arm. 'Come on, Patrick. I'm chucking you out.'

He pulled himself free and turned back to Dan and the twin. 'What do you think of my work?' he asked them. 'It's shit, isn't it? Glossy but shallow. Obvious, crude, derivative. Where's skill? Where's vision? Where's originality? No, don't say it. Ironic, referential, knowing, post-modern. That's no substitute.'

Dan and the twin were silent, their mouths hanging open. I took a firmer hold of his skinny elbow and dragged him away. He didn't resist, though he did seem concerned that our forced march to the doors was slopping the wine out of his glass. He tried to drink it down as we marched, but that just spilt most of it down his shirt. 'This is fun,' he laughed. 'I should get out more often. I really am enjoying myself.'

I dragged him out onto the pavement and half-way up the street. Then I let him go. 'Clear off, Patrick,' I said. 'Go home. Get sober.' He stood there, looking at me, a knowing smile on his thin face, nodding absently to himself. I wanted to punch him. Hard. So I turned and left him there and went back to the party.

A small platform and a microphone had been set up at the far end of the gallery, where Scott had said a few words of welcome at the beginning of the evening. About half an hour after my return, a loud burst of painful static rang through the gallery as the mike was turned back on. Everyone looked up at the stage. There was Patrick, mike in hand, about to address the audience.

'Hello, everyone,' he said. The murmur of the crowd died down. 'I'm Harry Jutting, as I'm sure you all know.' Heads turned to look at me. Puzzled faces, uneasy smiles. 'I thought I'd just take this opportunity to say thank you for being kind enough to come here this evening and look at all this shit, and for being stupid enough to buy it, especially at the mad prices we're insolent enough to ask for it.' There were gasps from the audience, awkward laughter – what is this? Some sort of entertainment? A stand-up comedian? – an angry muttering. I caught sight of Scott on the far side of the gallery, his face white with fury and alarm, gesturing urgently to some of his assistants. I pushed my way through the crowd towards the platform. 'My own work, well, it's just a joke, really, I

154

thought it up for a laugh, on the spur of the moment, I never meant it for real, for anyone to take it seriously…' The mike was suddenly turned off, Patrick stopped talking in surprise, there was a moment's terrible silence. Then a loud murmuring rose from the crowd and he started to speak again but his unamplified voice wasn't loud enough to rise above it. Then I was there at the platform. 'Ah, hello again,' he said to me. 'Just in time. Can you help me to get this thing working?'

I hit him. Hard. With my right fist. In the face. He went over backwards, his bum on the platform, his back against the wall, umph, the breath knocked out of him. I picked him up by the collar of his shirt. He seemed to weigh nothing. He was laughing and sobbing at the same time, laughing and whimpering. There was blood all over his face, from his nose or his mouth, dripping onto his shirt. I could feel him shaking all over. I tried to get him to stand up but his legs didn't seem to want to support him. I half-dragged, half-carried him out of the gallery, the crowd parting before us. Through the glass doors, out onto the pavement again. A few passers-by gasped in shock and surprise, shot us glances of horror and alarm, gave us a wide birth. A taxi came by with its light on. I flagged it down and opened the door and bundled Patrick inside. I gave the cabbie a tenner and the address of the squat and off it went.

I watched it disappear, down the street and round the corner, and wondered if I could ever go back into the gallery. I knew I had to. I took a deep breath and back I went.

A round of applause greeted me as I stepped in off the street. The atmosphere in the gallery was electric. The crowd was buzzing with the excitement and the mystery of it, laughing with relief that the embarrassment of it was over, still bristling with anger and indignation, but this

155

anger and indignation was now focussed against the unknown, uncouth gatecrasher who had at least got what he deserved. And Scott was already getting his assistants to circulate the rumour that this was all scripted and stage-managed, that it was some sort of post-modern entertainment. Performance art.

Trust Scott. Sure enough he turned a PR disaster into a PR triumph. The incident became well-know. Legendary, even. It did the Pyramid and my work no harm whatsoever. On the contrary. It gave his reputation for cleverness and mine for daring one hell of a boost. Yes, 'Bang!' was another success for the both of us.

*

But I was still pissed off with Patrick. He might have thought it was an amusing joke, but I didn't. I went down to the studio the next day determined to have it out with him. I wanted him to know that I was prepared to break his nose again or smash more of his teeth out if yesterday's punch hadn't knocked enough sense into him.

But Patrick wasn't there. The studio was deserted, and rather eerie. I hadn't been there for quite a while. I had a feeling that something had changed there, but I couldn't put my finger on it. It looked the same. It sounded the same, with the growl of the down and outs quarrelling over drink drifting in from the tow-path under the bridge. The only difference I could see was that the place was now almost entirely Patrick's. His work was everywhere. I had a good look at it while I waited impatiently for him to turn up. As far as I could see, none of it was finished. It all had an experimental, work-in-progress feel to it. But it was all very interesting. Interesting? It was bloody fascinating.

My anger and impatience faded as I examined it. Oil on small canvases. Collages. Watercolours. A few abstract sculptures knocked up with scissors and glue out of cardboard boxes. A pile of sketch books. Patrick's genius – yes, that was the word – shone through all of them. So why was he still unsuccessful, obscure, ignored? Well, the answers to that were clear enough to me. Success of course means commercial success; the art market being a market, I could see why dealers and galleries wouldn't want to take a punt on Patrick.

First of all, there was his technical skill. He could draw like an old master. But this brilliance, though of course ageless, could make his work look old-fashioned. Collectors have been brainwashed by the self-consciously punky and primitive and hip for so long that they're frightened and intimidated by real skill, which they can only associate with past, more accomplished ages. Second, there was the absolute seriousness of his purpose. Again, collectors are so used to jokey, ironic post-modernism that anything serious is taken as a rebuke, as a challenge few are up to. After all, the slap-dash, tongue-in-cheek, only-kidding approach is very easy to live with. It encourages you to slouch around, to slob out morally and spiritually; whereas a serious approach makes more demands on you - it tells you to sit up straight, tuck your shirt in and pay attention. Third, there was his uncompromising attitude to his subjects. He refused to use any of the usual tricks for grabbing attention or sweetening the pill; none of his work waved sex or violence in our faces; none of it tried to shock us with extremes or seduce us with flattering, patronising, meretricious, easy-entry borrowings from trendy low culture – there were no references to football, rock music, horror movies, gangster movies, soap opera, fashion, pornography, tabloid journalism, advertising, animation, computer gaming, etc, etc. Fourth, and most crucial, there was that unfinished, incomplete element; his work was still exploratory, experimental; and it wasn't entirely clear at that stage whether he would find his way to where he wanted to go or get completely lost, whether the experiments would succeed or fail. The real problem was that he was already exploring territory no one else had yet discovered; that he was testing by experiment theories that no one else had yet formulated.

In another age he might have found a rich and understanding patron selflessly willing to support him over a lifetime. But in this age, where there are only dealers looking to sell fashionable pieces here and now and quickly, he didn't stand a chance.

There was a fifth reason, which I didn't identify that morning and wouldn't identify until much later. As his work progressed, the stresses and strains of his solitary journey were becoming more and more apparent. Some of his pieces – the most recent ones, I was to find out later – were very disturbing indeed. Not in their subject matter, but in a kind of distortion of material and method. There were definite hints at an approaching crack-up or melt-down. You could almost hear the creaks and groans of an over-burdened building in danger of collapsing. But there was nothing inevitable about it. One or two bricks in the right place might just stabilise the whole structure; on the other hand, just one or two bricks taken from the wrong place might bring it crashing down.

By early afternoon I realised that Patrick wasn't going to turn up that day. I wasn't disappointed. I was glad. It would give me time and freedom to explore his stuff. I made myself a cup of coffee (instant, and black – the only milk I could find was off – solid and green) and hunted out a packet of biscuits (opened and stale, but untouched by the mice) and sat down. My mind was racing. I felt thrilled, excited.

I can use this, I thought, even if he can't. I can use a lot of this. I can follow in his footsteps, at least some of the way, into the foothills of his mountain ranges, perhaps, into the outskirts of his cities. He can't sell his work, but I can. I could see how it could be taken and tweaked and adapted, how it could be made palatable and accessible. Stir in some of that missing irony, put a twist in it to get a smile or a laugh the way an advert makes a joke. Add hints of sex, hints of violence. I remembered those sketches I'd rescued from his waste-paper bin a year or two ago and covered with obscene but funny cartoons and sold at that very first exhibition in the deserted factory way out east. Yes, that kind of thing. That would do it.

I took as many photos as I could. I sat down with his sketch books and spent hours going through them. I began by marking pages which I could cut out and take away with me, but in the end I decided to pocket the last three sketchbooks in their entirety. It was late evening by the time I'd finished. I wrote out a letter telling him that I was evicting him from the studio and he had a week to clear all his stuff out and return the key. Then I would change the lock. He'd be prosecuted for trespass if he ever tried to get in after that.

I left the letter on his desk. I found a plastic bag (from a local off-licence) and slipped the three sketch-books into it. Then I locked up and walked away. The three down-and-outs on the tow-path beside the stinking canal waved their bottles at me, inviting me to join them, excited by my bulging bag. I laughed and gave them the finger. They shouted angry obscenities after me. I wondered about going back and pushing them into the water. It would be fun. Give those filthy, stinking, disgusting bastards a bath. But I decided against it. I didn't want to risk those sketch-books ending up in the canal.

Chapter Eight

I went back to the studio eight days later and all Patrick's stuff had gone. The only thing he'd left behind was a note on my desk.

'I can't find three of my sketch books. I really need them. If they turn up, please send them on to me. Please look for them. Please send them. Please. I really, really need them.'

I screwed the note up and threw it away. He hadn't returned the key but it didn't matter. The locksmith came later that day and changed the lock.

He tried phoning me that evening, but I didn't pick it up. He left a rambling voice-message about his sketch-books, about how important they were to him, begging me to look for them or let him back into the studio so he could have another search for them, turn the place upside down if necessary. He sounded desperate, almost panic-stricken. I didn't bother phoning him back.

He tried phoning me or e-mailing or texting every day for the next fortnight. Each message was more desperate and rambling than the last. In the end they were barely coherent. I ignored every one. Then they stopped. I waited another week and then I went back to the studio and got to work.

I'd guessed that the longer I left it, the less likely I was to find Patrick besieging me at the studio, knocking on the door at all hours while I was trying to work. And I was right. There were no interruptions, and I worked hard every day. But Patrick hadn't disappeared. A week later, I heard that someone had turned up at the Pyramid claiming to be me, wanting to talk to Scott about some ideas for new work. The impostor had been shown the door. His description fitted Patrick. Scott showed me the CCTV

160

footage of the incident. The film was grainy and silent, but sure enough it was Patrick. There he was, skinny, twitching, nervous, but protesting and indignant as he'd been manhandled out onto the pavement. 'He wasn't joking,' said the assistant who had spoken to him. She was very puzzled. 'I don't think he was even pretending. It was as if he was convinced he really was you, as if he actually believed it.'

A few days later, someone walked into a rival gallery, claiming to be me. The impostor had insisted that he'd broken with the Pyramid and was looking for new representation. Would the gallery be interested in offering him a contract? They had been polite but non-committal with him, and had contacted Scott the moment he'd left. After that, hardly a week went by without hearing about the impostor and one incident or another; someone claiming to be Harry Jutting had contacted a journalist to offer an interview, or phoned a critic to argue about something he'd written on me, or tried to buy art materials in my name, or introduced himself as me at a party or private view.

Scott thought we should take it seriously, contact the police and get legal advice. But I didn't want the fuss. Not that I wasn't bothered about it. I was furious. I just wanted to sort it out in my own way. Sooner or later our paths would cross and I'd give Patrick such a beating that there wouldn't be a single illusion left in his skull. After a while my ghostly alter-ego became something of a joke, adding another layer to the Harry Jutting legend. Articles appeared in the art press with headlines like 'Everyone Wants to be Harry Jutting' and 'Why One Harry Jutting Isn't Enough'. So in a way Patrick's mad behaviour did me a favour.

It did me another big favour, too. One evening I came back from a day's work at the studio to find Stella waiting in the lobby. I hadn't seen her for months, not since her last visit. I wasn't expecting to see her ever again. I certainly wasn't expecting to find her waiting at home for me after the last time. She was waiting on one of the leather and chrome armchairs again; but she wasn't sprawling in it this time. She was sitting forwards with her head in her hands and her elbows on her knees. As I approached the big glass doors I could see her shoulders shaking. She was crying. I could hear her sobbing when I opened the door.

She sat up suddenly as I came into the lobby. She shot me a glance of alarm and embarrassment then put her head down and was busy doing something to her face with a handful of soggy, balled-up tissues. She hadn't meant me to see her in such a state. Her face was paler than ever, round and puffy. Her panda eye-shadow was streaked and blotchy. I was shocked, and strangely excited. Here was a different Stella, no longer bossy and self-confident, but vulnerable and hurt. She wasn't even wearing black jeans and a leather jacket. She was wearing blue jeans and a big green sweater. That was almost as big a shock. I'd never seen her wearing anything other than black jeans and a black leather jacket before.

My heart was thumping as I looked down at her. She's here, I thought. She's come back. And she's vulnerable. Now's my chance to get even with her. Play it cool, don't rush things, be clever and patient. Her legs looked even better in blue jeans than they had in black. There was more of a suggestion of hip and thigh, somehow. Perhaps that was the absence of the jacket. The sweater was shorter. And more clingy. Though big and thick and baggy, the wool clung in the right places. Her breasts... yes, she had breasts, all right.

I crossed the lobby to the lift doors and pressed the button. There was a whir as the lift was summoned, a judder as it arrived, and then the doors pinged open. 'Come on, Stella,' I said gently.

Stella nodded and stood up, still not looking at me, still trying to hide her face, and followed me into the lift. She was no longer sobbing, but her sniffs echoed around the little space as we shot upwards. I remembered the last time we'd been in that lift together. Then I'd been the one who was hardly in control of myself, giving her the upper hand. Now it was the other way round. Now the boot was on the other foot.

We came out into the loft. I went into the kitchen area and put the kettle on and made a pot of tea. I dumped my leather case on the floor. It contained Patrick's three sketch books. I'd got into the habit of carrying them to and fro between the studio and the loft, working from them during the day, leafing through them and mulling over them at night. I didn't look at Stella, I didn't talk to her. Let her get herself together, let her tell me what it's all about. I carried the loaded tray over to the low table between the two sofas.

Stella had found the bathroom – I could hear her in there, turning taps on and off, no doubt sorting her face out. She came out and crossed the floor slowly and sat down uncertainly on the sofa opposite me. I poured the tea and passed a cup to her and when she looked up and nodded in thanks I had another surprise. The panda eyes had gone. She'd washed off all the eye-shadow. It was the first time I'd seen her eyes as they really were. I'd always thought that she wore so much eye-shadow because her eyes were small. I'd imagined tiny piggy-eyes. But they weren't at all, even now, slightly blood-shot and puffy as they were after weeping. They looked clean and fresh, pale grey; a mask had been removed and here was an individual's face, unique and revealing. Clear and open and sincere. It was Stella's face all right.

163

'It's Patrick,' she said. 'He's having some sort of breakdown. I don't know what to do.' Her eyes welled up again. She put her hands up to cover them and took a deep breath. I waited, saying nothing, while she fought to hold back the tears. After a while she carried on. 'He's always been highly-strung, of course. Nervous and sensitive. But something seems to have set him off, pulled some kind of trigger.'

I put down my mug of tea. 'Any idea what that might have been?' I tried to look and sound as concerned and sympathetic as possible.

She looked at me with those strange, naked eyes. They were full of hurt and confusion, and accusation. 'I think it's something to do with you, Harry. He hasn't been the same since we lost touch with you, since you went over to the Pyramid and moved in here. But he's gone downhill really quickly since the two of you... did you have some kind of bust up? He says you've kicked him out of the studio...'

'No!' I said, aghast. 'I explained to him, I needed more space now that I'm with Scott. Scott's got all kinds of plans, demanding plans. Ideally I needed the whole studio - I might even have to hire a couple of assistants – but I said I was sure there'd always be room for him. We talked it over. He understood. But it was Patrick who insisted on moving out.'

She looked at me, frowning.

'I didn't want him to go. Honest, Stella.' I laughed ruefully. 'And I'm not saying that to sound noble. You know me, Stella. I wanted Patrick around for selfish reasons as much as anything. You know I hate being on my own. I get bored and lonely. More to the point, my work has always owed a lot to Patrick. I've always appreciated his ideas and input. Relied on them, really. I don't know how I'm going to get anything done without him.'

She nodded thoughtfully. She seemed to believe me. 'And he says he's lost some sketch-books. You can tell it's a huge blow. It's really knocked the stuffing out of him.'

I glanced over to the kitchen, at my bulging leather case dumped on the floor. 'I know. He's asked me about them. He kept on phoning me and e-mailing me and texting me about them.'

'He goes on and on about them. He's up in the middle of the night, every night, turning the squat upside down looking for them. He says they're his road map, the key to everything he's trying to do. Without them, he's completely lost. He's losing track of everything, including who he is. If we could find those books, Harry, if we could get them back to him... I'm sure their loss, more than anything else, is what's really triggered his breakdown... Could he have left them in the studio?'

I sighed, and shook my head. 'I've looked everywhere. I've searched the studio from top to bottom. I've turned the place inside out...'

'But they must be somewhere! We must find them, we must get them back to him!'

'Oh, Stella, if only it was that simple. But I don't think it is, I'm afraid. You see, I don't think those missing books exist. I think he's imagining it. He did have a whole pile of sketch-books on his desk, but I saw him go through them when he was packing. He counted them and boxed them all up and away they went. I think it's just another illusion. A symptom of his condition, not a cause of it.'

She stared at me, blinking. Then something inside her seemed to crumple and her head was in her hands and she was sobbing again. 'Oh, God. Surely there's something we can do. Surely...'

I got up and went round the back of her sofa and put my hands on her shoulder as if to comfort her. She didn't stiffen, she didn't shrink away, something inside her seemed to soften and I heard a little moan of gratitude and appreciation. I went to the little table, picked up the tea-pot, took it into the kitchen and topped it up with hot water from the kettle. Then I quickly took the leather case and stuffed it away in the back of the broom-cupboard, well-hidden.

'I'm so worried, Harry,' she said. 'I'm really frightened. He's stopped working, and you know what Patrick was like, always painting or drawing. He said to me years ago that sometimes he thought it was only his work which stopped him from going completely mad. I don't know what he's going to do, to himself or someone else. You can't imagine what he's like, Harry. I'm terrified for him...'

With her elbows on her knees and her head in her hands, I could see that her breasts had swung forwards and were pressing themselves against the fabric of her sweater. I saw that she wasn't wearing her usual high-heeled boots but a pair of simple flat pumps in pale tan leather. Her ankles were slender and delicate. One of the pumps had slipped off. The toes at the end of her naked foot were tipped with coral-pink nail-varnish.

I walked over to the big window, giving her shoulders another comforting squeeze as I passed behind her sofa. The thick dark mass of her hair had been pulled to one side, forwards over her right shoulder. I glimpsed the bare skin on the back and left side of her long pale neck, the left collar-bone disappearing under the loose collar of her sweater, a flash of black bra strap. A hint of cleavage from the shadows where her sweater gaped below her throat. Images repeating themselves in front of my eyes as I stood at the window, staring down into the darkness and the scattered lights below.

'We've got to help him, Harry. He says you've completely cut yourself off from him. I think that's really hurt him, damaged him. He's very confused about it. Sometimes he seems to think he's you, Harry. Perhaps if you saw him again, talked to him? If you two were friends again, it might help, he might get better…'

I shook my head, and turned away from the window. Stella was staring at me, imploringly. I held her eyes, and tried to look as worried and concerned and sympathetic as I could. 'I know about Patrick, Stella. I've heard about him. There are stories… I've been wracking my brains for the last two or three weeks, trying to work out what to do, how to help him. My first thought was to get back in touch with him, see more of him, like you suggest. That was my first instinct. But I didn't want to rush in and make things worse. After all, I'm no psychiatrist. It's a delicate, precise science and I know nothing about it. So I thought I ought at least to take some expert advice first. The wife of one of Scott's clients is a psychiatrist. I got Scott to put me in touch with her. It was just as well I did. I had a long talk with her, and she said the one thing I mustn't do is try to contact him. If I'm part of his problem, I must stay out of his way.'

Stella was staring at me, frowning, concentrating hard. Did she believe me?

'She was in no doubt about it. I must stay away from him, she stressed. If I didn't, I could precipitate a total crash. It could be disastrous. But it wasn't all bad news. She said that his condition could improve, that such cases do often resolve themselves, as long as the initial stimuli don't re-present themselves.'

Stella was still staring at me.

'I'm just as worried as you are, Stella. Just as eager to do whatever I can to help him.' Had she swallowed this shit? I'd made it up on the spur of the moment. Did it show?

Suddenly she was on her feet and stumbling towards me. She was beside me at the window. She was reaching out and taking my hands. 'Oh, Harry. So you know about him? So you're concerned, too? Yes, I can see you are. Harry, that's so good of you, to take advice, to try and find out... Harry, I'm so sorry, the things I said last time I was here, the things I said about you... I'm sorry...'

I closed my eyes and shook my head. 'But what can I do? She said I must stay out of his way. Do nothing. But that makes it worse. I want to do more... Poor Patrick, I want to help him... I feel so helpless...' I freed one of my hands and rubbed my eyes, my brow.

Stella put an arm round me. 'I know,' she said softly, comfortingly. 'I know.'

'I want to help him so much, because after Gary... I feel so bad about what I could have done for Gary, what I should have done. I feel terrible about it. Some nights I can't sleep, thinking about what Gary's going through. And it's all my fault...' Both hands were covering my face now, and there was a sob in my voice. 'I keep thinking, if I could help Patrick, that would be a small step towards making up for it... a start in the right direction... But I have to do nothing, and that feels terrible...'

Stella had both arms round me now. Her head was on my chest. 'Harry,' she murmured.

'But it must be worse for you,' I said. 'You've known Patrick for longer than I have. You see him every day. I can't imagine how awful it must be for you.'

I put my arms round her. Her own arms tightened. She snuggled closer. 'I feel bad, too,' she said. 'I've been a bit of a bitch with Patrick lately. He's been so needy, and I've... I've been having a bad time myself. Harry, the

168

band's split up. We've been breaking apart for months, ever since that tour in the summer... And I've been all wound up in that, like a selfish bitch, while poor Patrick...' She started sobbing again.

'Oh Stella, I'm so sorry. The band... that's terrible... that was your life...' I put every ounce of sympathy and concern I could manufacture into my voice to hide my excitement, my sense of approaching triumph. Got you now. Got you... I put a hand on her hair. I stroked it, the thick, glossy, black mass of it. I twined my fingers in it, and she didn't pull away. I could smell her perfume, feel her body pressed against me.

'I feel so lost, Harry. I don't know what to do.' She was crying now. I could feel her shaking in my arms. 'I feel so lonely. I don't know what to do...'

'Stella...' I brushed her hair away from her cheek. I bent down and kissed it, her skin smooth on my lips, her tears salty on my tongue. She held me tighter, and moaned, and turned her face to mine, her mouth open, her eyes closing. Our lips met. I felt like laughing and cheering. Over her shoulder I could see my big bed in the corner, wide and open and softly lit, waiting for us.

*

It was OK. I mean, sometimes the anticipation is so great that the realisation can be a bit of a disappointment, can't it? I'd been trying to get through Stella's guard for so long, as a sort of joke at first, and then as a challenge to be taken seriously, that perhaps I was expecting too much when that guard finally went down. But it was OK. It was all right.

And she did drop her guard. Those famously formidable defences collapsed dramatically. There seemed to be so much she wanted to get off her chest, mentally

169

and physically; and now that the chance had at last presented itself, now that she was no longer fighting against it, she shed it all as thoroughly and swiftly as she could. I'd never known her to talk about herself much; that was something I'd always felt she was anxious to avoid; that was perhaps what was behind her concern for other people. If she was talking and thinking and acting for others, then she wouldn't have to talk or think about herself. Well, she talked that night. She talked about herself for hours. By the time she'd finished I knew more about her than her own mother did.

Patrick had hinted at a shadow in her past, that afternoon in the studio when he made me swear that bloody stupid promise about her. 'Problems,' he'd said. 'Terrible things.' More than anything else, those hints had tickled my fancy, had teased my imagination. Whatever could have happened to her? Childhood abuse? Rape? The tragic death of a twin?

No, nothing of the sort. Just something simple and trivial - a routine piece of gynaecological surgery at puberty. I laughed when she told me. I couldn't help myself, I'd been expecting something horrific, traumatic, dramatic. She was dumfounded at first, puzzled by my reaction, then she was angry. Really angry. She wanted me to apologise, but I didn't. I made her show me the scars – she refused to, at first, she got quite upset – and when I finally spotted them I laughed even more, they were so small and faint. I'd never have noticed them. When I told her, she went all quiet and thoughtful. And then she started laughing too. She even thanked me. She said she'd been worried about the whole thing for so long. It had obsessed her. It had dominated her consciousness. And now a simple piece of brutal, callous humour had put it all into proportion for her.

She fell asleep just before daybreak, snoring happily. I got up and went to the loo and found her bag lying by the sofa. I sat down and had a good look through it. The usual rubbish. Purse, make-up, perfume, brush, comb, keys, tissues, etc. And a big note-book, bound in black leather. I flicked through it. Scribbled song lyrics. For the rock group which was no more. Some of them I recognised, some of them I hadn't heard, and probably never would unless she found a new band.

'Tease it?
Try that on me and I'll
Freeze it.
Get down on your knees and
Squeeze it.
I won't do that for you, so
Leave it!'

I chuckled. Perhaps it was a good thing the band had split. Stella couldn't go on playing the domineering bitch-virgin – untouchable but knowing - for much longer now. I flicked on, past a couple of pages of abstract but very angry doodling. Then more lyrics. No, these scribbles were different. Not rock lyrics, but poems. They were longer, their form and content were more complex. Thoughts and observations which were subtle and personal. Images which were vivid but not at all straightforward. As soon as I started reading them, I knew that they were private work, not intended for the public stage. And recent work – less than a dozen pages of it, and then into blank pages. I read and re-read those pages, and it occurred to me – surely I wasn't imagining it – that there were references to Patrick in there, and Gary, and myself. There were certainly references to Patrick's work – some of her phrases were clearly inspired by some of the canvases I'd seen (and photographed) in the studio. If I was right, some of the references to myself weren't flattering – monsters,

171

deformed animals, illness – and I felt a stab of anger. But that was quickly replaced by a wave of excitement. I could use all this in the work I'd been busy on for the last month. It would be a perfect fit.

I checked on Stella to make sure she was still fast asleep – she was, though she had turned on her side and was no longer snoring – then I sat down with pen and paper and carefully copied out the dozen pages of scribbled verse. When I'd finished I hid the copy with Patrick's sketchbooks in the leather case in the broom-cupboard and put Stella's notebook back in her bag. Then I went back to bed. I accidentally woke Stella up, which was a shame, because I could have done with a rest.

I don't know what Stella might have been expecting after that night. I'd made no promises, suggested nothing, requested nothing. But just to be on the safe side, I stayed away from the loft for the next week. There were phone messages and texts and e-mails, of course, but I ignored them. I didn't reply to any of them. They followed the familiar pattern. Soppy at first, then puzzled, then angry, then upset. Stay out of her way, I thought, and she'll get over it. They always do.

The messages went on for a couple of weeks ('Where are you, Harry? What's happened to you? Why are you ignoring me? Why won't you answer me? You bastard..!') then they stopped. But I didn't really give Stella a second thought. I was too busy. I was back in the studio, working hard. It was strange and exciting to be working with paint and brush and canvas again, rather than just sketching ideas out and handing them over to Scott and then getting the finished article back from the unseen team of skilled labourers who had actually built the thing. And the work went well. Each piece began as a reproduction of one of Patrick's canvases, or as a scene inspired by one of the ideas in his sketch-books. Then I added a line or lines

172

from Stella's poetry to it – stencilled, or sprayed, or in a collage of print cut from newspapers and magazines, or inked in immaculate calligraphy – around the edge of the canvas, or scrawled right across the centre, or swirling around in a corner, or scattered across the whole surface, odd words here and there. Finally I added my own graphics, usually in garish spray-paint, like graffiti or street art. These graphics were cartoonish and comical and obscene. They were meant to comment on the work or undermine it in a jokey, piss-taking sort of way. This layering gave each piece a depth and complexity which was very satisfying, and a sense of tension and contradiction which was dynamic and disturbing. Scott was delighted with them. He couldn't wait to exhibit them. I worked in a blaze of speed and urgency and inspiration, and the show opened less than two months later.

It was the first time I'd had a Pyramid show all to myself. It was fantastic. The gallery was packed for the opening night party. All Scott's biggest clients were there – collectors flew in from the four corners of the globe for it. Art critics from the broadsheets jostled with gossip columnists from the tabloids. TV cameras added their brilliance to the gallery lighting. There were actors and stand-up comedians and TV personalities and models and even one or two sports stars. All Scott's stable were there – Dan Woodhill, the Pedlar twins, Trudy Whitfur, all the rest, all the big names – and it was clear that this show would well and truly put me into the stratosphere alongside them. It was going to be a great evening. For three months I'd been sober and celibate and hard-working and well-behaved. Here, assembled for my pleasure, were beautiful women, intoxicants of every imaginable type and at least three journalists who I had a grudge against and who might be goaded into a fight if I insulted them aggressively enough. Here was a vast audience expecting some epically rebellious behaviour, and I had no desire to disappoint them.

But before I'd even finished my second glass of champagne, I spotted a face in the crowd – a lonely, uninvited, questing face – and all of a sudden the fizzing, chilled, golden wine seem to go flat and cloudy and luke-warm. It was Stella.

'Shit,' I muttered. 'What the fuck's she doing here?'

Trudy Whitfur – she was just coming out of her second gay phase, as documented exhaustively in her work, and she'd been flirting with me ever since I'd arrived - turned to see who I was talking about.

Stella had only just come in. She was hesitating in the doorway, alarmed by the crowd, peering around for something. For someone. For me. Shit. I ducked behind a corner and peered round at her. She didn't look well. She looked thin and tired, her normally pale cheeks were flushed and feverish. Blue jeans, grey sweater, no make-up. Her face looked even more naked than it had the last time I'd seen her. And she'd had her hair cut. That magnificent, long, thick, black mane had gone. A short, shaggy urchin crop had replaced it. It didn't look bad on her. In fact, it rather suited her. In fact... No, don't think about it. Think about staying out of sight. Think about getting her chucked out.

Trudy was laughing. 'What's the matter, Harry? Old girlfriend? Ex-wife? Shall I call her over? Hey!' she shouted 'Hey! He's over here!'

'Shut up, you bitch,' I hissed. But Stella hadn't heard. The noise in there was already a deafening roar. I could still see Stella scanning the crowds for me, frowning with concentration, dismayed by the size and density and clamour of the crowd, needle in a haystack. Then she squared her shoulders, took a deep breath, and began to push her way across the room. 'She's not invited,' I muttered. 'She shouldn't be here. Tell Scott. Get those hired gorillas to chuck her out.'

'What's her name?' Trudy giggled. 'If I bring her over, will you introduce me?'

I swore under my breath. Where are those gorillas? Why did they let her in? Why aren't they chucking her out? But then I saw Stella glance sideways at one of the canvases for the first time. She stopped, blinked, peered closer. She looked puzzled at first, and then shocked. Eyes wide, hands up to mouth. She was reading the words on the canvas. Her words. Her poetry. She turned to look at another canvas. And another. I couldn't see her face any more, her back was to me. Shit, I thought, chuck her out, chuck her out now. But she didn't need chucking out. Suddenly she was pushing her way back towards the door, struggling, fighting as hard as she could to get away, to get out.

'What's the matter with her?' Trudy was no longer laughing. 'She looks like she's going to be sick…'

She burst out of the crowd on the far side of the gallery, where it thinned out by the door. She stumbled and staggered out onto the pavement, and through the big plate-glass windows I saw her tall slim figure turn and run off up the street.

I laughed with relief. She's gone, I thought. Nothing to worry about. Why on earth did it bother me in the first place? I drained my glass and a passing waiter immediately refilled it. Sure enough it was chilled and bubbling and golden once again. 'Now,' I turned back to Trudy. 'You were going to tell me what those Czech girls were doing when you returned to the hotel…'

It was a great evening. A great night. I didn't get home until two days later, at ten o'clock in the morning. I slept for a couple of hours, had a shower, made some coffee, and turned my mobile on. There was a text message waiting for me. From Stella.

'I'm going to kill myself. You know why. It's all your fault, you bastard.'

I stared at the little screen. I was still tired, still hungover, but that message hit me like a massive jolt of electricity. I felt a moment of shock, heard a distant wail of approaching panic at the back of my mind, a distant moan of dread. I shook my head, trying to clear it. I gave an angry laugh. Stupid bitch. Play those games with me, will you? Well, you're not the first. Others have tried it with me, and I've always won. Empty threats, emotional blackmail, guilt trips, they don't work with me. Pathetic. I'm surprised at you, Stella. I thought there was more to you than that.

I strode across the room, restless with fury and alarm. I strode back to the kitchen and poured myself a cup of coffee. My hands were shaking. She's just playing a game, I told myself. An empty threat. She's just like all the others. Just trying to screw my mind. Why should she be any different?

I read the message again. I checked the time and date. Three twenty-two am, yesterday. Some five or six hours after I'd seen her in the gallery. I looked at my watch. One-thirty in the afternoon. Over thirty-two hours ago.

What if she wasn't joking? What if she isn't playing games? What if it wasn't just a threat, empty or otherwise? This is Stella, you fool. Think about it. Serious Stella. Stella the sincere, Stella the humourless. She doesn't do jokes, she doesn't play games.

Phone her. Phone her now.

My fingers stabbed my mobile, I was scrolling through my Contacts, then I stopped myself. Don't be an idiot. Calm down. Think hard. Be cool. Don't phone her. Do not phone her. If she's playing a game, if she's trying to screw you up, then you must not pick up the ball. You must refuse to play. You've been here before, you know what to do, don't fuck up now. And if she isn't, well, thirty-two hours is a long time, she sent that message ages ago, what can you do about it now?

I forced myself to delete the message.

I was just about to turn the phone off when it rang. It shook and trembled in my hand like a living creature, frightened and alarmed, screaming at me in panic. It took me by surprise. Before I knew what I was doing I'd answered the call and was pressing the thing to my ear. 'Hello?'

'Hello, is that Harry?' A girl's voice. Not Stella. A voice I didn't recognise. Young, light, a trace of some kind of an accent – Australian? The tone – serious, formal, but not official - a tone the caller wasn't used to.

'Yes?'

'You're a friend of Stella McNye?'

'Well… I know her…'

'Listen, I'm really sorry to bother you, my name's Jane Belton, I don't think we've met, I moved into the house in Navarino Row a few weeks ago, the house where Stella lives? I'm afraid I've got some bad news. We've been going through the names on the Contacts list on her phone, trying to work out who we ought to tell… She's been sending you a lot of messages recently, so I thought… I thought you must be close friends or something..? I thought you'd want to know…'

I didn't say anything. I waited for her to continue.

'Yesterday morning I found Stella in the bathroom… she was lying on the floor, unconscious… she'd taken a lot of pills, sleeping pills or something. An overdose. A suicide attempt…'

She paused, but I didn't speak. I couldn't speak.

'She's Ok. She's in hospital. She was lucky, I woke up in the early hours, I needed to go to the loo, otherwise… Perhaps I'd heard her, heard something, perhaps that was what woke me up… Anyway, I found her just in time. Another ten minutes or so, the doctor said, and… well, they got her to the hospital, and it was touch and go for a while, apparently, but she's Ok now. I've just been to see her…'

Pills. Hospital. The stupid bitch. The stupid, stupid bitch.

'I thought you ought to know. If you're a friend of hers. I thought I ought to let you know. I thought you might want to visit her in hospital, take her some flowers or something… I'm trying to contact all her friends. It would really help her, I think, if everyone rallied round…'

'Right. Right. Yes. Of course.' The words came automatically. I wasn't thinking. I didn't even know I was speaking.

'She's in the Homerton. Ward 5B. She'll be in there for a few days yet. The visiting hours…'

I listened to her without really hearing her. Eventually she said goodbye, and I said goodbye, and I rang off and turned the phone off and dropped it on my bed. I sat down on my bed. I tried to think about what I'd just heard, but I couldn't. I didn't want to think about it. I felt very tired all of a sudden. I felt… I rubbed my hands over my face. I looked at my hands. I suddenly wanted to wash them, for some reason, give them a good scrub. I wanted to take a shower. But I'd just had a shower. I lay back on my bed and began to drift off straight away. But a minute or two later something snapped me wide awake and I lay there, tossing and turning, my mind grinding feverishly but not getting a grip on anything. Sleep was suddenly a long way off now. I sat up. Coffee. There was coffee in the kitchen…

I drank the coffee. My eyes drifted round the empty apartment. What was I going to do now? I had to do something. What could I do? Go to the hospital. Visit Stella. No. No way. My mind recoiled with horror from the idea. If the stupid bitch wants to try and top herself, then that's her affair. Nothing to do with me. No way am I going anywhere near her, anywhere near that hospital. Stupid cow. What did she think she was doing?

The flat seemed very empty. And very quiet. I could put some music on, full blast. I could turn the television on. There was beer in the fridge... But I knew it would be no good. I'd still be on my own. I didn't want to be on my own. I had to get out. I had to go somewhere...

And then I suddenly remembered that I was supposed to be at the gallery that afternoon. An interview. They'd be waiting for me even now, Scott, and the journalist, and the photographer... The memory hit me with a huge wave of relief, desperate relief. I was late, but not too late. I could still make it.

*

The gallery was closed. It was Sunday afternoon. That was why the interview had been arranged for that time, so the press would have exclusive access to the artist and his work. Nevertheless, there was a solitary member of the public on the pavement outside, knocking on the glass door, trying to get in. A young man, short, slight, shabbily dressed. I saw him as I walked down the street. I recognised him when I was two or three doors away.

It was Patrick.

He was trying to communicate with someone inside the gallery. An assistant on the other side of the glass door was mouthing and gesticulating at him, trying to tell him that the place was closed, to come back tomorrow.

'What? Why is it closed? I don't understand. Why won't you let me in?' He sounded puzzled and bewildered, but cheerful and amused, as if this was some kind of game. 'But it's me!' he laughed. 'Don't you recognise me? Come on, let me in.'

The assistant unbolted the door and opened it, to give this difficult member of the public a definitive bums-rush. 'Look, we're closed. We're open tomorrow, at…'

But Patrick slipped past her, inside, still laughing good-naturedly. 'You can't lock me out of my own exhibition! Don't you know who I am? No, you're new, aren't you? I don't think we've met before. I'm Harry Jutting, of course. But you ought to know that, even if we haven't met.'

Patrick held his hand out. The assistant, young and female and attractive, had already let irritation crack her icy professional façade. Now it was followed by confusion and incomprehension. She took Patrick's hand and shook it, staring at him with her mouth open and her brow furrowed. She shook her head, tried to speak, but Patrick was already making his way deeper into the gallery, examining the canvases around him.

'Look, we're closed!' she said, gesticulating angrily. 'Are you pulling my leg? You'd better leave, please. Now. Or I'll call…' She turned, flustered, as I came into the gallery behind them. 'Ah, Harry!' Her eyes flashed with relief and her waving hands appealed for help. 'Thank God! This…'

'What!' Patrick, peering at the canvases, gave a roar of anger. 'What have you done to my work? Who did this? Who?' He turned on the assistant. He suddenly looked wild, furious. Mad. His eyes were narrowed, his teeth were bared, and there was perspiration on his pale, thin face. His skinny limbs were shaking. He pointed a trembling finger at the assistant. 'Did you let them do this?' he shouted. 'My work! How dare you!'

There was movement at the back of the gallery, and there was Scott, stepping out of his office, roused by the sound of raised voices. His eyebrows shot up in alarm as soon as he saw Patrick. 'Oh, shit! You again!' He reached inside his jacket and pulled out his phone. 'You're trespassing. I'm calling the police. If I were you I'd clear off, before…'

Patrick grabbed hold of a canvas by its frame and tried to pull it off the wall. An alarm started ringing, right there in the gallery, ear-splitting, brain-scrambling, agonising. 'I'm taking them away!' Patrick shouted above the din of it. 'All of them! They're mine! You can't do this to them!'

I grabbed his arm. 'Patrick..!'

He shrugged me off, still trying to wrestle the canvas off the wall. I took hold of him again and pulled him away. The picture fell to the floor, wood cracking as the frame broke. Patrick turned on me, crouching, gasping for breath as if he'd been running a race. He squinted at me, unrecognising at first, and then his eyes slowly focused on mine. He really did look very ill. Tired and hungry and anxious. And very angry. But also, somehow, very sad.

'Patrick,' I said. The alarm was still screaming. 'Clear off. Or I'll beat the shit out of you.' I meant it. I was as angry as he was. A cold anger, seething towards boiling point. Anger at Stella for screwing up, for behaving like a mad bitch. Anger at Patrick, coming here to dump on my parade, the mad bastard. It was all building up, it had to explode, someone had to pay for it and here was Patrick, no one more deserving. Go ahead, Patrick, make my day.

'Patrick?' he said, still squinting at me. 'Who's Patrick? And who are you?' Then something like recognition crossed his eyes. 'Ah! Yes! I know who you are!' I started to drag him towards the door. He struggled hard in my grasp. He was wearing a big overcoat, old and tatty, there was something heavy in one of the pockets, swinging and dragging at us as we lurched across the floor. 'You're the impostor! You're the madman going around pretending to be Harry Jutting! Pretending to be me! Stealing my ideas! You fucking thief!' Patrick was shouting, screaming. The alarm was clamouring. Scott was shouting into his phone. 'I've been looking for you!' Patrick yelled and spat. 'I've been waiting for you! I was hoping to find you here today! That's why I brought this with me!' He suddenly broke away from me, stepped backwards, and reached into his coat pocket, grabbing and tugging at the hard, heavy, awkward weight there. He untangled it from his flapping coat. He pulled it free and pointed it at me.

A handgun. A big, heavy, black-grey, wobbling revolver.

The assistant started screaming. Scott stopped shouting. The hand holding his mobile fell to his side. Everything seemed to slow down, to stop, to freeze. Sounds faded. Even the alarm seemed to fall silent. Fuck. Oh, fuck...

'Patrick...' My own voice seemed to come from a long way away.

Patrick smiled. 'I've got to get rid of you. You're not me. I'm me. You're trying to take me over. Stealing my work. Doing this to it. Telling everybody you're me. You can't take me over. You can't get rid of me. Because I'm getting rid of you.'

He thrust the gun at me. I backed away from it. His hand shook. The gun shook. The blind eye of its barrel stared at my own left eye, then at my right, then at my left, as if daring me to blink. Then his grip tightened and he pulled the trigger.

There was a massive explosion. An angry whine blasted past my left ear, something cracked and splintered off to the left behind me. Everything sprang into life again. The assistant was screaming, the alarm was dinning, Scott was

182

yelling into his phone. Patrick was still smiling. He was waving the gun, coming towards me. There was smoke in the air between us, a burning smell in my nostrils, sharp and acrid.

I backed away as fast as I could. A mad, blind, crouching scramble. Fear twisted my guts and squeezed my bladder. I struggled for breathe and heard a low moan of terror. My own. Patrick came after me. I bumped up against a hard obstacle. The gallery wall. My hands groped the plaster behind me, the wooden frame of another canvas. Solid, no way through. Patrick shouted, tensing his whole body to squeeze the trigger.

The second shot was even louder than the first. I felt the blast of it pass overhead, heard it crack into the wall, saw dust and chips flying. I dived sideways. The nearest door was over there, off to my right. I made for it as fast as I could, a scrabbling dash, almost on all fours. Was it locked? It wasn't. I crashed through it. The outside world. Fresh-air. Daylight. Safety? No. I wasn't in the street. I was in the yard behind the gallery. I'd come out of the back door, not the front. Abstract sculpture, paved area, wooden bench, three white-washed brick walls, glass-walled rear of the gallery. Nowhere to run. Nowhere to hide. I was trapped.

Patrick came through the door after me. He didn't seem to be in a hurry. He looked around the yard. He didn't seem to see me at first. I was behind the bench, leaning heavily against it, gasping for breath as if I'd just run a marathon. His eyes found me and he came forwards, quite calm, the gun held out in front of him. I could feel terror jerking me around like a puppet. Hot and cold shivers. Icy sweat. My shirt was drenched with it. I stank of it.

'Stella,' he said absently. Then he frowned and shivered. 'This is for Stella,' he said, no longer calm. 'You know what you did to her. You tricked her. You told her you were Harry Jutting. She'd never have… And then you…' He shook his head, then nodded. 'You said you wouldn't. You promised. You bastard! I told you what it would do to her. You promised!' He was shouting. His thin features – his eyes and his mouth – were popping all over the place. He was kind of sobbing. Kind of hissing between gritted teeth. There was sweat running down his forehead, tears on his cheek. He was holding the gun in both hands and pointing it straight at me, but it was wobbling wildly and it was almost as if he'd forgotten about it, as if some sort of storm going off in his head was distracting him from it.

I sprang forwards and slapped him across the face. A hard back-hander. He cried out in alarm and surprise and I slapped him again. Fore-hand, even harder. I heard the blow echo around the yard, felt my hand stinging and tingling. There was a moment's shocked silence as if the white walls and the glass wall and the sculptures were holding their breath, and then Patrick began to cry. Tears burst from his eyes. He sobbed and wailed. His whole body shook with it. His hands went up to cover his face and he seemed to crumple with it.

I was going to hit him again. Properly, this time. My right fist was already raised, ready to strike. But he turned and ran before I could land the blow.

He was gone, the glass door swinging to and fro – plaff plaff plaff – behind him. I was alone in the yard again. The alarm suddenly stopped ringing. Police sirens rose in the distance, swelling louder, coming closer. Scott and his beautiful assistant – faces drawn and pale – came rushing out into the yard. Behind them was a man in a leather jacket – the journalist? – and behind him, yes, a bearded man with a camera. Their faces were flushed with excitement and they were struggling hard to keep the

184

delighted grins off their faces. What a scoop! Interview? Sod that. This'll make our names. What, the bastard's still alive? Not even wounded? No blood, no ambulances? Well, you can't have everything. Still, he's shit scared. Look at him. Get a photo of that.

I'd knocked the photographer to the ground and I was grappling with the journalist when the police came out through the gallery and separated us. Somehow Patrick had slipped past them but they were eager enough to get the cuffs on me. Scott talked them out of it, which can't have been easy because I was trying to kick and nut them at the time. But what did they expect, the stupid bastards.

Chapter Nine

They picked up Patrick later that day, at the squat. He didn't put up any resistance whatsoever. He seemed puzzled by the whole thing, apparently. He was arrested and charged and locked up in a police cell. They weren't going to let him go, even though he didn't seem particularly dangerous any more, but they didn't send him to prison either. He was transferred to some sort of psychiatric hospital, for tests and assessment and things while he was on remand.

The whole episode affected me badly. I thought I'd get over it, the shock and fear, after a couple of days, or a week or two, but I didn't. It just got worse and worse. I didn't go out at all. I couldn't go out. I locked myself away in my apartment. I had the television on all the time, I played loud music, but I couldn't concentrate on anything I watched, I couldn't really hear anything I listened to. I tried reading – I'd never been much of a reader – but the words made even less sense than usual. I didn't work. I couldn't contemplate as much as doodling in the margin of a newspaper. The very thought of it made me feel sick. The only thing I did do was drink, and luckily there was plenty of booze in the place. Beer, whisky, gin, vodka, rum. I managed to shrink all my anxieties into the single worry about what would happen when the booze ran out. It was still terrifying, but somehow less terrifying and more manageable than all the other shit it managed to keep submerged.

Someone had tried to kill me. I had escaped death by a whisker. Is it any wonder I felt like the stuffing had been knocked out of me? I couldn't really understand how and why I was still alive, that was the thing. If I thought about it, I realised that I had been very, very lucky, and that's why I tried not to think about it. It made me shiver and sweat and want to throw up when I realised how close death had been. Those first two shots had missed, even though Patrick had been so close. He'd had me cornered in the yard; if he'd just blasted away, if I hadn't seized the initiative and slapped him… But whatever had made me do that? What an incredibly stupid, foolhardy thing to do! I felt ill every time the memory of that came back to me. I couldn't understand why I'd done it. Yes, it had saved me, but it could just as easily have finished me off.

And what if he tried again? Surely I wouldn't be so lucky a second time? Yes, he was locked away – but that was only for the time being. They couldn't lock him away forever. And if not Patrick, why not someone else? If one person had wanted to kill me, why shouldn't others want to kill me as well? How many other people might be nursing a murderous grudge against me? That was a question I didn't want to think about. Why did anyone have a murderous grudge against me? Another question to run away from. And what about the random nutters out there, the psychos that didn't have anything personal against me but would nevertheless shoot me or knife me or push me under a bus without hesitation should I happen to be to hand when the urge took hold of them? There were so many questions to hide from. No wonder I was drinking the place dry.

I wasn't sleeping, either. Every now and then I kind of passed out – either from sheer exhaustion or from extreme intoxication – but after a moment or two's oblivion some dream or nightmare always shook me awake, wide awake, with no hope of drifting off again. The dreams were like visions, weird visions, vivid and jumbled-up memories. There was Patrick in the gallery with the gun, of course, over and over again. But there was also Gary, strangely enough. Or rather, not Gary, but a desperate quest for Gary, something important I had to give to him, and always some sort of huge obstacle in the way – a high wall, or an impassable mountain, or a vast sea. And there was also Stella. But I was always hiding from Stella. She was dead, somehow, but was coming after me to get me, too, to kill me; a horrible game of hide-and-seek which always ended with her finding me trapped in a corner, with terror jerking me awake as the knife plunged or the gun exploded.

I was awake night and day for weeks, alone in that big millionaire's loft. I'd never really liked the place, never really settled into it as a home – never fully unpacked, even - and now I began to really hate it. It was like a hotel-room I'd booked into for just a couple of nights but had ended up having to live in for weeks on end. A hotel room abandoned by room-service, maid-service, laundry-service. There were rare, lucid moments when I realised the place was a sty, a slum – dirty clothes strewn all over the furniture, empty bottles and cans rolling around on the wooden floor, black bags of stinking rubbish spilling out of the kitchen, mugs and glasses and plates and dishes piled up on the work-surfaces waiting to be washed-up – but I had neither the will nor the energy to do anything about it. Finally it was like a prison cell. It seemed to get smaller and smaller as I paced restlessly from windowed wall to front door and back again, from kitchen to bedroom and back again. I realised I had to break out of it or I'd be trapped in there for ever.

But where to? I thought about dropping by the gallery, having a chat with Scott. But that idea filled me with panic. The place was associated with my narrow escape from death, of course, but there was more to it than that. It was the whole question of work. I didn't want to think about it, but what was I going to do now that Patrick was as good as on another planet? What kind of work would I

188

manage without his… his help, shall we say, his inspiration? Would I be able to manage any work without him? These were questions I could hardly bring myself to address, let alone talk through with Scott when he asked me, as he surely would, 'Well, Harry dude, what next?'

I still had those sketch-books, of course, and I flicked through them fretfully for hour after hour. But they no longer spoke to me. I found I couldn't understand them as I'd understood them before the exhibition. I couldn't see where he was going, what he was trying to do. They were no use to me any more. Except… they did now seem to point me somewhere, but it was in a direction I hadn't sensed before. It was a direction which questioned the whole point of the activity he was engaged in. The doubts and fears about his vocation, which he'd tried to talk to me about before and which had become more acute recently, I could now see looming larger and larger in the experiments those sketch-books contained. How come I hadn't seen that before? They were explicit in some quotes he'd copied out here and there on blank pages or in margins or scrawled across unfinished work. I found myself returning time after time to those texts, and their words began to haunt me, as I'm sure they'd haunted Patrick.

'Both Judaism and Islam regard artists and artistic creation as evil and blasphemous,' he wrote. 'God is "musawwir", the "maker of forms", the only Artist, the sole Creator. Anyone who paints or sculpts is trying to usurp His power, is challenging God as a rival, is suggesting that God's creation is inadequate, incomplete, imperfect. The artist wants us to cherish and value him and his work with a reverence which is due only to God and His works; he tempts us into a form of idolatry. The artist tries to seduce us away from the true and good world that God has created, to the false and bad world that he has created.'

There were scribbled quotes from the Bible - from Exodus ('Thou shalt not make unto thee any graven images, or any likeness of any thing that is in heaven above, or that is in the earth beneath, or that is in the water under the earth...') and Deuteronomy ('Take therefore good heed unto yourselves... lest ye corrupt yourselves, and make you a graven image... which the Lord thy God hath forbidden thee...'). There were scribbled quotes from the Hadith, records of the traditional sayings and deeds of Mohammed the Prophet - something about angels not entering a house in which there is a dog or a picture, and about painters of pictures being punished in the fires of hell and on the day of resurrection.

Patrick's lonely doubts and fears, tormenting him and slowly destroying him, growing and hardening until they split his brain open. They were all over those sketch-books, I could see it now, they were in every brush-stroke and pen-mark and pencil-line. It was fascinating but frightening. I didn't like to think about it. I didn't like to imagine him sitting there all alone in the empty studio with these furies tearing at him. I could almost feel those creatures' claws in my own brain. I could almost imagine closing my eyes and reading those words written inside my own head. In Patrick's hand-writing. It was almost as if, having taken over his work, I was now taking over his ideas. Or were his ideas taking over me?

*

If my apartment was like a prison cell, those scribbled quotes were like the words of the judge who had condemned me to a lifetime of solitary confinement there.

I had to break out, and one day I did break out. I screwed up my will-power and took a deep breath. I rushed out of my front door, into the lift, through the lobby and didn't start breathing again until I stood on the pavement in the rain and the half-forgotten roar of passing traffic.

I made my way to the clinic where we'd been giving blood for the Montezuma's Revenge project. I didn't know where else to go. I couldn't wander aimlessly – I sensed that somehow the prison walls would catch up with me unless I did something purposeful to keep them out of my mind. I lay down as usual on the clean white bed in the clean white room, and let the clean white nurse do what she always did (but which I could never bring myself to watch) to my left arm. Only then, lying there with nothing else to do, did my thoughts start to creep up on me again. They were like unwelcome hospital visitors intruding on the peace of convalescence. The words of those quotes began to echo around my skull again, solemnly intoned in some judge's god-like voice.

In a moment of panic I imagined Gary or Stella or Patrick coming into the clinic to give blood while I was lying there. But the moment passed quickly. Don't be stupid, I told myself angrily. Impossible. None of them is in a position to come here, none of them would want to ever again. So is the project done for? No. I knew that we had collected almost enough blood for it, that this last donation would probably do for it, that the wild-flower seeds – carefully selected for their colours – were ready and waiting.

This brought on another moment of panic. If those words which I was trying to block out were true, then what we were doing was wrong, a damnable transgression, to be punished by forces we couldn't hope to challenge. And those words had to be true. Patrick – so bright, so gifted, a genius - had uncovered a great and frightening

191

truth. Look what had happened to us. Gary, and Stella, and Patrick. All suffering, all punished. And me – was I being punished, too?

That stern judge's voice seemed to laugh. You? It seemed to say, harsh and jeering. Are you in prison? No. Are you in hospital? No. Are you in a lunatic asylum? No. But your friends are. Your friends, Harry. And why are they there? Who put them there? Who? Think about that, Harry. Whose fault is it?

I tried not to think about it. I had been trying not to think about it for ages, so it seemed. But now, at last, there was no way of avoiding it. Gary and Stella and Patrick were the only people who had ever been anything like friends to me, and where were they now? Gary was in prison. Stella was in hospital. Patrick was in a lunatic asylum. And I had put them there. It was all my fault.

Guilt. It was a novel, terrifying experience. I broke out in a cold sweat, a hot sweat, I trembled, I felt sick. I had to repent, I had to make amends. I had to find them, I had to apologise to them, face to face, beg for forgiveness, promise to put things right... But I knew that I would never be able to put things right, would never be able to make amends. And without that, any apology would be worthless, forgiveness would be impossible. But I had to do something...

There was nothing I could do. Except stay out of their lives, forever. I had come into their lives and something in me had done them irreparable damage. If their lives and mine remained entangled, then they were sure to suffer even more damage. I had to get out of their lives, get away from them completely. For their sakes. It was all I could do.

Something in me. I didn't quite know what it was, but I knew that it had destroyed three other lives. Whatever it was, I had to destroy it, before it could destroy any more lives. That was something else I could do.

I looked down at my left arm. I could see the blue vein on the inside of my elbow, the dressing across it, the plastic tube leading out of it, full of blood, red blood, my blood, flowing out of my body, pumped by my heart out into the clear plastic sack there, already half-full of red life. I had never dared to look at it before, all those times I'd been here to give blood, and now the sight of it gripped me with a horrid fascination. My right hand twitched to seize that tube, rip it out of my left arm, let the red blood flow out of my body, let it pump out all over the white bed, the white walls, the spotless tiled floors. That would do it, that would finish it all now and forever, that would make sure that no one else would end up like Gary or Stella or Patrick.

But I didn't want to die. I knew that, from the narrow escape from death I'd had at the gallery. And I knew that it would be wrong, that killing myself would be just a fourth crime to add to the first three. Just another act of waste and destruction. And I knew that it wouldn't get Gary out of prison, or Stella out of hospital, or Patrick out of the lunatic asylum.

But I had to get out of their lives, and I had to change. I had to find that part of me which had hurt them, and destroy it. I had to kill Harry Jutting and become someone else. I had to start a new life, a different life, a good and virtuous life, a long way away. I was already changing, I could feel it. I was beginning to hate Harry Jutting and everything he had been. I could feel a new person, a new self, beginning to emerge from the old. I was sick of the life I was leading. I had to leave it all behind, go somewhere else, start again.

But that wouldn't be easy. Harry Jutting was famous, the world wouldn't let him disappear, wouldn't want him to change. The world would follow me, I was sure, it would follow me wherever I went and refuse to see me as anyone other than Harry Jutting. I would have to trick the world. I would have to persuade it that Harry Jutting really was dead. Dead and buried.

A dead body, a death certificate, a funeral, to lay the old Harry Jutting to rest. And a new name, passport and National Insurance number for a new life. It would be difficult, but not impossible if I had the right technical help. And I knew just who would be able to give me that help. It would be expensive. It would cost a fortune. But Harry Jutting had a fortune, and he would willingly spend it all on an escape into a new life.

*

The body lies face-down on the floor between the sofa and the big windows. A young man's body. About the same age as Harry Jutting, the same height and build, the same colouring. A handgun lies on the polished wooden tiles beside him, as if it has just slipped from the grip of his right hand. A pool of blood spreads out from his head. His fair hair is soaked and dark with it. An exit wound is evident on the top of his crown. The body is dressed in black jeans and a grey t-shirt, and is bare-footed. The big open-plan apartment is dimly lit but the central heating is turned up high. It is very hot in there, and it stinks. The sink and the work surfaces in the kitchen are crowded with plates and dishes waiting to be washed up. Black bin-liners, full and bulging but still open and untied, crowd the kitchen floor. Empty wine-bottles and beer-cans roll about underfoot throughout the apartment. The television is on, and the volume is loud – an American sit-com, spilling witty one-liners and loud canned laughter into the apartment. A lap-top computer is open on the coffee-table by the sofa. It displays a word-processed suicide note. Apologies to friends betrayed, regrets for lives destroyed. No point in going on.

The front door is slightly ajar. Any moment now, a neighbour – alerted by the sound of a gun-shot – will push it open and peer inside and find the body. She will call the police. The police will arrive and call a doctor. The neighbour will identify the body as Harry Jutting's and the doctor will sign the death certificate.

The death will go unrecognised, officially, for what it is – a gang-land execution. The young male victim, an enforcer for a south London gang, has been hit in revenge for killing one of their number who had been double-crossing them for an east London gang. Or something even more unsavoury and complicated. The neighbour – who isn't really a neighbour – has been paid to lie. One of the policemen is in the pocket of the east London gang. The doctor is a cocaine addict; he is supplied by the east London gang and will do whatever they tell him to do.

A week or two later, Harry Jutting will be buried in an east London cemetery. His funeral will be attended by Scott Feathers of the Pyramid and by representatives of other commercial galleries, by a handful of art-critics, and by a cluster of girls from various PR agencies. Many of those present will have slept with Harry Jutting in the last year or so. Many of them will have got drunk with him. Many of them will have made a lot of money from him. But no one who will stand by his grave can claim to have known him well, or to have known him for long. No real friends will be present. Real friendship just isn't something that Harry Jutting ever did.

PART III

'…Through a circle that ever returneth in
To the self-same spot…'

Edgar Allan Poe, *The Conqueror Worm*

'At such extreme temperatures (over 1200 degrees Celsius when firing porcelain), the contents of the kiln can undergo astonishing and unpredictable transformations. Sometimes such transformations are felicitous; sometimes they are disastrous.'

The Potter's Craft (1932)

Chapter Ten

The strange and unreal landscape of central London loomed ahead of me. There were its science-fiction landmarks. The towers of Canary Wharf, huge and ominous, giants guarding a forbidden gateway. The Millenium Dome, vast and low-lying, a predatory sea-monster emerging from a futuristic ocean. Suddenly the mouth of the Blackwall Tunnel gaped - a wide, roaring, hungry blackness swallowing the road ahead - and down I went into the heart of it.

I'd always felt a moment of disorientation whenever I came up out of the tunnel. But this time the feeling stayed with me. And it got worse as the city's endless streets and ever-taller buildings and hurrying crowds and impatient traffic-jams engulfed me.

I thought I'd know the way to Navarino Row, even after all these years, but the streets had changed. Landmarks had disappeared, unfamiliar buildings had taken their place. Roundabouts, traffic lights, one-way systems, had been moved or removed or inserted. I got lost time and again, taking the wrong turning, or failing to find the right turning, or getting stuck in the wrong lane. I began to wonder if it was still there. It could have been bulldozed years ago, reduced to rubble from one end to the other, cleared and then built over with a new super-store or block of flats or high-rise offices. Easily, old and crumbling and rotten and condemned as it was. I hadn't thought of that. I felt lost, and confused, and afraid. What was I doing here? Everything was wrong, nothing seemed to fit.

And then I found it.

Even then, I wondered if I'd made some sort of mistake. If I was imagining it, or if it was another street altogether. It had changed so much that it was barely recognisable. Its terraces looked brighter, cleaner, newer. But exactly what had changed? They were the same old houses, nothing had been knocked down, no new ones had been built. They were familiar, yet unfamiliar at the same time. I remembered them as a ruinous slum; but now they looked like the kind of houses you might want to live in. The brick-work was no longer a dirty-grey or black; it had been cleaned up, and now showed pale yellow and warm red. There wasn't a broken window or a dirty lace-curtain in sight. All the external woodwork – window frames and doors and door-frames – had been renovated and freshly painted, gleaming whites or delicate pastel shades of pale blue or light yellow or dusty green. Cracked plaster had been re-plastered. Guttering and drain-pipes were new. Roofs had been re-tiled, with genuine slate. The pavements were clean. The little front gardens were clear of rubbish. Hedges were neatly trimmed, and new little fences still smelt of creosote. There wasn't a single rusting carcass of an abandoned car in the road; all the vehicles parked there looked new and well-cared-for. The late-spring sunshine helped, but I knew it wasn't an illusion; Navarino Row had transformed itself into an estate-agent's orgasm.

I rode slowly along the street until I came to the end. There was number forty-seven. I stopped the bike in the middle of the road and looked up at it. It was as bright and clean as all the other houses. It looked very pretty indeed. Small, charming, simple, but beautifully proportioned. A classic flat-fronted, sash-windowed, nineteenth-century end-of-terrace London house. The dirty, ugly, starving and diseased street-urchin had been taken in by kind and wealthy benefactors, had been washed, fed and re-clothed, and had emerged the beautiful child its mother had always known it to be. It was miraculous, incredible. And downright sinister.

Had the tower-blocks gone? I hadn't noticed them. I looked up. Where were they? Surely not… No, they were still there, grey and ugly and lowering as always, but somehow they'd been pushed into the background. I remembered them as dominating the terrace, as the terrace lost in the darkness of their shadow, but now it was the other way round, it was the bright terrace you noticed, and the ugly tower-blocks that seemed to recede out of sight.

A sound and movement brought my eye back down to number forty-seven. The front door was opening, voices were drifting out. And the sound wasn't a harsh, profane cockney scream, either. A tall, slim, pretty girl came out onto the doorstep. She had long, clean fair hair and good skin. She wore pale-grey leggings which showed off her legs, short boots, and a loose, thin, pale-blue woollen top. One hand gripped a graphic artist's portfolio, the other waved to the figures which emerged in the doorway as she tripped down the steps. 'Goodbye, darlings. Mummy loves you. Be good for Sonia. I'll be back in time for tea. And Daddy will take you to the park this afternoon. Bye bye.'

A small child with long blond hair – boy or girl? – waved back from the doorstep. He or she stood beside another young woman, short and dark and thick-set, who held an infant in her arms. 'Say bye-bye to Mummy, Hugo. Say bye-bye.' Her voice was clear but heavy and clipped with Eastern European consonants. Hugo continued to wave but remained sullen and silent. 'Dora waves bye-bye. Bye-bye, Mummy.' She waved the impassive babe's hand at the world in general.

The girl clicked the garden-gate shut behind her, shot a suspicious but fearless glance at the inquisitive motorcyclist who had stopped in the middle of the road right outside her house, and then hurried off down the street.

I put the bike in gear and turned round slowly. I rode back up towards the high street. I felt puzzled and alarmed. The Ellerby Arms - was it still there? I hadn't noticed it on the corner when I'd turned into the street. I'd been looking out for it, and then the turning had taken me by surprise, and I hadn't seen it… But it was still there. Or at least, a pub was still there. Or at least something, a pub, or bar or café or restaurant was still there. It called itself The Ellerby, but it didn't look like the pub I remembered. It didn't look like a pub at all. The front was all glass, three big windows. Anything which wasn't glass had been painted cream. There were chairs and round tables out on the pavement, continental-style, and an awning overhead. A few of the tables were occupied. I saw wine glasses and coffee cups, and a single pint glass. And food – green, frondy salads on white plates, splashed with oily, herby dressings.

I pushed open the door and went inside. It was so clean and bright. The walls were a pale cream, the floor and most of the furniture were pale stripped wood. The bar had moved. It was open and L-shaped, the longer leg facing the tables and chairs and the glass front, the shorter leg facing a more intimate corner where comfy-looking leather arm-chairs and sofas stood around a low coffee-table festooned with style magazines. The place was doing a brisk lunchtime trade, but the crowd was relatively quiet; young men and women, affluent and casual, hip in appearance – not a suit or tie in sight – but serious and intense as they crouched over shared screens, tapping keyboards and discussing prototypes and pitches.

Where was the small, dark, pokey, dirty pub I remembered? Where was the filthy carpet, the juke-box, the dart-board, the cigarette-smoke, the plastic beer-puddled tables? And where were the regulars, middle-aged men looking older than their years, their faces nicotine-yellow or high-blood-pressure red, flabby with too much beer and chips or scrawny with too much scotch and fags, but loud and funny, and alive here as they probably weren't anywhere else?

I sat down at the bar and ordered a coffee. 'I used to drink here ten or fifteen years ago,' I said to the boy behind the bar. He put a tray down in front of me. White cup, white bowl with brown sugar cubes in it, white milk jug, cafetiere, on a clean white cloth. He'd moved a couple of bowls along the bar to make way for it. I peered into them. 'Olives, balsamic vinegar, artisan bread? It was sawdust and pork-scratchings back then.'

He laughed politely. 'Everything's shifted east since then,' he said. 'This is now the centre of town. The East End is probably somewhere out in the North Sea by now. Heard of Silicone Valley, California? Well, Silicone Roundabout, London, is just up the road here. Everything that's hot in London - clubs, art galleries, video makers, computer gamers – they're all right here right now.' He nodded towards the low coffee-table behind me. 'See those magazines? Read in New York, Paris, Beijing – all published within a stone's throw of this place.'

'You used to have rooms to let upstairs. You know, bed and breakfast? I need somewhere to stay for a couple of days. Perhaps a week.'

I wasn't sure that he'd heard me. The place was busy, and someone was calling to him from one of the tables. 'Don't know about that, mate,' he said as he hurried off. 'Hang on there, I'll ask the boss in a second.'

I poked through the pile of style magazines while I waited. A headline on the cover of one of them brought me out in a cold sweat. 'Harry Jutting. Gone But Not Forgotten'. I picked it up. 'Forwards Backwards'. What kind of a name was that for a magazine? Rang a bell, somehow. I flicked through it. 'Ten years after his tragic death, the original Shoreditch bad boy is about to hit us with a new work and a movie of his life...'

'Yes, sir? You were asking about a room?'

I jumped, startled, and dropped the magazine back onto the table. The landlady was clean and bright like the pub – well-groomed, short blonde hair, gold ear-rings and necklace, a tan which was probably winter holiday rather than sun-bed, trim in black jeans and white t-shirt – but she was older than everyone else in there, and there was definitely something of the authentic Ellerby Arms about her, something of the old East End. She was brisk and business-like and no-nonsense. She left the smiles and the PR to the drama school students she employed as bar-staff – and her voice echoed with the sharpness and stretched vowels of the born cockney. She looked me up and down, as if she wasn't sure she wanted to let a room in her pub to my type.

'Yes. This place used to do bed and breakfast ten, fifteen years ago. I knew the people who owned it back then.' I watched her carefully. 'I was a mate of Steve Smith. His Uncle Jeff ran the place. Steve still around, is he?'

Her eyes froze with fear and alarm. She looked away for a second, frowning. Then she swallowed, and sighed, and looked up at me again, blinking, as if seeing me in a new light. 'OK.' She nodded. 'How long did you want the room for?'

'A week?'

I followed her upstairs. It was dark, and stank of cigarette smoke. She flicked a switch and a bare electric light bulb on the landing ahead pushed hard against the shadows but didn't really move them. The cracked lino on the floor and the grubby wallpaper seemed familiar – they certainly didn't look like they'd been changed in twenty years. I felt a sudden stab of hope and relief. Yes, this was more like it. Perhaps something of the past was still here, after all. Perhaps everything hadn't changed.

The two rooms were exactly as I remembered them. The same drab carpet, the same dark wall-paper. And they didn't look like they'd been used much since I'd last seen them, either. No en-suite here, and yes, there was still a chamber-pot under each bed. I took the one looking out onto the high-street – the one looking onto the back-yard was quieter, but I remembered Steve's description of what had happened in there one night when he was a kid – one of Scotland Yard's great unsolved crimes. The room had been re-decorated, but Steve swore the blood-stains re-appeared on the wall-paper on every anniversary of the event.

She wanted cash in advance, and I didn't argue. 'Any idea how I might link up with Steve again?' I asked casually as I counted the notes out into her hand. 'It would be great to see him again. And I'm sure he'd be happy to catch up with an old mate like myself.'

She looked at me with narrowed eyes. Had her tan faded a shade or two, or was it just the dim light on the staircase? 'What did you say your name was?' Up here, in the stuffy, dusty half-darkness, her cockney twang was unrestrained.

I counted out the last of the notes, then paused. I hesitated for what seemed like an age. Then I made my decision, and forced out my reply. 'Harry,' I said. 'Harry Jutting.'

*

I closed the door and closed the curtains and lay down on the bed to rest for a moment. I was tired, I hadn't slept much the night before, at the motel. But I was too confused and disoriented to sleep. I felt uneasy and alienated. I could hear the animated buzz of the cheerful young men and women drinking and eating downstairs in the light, clean bar. There was no place for me and my dark quest in this bright new world. And I was worried. I had come here to uncover and interrogate an old life, but now I couldn't imagine it was still there, or if it was it must be so deeply buried that I had little or no chance of reaching it.

I was a fool to come here. I didn't want to be here. I wanted to be back at the cottage, I wanted to be with Helen and Liz and Richard. For a moment I thought about getting up, getting out, getting on my bike and riding away, out of London, going back home, abandoning this hopeless, pointless quest. What did I think I was doing here? I had no plan, no strategy, no idea.

But I knew I couldn't go back. Going back meant giving myself up to the police, being arrested, tried for criminal damage, death threats, even perhaps murder. It meant prison, it meant separation from Helen and Liz and Richard for years, perhaps for ever. I began to panic at that thought. I must phone Helen, I must talk to her. There was a pay-phone down in the hallway off the bar, I'd noticed it on my way upstairs. But I didn't move. I was too frightened to phone her. Would she speak to me, after everything I'd told her yesterday? Perhaps she had learnt even more about Harry Jutting since then. I hadn't yet posted the manuscript to her — I'd brought a jiffy bag and sealed it up and written the address on it and now had to find a post-office — but the police must have spoken to her again, must have told her more about me, shown her press-cuttings, articles, photos, news footage. Dear God. Would she ever want to speak to me again? Would she ever want to see me again?

No. I couldn't go home. Not yet. Not until I'd solved the mystery which had brought me back to London. I had to stay here and find out who had betrayed me, and how, and why.

Three people. Stella, and Patrick, and Garry. One of those three had betrayed me, I was sure. One of them had found out that Harry Jutting wasn't dead, that he was still alive, they had tracked me down and betrayed me to the police. But how had they done that? How had they discovered the secret of Harry's death?

There was only one way they could have done that. Only one person, apart from myself, knew that secret. Only Steve Smith had known. Only Steve Smith could have let that cat out of the bag. Whoever had betrayed me must have learnt my secret from Steve Smith.

A plan. I needed a plan. Well, the first step was obvious. Track them down, all four of them. Steve, Gary, Stella and Patrick. I was sure that was going to be tricky enough in itself. Ten years… anything could have happened to them in that time. I had no idea where any of them were. They could be anywhere in the world. What were the chances that all of them or indeed any of them were still in London after all that time? But the search had to begin here, at least. I'd already thrown out a line to Steve Smith, and I would have to wait patiently to see if anything bit on it. As for the other three, Gary and Stella and Patrick…

Patrick. I shivered. It wasn't entirely true that I didn't know where any of them were. I knew where Patrick was, of course. But I didn't want to think about it. I didn't want to know anything about it. In my mind's eye I saw rain falling on a garden. A green lawn, a statue of rearing horses, a fountain. Cedar trees in the distance. A garden seen through a window. A big, plate-glass window. And inside the window, in the room… I closed my eyes tight

207

and shook my head violently to get the vision out of it. The vision fell away all right, but a soundtrack replaced it. Behind me, the sound of a game of table-tennis. Ker-pock ker-pock ker-pock ker-pock. But beyond that, in the distance, what was that noise? Screaming? Who was screaming? Why were they screaming? Ker-pock ker-pock ker-pock…

I stood up suddenly. I walked from the bed to the window. I looked out through the gap in the curtains to the busy high street below. The curtains were dusty, the windows were filthy, I could hardly see anything out there. I was breathing heavily and I could feel sweat trickling down my spine. So I know where Patrick is. So what? It was just my imagination. My imagination, and guilt… Loony bin, psychiatric hospital, secure unit, lunatic asylum… Everyone can imagine them, everyone's seen the movies, read the chillers. But who knows what they're really like? They could be completely different in real life. Who knows? Calm down. So I know where Patrick is. So it makes my job easier. Patrick's box ticked, a call out for Steve, just Stella and Gary then.

And then? Once I had tracked them down, what then?

I had no idea. But instinctively I felt that it would be no use being too subtle. Bold action was what was called for. A sudden confrontation, the truth emerging from shock and surprise. In confronting Stella and Gary and Patrick I could expect surprise and amazement from them – massive surprise and amazement – mind-blowing incredulity even. What! Harry Jutting! Back from the dead! That was the only reaction possible. But one of them would be faking it. And it all came down to spotting which one was faking it. That was the crucial task, and I was sure I was up to it. Hesitation, caution, exaggeration, contradiction, whatever gave the game away – and something was sure to give the game away – I was confident that I would spot it.

But I had to hunt everyone down first. Information. Where could I go for information? Who could I ask? When the four of us had lived together at forty-seven Navarino Row all those years ago, we had been students at the same art college. Would that college keep records of the lives and careers of its students after they had left? It was worth a try.

*

I left the bike in the tiny car-park behind the pub and walked up the High Street to the underground. The High Street… I remembered broken windows and rubbish and drunken down-and-outs begging. Cheap takeaways, charity shops, off-licences. Empty premises boarded up with sheets of corrugated iron and chip-board. But now I passed a delicatessen offering half a dozen different types of sun-dried tomato, a sherry and tapas bar, a book and music shop with free wi-fi, a vintage clothes shop which looked like something from Savile Row c.1910. The pavements were clean and there were no empty premises. Polite, intelligent, pleasant-looking young couples drifted in and out of the shops, speaking languages I didn't recognise. But they didn't have the lost, uncertain look of tourists. Students, I guessed, or young entrepreneurs after the opportunities and star-dust London once again seemed to be offering the world.

There were two policemen outside the underground station.

They were casually scanning the crowds coming in and out. There was nothing to suggest they were any different to any other policemen you might see outside any other underground. But the sight of them shook me up. I turned away and went back up the high street and dodged into a side-road, my heart thumping and my breath struggling to get out of control. I stopped and listened. There were no shouts, no running feet, no sound of pursuit.

I fought to get a grip on myself. What was the matter? Yes, I was a fugitive from the police. Yes, I could vividly remember the sight of the police-car in the farm-shop's car-park, of the police in the cottage. But at the same time I knew that those two policemen, here, miles away, in the middle of a big city, couldn't possibly be looking for me. So what was the matter? I could feel something, and it wasn't fear, or not just fear. What was it? I groped for it, touched it, fingered its shape and texture. It felt like guilt. Guilt? But what had I done? Why should I be feeling guilt? Guilty of what? I wasn't hiding because I was guilty, I was hiding because I was innocent! Wasn't I? Of course I was!

I took ten deep breaths and marched out of that side-street, up the road and into the underground station without giving those two policemen a second glance.

I got out at the West End and walked through the busy streets to the college's central site. I tried to prepare myself for what I might uncover. Stella and Gary. What directions had their lives taken over the last ten years? Where do you go after a suicide attempt lands you in hospital? What do you do after a spell in prison for aiding and abetting organised crime? What kind of lives can you build on those foundations?

I couldn't find the college. It wasn't there any more. There was a brand new office block on the site, a glittering tower of glass and steel. I asked the uniformed concierge at the reception desk inside the building's huge lobby. The college had moved out two years ago. It had become part of a new University of the Arts; its campus was in a canal-side park just north of King's Cross. He showed me on a map how to get there.

I took another underground train. I felt tired and hungry, lost and disoriented. I dozed for a couple of stops, thinking about Helen and Richard and Liz. I suddenly missed them terribly, it was somehow both sweet and painful to think about them. I slipped in and out of a daydream, Helen and I were in the garden outside the cottage, Richard and Elizabeth were in a paddling pool, Richard gurgling happily and splashing his arms and legs while Helen held him carefully in the water, Elizabeth asking anxiously 'Are you sure he isn't supposed to have a nappy on, Mummy? What happens if he wees or poos in the water?' I could see them, I could hear their voices, I could feel Helen's warm bare shoulder under my hand, shaking as she laughed.

'He'll go to prison,' Stella said. 'And you'll end up in hospital.' Helen wasn't there any more. Somehow she'd turned into Stella McNye. She looked at me, her face lined and grey and emaciated, hatred and anger in her eyes. 'And it will all be your father's fault.'

I snatched my arm away with shock and horror. Elizabeth began to cry. Richard... Richard had disappeared! Where was he?

I woke up suddenly. The train had stopped and the doors of the carriage had just swished open. Kings Cross. I jumped up and made it out onto the platform as the doors began to close again.

Acres of industrial wasteland behind the railway station had been beautifully landscaped. The brand new University spread out away from the sparkling canal, sleek, low-lying brick and steel and glass buildings which incorporated lawns and leafy plazas and renovated and converted Victorian warehouses. There were students everywhere, young and slim and beautiful and happy, sunning themselves on the grass, chattering in groups in the plazas and on the bridges over the canal, hurrying purposefully to and fro. I thought of the gloomy corridors and dusty lecture halls and cramped studio space of the ancient buildings we'd known fifteen years before, and felt even more lost and out-of-place than ever.

The receptionists seemed puzzled by my enquiries, but they were helpful enough to send me to the library. The librarian said they did keep records, not complete, of course, it all depended on how closely each alumnus chose to stay in touch with the college. Could she give me any details they might have about two people who had been students at the college ten years ago? No, she couldn't. Not allowed to. Data protection. Could she at least tell me if she had any information on them? She peered at me, frowning, then sighed and asked me for names and dates. She tapped at her keyboard then sat back, eyebrows raised.

'Ah yes. Here we are. I can't show you, I'm afraid, but we do have something for Stella... ah... ' She squinted at the screen. 'She doesn't call herself McNye any more.' She looked at me. 'I can't show you anything, I'm really sorry. But why don't you Google her?'

'Google?' I asked, puzzled.

She stared at me. 'Google, you know, put the name through an internet search?' I shook my head, and she tried again. 'Do you have a Blackberry? An iPhone? An iPad? Your mobile – is it a smartphone?'

'A what?'

'Does it have access to the internet – your mobile phone?'

'No, no, I don't have a mobile phone.'

'But your computer then, at home..?'

'I don't have a computer.'

She stared at me, blinking, her mouth open. 'Where have you been for the last ten years?'

I didn't say anything. I couldn't think of anything to say. Suddenly I wanted to get out of there, quickly.

She seemed to take pity on me. 'Look, there's a website mentioned here, in her details. Public information, you know? Anyone can look at it. I can give you that.' She looked at me again, and shook her head. 'No, I tell you what, I'll print it out for you. All the stuff about her on this website it mentions.'

'Thanks.'

'Don't mention it. And the other guy. What was his name? I'll see if we have anything on him. See if it points to anything on the net.'

'You're very kind. I really appreciate it.'

She stapled together two bundles of A4 sheets and stuck them in a folder for me. I resisted the temptation to look at them there and then and left the building with my heart thumping in anticipation, my right hand gripping the folder tightly as if it was a living thing that might break free and run for it if I gave it a chance.

I made my way back to Kings Cross. I found a café in the station and sat down to look at the papers over a cup of tea and a sandwich.

The first thing I saw was a photo of Stella. A head and shoulders shot. She was wearing a simple, tailored white blouse. That great black cloud of hair hanging over her shoulders had gone. It was cropped short above her ears and around her slim neck, but it was still thick, and subtle auburn touches had lightened its colour. It was the face you noticed now, not the hair. It was the same face, but slimmer, and somehow more strongly defined. You noticed cheek-bones, a high, clear, elegant brow. It was no longer deathly pale, but lightly tanned. The scarlet lips had gone, the panda eyes had gone. If she was wearing make-up, it was too carefully done to notice. Something silvery glittered at the tips of her ears and round her throat. She was smiling. She looked well. Very well indeed. Confident and comfortable and businesslike. Fit and healthy and happy. Grown up. She looked great. She looked beautiful.

I looked at the picture and felt a strange burst of joy. It was relief, yes, but something else, something I didn't understand. A ghost stirring from the past, perhaps, but a ghost I didn't remember. A ghost bringing a warmth and happiness which puzzled me even as it cheered me.

I shuffled through the papers impatiently, skimming the text, pouncing on more photographs. They were pages from the website of a PR company. Stella's company. Foreman Blue Sky, it was called. And Stella McNye now called herself Stella Foreman. What? Why? Ah, of course, she was married… There was a picture of her with a small, slim, dark-haired man. They were standing close together, in an office, against a high window, smiling happily. He looked bright and energetic and confident, and yes, fun. Tanned. A white shirt, rather like hers, black trousers. David and Stella Foreman, the caption said, the owners and joint managing directors of the firm they founded four years ago, a year after they married.

I felt something twist painfully behind the ghost's gifts of warmth and joy. It felt almost like bitterness, regret, sadness, anger… Cruel ghost… But why? I was glad for Stella, genuinely happy for her. For both of them, Mr and Mrs Foreman. There they were, successful and prosperous. Stella was in a good place, and I was relieved. She deserved it. She had earned it.

Foreman Blue Sky seemed to specialise in PR for the music and entertainment industry. There were details of clients – pop groups and actors and film production companies – names and faces which meant nothing to me but which glowed with the aura of success and fame. I ignored them and searched for contact details – there they were, the office address, phone and fax number, e-mail… London EC1. Yes! London! She was still here, I had found her, she was within arm's reach! EC1. Clerkenwell. Just down the road! I laughed, my heart thumping with triumph and excitement.

The second bundle of papers was scrappier. There were copies of newspaper articles covering a court-case brought against an American movie star by a photographer, a case of assault and criminal damage. The photographer had been taking shots of the actor coming out of a London restaurant and the actor had punched the photographer and smashed his camera. In another court-case, an Italian pop-star had brought a case against the same photographer for harassment. The photographer had been trying to take shots of her through the windows of a London hotel. He'd been seen on a neighbouring roof-top, on a fire-escape, hiding among the dustbins outside a bathroom, even inside the hotel in the uniform of a bell-boy. There was an account of a legal dispute between a glamour model and the photographer over the copyright of some intimate photos. In another article, police spokesmen were suggesting that there was something sinister and criminal about the graphic and disturbing crime-scene snaps taken by the photographer who always seemed to arrive long before the police. Where did he get his information from? There were extracts from a parliamentary enquiry into press corruption, and the photographer's name seemed to come up time after time. The photographer's name was Gary Hughes.

There was a website – HughesViews – but it seemed to be a members-only site. I scanned the registration page for an address, but couldn't see one. There was a self-portrait shot of Gary, however, and if it hadn't been titled I doubt that I would have recognised it. It was a shot of a tanned and muscular young man. Blond crew-cut. Black t-shirt. Arms crossed to show off strong bicep and shoulder. Staring unsmiling at the camera. An aggressive, challenging, confrontational, give-a-shit stare. The shot had been lit to make the subject look tough and handsome, glamorous and dramatic, like something from a film noir, except it was in full colour. It was a bit overdone, a bit camp.

Was that really Gary Hughes? I looked closer. Yes. The eyes – I knew those eyes. It was Gary, all right. Everything I read in that bundle seemed to fit the Gary I'd known. It wasn't wholesome reading. What did I feel about it? Again, my reaction was strange, puzzling. It was mainly indifference. Here was an unpleasant character. I hadn't liked him all those years ago, and no doubt I wouldn't like him when we met up again. That was all. Guilt about the way I'd treated him? Sympathy and compassion for the shabby life he had chosen? No. Not really. The ghosts were silent, absent.

Where was he? How was I going to find him? Was he still in London? Almost certainly yes, given the kind of life documented here. And if he was in London, I would find him.

I turned back to the first bundle and checked Foreman Blue Sky's EC1 address again. I borrowed an A to Z from the waiter and looked it up. South of the Angel, north of the Barbican. Twenty minutes stroll away. Easy.

I found it in the middle of a nest of Clerkenwell's picturesque one-way streets. But I couldn't get very close. FBS's offices were in a big Victorian school building which had been converted into luxury apartments and business premises. At the front, what I guessed had been the playground was now a car-park. At the back, there was a garden, a lawn and trees. The whole complex was walled and gated. There was a big iron gate for cars and a small iron gate for pedestrians, with a porter's lodge beside them. I peered through the iron bars. The car park was full of expensive vehicles – Jags and Porsches and Mercs, a

Maserati and an Aston Martin. The building was tall and handsome, its wide south front bathed in the clear spring sunlight, red and yellow brickwork glowing. There were scores of offices in there, dozens of apartments. Which windows were FBS's? Stella was in there somewhere, right now. But where?

The blast of a car-horn sounded right behind me. I jumped, startled. I turned round. I was in the way: a big shiny car was turning in off the street. I stepped aside. The iron gates opened automatically and the car swept past.

'Can I help you?' A window had opened in the porter's lodge. A young man – red-haired, white shirt, blue jacket and tie which could have been some sort of uniform – was peering out at me.

'No... thanks... it's OK...' I waved awkwardly. I was still startled. I felt furtive and flustered. The young concierge looked pleasant enough, but something about him made me feel guilty. I slunk off, heading for Farringdon Underground.

*

I got the underground to St Paul's and walked over the Millenium Bridge to Tate Modern. I approached the place with something like dread. I'd never liked it. Dark and gloomy and hostile. I'd always thought of it as one of Blake's dark satanic mills, I'd always thought it cast a pall of depression over any work it exhibited. But now I had good reason to hate it.

There were posters outside showing a big glass case containing a dark and shadowy human figure, life-sized, standing with its feet apart and its arms outstretched. From the way it was shot, it was difficult to tell what material it was made from. In fact, it looked more like a real body than a sculpture. The artist's name was printed

217

in big letters along the top of the poster, the name of the work along the bottom.

Harry Jutting. Montezuma's Revenge.

A pile of leaflets showing the same image stood on the counter of the information desk just inside the entrance. I picked one up and read it as I followed the crowds into the airless, windowless interior. 'On the tenth anniversary of Harry Jutting's death, Tate Modern is exhibiting a new and posthumous work by this tragic and enigmatic comet who still burns bright in the art firmament. Montezuma's Revenge promises to be one of Jutting's most exciting and interesting pieces. The exhibition, which also includes other work by Jutting from the Tate's own collection, offers an opportunity to re-assess this artist's creative achievement, now that the dust stirred up by his near-legendary life has had time to settle. Slowly revealing itself over a finite life-span, this unusual work will repay repeated visits…'

I found the piece in a small, windowless gallery on the first floor. It was crowded, to my surprise and dismay. Listening to the murmured chatter around me, it was clear that Hobson's mysterious death had handed the gallery's marketing and PR department a coup they could only have dreamt about. Art Crash Express might never be completed, but Harry Jutting's name was riding high on the back of the wider and more popular fame of a murdered soap-opera star.

'Did Hobson do that then, that actor guy from First Orders?' a girl whispered to her boyfriend at my elbow.

'Nah, you idiot. What's his name, Jutting, Harry Jutting, did it.'

'Harry what? Who's he?'

'The artist bloke, you know, the character Hobson was going to play in that movie. Before he was done in.'

'Oh. So he was real, then, was he? Harry whatsit? Not just a character in a movie?'

'No, he really existed, you silly cow. The movie was like a documentary, no, what do they call it, non-fiction, you know, based on the artist geezer's life.'

'Oh.' They peered up at the glass case. 'But what is it?'

What was it? I looked up at the dark figure. The cast of a human body, made from a porridge of human blood and plant seeds. Frozen solid, and preserved for ten years in this glass case which has carefully monitored and maintained its temperature at below zero. Until now. A week ago, the case had been taken out of storage in the depths of the Tate, its thermostat had been adjusted, special lights had been installed to promote photosynthesis, and it had been put on display. Each day, the temperature inside the case was being allowed to rise bit by bit, until eventually the frozen sculpture will have thawed out, offering the seeds the warmth and the moisture and the nutrition to germinate, to put out roots and shoots and finally to blossom, until the whole sculpture would look like a flower-man, a human being made of bright and colourful blooms. And then the flowers would wither and the plants would die, the figure would decay and collapse, and this work would be no more. Fertility and decay, nature's twin faces. The beauty of life, the horror of death.

But I was going to destroy it before anyone would see any of that.

I looked closely at it. The casting had been done well. Very well indeed. The material, rough though it was, muddy, dark brown, studded and speckled with grains and wormed with roots and shoots, nevertheless showed clear details of musculature, bone structure and male genitalia. The face was anonymous enough, but all the features were clearly identifiable. I peered at the surface. There were

219

patches already wet and glistening and viscous like wet mud, other patches which shone and glittered like defrosting ice, others which still looked frozen solid. I looked at the thing's feet for signs of liquid puddling on the floor, but there were none. The whole thing should hold together, rather than just melt and collapse into a liquid mess, thanks to the organic gelling agent which had been mixed into the porridge, and to the roots and shoots which some of the seeds had been allowed to put out before they were added.

'Blood? Real human blood?' The girl beside me shivered. 'Ugh. Disgusting. Gives me the creeps. Let's go.'

'Me too,' her boyfriend whispered. 'Let's go back to the dodgems in the boiler-room. They were fun, weren't they? I'll beat you this time.'

It would be easy, I thought. Just break the glass case. Without its bubble of controlled temperature and atmosphere the whole thing would be done for. Smash it with something heavy. A brick or hammer smuggled in under your jacket. Or just put your shoulder to it and heave the thing over. For a moment the sound from the crowd around me faded and I heard a faint hum coming from the exhibit. Electricity. Perhaps it would be as simple as flicking a switch. Turn the power off… I walked round its plinth, a big box of white wooden boards. There was no sign of plug or flex. The cables must come in under the floor and up through the inside of the box. There was what looked like a service-panel on the back of the box, screw-heads visible in each corner. A screw-driver and a caretaker's white over-alls, would that do it?

I glanced at the work on the gallery walls. I recognised them all, and the recognition made me feel sick. Half a dozen pieces, pretty representative of Harry's brief but dramatic career. I would have to destroy them as well, all of them. There were information panels on the wall, but I didn't bother reading them. I could guess what sort of garbage was written there.

My attack would have to be very carefully planned. It wouldn't be easy. I mentally ran through the obstacles. The crowds, the number of pieces to be destroyed, the distance to the exit. The more time it took, the more people there were around to stop me, the further I had to go to escape, the less likely I was to get away with it. But it wouldn't be impossible. Anyway, getting the job done and getting away with it were two different things, the first easier and more important than the second. As long as I could get the job done, I'd always been prepared to take risks about getting away with it. But now I knew I couldn't afford to get caught. Not now, not yet, not until I'd solved the mystery which had brought me back to London.

No, this job would have to wait until I'd found out who had betrayed me, and how, and why.

I left the Tate and went and sat on a bench overlooking the Thames and got some fresh air into my lungs and fed my eyes on the sunlight sparkling on the river's surface. Montezuma's Revenge. A statue coming alive. A dead body which wasn't dead. A sleeper waking up after a ten-year slumber. Four people had given their blood, had shared their blood, had mixed it together, to give birth to… whatever new life was stirring in that big glass case in the little gallery, windowless and harshly over-lit, in the bleak black giant of a building behind me. Four people. Myself, and Stella, and Patrick, and Garry.

I had a curry in Brick Lane on my way back to Navarino Row – not everything had changed in the East End, after all – and while I ate I read through those papers again. I looked at the photo of Mrs Foreman, happy with her skinny little husband at her side, at the photo of Gary Hughes, a narcissistic portrait of arrogant complacency. Which one of you has done this, I wondered? Which one of you has separated me from Helen and Richard and Elizabeth? Which one of you has driven a wedge between me and all I love and care for in the world? I was looking forward to calling Helen. I had a whole conversation with her in my imagination, I could hear her talking and laughing, I spoke to Elizabeth too, and answered her innocent questions, and spoke to Richard and listened to his excited gurgles.

I tried phoning home as soon as I got back to the Ellerby that evening. But there was no answer. I tried several times, but it was no good. I missed Helen and the children, I desperately wanted to talk to them. Not being able to only made it worse. And the silence only added worry and anxiety to my sense of isolation and longing. Why wasn't Helen answering the phone? Had she guessed it was me, and decided not to answer it? She must be so angry with me. Yesterday she had been stunned and surprised. But now the shock had worn off she must be furious with me.

Or perhaps she wasn't at home. Why wasn't she at home? Where was she? What had happened to her?

I thought about the last time Helen and I had spoken. Was it only yesterday? About what we'd said to each other. Or rather, what I'd said to her, and what she hadn't said to me. 'Please tell me nothing has changed,' I'd begged. 'Helen, please, tell me!' And she'd been silent. She hadn't answered. She'd refused to answer. And now she wasn't answering the phone when I called.

Well, what did I expect? Only a fool could hope that nothing had changed. Helen was unconventional, she lived by her own laws and standards. Nevertheless, those laws were real, those standards were high. She was an idealist. In the years before I met her, she had lived a life of protest in defence of those ideals. She had handcuffed herself to bulldozers to stop developers destroying acres of wild downland, she had lain down in the road in front of lorries delivering building materials to sites where new nuclear reactors were being constructed, she had lived through freezing winter months in a hut in the tree tops to stop road-builders cutting down ancient woods, she had been beaten up by private security guards, she had been arrested more than once. She had carried those same high standards and ideals into her private life, and I had failed them. I had let her down. I had disappointed her. Would she ever speak to me again? Would she ever want to see me again? Those questions were terrifying. I couldn't bring myself to think about them.

I tried to think about what Helen and the children were doing. I tried to imagine her feeding them, bathing them, putting them to bed. A comforting, familiar routine. Normal life. But of course I had destroyed all that. Normal life had come to an abrupt end the moment police had knocked on our door. That's what the silence at the other end of the phone meant. Perhaps Helen was in police custody, helping them with their enquiries. Perhaps the children had been taken into care. No, that possibility was too painful, too frightening to even consider.

That night I dreamt that I was walking along the beach with Helen and the children. The wind was blowing and it was cold so we weren't saying much to each other. Then we noticed something washing to and fro on the shore-line ahead of us. It was a body. It was the body of Stella McNye, pale and bloated and drowned. The children were frightened. I didn't know what to do with it. Somehow I got it back to the cottage and locked it away in the bathroom. I was standing in the sitting-room, with Helen and the children, we were all shivering around the fire, trying to get warm, when a banging from the bathroom door began to crash through the house.

'She's alive!' a voice shouted from behind the locked door. It was Gary's voice. 'Alive! She's alive!' The banging got louder. 'Let us out! Let us out!'

I woke up suddenly. The banging was still echoing around the room. No, it wasn't a banging – it was a loud tapping. It was very dark. I didn't know where I was, for a moment I thought I was at home in the cottage, then I remembered the motel, then I remembered…

'Mr Jutting?' A voice half-called, half-whispered over the tapping. 'Mr Jutting? You awake?' I recognised the voice – it was the landlady's voice, more cockney than ever. Mista Ja-ing… She sounded urgent, alarmed.

I groped for the light, found it, turned it on. What was the time? One thirty-five. In the morning. There was a dim light showing under the door. I got up unsteadily and opened it.

'I'm sorry, Mr Jutting, sorry to wake you…' The landlady was wrapped in a quilted dressing-gown. Her hair was a mess. She was wearing no jewellery or make up. She looked and sounded very frightened.

And she wasn't alone. There was a man beside her, bulking indistinct in the dim light, a big mass of black leather, black denim, cropped hair and stubble. He stepped forwards and a face emerged from the shadows. A tough face, broad and hard, small eyes, flat nose. He looked pissed-off. Who wouldn't be, doing business at this time of night? I didn't know him, but in a flash I guessed what he was about. He frowned at me, and jerked his head, a mimimal gesture back down the corridor. 'Come on, then,' he grunted. 'Other room.'

Chapter Eleven

The other room. The room overlooking the backyard. The room where… The night air was cold on my bare skin. I'd been woken suddenly from a deep sleep. I knew who was waiting for me in the other room. No wonder I was shivering.

'Hang on.' I found a sweater and a pair of jeans and pulled them on with trembling hands. 'OK.'

I followed the heavy's leather-clad back and plodding step down the dark corridor. His big jacket was stretched tight over the bulk of his torso. I could hear his breathing – a curious wheezing snort. It sounded very loud in the silence of the night. The bare light-bulb on the landing ahead was fighting its losing battle against the shadows. A dim glow flowed up the stairs from the shuttered bar below. I heard the sound of a chair scraping on the floor down there. A trickle of light crawled towards us from under the closed door of the room ahead. In the semi-darkness, the patterns on the ancient wallpaper were sinister smudges and stains. The cracked lino felt cold and damp and gritty under my bare feet.

There was another heavy waiting outside the closed door. He was in leather and jeans like the first man, but he looked younger and lighter and faster. He stepped towards me with his hands out, and he laughed when I flinched back. 'Hold on,' he grinned. 'Gotta frisk you, mate. You wired-up? Tooled up?'

'Nah, I seen him in his boxers,' the first man said. 'He's clean.'

The second man shook his head. 'My bollocks on the line here, Pete, not yours. Come on, mate. Arms up. Imagine you're at the airport. Going on holiday. Happy thoughts.' I stood still while he frisked me. 'Ok, Pete, you were right, don't make a fuss about it.' He straightened up and knocked on the door. 'In you go.'

I opened the door and stepped into the room.

Steve Smith was sitting in the armchair by the window. The curtains were closed and the main light and the bedside light were on. It seemed very bright in there after the gloom of the corridor and landing. I could see Steve with such clarity he was almost like a hallucination. He was wearing a navy blue suit, a white shirt, a pale blue tie. His black leather shoes were polished to a high shine, there were gold rings on his fingers, a gold bracelet on his right wrist, a chunky gold watch on his left. He was deeply tanned. He looked bigger than I remembered him - in ten years he'd gained a lot of weight. The suit did a good job of hiding it – you only noticed the powerful shoulders, the deep chest – but his face and his hands were fuller and fleshier and I could imagine the gut straining against the waist-band. His face had that same hard, dull look about it which I remembered; a look which could easily be mistaken for stupidity, but in fact was the sign of someone who took a completely ruthless and clear-eyed view of the world because they weren't hampered by the least scrap of imagination. There were deep lines running from his nose to the corners of his mouth which made him look bitter and cruel and middle-aged. He'd lost a lot of hair as well, and there were hints of grey in his receding crew-cut.

He sat very still with the alert stillness of the violent criminal, of the predatory animal instinctively preserving its energy for when it was really needed. He looked powerful and prosperous and frightening.

He looked at me as I came in through the door. He frowned, and peered closer. 'What the...?' He sounded irritated and impatient. 'Who the fuck are you?'

'Steve.' I laughed uneasily. 'Don't you recognise me?' It was the beard and the long hair. 'OK, I need a shave. And

a hair-cut. And ten years is ten years. But all the same...'
My voice trailed off. Uneasiness was turning to fear. What
was I doing here with this dangerous animal? What was I
thinking of?

He was still peering at me, still puzzled and annoyed.
Then he shook his head slowly in recognition. 'Oh, yeah. I
see it now,' he said without much interest or surprise.
'Yeah, you're the one... the one who... Yeah, I remember.'
His voice rose with sudden irritation. 'But what the fuck
do you want? And what the fuck do you mean by giving
that name to Suze?'

'Yes, Steve, I'm sorry, I never use that name, I know I
shouldn't use it, mustn't give anything away, but I couldn't
think how else to contact you.'

'But why the fuck would you want to contact me?' He
looked genuinely puzzled. Bewildered, even.

'Steve.' I laughed awkwardly. 'Someone knows who I
am. Someone knows what happened ten years ago, what
you did for me. They must have found out somehow, I
don't know how. But it means I'm in danger, I'm in
trouble. And that means you might be, too. I was
wondering if you might have any idea...'

'What the fuck are you talking about?' He was even
more alert but no longer still. He was leaning forward in
the chair, tense and angry. 'Danger? Trouble? Who the
fuck are you to tell me I'm in danger? You fucking
threatening me or what?' His eyes went up over my
shoulder and I realised with alarm that the big heavy who
had got me out of bed had followed me into the room and
was standing behind me. Steve was giving him some sort
of signal.

'No, Steve, no. No way. But someone's making trouble
for me and I have to find out who they are and how they
found out about... you know... I swear I haven't told
anyone. Never. My secret... our secret... what you did for

227

me… I've guarded it carefully for ten years, I promise. They couldn't have found out from anything I've said or done. And there's only one other person who knows… you, Steve. No one else. Could anything you've said or done… could anyone have… have you any idea who..?'

'I've no idea what the fuck you're talking about. Secret? What secret? What have I done for you? Bugger all, mate, I've never done anything for you. What the fuck are you talking about?'

'But, Steve…'

'Listen, you mad fucker. I remember you. I know who you are. I remember what happened to you. But if you try and mix me up in any of your mad ideas, I'll fucking kill you. If you go around saying anything about what I might or might not have done, I'll fucking kill you fucking painfully. All right? You fucking understand?'

'Steve, please, I need your help…'

He looked up past my left shoulder again, and nodded. I heard a grunt of exertion from the man behind me and at the same time felt a sudden blinding pain explode in my right kidney. Then I was on the floor, lying down. I had no memory of having fallen over. But there was a sharp pain in my shoulder and head where I must have hit the furniture going down. My eyes were closed and when I opened them I could see the filthy carpet right under my eyes and a close-up view of the dust and muck under the bed. The carpet smelt foul, and felt damp and crusty against my cheek. The pain in my back was overwhelming and I couldn't move. I saw feet in big black shoes walking round past my face. Then I heard another grunt of exertion and the heavy kicked me in the gut and a new explosion of agony shook me from head to foot. I curled up, coughing and retching. I heard the curious wheezing snort of the heavy's breathing get louder as he leant down and grabbed a handful of my sweater and hauled me to my feet. I couldn't breathe. I was choking for breath and retching like a dog about to be sick all at the same time.

'That's for wasting my time,' Steve said. His face swam in front of me as the room swung up and down and from side to side and the light seemed to blink on and off, on and off. He looked bored and pissed off, ready to move on and move out. 'I've got a plane to catch in a few hours time. A business meeting in South America tomorrow, thousands of miles away. And here I am, wasting half the night listening to your shit. Last thing I need. I'm a busy man and I don't like people pissing me about. Now listen. I know what you are, I remember what happened to you, I feel sorry for you, so I'm letting you off lightly, you fucking lunatic. My advice to you is, piss of back to that safe place you just ran away from. Stay there and keep your nose clean and your mouth shut. And piss off quickly, before I change my mind.'

The heavy was still holding me up, a fistful of my sweater in his left hand. He swung his right and it hit me in the gut like a canon ball. Then he let me go, pushing me back onto the bed. I collapsed on the bare mattress, bounced, and rolled off onto the floor. Footsteps left the room, the door slammed shut, and I was on my own, throwing up the Brick Lane curry all over that stinking carpet.

*

The landlady helped me back to my room. She kept apologising, as if she'd been sick on my carpet and not the other way round. I could hardly talk, but I managed to let her know that I'd clean it up in the morning.

'No, no! That old carpet? I should have thrown it out years ago! High time we had a new one, you've done me a favour, really and truly.' She looked and sounded relieved.

She hadn't been left with any corpses or severed limbs to dispose of. She wouldn't have to re-decorate the whole room. The police weren't hammering on her front door or trying to close her pub down.

I fell into a deep sleep the moment I hit my bed. Fear and exhaustion knocked me out. But I woke up after only an hour, and I couldn't get back to sleep. My guts and my back hurt too much, and my mind was racing. Part of me wanted to forget all about Steve Smith, to wipe all recollection of him from my memory. But another part of me wanted to go over every word of our interview, examine it from every angle, find out... what? What had it told me? What could I learn from it? I forced myself to remember what he had said. I dragged every word and phrase up from where my terror and anxiety were trying to hide the whole experience. I went over them again and again. He had tried to deny everything. That was hardly surprising. I should have expected it. What on earth had made me think he might have been helpful and co-operative? Denial and threats. And a taste of what was in store for me if I refused to let sleeping dogs lie. I should have known that was all I could hope for.

And yet I was puzzled. There was nothing in anything he had said or how he had said it to suggest that he might ever have let slip anything about my secret. Our secret. On the contrary, his very denial of it seemed to suggest he was just as anxious as I was to keep it buried.

And there was something else I wanted to think about. An idea – a suspicion – which had hit me just before the heavy's fist did. Could it be Steve Smith himself who had betrayed me? Perhaps he hadn't after all revealed anything to Stella or Gary or Patrick. Perhaps it hadn't been any of those three after all. Perhaps it had been Steve himself. No. No, the more I thought about it, the more absurd it seemed. He had no reason to do it – he had nothing

230

against me, whereas each of the other three did. And he had every reason not to do it. He had a lot to lose. If word got out that Harry Jutting was still alive, if the police ever found out how his death had been faked, who had faked it... Steve Smith had everything to lose from such a revelation. No, the idea was absurd.

So Steve Smith was giving nothing away. So I was no closer to solving the mystery. Well, what had I expected? Steve Smith's day-to-day survival must depend on concealment and denial. It must be second nature to him. But not to Stella, or Gary, or Patrick. One of them would give themselves away. I was certain of it. A tone of voice, an unguarded expression, a look in the eye, that was all it would take. Proof? I didn't need proof. The truth would out. None of them was so devious and steely and self-controlled that they'd be able to hide it once I confronted them.

I lay awake, trying to toss and turn my way out of the pain in my back and gut, listening to the traffic growing louder and louder in the high street outside the window, seeing the grubby details of the shabby room emerge from the darkness as it got lighter. I wanted to phone Helen, to hear her voice, but I didn't want to disturb her. It would wake the children up, and the one thing that comforted me as I lay awake was imagining Helen and Elizabeth and Richard fast asleep far away, at rest and oblivious and safe, their dreams soothed by the faint rumble of the sea rising and falling beyond the marsh.

At seven o'clock I got up and had a shower and brushed my teeth to get the stink of vomit off me. I got dressed and let myself out of the pub without waiting for breakfast. Just the idea of coffee made my sore guts twist painfully and my battered kidneys throb. And I wanted to get to Clerkenwell as soon as I could.

There was a shock waiting for me on the underground.

The carriages were packed. Rush hour. The world on its way to work. I stood all the way – it was only a few stops. Most of the people sitting down were reading copies of the free newspaper handed out at underground entrances. A woman beside me, her eyes closed as if asleep, had one folded on her lap. I peered at it dully – and a headline caught my eye like a hook gaffing a fish. I jumped, physically, as if I'd just touched an electric fence.

'Vandal Targets Works of Art by Montezuma's Revenge Artist'.

I tried to focus on the tiny print, but I couldn't quite read it. The paper was a few feet too far away. It was rocking and shaking and swaying with everything else in the carriage. And the woman stirred every now and then, without opening her eyes, shifting her knees and sliding her hands over the paper. Her right hand ended up resting on the paper, her wrist obscuring the column I was trying to read.

I glanced around to see if I could read anyone else's paper, but everyone seemed to be on a different page. The man on my left caught me trying to peer over his shoulder. He sighed angrily, moved away from me, and folded up the paper as small as he could, hiding everything but the article he was reading.

I looked down at the woman with the newspaper on her lap. Was she asleep? Her eyes were still closed, her head was resting at an awkward angle, her mouth was slightly open, and her chest was rising and falling slowly and regularly. Yes, she must be fast asleep. Could I reach down and take her paper without disturbing her?

The train came into a station and ground to a halt. The woman opened her eyes, sat up, and looked around. The doors shuddered open and even more people surged in and out of the carriage. She looked down to check her bag – still there on the floor at her feet. She picked it up and stuffed the folded paper into it and sat with it on her lap as the train took off again.

The next stop was Farringdon. My stop. I got off and followed the crowds along the platform and out of the station. On the pavement the crowd flowed around a couple of youngsters in baseball caps and t-shirts advertising the free newspaper, bundles of it under one arm, the other hopefully thrusting copies at the indifferent multitude hurrying past. I took a copy from each of them – they were surprised and delighted – and made my way up to Clerkenwell Green.

There was a church beyond the green. The churchyard had been turned into a small park – grass, trees, benches, dog-walkers throwing balls and sticks and picking up steaming piles with plastic bag gloved hands. I sat down and opened the newspaper. My hands were shaking. I read the piece quickly, my heart thumping as my eyes skimmed and raced over the print. Then I read it again, slowly.

'A number of works of art have been attacked and destroyed over the last six months in what appears to be a well-organised and concerted campaign of cultural vandalism. The criminal or criminals have launched at least seven separate attacks on paintings and sculptures by the well-known and controversial rebel punk artist Harry Jutting. Items worth many thousands if not millions of pounds have been deliberately destroyed. Private homes, commercial galleries and public exhibitions around the country have been broken into or subjected to hit-and-run raids. Security has been stepped up at Tate Modern, where Montezuma's Revenge, a posthumous work by Harry Jutting, is being exhibited to mark the tenth anniversary this year of his death.

'The motivation behind this curious but serious crime remains unclear,' said Inspector Morris of Scotland Yard, the police officer in charge of the investigation. 'But I would guess that the individual or individuals responsible has some kind of personal or aesthetic grudge against Mr Jutting and his work. No work by any other artist has been touched during these attacks. And nothing has been stolen, so personal gain does not appear to be a motive.'

Inspector Morris refused to confirm or deny that his investigations are part of the broader investigation into the mysterious death of James Hobson, the actor who was playing the part of Harry Jutting in the film 'Art Crash Express', a dramatised account of that artist's life. Hobson's death has brought filming to an abrupt halt, and it is uncertain whether the movie will ever be completed. But it is known that Hobson received anonymous written warnings and death threats from someone who appeared to have 'some kind of personal or aesthetic grudge against Mr Jutting and his work'.

For at least six months these attacks, apparently random and scattered, have largely passed unnoticed and unremarked. Only now are they recognised as connected, as part of a concerted and prolonged campaign. The police and the art world are at last putting two and two together, thanks perhaps to the raised profile of Harry Jutting's name in the wake of Hobson's tragic and dramatic death, and to the much-anticipated unveiling of Montezuma's Revenge.

'The public response to Montezuma's Revenge has been wonderful,' said Dr Mary Stanhope, the curator in charge of Tate Modern's smash-hit exhibition. 'People have been queuing up to see this intriguing piece, many of them returning over the weeks to inspect the changes to this fluid, dynamic work. I don't believe that the events now subject to this criminal investigation constitute any kind of threat which would discourage our public. But I can assure you that Tate Modern has taken every precaution necessary to protect our holdings and to safeguard the welfare of our visitors, which is of paramount importance to us. Nevertheless, I would urge the public to be especially vigilant...'

I shouldn't have been surprised. I'd been expecting it for some time now. The only surprise was that it had taken so long for anyone to join up the dots and spot the common factor - Harry Jutting - linking all those demolition jobs together. But it was still alarming. Another pack of hounds was loose on my trail. They might not have caught my scent yet, but I could hear them baying in the distance.

Eight-thirty in the morning. I'd guessed that there would be a lot of traffic in and out of the converted Victorian school-building where Stella had her offices. People coming into work in the offices, residents going out to work. I was right. Both sets of gates – pedestrian and vehicular – were continually swinging open and closed. Some pedestrians were using security fobs to open the side gate, others were just following cars in through the main gate. I tagged on behind them and got in without any questions asked. I strode across the car-park towards the main building as if I knew exactly where I was going.

But there were at least twenty sets of offices in there. Which ones were Stella's? How would I find them? I peered through a glass door into the building. There was a row of numbered intercom buttons beside it. Each button had the name of a business against it. None of them said Foreman Blue Sky. Below was a swipe pad. Someone reached past me and scraped their security fob across the pad. The glass door clicked open, they disappeared into the building, the glass door clicked closed again.

The numbers were seven to twelve. What was Foreman Blue Sky's number? Their address? Nineteen. I walked on, round the building. Another glass door. I looked at the numbers. Thirteen to eighteen. I walked on, turned a corner, found myself in the garden at the back. Another glass door. Numbers nineteen to twenty-four. And there, beside the button for number nineteen, was the name – Foreman Blue Sky.

I pressed the button. A voice sounded through the intercom. 'Hello?'

My mouth was dry. I licked my lips. 'Package for Stella Foreman.'

'Come on up. First floor'

The glass door buzzed open. I stepped inside. Lift doors on the far side of the small lobby. I got into the lift, pressed the button for the first floor. The lift shuddered into life, rose, shuddered to a halt. The doors opened. I stepped out into another lobby, a reception desk in front of me, office doors to left and right.

'Good morning?' The girl sitting at the desk was a bit too bright and cheerful for first thing in the morning. There was a big row of framed photos and posters all along the wall behind her. Clients – faces and events. 'Can I help you?'

'Package for Stella Foreman,' I said again. 'Is she in?'

'Mrs Foreman won't be in till nine. But you can leave it with me, if you like.' She looked me up and down, puzzled. I didn't have a package. All I had in my hand were the rolled-up newspapers. She frowned. 'I'll see that she gets it, as soon as she arrives.'

'Nine o'clock.' I hesitated, uncertain. I looked at my watch. Another twenty minutes. 'I'll come back.'

'You can wait here, if you like.' She indicated the sofa and coffee table beside the reception desk.

'No. No, I'll… I'll come back.' I took the lift back to the ground floor, went back out into the fresh air and sunlight. I felt foolish – why didn't I want to wait in reception? - but relieved. Somehow the tension of waiting twenty minutes up there would have been unbearable. But out here it would be different. I breathed in and out deeply, then walked back round to the car park at the front of the building. I sat down on a wooden bench against a wall and watched the cars come and go. My heart lurched with each car that came in. I watched closely as they came to a halt, as the doors opened… A Merc drove in, came towards me, turned aside. The sunlight caught the windows as it passed, and I couldn't see inside. It parked in a marked space a dozen steps away and the driver's door opened. A small, wiry man stepped out. Dark-haired. Navy blue suit, white shirt, no tie. I recognised him immediately. David Foreman.

The passenger door opened and a very tall, slim woman got out. I noticed short-cropped auburn hair, a blue dress, bare arms, bare legs, high heels. Something glittering at throat, wrist and ears. She had a blue and white checked jacket in one hand and a black leather handbag in the other. She put the bag on the ground, shut the car door, and slipped on the jacket. The man locked the car. They smiled at each other across the top of the car. The woman said something I couldn't hear and they both laughed. She picked the bag up, the man came round and took her hand, and they both walked away from the car.

Stella. Stella McNye. Stella Foreman. I was on my feet now. They both glanced at me as they walked past, just for a fraction of a second, the man's glance blank, not seeing me, Stella's glance almost a smile, politeness to a stranger, fleeting, unrecognising.

'Stella!' I tried not to raise my voice. I tried to speak just loud enough for her to hear, but it came out almost as a shout. 'Stella McNye!'

They stopped and turned. The man peered at me, politely at first, then he frowned, concerned, as if he wasn't exactly reassured by what he could see. But I hardly noticed him. Stella looked at me, and I focused on her as closely as a camera-man filming the leading lady. She looked puzzled. She didn't recognise me. She looked me up and down, looked almost worried, as if I was the kind of stranger she wouldn't want to be accosted by. Then something flashed through her eyes, alarm and perhaps recognition, and she peered closer. She gasped. Yes, she recognised me. Amazement and something else flashed across her face, anxiety perhaps, no, more like concern, embarrassment even. Then she was smiling. And the smile seemed genuine.

'Is it..? Yes, yes it is! Well, hello! How are you?' She came towards me, her hands out, laughing. Her face... Her complexion was wonderful. Lightly tanned, pale lipstick, a hint of eye-shadow... She looked even lovelier than her photo. I took her hands. They felt warm, and firm rather than soft, and then we were embracing. I could smell her perfume, feel her short, clean hair against my cheek... Then she broke away, and turned to her husband. 'It's OK, David. It's all right.' But he didn't look reassured. He was still frowning at me. 'An old friend... it's OK.' She turned back to me. 'Shall we... shall we go for a coffee somewhere? Breakfast? I haven't had breakfast. Have you had breakfast?' She sounded a little uncertain, a bit nervous, and solicitous, concerned, but at the same time pleased and willing.

'Yes, I... No, I haven't.' I stumbled over the words. 'Yes, please. Good idea.'

'Stella…' The husband's voice was uncertain, almost a warning.

'Don't worry, David. We'll just drop into the Kitchen. I'll be back in time for the Blackwater meeting.' She kissed him and he nodded, still uncertain. 'Hold the fort till then?'

'Ok,' he said. 'But don't be late.'

'All right,' she said. 'Come on, then. It's just round the corner. Out of the gate here.'

Stella took charge, leading the way to the café, directing me to a table and buying the coffee and pastries. She was still Matron. But what had seemed bossy and fussy ten years ago now seemed comforting and even flattering. Almost maternal. It inspired confidence and affection and gratitude – I could see how and why her business was thriving. She was on cheerful, first-name terms with the people behind the counter. One of them insisted on carrying her order over to our table for her, and I didn't see them do that for any other customer.

'Thanks.' I sipped at the cup, wincing. The pain in my gut and back stirred, then settled. No, I wasn't going to throw up. What a relief. I gulped more coffee. It tasted good. The pain began to recede. I put the cup down and stared at Stella. She looked fit and well. She looked like she took winter holidays in the sun, and jogged every day and worked out in the gym three times a week. Her face was no longer pale and puffy and half-hidden by an unruly mass of long dark hair; it was slim and delicate, with a good bone-structure now evident. Her cropped hair set it off nicely, merely framing it and no longer distracting from it. 'You're looking good, Stella,' I said. 'You're looking great.'

She laughed. 'You should have seen me half an hour ago. You should have seen what I saw when I got out of bed and looked in the mirror.'

'And successful,' I said. 'I'm glad, Stella. I'm really glad for you.' I felt strangely, unaccountably happy. Just being here with Stella, seeing her, hearing her talk. 'PR? You, Stella?'

'Yes, indeed. I fell into it by accident, more or less. But I liked it straight away. And soon enough I found I wasn't bad at it.'

'Your own company?'

'Well, I've been lucky. I met David a year or two into my first job. We set up on our own, and things have gone pretty well for us ever since.'

Her right hand held her coffee cup, her left fiddled with the pastry on her plate. I saw the band of gold and a circle of diamonds on her ring finger. Something stirred behind the happiness, something sharp and bitter, like the pain which stirred from time to time behind the sweet taste of the pastry and the mellow smoothness of the coffee. I felt I ought to ask about David, how they met, whether they had any children, but I didn't want to. 'Don't you miss the rock and roll?' I said.

'No!' She laughed again. 'I grew out of that pretty quickly, after... well, you know.' Something like a frown passed over her face, then she was smiling again. 'Besides, we've got a few rock stars on our books, so I'm still in on the scene. But between you and me, those clients are always the ones who are a pain in the arse. I see what it's really like, and I can't say I envy them.' She shook her head. The diamonds in her ears caught the light, sparkled like her eyes. 'But what about you? How are you? What a surprise, seeing you again, I mean, a bit of a shock to be honest, I'm sure you understand. But how are you? Really?'

'OK.' I shrugged. I felt a strange reluctance to talk about me, about my life.

Stella was looking at me strangely. There was concern in her eyes, a sincere concern, but something wary and guarded as well, like some sort of instinct warning her to keep me at arm's length in spite of the concern.

'Really,' I said. 'I'm fine.' But I was amazed to realise that I suddenly felt like bursting into tears.

'Are you sure?' She put a hand out towards mine. It was a beautiful hand, long-fingered, well-manicured, subtle nail-varnish. But I pulled my hand away before she could take it.

'Yup,' I said. I wasn't going to burst into tears. I was determined. I would sit here and chat cheerfully with Stella McNye and be happy.

'Well, it's wonderful to see you. I didn't know you were… I didn't know you were in town. How long are you here for?'

'A couple of days. A week, perhaps. I'm just… just sorting a few things out.' I didn't know what to say. I wanted to blurt the whole thing out, tell Stella all about it, ask her to her face if she knew who was behind it all. Was it you, Stella? Was it? I was on the very verge of doing so. But I held myself back. Be cautious, be wary, be cunning. Circle the subject, drop pebbles into the pool, see how she reacts. 'I dropped by Tate Modern the other day. Had a look at Montezuma's Revenge. Have you seen it?'

Another frown passed over her face. The laughter went, the smile went. She looked down at her plate and poked her pastry with a fork. 'No. I don't want to see it. I don't want anything to do with… those days.'

I felt a fierce stab of sympathy for her, a stab of anger, of outrage. 'No. I understand. Those days… they should be chucked in the bin. Put through the shredder. Fed into the furnace. Along with Montezuma's Revenge and all the other rubbish from then. They should never have kept it,

241

the bloody monstrosity. They should have pulled the plug on it as soon as…'

'All right, all right, OK…' Stella had one hand out. She was glancing from side to side, around the café. The people at the other tables and the staff behind the counter were staring at us. What were they looking at? Had I been shouting? 'Sit down. It's Ok. Sit down.'

I sat down. I didn't remember standing up. 'Sorry,' I said. 'But I know what you mean…'

'Yes. Quite.' She laughed uneasily. 'I just don't think about it these days. But it's been difficult, just recently. That film – Art Crash Express – they wanted me to come on board, as some sort of consultant, you know, the inside story, that's what they wanted, the people making the film… But I refused. And then they wanted us to do the PR for the movie – we do a lot of that at FBS – but again I refused. I don't like turning work down, we could have done with the business, but there was no way I was going to have anything to do with it. David understood, thank goodness.' She sighed. 'Not that it makes any difference now. They'll never finish it. They could get someone else in, re-shoot it, but I've heard that's just going to be too expensive. There's insurance, of course, but you know what that's like. No, they'll bin the whole project.'

'Good!' I said. 'What were they thinking of? Real life – why can't they leave it alone? Isn't it good enough for them? Why do they have to copy it and transform it and twist it into something false and artificial, some kind of fantasy they can re-package and prostitute?'

'Yes. I dread to think of the liberties they were taking. They offered to show me the script. They wanted me to read it. No way. Either they got it wrong and it was a travesty or they got it right and it took me back to somewhere I didn't want to revisit. Either way I wanted nothing to do with it. Do you know who they had lined up to play my part?' She laughed incredulously, leaned closer across the table. 'Eve Pauli! You know, played Simone in 'Cat Catcher.' Can you believe it? She's blonde, for heaven's sake! And she's tiny! About half my height! And she's all bum and boobs! Hers are about ten times bigger than mine! What a cheek! Honestly, am I a sexy little Swedish art student? Was I ever?' She shook her head, still laughing. 'And if that was an unlikely piece of casting, did you hear who was going to play your part?'

'Yes, of course. James Hobson. Everyone knows that now.'

I heard the café door open and shut behind me as someone came in. Stella was staring past me, presumably at whoever had come in. I glanced round. A big man in a big overcoat. The collar was turned up and I couldn't see his face properly. I heard his voice – deep, slight Latin accent – as he ordered coffee to take away. He paid for it, glanced across the café at our table, at us, then he was gone, the door banging shut behind him.

I turned back to Stella. Her eyes came down from the door and met mine. She looked like someone had slapped her round the face. For a moment her eyes were blank with shock. Her tan had faded and her face was white. She looked at me, frozen, motionless, then she blinked rapidly a couple of times. A deep blush spread slowly across her cheeks. 'Right,' she said. 'Yes. Yes, of course. I see.' She put a hand to her blushing cheeks. Her fingers were shaking. 'Yes. OK.'

'What?' I exclaimed in alarm. 'What's the matter?' I half rose in my chair and looked round. The man had gone. I wondered madly about running out after him but he was probably half-way to Farringdon by now. 'Who was he? That man?'

'Who?' She frowned, looking back at the door, then shook her head. 'No. No, it's nothing.'

'Are you sure? I can go after him.'

She shook her head again. 'No, really.' She sighed deeply and ran a hand back through her cropped hair. Her tan was returning but she looked tired now, and worried. She looked at her watch. 'Goodness, is that the time?' She stood up. 'I'm going to be late for that meeting. David will be furious.' She was fiddling with her handbag, putting things back in it, mobile phone, keys, purse, and I had the feeling that she didn't want to look at me.

I felt panic approaching. Stella was going. I didn't want her to go. I was so happy, because she was here with me, but she was going to go and I wouldn't be happy any more. 'Stella,' I said. 'Don't go. Please. Stay here with me, just a little bit longer.' I stood up, too. 'Please.'

She shook her head and laughed, still fiddling with something inside her bag. It wasn't amused laughter, it sounded like hopeless laughter, the laughter of despair. 'I'm sorry,' she said. 'I've got to go. I really will be late.' She seemed to be in a hurry, eager to get out and away. Was she planning to run after that man? Who on earth was he? Then she did look at me. She wasn't smiling any longer. The concern had returned to her eyes, and I could see a new alarm and anxiety there. She was serious. 'Listen. It's been lovely... really... thank you for...' Suddenly, and amazingly, her eyes filled with tears. 'You really need... you need to look after yourself...' She turned away, blinking, took a tissue and a pen from her bag and scribbled something on the back of the café bill. 'Call me if you need help. Any time. You know where I work. I guess you know the phone number there, the e-mail address. Here's my mobile number.' She pressed the paper into my hand. Then her arms were round me and she was hugging me tight. 'Take care.' Then she was gone.

I sat down slowly. I looked at her empty seat, pushed away from the table. I looked at her empty coffee cup, and at her plate. Her pastry was still there, she'd hardly touched it. There was a crumpled paper tissue abandoned in the middle of the table. I reached out and touched it. It was damp. My left cheek felt cold and wet. I put my hand up to feel it. Tears. Stella's tears, when she'd hugged me. What had upset her so suddenly? That man. Who the hell was he? I tried to remember the expression on his face as he'd turned towards us and looked at our table, but all I could see was his turned-up collar and his long, dark hair. Had Stella left so quickly because she wanted to rush out after him? Had she managed to catch him?

I wanted to rush out there myself, follow her, find them both, spy on them, discover what it was all about. But I knew I couldn't do that to Stella. I sat tight until they'd had time to get away and there was no chance of catching up with them. Then I left.

Chapter Twelve

I was almost back at the underground when I realised I'd forgotten to ask Stella about Gary Hughes. I was relying on her being able to tell me how I might find him. I had no idea where he was living and working, beyond the guess that he was still in London somewhere.

I pulled out the paper on which she'd written her mobile number and peered at the digits. I looked round for a phone box. I couldn't see one. I shook my head. I can't phone her now, I thought. She may have made that meeting, however late. Don't disturb her now. I'll find a phone this afternoon and try then.

There were more youngsters giving away a different free paper – the Standard, this time – outside the station. I absently took a copy and walked on past the underground without going in. I had nowhere in particular to go to. Besides, I wanted to think about the meeting with Stella, and I could do that best on my feet, wandering aimlessly.

Could Stella be the one who had discovered my secret? Could she be the one who had given me away? No, not Stella. Somehow I was certain of it. Why? How had she reacted to my re-appearance? What was it about that reaction which had convinced me? What had I sensed in it?

I tried to think about it. But it was confusing. Her reaction puzzled me. She'd been surprised, yes, she'd been amazed, and yet... something wasn't right. And there'd been something else behind it all, something unsaid, something I couldn't read or understand. I couldn't work it out. Nevertheless I was sure that she wasn't the one I was after. Somehow the meeting had convinced that it wasn't Stella. It had to be Gary or Patrick.

I walked through Smithfields and on to the Barbican. I sat down on a bench by the fountains, watching the ducks on the water paddling across the rippling reflections of high-rise concrete and plate-glass windows. I put my bundle of newspapers down. I still had the two copies I'd picked up first thing, and now that Standard. I idly flicked though the Standard, half my mind still on Stella's words, on her clothes, on her laughter. Then it hit me, another headline, a powerful straight right following on from the exploratory left-jab of the earlier article. It was bang on target and my brain reeled with the blow's impact.

'Body of 'Montezuma's Revenge' Artist to Be Exhumed.'

I had to read those eight words three or four times before my mind was capable of taking in any more, and even then my eyes skimmed and skidded all over the text with panic and alarm. The remains of Harry Jutting were to be dug up and subjected to DNA testing. Harry Jutting, the creator of 'Montezuma's Revenge' currently on display at Tate Modern, committed suicide ten years ago and was buried in Walthamstow Cemetery. But now it would appear that police have doubts about the identity of that body. They have been given authority to open the grave in an attempt to prove or disprove those doubts. The police have issued no more than a brief statement about this new investigation, and refuse to say whether it is connected with the ongoing investigation into the death of James Hobson, the actor who was playing the part of Harry Jutting in the film Art Crash Express when he died, or with the investigation into the recent campaign of vandalism against Jutting's work…

I felt dizzy and faint. My sight misted over but my mind was racing. Ten years buried underground, mouldering in the darkness among the worms and the dank earth, surely there would be nothing left to test? And

247

even if there was, what were they going to test it against? Surely he was too much of a bastard for anyone to have treasured a lock of his hair or a collection of his nail clippings all this time?

'Geologists and forensic scientists are confident that the police will be able to recover sufficient remains for testing. And samples of Harry Jutting's DNA are readily available. Ten years ago, he gave a large amount of blood for the creation of Montezuma's Revenge, the work currently on show at Tate Modern. A surplus of that blood remains frozen in the stores of the clinic where it was taken. Scott Feathers, who represented Harry Jutting and whose new gallery, Pyramid East, has just had such a triumphant opening in Hoxton, commented...'

Bloody hell! That's my blood! It still belongs to me! The bastards can't have it! They have to ask me first! The bastards!

Anger and fear. I stood up quickly. I had to keep moving. Who knows how many packs had been let loose on my trail now? The hounds were closing in on my scent, closing in on me. They were snarling and snapping as they ran, ready to tear off every layer of my safe disguise, eager to dig and dig until they'd uncovered the den where I was hiding. And then they'd have me, helpless and defenceless, completely at their mercy. No. That wasn't going to happen. I might be running out of time and space, but they hadn't found me yet. And they wouldn't, as long as I kept moving.

I wound my way out of the Barbican and found myself heading for Saint Paul's. Beyond St Paul's was the river. And beyond the river loomed the black fortress of Tate Modern. There it was, ominous, evil, heavy with danger, a great dark storm-cloud lowering on the horizon. The Millennium Bridge drew me over the river towards it as irresistibly as converging lines of perspective draw the eye up and across a canvas towards the unavoidable vanishing point.

The crowds were queuing to see Montezuma's Revenge now. The line went all the way along the passage and twice round the hall. And security had been tightened up. There was a bag search at the head of the queue, and twice as many gallery assistants in the room with the exhibit and guarding the door outside. The exhibit itself had been roped off so no one could get within a yard of it. That made the room even more crowded. And it made the exhibit itself seem even more like an object of reverence and worship than ever before, a dark idol dominating the cramped temple and its heaving crowd of eager devotees.

The idol was coming alive, slowing waking up from its ten year slumber. A bright blue blossom was bursting out of its left eye-socket, a pale yellow flower was opening from its right nipple, and a rosette of deep red petals was unfolding from its groin. Writhing green shoots and thrusting pale buds were everywhere emerging from its body, breaking through the reddish-black crust of its skin. There was something strange and disturbing about the figure's stolid passivity. Why did it just stand there, when all this bright, colourful vitality was bursting out of it? It was almost as if you expected it to start moving, walking, dancing, to start coming to life indeed.

I stared at it. My blood, Stella's blood, Gary's blood, Patrick's blood. Jettisoned from a past, unwanted, dead life. Moulded into a body, buried for ten years in dark, freezing basements, then dragged up and out into the warmth and the light, to moulder in public and surrender its secrets to a clamouring, baying crowd.

I thought about the cemetery in Walthamstow. I saw the clouded polythene tent the police had erected around the grave. I could feel the warm, stuffy privacy inside it; there were men with spades digging, sweating, uniform jackets off, shirt-sleeves rolled up. Silence but for the heavy breathing of their exertions and the thud of their tools and the rattle of shifted earth and stones. And the occasional exchange of sardonic wise-cracks which only emphasises the bleak seriousness of their task.

And somewhere there was a brightly-lit and gleamingly-clean laboratory, ready and waiting to receive the digging policemen's grisly harvest. The putrid remains would be laid out on a shining white table, and highly-trained scientists in sterile robes would bend over it and begin to desecrate its mysteries with their brilliant brains and expensive equipment.

I could smell the remains the men were digging up. It was the disgusting stench of foul secrets hidden underground, buried and left to rot in the dampness and darkness where nobody should be able to sniff them out. It was as if I could smell the air inside that sealed glass-case in the middle of the room, the throat-grabbing stench that dark figure was rotting away into, was suffocating on. I could see the remains emerging from the dank soil and rotting woodwork, crumbling black matter threaded with pale roots and translucent worms and bursting with maggots and minute, crawling, many-legged horrors. Bag them up. Yes, get them up and out of sight. Shovel them into the big black plastic bags, seal them up and pass them on. But the stench lingers, the stench…

I was going to be sick. I tried to push my way out. The room was crowded, the door was blocked. Push. Push! Feet trodden on, ribs elbowed. Sorry, sorry. Annoyed frowns, indignant exclamations. Then out, down the corridor past the restless queue, into the echoing hallway, down the stairs. Outside. Fresh air, and a cloudy sky, the sound of traffic and the sight of the river, broad and calm and silver, vast water flowing by on tide and current. I breathed in deeply, the waves of nausea passing, fading, dissolving to nothing in the cold air.

I would deal with it. The statue, the idol, the monstrosity. I would finish it off in due course, put it out of its misery. I would kill it off once and for all, see it dead and buried, out of sight and out of mind for evermore. But I had other work to deal with first. I shivered. Stella. I had to talk to Stella. I wanted to talk to Stella.

I found a phone-box by the river at Southwark. I fed the slot with coins and punched in the number of Stella's mobile phone. It was lunch-time. She should be free to talk. The call was answered almost straight away.

'Hello?' Stella's voice. Bright and warm. I was feeling better already.

'Hello Stella. It's me. Listen I…' I faltered.

'Sorry? Who is this?' An apologetic laugh. My fault, it said, not yours.

'It's me. Harry. This morning…' I faltered again, but this time silence followed. For some moments I could sense and almost hear agitated breathing, swallowing, an amplified heart-beat. Was I imagining it?

'Ah, yes. Yes. Right, OK, yes. Sure.' The brightness and the warmth were struggling with confusion and uncertainty.

'Sorry, Stella, have I caught you at an awkward moment?'

'No, no. No problem. Don't worry.'

'Thanks for breakfast, Stella. It was great to see you again.' I remembered the feel of that first embrace in the car-park, the softness of her hair, the scent of her perfume. The happiness I'd felt in the café was returning. 'But I forgot to ask you something. Something important.'

There was another pause. I could sense tension, suspense. 'Yes? OK, well, it's probably my fault. I'm sorry for rushing off like that.'

'Did you make the meeting?'

'I did, thanks. The client was a bit late himself, later than me, so no harm done.'

'Good.' Did I believe her? She was holding something back. She was putting up some sort of front, I could feel it. 'Stella, I forgot to ask you about Gary. You remember, Gary Hughes?'

She groaned, and laughed. 'That poisonous little toad. What about him?'

'Do you know how I can find him?'

'I do, but I wouldn't bother, if I were you. He's gone from bad to worse, has Gary.'

'Are you still in touch with him?'

'I try not to be. In this business, it's hard to avoid people like him. They can be useful, to be honest. If your client wants their photo taken at a certain time, in a certain place, with a certain person, a word in the right ear can do everyone a favour. But it's a two-edged weapon. They're just as likely to take a photo of your client in exactly the place and time and company you don't want it taken. More likely. They're all evil parasites, even the useful ones. And Gary's one of the worst.'

'Where can I find him?'

Another burst of sardonic laughter. 'Wherever there's a compromising photo to be taken. Wherever there's privacy to be invaded. Wherever there's a newspaper buying a picture of a celebrity behaving badly or looking like crap, a picture a celebrity doesn't want publishing. Or does want publishing, for that matter – is there such a thing as bad publicity any more? Wherever there's a blackmailed celebrity trying to buy back such a picture. Wherever there's free booze or free drugs or malicious gossip.'

'OK. Do you have an address? A phone number?'

'Seriously, are you sure you want to? Sure you know what you might be letting yourself in for? Someone like Gary, he can do a lot of harm, if there's something in it for him, even if there isn't, just for the hell of it. He wouldn't think twice about it.'

'I'll take my chances.'

Stella sighed. 'OK. But think very carefully about it before you do anything. All right? Hang on.' There was a pause. 'Got a pen?' She read out a number – a mobile phone number – and I scribbled it down. 'One other thing about Gary. You know the producers of 'Art Crash Express' wanted to get me involved with the movie? And I wanted nothing to do with it? Remember? Well, they approached Gary Hughes as well, and he was so keen he more or less bit their arm off. I heard him boasting about it. He reckoned they were taking him on as a script consultant, they were going to give him a production credit, he was the official on-set photographer, blah blah blah. Probably all bullshit. Except the photographer bit. That rings true enough.'

'Thanks, Stella.' I paused. I wanted to talk to her about the piece in the paper, about the grave they were digging up, the tests... But I couldn't bring myself to mention it. There was still something about her, about her attitude to me, that I didn't understand, that I didn't trust.

'By the way, how can I find you?' she said. A casual enquiry. But the casual was unconvincing. The tension and suspense it was trying to camouflage were too evident. 'Where are you staying?'

'Why?' I said.

'Why not?' She laughed uncomfortably. 'You know how to find me. I gave you my mobile number. I don't even have your mobile number.'

'I don't have a mobile.'

'Come on. Everyone has a mobile.'

'I don't.'

'Ok. All right.' She wasn't going to push it. 'Listen, I meant what I said this morning. Look after yourself. And if you need help – just call me. Any time. All right?'

I didn't know what to make of that. I didn't say anything.

'I've got to go now.' She paused, listening. 'Are you still there?'

'Who was that man, Stella? The man who came into the café this morning? '

'Who? What man?'

'He came into the café and ordered a drink and looked over at you then left. And you rushed off straight away. As if you were running after him. Or running away from him.'

'What? I don't know what you're talking about.'

'Big man. Big coat. Middle-aged. Collar turned up. Long dark hair. Italian accent?'

'Who? I don't know. I don't remember anyone... Listen, that's not... you're...'

'Ok. None of my business. Don't worry.'

'No, you're mistaken...'

'Ok, Stella. Thanks. Bye.'

I rang off. But I couldn't get the man out of my mind. It was almost as if I was jealous of him. Jealous? Why should I be jealous? I wasn't even jealous of her husband. Why should I be jealous of her husband? David Foreman. David bloody monkey-man Foreman. Husband of the happy and successful Stella Foreman née McNye. Husband and wife. Partners in business. I remembered them getting out of the car that morning, smiling at each other, laughing, walking off hand-in-hand. Why had that hurt?

She hadn't even introduced me to her husband. She hadn't asked me up to the office. She'd hustled me off to the anonymous café as fast as she could. But of course she had, I told myself. What else could she do? She did just the right thing. Considering the shock it must have been for her, she acted surprisingly cannily. I should be grateful to her for concealing my identity, for keeping the secret... Though it will soon be out for all to know, once that grave's open and those scientists get to work...

I pumped more coins into the phone and rang the number she'd given me for Garry. The dialling tone rang. And then a recorded message. 'Give me the gossip, bitch. And make it hot and spicy. Now!' There was a bleep for recording. I rang off. It had been Garry's voice all right. No mistaking it. Voices don't change, at least not as much as faces do. I rang the number again. Give me the gossip, bitch... I took a deep breath and spoke quickly.

'She's big and beautiful and she's here from the States. She's working at Pinewood and living at Brown's Hotel in Mayfair.' The words came out as if it was someone else speaking. 'You know who I mean. But you don't know she'll be having a pint in the Lamb and Flag in Lamb's Conduit Street with some very interesting company at nine o'clock this evening. Well, you know now. I'll introduce myself and we can discuss rewards when you get there at eight-thirty.'

Bait. Deception. That should work. I felt the satisfaction of a hunter laying a well-set trap. But I also felt disgust. Hunting and hunted, spying and spied-upon, suspicion and dishonesty. I was sick of it. I was tired and hungry, I'd had enough of the noise of traffic and the sight of crowds and the reek of petrol and diesel, I was sick of the relentless onslaught of man-made images trying to sell me things, shouting at me from advertising hoardings, from the sides of buses, from posters on the underground, to buy, spend, spend, buy. I wanted a view of hills and the sea – the real thing, not a copy of it – honest beauty, natural beauty. I wanted fresh air, and silence punctuated now and then by the lowing of cattle or the cry of gulls or the distant rattle of shingle and surf. I wanted Helen and Liz and Richard. I wanted to go home.

I pumped the last of my coins into the phone. I dialled the number and listened anxiously to the dialling tone. I imagined the sound of it ringing through the little cottage, Helen starting up from the ironing or the cooking or the washing-up. Or perhaps the cottage was empty – Helen could be out with the children, or at the farm-shop – and the phone would ring on unanswered.

'Hello?' Helen's voice. She was in. She had answered the phone!

'Helen…' I stuttered. 'Helen, it's me…'

'Will? Thank god… Where are you? Are you… how are you?'

She was talking to me! Helen was still talking to me! The relief… The sound of her voice… It calmed and soothed me. Something inside my head and my chest was being gently untangled, untied, shaken loose. Straightened out and relaxed. There was a stab of guilt – I remembered Stella turning to me as I'd called out to her that morning – but it swiftly passed. Stella was nothing, to me at least. Her life and my life, they were separate, they were meant to be separate. The course of my life pointed towards Helen and Liz and Richard, Stella's pointed in another direction entirely, a direction which held no interest for me. I could see that now, I was sure of it.

'Will? Will? Are you there?'

'Yes. Yes, I'm still here.' I was listening hard to the silence behind her voice, listening for Liz and Richard, their voices or footsteps in the background. But I couldn't hear them. 'The children – how are they? Are they with you?'

'They're… outside. Out in the garden. They're OK, Will. But Liz… Liz keeps asking when you'll be coming back, and where you've gone, and why... and I don't know what to tell her.'

'Tell her the truth. Tell her I'm in London, seeing old friends, and I'll be back soon. I'll tell her now, if you get her to the phone.'

'How soon?'

'In a while. I don't know... another week, perhaps.'

'I have to see you, Will. The police, they've been talking to me, asking me questions, telling me things...'

'That's OK, Helen. Be honest with them. I don't want you getting into trouble.'

'Can I come and see you? I can bring the children. You'd like to see them, wouldn't you?'

'Yes. I would. But not here. Not in this hell-hole. I don't want them ever to set foot inside this stinking city. I'll be back soon enough, Helen. I can't wait.'

'But where are you staying? Where are you phoning from?'

'Better if you didn't know, Helen. If I told you, you'd have to tell the police.'

'No, Will, No, I wouldn't.'

'You'd be in trouble if you didn't. And I don't want to get you into trouble.'

'You can trust me, Will. I don't care...'

'You've got to care, Helen. You've got to look after the children, and you've got to look after yourself.' I swallowed hard. 'I love you so much, Helen. You and the kids. I love you all so much. This is hell, being away from you. I hate it.'

'Then come home, Will. Right now.'

'I can't.' But even as I said it, I thought, can't I? Why don't I? Just get on the bike, turn your back on this torture, get out of it... 'Are the thorn trees still blossoming along the dyke?'

257

'Yes! And the apple trees. You should see them. Pink and creamy, like strawberry ice-cream, or raspberry meringue.'

'Plenty of bees?'

'Plenty. And there was a goldcrest in the garden this morning. It looked like a humming-bird, ridiculously exotic in the gloom and the drizzle.'

'And Liz's tadpoles?'

'They've got legs now. They'll soon be frogs.'

I nodded. I could see it all. It was so vivid. There were tears in my eyes. I brushed them away with my sleeve.

'Will? Will? Are you there?' There was a note of panic and desperation in her voice.

I was thinking of the hill, and the lane, and the cottage, imagining them, the garden, and the studio... That reminded me... 'Helen, can you do me a favour? Can you unload the kiln, please? I left a batch in there. Glaze-fired.'

'Yes. Of course. But Will... where are you?'

'I've got to go now, Helen. I'll phone again tomorrow.'

'Can't I call you? Can't you let me know where you're staying? Isn't there a phone number there?'

'I've got to go, Helen.'

'Will..! Will..?

'I'm sorry, Helen. I'm really sorry.' I rang off. I felt terrible. Then I realised I hadn't spoken to Liz, and that made me feel even worse. And I still hadn't sent her that manuscript. I must find a post-office tomorrow...

*

It was dark when I walked up Lamb's Conduit Street and into the Lamb and Flag. It was just before eight-thirty. I had no idea whether Gary Hughes had swallowed my bait, but somehow I felt sure that he had. I didn't know how he'd react when he realised he'd been tricked, but it didn't bother me. By then he'd have seen a ghost. My ghost. A dead man walking. Would his amazement be real or faked? That was the only question which mattered.

The pub was pretty full when I arrived. It was hot and noisy. Youngsters from the offices down towards Theodbald's Road, laughing and drinking, lads with ties loosened and top shirt-buttons undone after a hard day at the office, girls with legs crossed under tight skirts, stockinged feet jigging high-heeled shoes up and down on pointed toes. I took my orange juice and stood in a corner with a view of the front door.

The place began to thin out. Empty pint glasses were left on abandoned tables as drinkers began to drift off towards home or Kings Cross or the curry place round the corner. It was quieter. Fewer new-comers arrived. I peered at each one, as unobtrusively as I could. Would I recognise Gary Hughes? If that photo was to be believed, he'd changed a lot. But photos weren't to be believed, were they? I'd recognise him, I was sure of that. Would he recognise me? Of course he would.

I was thirsty. I drained my glass, stepped towards the bar to order another orange juice. I hesitated. I could smell beer and whisky. I felt a sudden longing for a pint, comforting and relaxing and nourishing, remembering its rich taste, bitter and yeasty. Or a measure of scotch. Sharp and fiery and stimulating. I needed something. It had been a long day, a day of shocks and surprises. I still felt shaken by my conversation with Helen. I still had half a mind to chuck the whole thing, to jump on the bike and roar away from the whole ugly, troubling mystery and this city which I hated and rush back to the people I loved as quickly as I could. I was still shaken by my meeting with Stella. My guts and back were still aching from the encounter with Steve Smith in the early hours. My nerves still felt shredded by the surprises in the newspapers.

Exhumation… The very thought of it and what it would reveal was almost enough to make me reach out for an abandoned but still half-full pint glass on the table beside me and empty it in one go.

No. I hadn't drunk for years, and there was no way I was going to start again now. I ordered another juice and turned away from the bar just in time to see Gary Hughes come in through the door.

Gary Hughes. The photo had made him look big somehow. But he was still short, even if he was no longer fat. He had a severe crew-cut, dyed blond. He had a deep tan, so deep it must have been spray-on or from a sun-bed. The contrast between the colour of his face and the colour of his hair was so great that the hair looked white and the face orange. He was wearing black – black jeans, black leather jacket, black t-shirt. He had a black leather bag slung over one shoulder.

His entrance was swift and furtive. He didn't pause when he came in though the door but headed straight for the bar with his head down, as if he didn't want to draw attention to himself. But he somehow managed to scan the whole of the place as he moved, his eyes picking out each and every one in there, without raising his head or breaking his step or bumping into any of the furniture. He came up to the bar right beside me. His eyes met mine for a second – no recognition or interest there – then he'd turned to the bar-maid and was ordering a vodka and coke. He paid, said something to her which made her giggle, then headed for a table in the corner from which he had a good view of the door and the whole bar.

I waited for a few moments, watching him. He downed his vodka and coke, put the empty glass down on the table in front of him, and took a magazine out of his bag. He pretended to read it, elbow on table, forehead in hand, but his attention was fixed on that front door. He sat very still.

No fidgeting, no shifting. I was surprised and impressed by his stillness and his patience. I'd never had much respect for Gary – had always despised him, really – but now I could sense that he had a new self-control and ruthlessness which I would be wise to treat with caution.

I went over to the table and stood in front of him. He looked up at me. He frowned, irritated. Still no recognition. I didn't speak. 'Yes?' He was annoyed and impatient and wasn't going to hide it.

'I know you,' I said. 'From way back.'

'Yeah?' His eyes went round me to the door. 'I don't know you. So piss off, will you, I'm waiting for someone.'

'Gary? Gary Hughes?' I nodded. 'Don't you recognise me, Gary?'

He peered up at me, still frowning. His eyes looked glazed, unfocused, wild. Was he drunk, or high, or something?

'Lose the beard,' I said. 'And the long hair. And ten years or so.'

The frown went. The eyes opened wide. The mouth opened wide. He half stood-up, pointing. 'Yeah!' he exclaimed. 'Yeah, I know you! I remember you!' He laughed. The pointing finger of his right hand became two pointing fingers, his hand became a gun. He aimed the gun at me, at my chest. 'Bang! Bang bang!' He laughed again. 'Yeah, you're the one... the one who... yeah! That's you!' He aimed at my head. 'Bang bang! Great stuff!' He sat down again, still laughing, and picked up his glass. He looked at it, surprised it was empty, and his frown returned. Yes, he was high, all right. There was no mistaking it. I could see it in his face, now I was close enough. I could hear it in his voice. His eyes were unfocused pin-points. His features had that slack, molten look of someone who'd been smoking dope all afternoon. I could even smell the whiff of it on him. 'Sit down,' he said. 'No, not there. Round here a bit. Here. That's it. Don't want to spoil the view.'

'Who are you waiting for?'

He glanced at me and winked. 'Secret. That's what it's all about, isn't it? Secrets. Mysteries.' He'd taken his jacket off and slung it on the back of his chair. He looked fit and strong. The t-shirt was tight-fitting and showed off his muscles. His pecs looked hard and well-formed. His shoulders bunched and rolled and shifted whenever he moved his arms. A thick black leather belt with a big silver skull-and-cross-bones biker's buckle showed off his slim waist. Big biceps bulged out of the shirt's short sleeves. His face, purged by jogging or step-exercises or weight-training of the fat I remembered, looked hard and bony. He looked like he was trying to imitate the thugs who had visited me the night before. But it was an unconvincing imitation. Like some sort of fancy-dress. Was he wearing make-up? There was something about the eye-brows, and lashes, and lips, didn't look quite natural. And the skin on his face was strangely smooth and unlined.

'I'm looking good, aren't I?' he giggled. 'Ten year's hard work. Weights, running, swimming, the lot. Yeah. Looking great.' His strange eyes turned on me, focused with great effort, scanned me from head to toe. 'But you look like shit. You're a mess, mate. Get a grip, if I was you. Get a hair-cut. Trim the old facials. Get yourself a steak and protein-drink every day. Bulk up, work out. Work on the tan. A bit of Botox now and then, why not?' He shook his head. 'Prison. I tell you, a man goes there, it sets him up or it knocks him down. It set me up, all right. And I've been on the up ever since.' His eyes were back on the door. 'Shit,' he said, glancing down at his watch. 'It's gone nine. Where the fuck is she?'

'Let me get you a drink. I owe you a few.' I didn't want him clearing off as soon as he realised he'd been stood up.

'Vodka and coke. Make it a big one.' He downed it as swiftly as he'd downed his first. 'Yeah, prison. Big decisions in there. No more bollocks, no more bullshit. That's what I decided. No more bollocks from anyone else. Never. Number one, that's what it's all about now. Me, the gorgeous Gary Hughes. Number one. Cheers, I'll have another.'

The place really was thinning out now. No one had come in since Garry's arrival. He was shaking his head and muttering to himself. 'Another no show. What a bummer. Perhaps she decided to stay in and have it off with that stud we all know she's into. Perhaps she went somewhere else. Perhaps someone's jerking me about. Who? Beryl. Yeah, bet he's the bitch.' He giggled. 'Well, I'll get him back, good and proper, right where he doesn't like it.'

I got him another drink and watched him knock it back. That strange sense of unreality, that nothing seemed to fit, that nothing was right, was getting stronger. It had been creeping up on me over the last two days, ever since I arrived in London, and now it was so potent I seriously wondered if someone had been spiking my orange-juices. It was as if I had been knocking back the vodka, not Gary. The vodka seemed to have little enough effect on him, apart from making him livelier and even more talkative.

'Haven't seen you since, what, before I went to the nick? I was a fatty then, wasn't I? A jolly little roly-poly. Trying to be everyone's friend and getting kicked in the teeth for it. Well, look at me now. Lean and mean and beautiful. I do the kicking these days and I don't care who gets it.' He glared at me and leaned closer. 'Sending me to prison, best thing anyone ever did to me.' Then he sat back and sighed. 'Even if I did miss all the drama and excitement, you know, when you… when you all… all that brilliant fucked-up bollocks. We all got fucked-up one

263

after another, didn't we? I was out first, so missed the really juicy stuff.'

'I saw Stella this morning - '

'Stella McNye?' he interrupted angrily. 'That stuck-up bitch? Thinks she's too good to work with an old friend like me. The favours I've done her… I might work in the gutter, but that's where you find a lot of the shit her clients need. She's too proud to go there herself, but not too proud to take that shit and cover it in perfume and sell it for a fortune. That's all her job is.'

'She said you've been involved with Art Crash Express.'

'Sure thing. They were desperate to have me on board. I was a script consultant, they were giving me a production credit, I was the official photographer on-set. Then that yob Hobson went and screwed up and it all turned to shit. What a stupid bastard.'

'Screwed up?'

'Got himself killed!' Gary shook his head, and laughed. 'Things were pretty wild on set around him, I can tell you. One big crazy party. Some of the shots I took, I'll be knocked off myself if they ever see the light of day. He was up to his neck and off his head on drugs all the time, he got half the cast following his example, there were dealers fighting each other, literally, to get at them. Madness. Chaos. Everything was behind schedule, everything was over-budget, the director had lost control of the actors, the camera-crew was getting really pissed-off. Great fun, though.' He laughed. 'Hobson had a whole crowd of dodgy hangers-on. His posse. Those twats he made that shitty record with. And some of his family, really fancy themselves as geezers, know what I mean? Mucking about, pretending they're businessmen like our old friend Steve Smith. Complete joke, of course. They have no idea. Family Smith could roll them up and snuff them out in five seconds.' He nodded. He looked thoughtful for a moment. 'Family Smith has been good to me. Real professionals. Efficient, thorough, careful. They know how to reward loyalty.' He glared at me. 'I went to prison for them. And I kept my mouth shut. I said nothing to the police. I said nothing to the court. The Family appreciated that.'

'Do you know what happened to him? Hobson?'

'Who shot him, you mean?'

'Is that what happened?'

Gary was sitting back with his arms folded, staring across the table at me. He was frowning. He was looking at me in an intense but strange sort of way. He could have been puzzled, or angry, or even accusing. I didn't know what to make of it. 'Yes, of course he was shot.' He unfolded his arms and leaned forward across the table until his face was very close to mine. I could see the make-up clearly now, and smell some sort of perfume, too sweet and sickly for after-shave. 'And I know who did it.' He spoke quietly, and he raised a pointing finger again, just as he had on recognising me, and the hand became a gun, and the finger barrels were pointing at me. 'Bang bang' he said softly. He raised one eyebrow, then he winked slowly.

'What are you suggesting?' I heard my voice shaking. What was he suggesting? Was he suggesting I did it?

'I don't give secrets away.' It sounded like he was trying to be reassuring. Why was he trying to reassure me? 'Information is valuable, and secrets are the most valuable type of information. Information, secrets, they're my stock-in-trade, aren't they? I'm not going to go around giving them away, am I?'

'What are you trying to say?' I suddenly felt cold. A moment ago it had been very hot in that bar, now I was shivering.

He shrugged theatrically, spreading his arms wide. 'I'm just explaining my business. How much do you think someone would pay me to tell them something like that? How much do you think someone would pay me to keep quiet about something like that?' He raised and lowered his outspread hands, as if weighing something in a balance, and moved his head from side to side. 'How much, do you reckon?'

'I've no idea whatsoever.'

'It depends on who that someone is, of course. For instance, how much would you pay me to keep quiet about something like that?'

'Why would I pay you anything?'

'OK.' He shrugged, and sat back, as if he'd lost interest in the matter. 'Just kicking a few ideas about, trying to imagine a market. Always helps to talk things through with a disinterested party.' But he continued to stare at me intently, as if he was expecting me to say more.

I didn't know what to say. I wanted to change the subject. 'Have you seen Montezuma's Revenge? At the Tate?'

'Montezuma's Revenge? Don't talk to me about bloody Montezuma's Revenge!' Gary was suddenly very angry. 'Four people made that piece! Three of them have been written out of the picture completely! Who sold it, how much did they get for it, and where's my slice? That's what I want to know! Where's my slice of the cash, and where's my slice of the glory? I wrote to the Tate, gave them chapter and verse, suggested they got me in, talking, taking photos, exhibiting my archive, all that bollocks, didn't ask for much, just wanted to show off really, get to be famous. And the bastards' lawyers wrote back, telling me to piss off or else! Well, I've got my lawyer on to it, and he'll sort them out! That's my blood in there, literally, and someone else has made a packet on it, I'll bet, and if I don't get my cut I'll want some of his blood instead!'

A muffled ringing began to sound from his bag. He unzipped it and took out a mobile phone. 'Hello?' He listened hard, and a big grin spread across his face. 'Who? Where did you say? When?' He glanced at his watch. 'Ok. Twenty minutes. No, fifteen. See you there!' He rang off, tossed the phone back into the bag, and laughed in triumph. 'That's more like it! A proper tip-off! Sound, reliable! Great target, too! We're talking a grand, two-and-a-half if the angle's right, five if something spectacular happens!' He tossed the magazine and one or two odds and ends into the bag. I caught a glimpse of cameras and lenses in there before he zipped it up. 'The money I make in this business, you wouldn't believe it! These eyes, that phone, a couple of cameras and genius rat-cunning! Better than a goldmine!' He was on his feet now, shrugging on his leather jacket. 'Want to come with me? Fancy a lesson in gutter alchemy? Shit into gold? Come on, quick! Quick!'

Without thinking I followed him across the bar to the door. He was more or less running.

'Of course, I've made a shed-load of enemies,' he was saying as we burst out of the pub and onto the pavement. The sudden cold, the fresh air, the noise of traffic, the darkness, it was like stepping through a portal into another dimension. 'But I don't give a shit. I'm not frightened of anything…'

A tall figure stepped out of the shadows on one side of the door and Gary ran right into it. I heard Gary grunt and then exhale loudly like a wheezy old man trying to get his breath – a long, choking rattle – and then the two figures parted and Gary was doubled up clutching his gut and the other man was standing with feet spread and fists raised preparing himself to land a second blow. He had a hooded sweat-shirt on under a leather jacket and the hood was up, hiding his face.

Gary was gasping and coughing, trying to get his breath, trying to speak. 'Not… not my face… please..!' he managed to groan.

But the other man was already swinging his right fist. Head down, weight going forward onto his left foot. Crack. The sound of it hitting Gary in the face was sickening. Gary's head snapped up and back and his legs buckled beneath him. He went down in the road on his hands and knees.

A second man had come out of the shadows behind us, on the other side of the door. He was also hooded – his hood was part of his leather jacket. He had what looked like a baseball bat in one hand. He saw me step towards Gary and he held the weapon up, brandishing it at me. A warning. Keep out of it. He stood between me and Gary, shaking his head, while his companion took Gary's leather bag and emptied it out onto the road. I could hear Gary whimpering and sobbing. His gear crashed and tinkled onto the hard ground. The first man began to stamp systematically on each and every piece, shattering the phones – I saw at least three – and cameras and lenses.

I heard shouting from further down the street, and screams. We'd been seen. Someone came out of the pub behind us and I heard him go back inside yelling 'Police! Call the police!'

The first man had finished stamping on the gear. He turned back to Gary who was trying to crawl away to the other side of the road. The man kicked him in the gut and he rolled over onto his back, howling. The man kicked him again. Then he whistled twice and his mate with the baseball bat turned smartly, weapon raised, and struck Gary's writhing body. Once, twice, three times. Then both men were off and away, running up the road and disappearing round the corner into Guildford Street.

The police and an ambulance arrived ten minutes later. Gary was still conscious but they had to put him on a stretcher and carry him into the ambulance. He was crying and kept on calling for his camera and his phone.

Chapter Thirteen

I went straight to bed when I got back to the Ellerby but I couldn't sleep. I kept on going over what Steve Smith had said to me, what Stella had said to me, what Gary had said to me. The more I thought about it, the more confusing and puzzling I found it all. There was something I didn't understand, something which wasn't right, which didn't fit, and I couldn't put my finger on it.

Gary... what had he been suggesting? Had been accusing me? Had he been trying to blackmail me? No. Nonsense. Why would he? I was imagining it. But why would I imagine something like that? And did he really know what happened to Hobson? Wasn't that something he'd want to keep quiet about, unless he was talking to the police? No, not Gary. He'd want to boast about it. That's what he was doing. He was just boasting, trying to impress me. Perhaps he didn't know anything. Perhaps he was just bullshitting, making it up. Yes, that was Gary. That's all it was. Bullshit.

I thought about him lying in some hospital somewhere. Who were those two men, why had they attacked him? They'd been waiting for him, perhaps it was them who had phoned him, to get him out of the pub, set him up. Well, someone like Gary, doing what he does, he must lose count of his enemies. He said so himself. But the violence still disturbed me. I remembered the sound of the blows – the crack as the fist hit him in the face, the thuds as the boot went in, the whack of the baseball bat. I remembered the sounds Gary had made. Begging and whimpering, crying and screaming.

The day had begun with violence and had ended with violence. Where had it all come from? London seemed a brighter, cleaner, more peaceful and prosperous place than

I remembered from ten or twenty years ago, but clearly the violence was still there, lurking under the surface, waiting to burst out again. Like a graffiti artist coming and going under cover of darkness, spraying fear and pain around in streets which had been spotless and decent in daylight. It seemed unreal, as if I'd dreamed it all or imagined it. But I had bruises and aches and pains to tell me that I hadn't.

I'd spoken to Steve and Stella and Gary. But I was no closer to solving the mystery. I'd thought I'd have it all more or less sorted by now, but I was even more in the dark than ever. There was one more person to speak to. Patrick. Perhaps everything would become clear when I talked to Patrick. Perhaps he would have the answers. Yes. It wasn't over yet. I still had to talk to Patrick. Tomorrow I would have to talk to Patrick. I knew where to find him. I would go and see him, talk to him…

I must have fallen asleep eventually, because I had very vivid dreams. I was holding a gun, a heavy handgun. I could feel it hard and smooth and warm in my right hand. It was the weapon that Patrick had brandished at me and dropped in the yard of the gallery before running off. I'd instinctively snatched it up and hidden it in my waste-band, under my jacket, before the police had shown up. No, it was the weapon I'd taken from the Russian body-guard in the house where I'd destroyed Dirty Flirt. Somehow they were one and the same weapon. In one dream I was sitting in my open-plan penthouse flat at night, in the darkness, staring out of the window at the brightly-lit but empty offices towering up on the other side of the river. The weight of the gun in my right hand was immense, I could barely hold it, but somehow I managed to lift it, my hand shaking and my brow sweating with the effort, until it was at my head, the hard barrel pressing against my temple, its oily, metallic smell filling my nostrils...

In another dream I was outside, in the darkness – night-time again – in a quiet London backstreet, a children's playground on one side, office blocks on the other. A row of lorries and trailers and caravans was parked all along the street, under the street-lamps. There was a coach parked there, too, and a number of mobile generators, their humming the only sound to break the stillness of the night. I was alone on the pavement, staring at this temporary, sleeping village. I could feel the gun in my hand, and I was glad of it. I could feel the rage in my heart, the anger. This village was the set and crew and cast of Art Crash Express, camping for the night, waiting for daylight when they would renew work on their monstrous project. Makers and purveyors of fantasy and falsehood and deception, of an unreal world, of an artificial life, which insulted and defied and denigrated the glory and beauty of the real world, the only world, the reality of life which each and every one of us had been granted as the greatest gift of all. They should be stopped. They should be taught a lesson. They had, after all, been warned...

In another dream I was inside. The light was very bright. It was dark outside. The echo of a gunshot was ringing in my ears, and the sharp stink of cordite was stinging my nose. I was standing in a cloud of smoke, and the smoke cleared to reveal a body at my feet. The body of a young man, big, well-built, lying face-down. His fair hair is dark and matted with blood. A dark pool of blood, glistening in the bright light, is spreading out from his head. He is still moving. One hand reaches out across the floor, slowly and blindly, the other twitches at his side. He groans. Then he begins to shake. For ten seconds his whole body trembles and shudders. Then he lies still.

Daylight grew slowly outside the ancient curtains, gradually pushing back the darkness until it was no more than shadows in the corners of the shabby room. I didn't remember waking up. Perhaps I'd never been asleep. Perhaps I'd been awake all night, and those dreams, so vivid, hadn't been dreams but memories. Memories? Nonsense. How could they be memories?

The sound of traffic outside grew louder, thickened, became daytime's constant rumble. I knew I had to get up, get washed, get dressed, have some breakfast and then climb on my bike and go and see Patrick. Just outside London, just beyond Epping Forrest, into the flatlands and empty horizons of Essex, that's where I'd find him. But I couldn't move. I didn't want to move. I didn't want to go there, I didn't want to see Patrick. I felt exhausted and strangely frightened. Later, I told myself. In five minute's time. In an hour's time. This afternoon... I needed more rest. Some sleep, then I'd be ready for it.

When Patrick had been arrested for shooting at me, he'd been taken to a police cell for questioning and then transferred to the psychiatric unit of a hospital rather than sent to prison on remand. They kept him in the hospital and subjected him to all kinds of head-shrinking tests and observations pending his trial. There was no way a dangerous gun-waving maniac was going to be granted bail.

Then, when it was announced that Harry Jutting had been found in his flat with a bullet through his head, the police naturally had their suspicions that Patrick might have been responsible. Particularly when ballistics, comparing spent bullets, discovered that the same gun had been used in both shootings. They'd never found the gun Patrick had waved at me in the gallery, in spite of their best efforts to recover it once they'd arrested him. They'd searched the squat from top to bottom. They'd searched the rubbish-tip of its backyard too. They'd questioned him relentlessly about it. He'd always insisted that he'd dropped it in the yard of the gallery before fleeing, but they hadn't found it there either. But they had no evidence to back up their suspicions, and every reason to believe that the death they had on their hands was a suicide. And they knew exactly where Patrick had been on the night of the death; he'd been under supervision at the hospital. It was easy enough for them to put two and two together and guess the truth - that I'd found the gun where Patrick had abandoned it, and concealed it (presumably somewhere about my person) before they'd arrived.

Their suspicions were academic, as it happened, because Patrick never went to trial. The doctors certified him insane. They sectioned him under the mental health act and sent him away to the secure unit of the asylum out in Essex. Who knows what they did to him – were still doing to him – out there. Analysis, treatment, observation, drugs, medication, containment, control. I didn't want to think about it. Was it any mystery that I didn't want to go out there to see him?

And what was the point, I asked myself as I lay on the bed staring at the ceiling, going over and over my excuses for not moving out of the room. What kind of conversation could I hope to have with a mad-man? What could I possibly hope to learn from a man whose mind had gone? Would I even be able to get in to see him, to talk to him? Well, yes, no doubt they had visiting hours, surely I'd be able to talk to him under supervision, but... Patrick was hardly my prime suspect. Of all three, Patrick was the least likely... And yet, I'd seen Stella, and I'd seen Gary, and neither of them had... So if it wasn't Patrick I was after, who on earth was it?

I closed my eyes and saw a flat, featureless landscape rolling away to the low, wide horizons and huge, empty skies of Essex. A monotonous landscape of ennui and despair, stripped of the props of perspective and landmark which enable the mind to keep its grip on what it sees. I didn't want to think about Patrick and his surroundings. But I could imagine them, that was the terrible thing. I could imagine them only too vividly. The border of mature trees and bushes enclosing the place, partly hiding the wire fencing and the security cameras. The immaculately-maintained lawns between the border and the core of buildings. The gravel driveway, the ornamental statuary and the fountains. All very soothing, very calming to look out on, and almost enough to distract the mind from the frighteningly empty and dreary landscape beyond. The landscape which the hedges and trees hide from view but can't wipe from the memory. It's always there, you're always aware of it, even though you can't see it.

That's what it's like in the movies, isn't it? All those movies set in lunatic asylums, they're all the same, they could all have been filmed on the same set. And I must have seen them all, judging by the vivid and prolonged way they replayed themselves inside my head that morning. You know the kind of thing. Wards and corridors patrolled by shuffling, catatonic figures in pyjamas. Sinister female nurses in pale-blue uniforms, smiles on their faces but dripping syringes held behind their backs. Sinister male orderlies in dark blue uniforms, banter on their lips but handcuffs and leather coshes in their pockets. A continual, low-level babble of voices in the background, murmurings, incoherent ramblings, one banal word repeated over and over again for hours on end until it resonates with some sort of occult significance. A babble which rises every now and then, randomly and unpredictably, to ear-splitting screams, brain-shredding shrieks. Hysterical. Terrified. Terrifying.

And the psychiatrist – an arrogant, complacent, hyper-intelligent man, middle-aged but athletic, bursting with mental and physical energy, lean and tanned and completely bald. Gold-rimmed spectacles, ice-blue eyes which see everything. Armoured in a spotless, immaculately-ironed white shirt, claret-coloured silk tie, grey trousers with a razor crease, black leather shoes polished to a dazzling shine. We've seen him in a dozen movies, haven't we, he could be played by the same actor, an actor whose age and costume never change.

Shall we give him an Austrian accent? And a German-Jewish name? Dr Hoffman, perhaps? Or Dr Schneider? No. That would be going too far. Let's call him Dr Allen. He speaks with the clear and precise authority of an Oxbridge educated scientist. But he has a surprisingly high-pitched voice for the Alpha-male that he is. And we'll give him a tic – a nervous twitch to confirm our suspicion that all psychiatrists are called to their vocation for personal reasons, by a subconscious fear that they themselves need treatment. Every now and then he tugs at the collar of his spotless shirt with the index finger of his left hand, raising his chin and twisting his neck, as if the collar is too tight. It isn't. It's just that a patient has given an unexpected answer to one of his questions, and he's having to reformulate his theories.

He has plenty of questions, and he repeats them every day.

'Tell me about Patrick Joyce,' he asks in the morning. 'Who is he? Where is he? How did you meet? Did you like him? Did he like you? Were you friends?'

'Tell me about Harry Jutting,' he asks in the afternoon. 'Who is he? Where is he? How did you meet? Did you like him? Did he like you? Were you friends?'

'Tell me about James Hobson,' he asks at night. 'Who is he? Where is he? How did you meet? Did you like him? Did he like you? Were you friends?'

He's in that brightly-lit room with you, the room echoing with the gunshot and swirling with smoke and stinking of cordite. 'Why is there a gun in your hand?' he asks in his precise, authoritative, high-pitched voice. 'Where did you get it? Why is there a body on the floor? Who is it? What have you done to him?' His pale-blue eyes see everything. The light flashes on his gold-rimmed spectacles. He knows the answers to all his questions, even though you tell him nothing. 'What have you done? Who have you done it to?'

I woke up with a start. The room was gloomy, but I could still see daylight fighting its way in through the curtains. The sound of traffic was as loud as ever. I forced myself to sit up on the bed, to stand up. I felt sick. I was trembling. It was hot and stuffy in there. I stumbled over to the window, thrust back the curtains, unlatched the sash and tugged it open. The roar and blare of the traffic was suddenly unbearably loud, the stink of diesel overwhelming. I slammed it shut again.

Guilt. I could feel it churning my guts and throbbing in my veins like an infection, a poison. I could taste it in my mouth like vomit. Was it any wonder I didn't want to see Patrick, when I felt so guilty about what had happened to him? Was it any wonder I felt so guilty, after what I had done to him, after the way I had treated him?

I opened the door and went out along the corridor to the bathroom. The noise from the bar downstairs was loud – laughter, raised voices, music, the rattle of plates and cups and glasses. People were talking and eating and drinking down there. Cheerful, normal, hard-working people. I guessed it was lunch-time. I locked myself in the bathroom and tried to ignore the noise from below and to forget what was going on down there. I wasn't interested in food or drink or company. I felt too sick to eat, the temptation to drink was growing stronger but had to be resisted at all costs, and the idea of crowds… I shuddered. There were only three people whose company I wanted. Helen, and Liz, and Richard. And only one place I wanted to go to. Home. I wanted that view from the hill, across the marsh to the sea. Walking up to the farm shop to meet Helen as she comes off work. Richard on my back, gurgling in my ear. Liz running on ahead, singing to herself, skipping along, stopping every now and then to pick up acorns or speckled egg-shells from the side of the lane.

I had to see them. I'd phone Helen, arrange a meeting. For tomorrow afternoon. Yes. I'd go and see Patrick in the morning, and seeing Helen and the kids in the afternoon would be my reward. I didn't like the idea of the kids coming to this abomination of a city, but I had to see them. And I could give the manuscript to her. I still hadn't found a post-office, hadn't posted it, but it didn't matter if I could see her tomorrow, hand it over to her then.

I went back to my room and threw on some clothes. I went down the stairs, to the hallway between the bar and the toilets where the ancient pay-phone hung on the wall in one corner, as dusty and unnoticed and old-fashioned as a Victorian stag's head. I tried to ignore the noise coming from the bar, tried not to imagine the crowds eating and drinking in there. I fed the machine with coins and dialled our number. I listened to the dialling tone and prayed. Let her be there. Helen, answer the phone, please, Helen –

'Hello?'

Helen's voice. I breathed out, a long sigh of relief. 'Helen, it's me…'

'Will?'

The sound of her voice, it was wonderful. I didn't want to speak, I couldn't speak, I just wanted to listen to her voice.

'Will, are you there?' She sounded relieved and glad, but also anxious.

'Yes, yes. Helen, it's great to hear you…'

'How are you, Will?' Was it my imagination, or was there something wary about her voice, a note of caution?

I felt a twinge in my guts and lower back. I wasn't going to say anything about that. 'I'm OK. But… but I'm really missing you, and the kids. I really want to see you. I have to see you. I've been thinking. Do you all want to come up to town tomorrow afternoon, we can have tea or something?' I remembered a café down the road I'd noticed the day before, half-a-dozen different home-made cakes and a dozen different types of tea.

'Yes! Yes, Will, that would be great!'

I told her about the café, how to get to the nearest underground from the main-line station, how to get to the café from the underground. 'It's only a five minute walk. I should be there by three – if you're there first, you can order a pot of Darjeeling and a slice of fruit cake for me.' I paused. 'But don't tell anyone where you're going. Don't tell anyone you're coming to see me. All right?'

'I understand, Will.'

We chatted about the children, and the farm shop, and the customers, and the farmer's children. Then she said she'd have to go, or she'd be late for work. 'Will, you…' she hesitated. 'There's something…' She paused. I waited for her to continue, but she didn't.

'What's the matter? Are you all right? What is it?'

'No. It doesn't matter.' I heard her sigh. 'We can talk about it tomorrow.'

'Helen, I love you so much. You and the children, nothing else matters to me. I miss you, I hate it here, I can't wait to come home.'

There was another pause. I tried to imagine what she was doing. Was she smiling? Was she crying? 'I love you too, Will. We all love you. Why can't you just come home? Come home right now.'

'I can't, Helen. I'm really sorry. But I'm nearly done here. Another couple of days. That's all.'

We rang off. I stood by the phone for a while, in its dusty corner. Then I went out into the street and walked for an hour, forcing myself to take some exercise and fresh air, though fresh air was in short supply. I walked down Navarino Row and across the playing fields to the canal. The playing fields weren't the sea of mud I remembered. The grass there was green and lush. Was that because kids didn't play football any more? And there were young trees shedding pink and white blossom everywhere, and I noticed that the grounds of the council estate around the tower blocks had been beautifully landscaped and were well-maintained, with an inviting-looking kids' playground and ornamental rocks and little grassy hillocks and flowering shrubs. It was familiar and unfamiliar, disturbing and disorienting, like a hallucinogenic distortion of reality. It didn't seem real at all. Even the tower-blocks themselves were eerily silent, no rap or rock pumping from open windows. It was almost like a painted stage set, its brightness and cheerfulness exaggerated to disguise its artificiality.

Everything had changed by the canal as well. All the warehouses and light-industrial buildings had gone – including Steve Smith's mysterious warehouse where Patrick and I had had our studio. They'd all been jerry-built twentieth-century shacks – concrete and breeze-block – so hadn't been converted into luxury period residences.

They'd been knocked down and in their place stood towering apartment-blocks – shining, futuristic, steel and plate-glass edifices flying the flag for the universal, anonymous twenty-first century city – ranked for a good half-mile each way along the canal and on both banks. The water of the canal was free of rubbish. There wasn't a supermarket trolley in sight. There were no groups of rowdy drunkards or lurking drug-addicts on the tow-path, and the shadows under the bridges didn't stink of piss any more. Young men and women on bicycles whizzed past, in both directions, cheerfully ringing bells to announce their approach. They looked hip and trendy and prosperous, bags bulging with lap-tops on their backs or shoulders, and ear-phones dangling wires into jacket-pockets, well on their way to the nirvana where everybody runs their own business in fashion or the media or computer-gaming and no one has to shave every day or clock in or wear a suit and tie.

I felt like a time-traveller from an earlier, darker, rougher age. A visitor who was being given a glimpse of this bright new future but knew there was no place in it for himself. A visitor who wondered whether the whole trip wasn't just an illusion sold to him by a fair-ground huckster.

I cut up to the main road at the railway bridge and made my way along the busy street back to the Ellerby. I passed the Underground and took a free newspaper from a boxed stack by the entrance. No one handing them out at this time of the afternoon. I brought a sandwich and a pint of milk on the way. I ate and drank in my room, sitting on my bed, leafing through the newspaper.

The shock was on page six. A small article way down the page, a few inches only, no photograph. A body had been exhumed from Harry Jutting's grave in Walthamstow. DNA from the remains had been checked

281

against DNA from frozen blood known to have been given by Harry Jutting when he was working on Montezuma's Revenge. The DNA had matched. Without discussing the suspicions which had prompted the exhumation and the tests, the police could confirm that the body buried in the grave ten years ago was indeed that of Harry Jutting.

*

I didn't go to see Patrick the next morning. I didn't get out of bed the next morning. I couldn't get out of bed until I'd decided whether it would be good or bad for Patrick if I went to see him, and I couldn't reach a decision. Some time in the night it had occurred to me that it would be bad for Patrick if I did go to see him. Who knows what sort of trauma or relapse or breakdown the sight of me, and the reminders of what I was responsible for, might precipitate in his fragile mind? I had done more than enough harm already, I didn't want to compound the damage, hadn't I decided all those years ago that the kindest thing I could do would be to stay out of his life?

No, no, I told myself. You're just thinking up excuses for not going to see him. Trying to justify your own cowardice, trying to disguise your weakness. Seeing you and talking to you could be a cathartic experience for Patrick, a liberating experience. Certainly talking to his psychiatrist, telling him exactly what happened between the two of you, filling him in on the background to Patrick's breakdown, would give Dr Hoffman or Schneider or Allen or whatever he was called valuable information which could influence his approach and treatment, refine it and improve it, make it more effective, more powerful. At the very least, I should arrange to see

Dr Hoffman or Schneider or Allen first, and he'd be able to tell me whether it would be good or bad for Patrick to see me.

But what was the point of going all that way if there was a possibility that they wouldn't let me see Patrick or talk to him?

The debate lasted for hours and hours. The question went round and round in my mind all night and all morning. Which was fine, because if it was busy on this issue, it didn't have to think about the issue of that body and my DNA. What had gone wrong with the tests? Could there have been some sort of cross-contamination? How reliable were DNA tests anyway? I didn't know. I didn't want to think about it. I just couldn't understand it.

I thought about Helen and Liz and Richard, locking up the cottage and taking a bus to the train station, getting on a train up to London. I was excited. I was looking forward to seeing them, I couldn't wait for the afternoon. I needed to see Helen again, to talk to her, to hear her laughter. Just a few days apart had proved how much I needed her. I needed her good sense and her good humour. I'd always needed her to tell me to relax, to laugh at things, not to take them so seriously. At mid-day I got up and showered and got dressed. I went straight out to the café, the thick wad of the manuscript in its jiffy bag tucked under my arm. I was much too early, but I had lunch there while I waited.

From two o'clock onwards I looked up every time the café door opened. For an hour I rode a tense and exhausting roller-coaster of hope and disappointment. Then, at three o'clock on the dot, there she was. Small, thin, her long copper hair in an untidy plait. Wearing an outfit - blue jeans, green sweatshirt, brown suede jacket - that I knew well. But I almost didn't recognise her. She looked tense and anxious. Care-worn. Tired. I'd never seen her looking like that before. And it was strange seeing her there, in the middle of a big city, in a busy café, coming in off a busy street. She looked out of place. I felt a pang of guilt, dragging her here into this alien environment, down into this cess-pit, away from the purity of her natural habitat. She smiled when she saw me, but it wasn't the devil-may-care grin I was used to. It was a forced, sad, uncertain smile, a smile which I should have guessed there and then was hiding something. I'd never thought that Helen would ever have to hide anything from me. I'd always been too worried about everything I was hiding from her.

She came in through the door and I stood up and stumbled towards her and we were embracing before she was half-way over to the table. She hugged me tight, her arms clinging round me and her cheek pressed to mine. I could smell the smoke from our wood-burning stove in her hair, and the sea, and the fresh spring grass from the marsh grazings, and the pure air blowing over the crest of the hill. 'Oh, Will, I've been so worried about you. I'm so worried.'

'Well, don't worry,' I said, laughing. 'I'm OK, aren't I?' I looked at her, and she tried to smile again. 'I love you, Helen. I've missed you so much. I love you so much.'

We sat down, and only then, strangely, did I realise the children weren't with her. 'Where's Liz?' I asked abruptly. The sharpness in my voice surprised me. 'And Richard? Where are they? Who's looking after them?'

'Don't worry about the children, Will,' she said. Her voice was calm and reassuring, but for a moment there was a shadow of something like guilt or shame in her eyes. 'They're in good hands. They're being well cared-for.'

'What do you mean? Where are they?'

We were sitting facing each other. She reached out across the table and took my hands. 'Trust me, Will.

You've got to trust me.' She looked me straight in the eyes. 'I've always trusted you. Will you trust me now?'

She looked serious and determined, as if she was forcing herself to do something she was dreading but nevertheless knew she had to do. I nodded. I felt fear beginning to creep up on me, like the cold in an old house when the fire goes out.

'There are things we have to talk about, Will, aren't there? Without the children. It's better if they aren't here, while we…' She broke off, and shook her head. She took one hand away from mine and rubbed her eyes. 'I could do with some tea. Have you ordered a pot?'

'What things, Helen? What are you talking about?'

'I'm parched, Will. Let's have something to drink first. Please.' She sighed. She looked very tired all of a sudden.

The tea arrived, and we were both silent and awkward for some moments while we stirred the pot and waited for it to brew and then poured it and added milk and waited for it to cool. She wouldn't meet my eyes while she busied herself with all this, as if she was preparing her thoughts for what she had to say and didn't want to give anything away before she was ready. Fear and panic were reaching out for me. I held my tongue, not sure I'd be able to control myself if I broke that silence. If I spoke, I wasn't sure I could stop myself from shouting at her. If I shouted at her, I wasn't sure I could stop myself from grabbing her and shaking her until she answered me…

'There are so many things you haven't told me, Will, aren't there?' She put her cup down and looked up at me. I wouldn't look at her at first, afraid of the accusation and anger and upset I would see there. But when I did look at her, I saw only pity and fear in her eyes. 'Would you like to tell me anything? What do you think I ought to know?'

'I told you. After the police came. Before I left. I told you everything.'

She shook her head. 'No, Will,' she said quietly. 'No.'

'I told you. I told you who I was. I told you what happened, why I had to change. Why I changed everything, my name, my life, everything. I was Harry Jutting, I admit it, I'm not proud of it, I'm ashamed of who and what I was.' I suddenly remembered the jiffy-bag. It was on the table between us. I pushed it across to her. 'It's all here, all written down, the full story, take it, read it…' But she didn't move. She was staring at me strangely. Oh God, I thought, is that it? Has she decided she can't love someone who was once a monster like Harry Jutting? 'But I'm not that man any more! Helen, please, you have to believe me, I'm not Harry Jutting any more!'

'No, you're not Harry Jutting. And you never were Harry Jutting, were you?'

I stared at her, shocked, my mouth open, my eyes blinking. 'What? What is this?'

'You told me you were Harry Jutting. You showed me that photograph, remember? The police have been talking to me, they've told me lots of things, they asked lots of questions - '

'What? And you believe their lies? Their gossip, their accusations?'

She shook her head. She was reaching into her bag, pulling something out, a piece of paper, a stiff sheet of card. Her hands were trembling. She was breathing quickly and heavily, I could see her shoulders moving, her breasts rising and falling under her sweater. She put the card down on the table. I could see now that it was a photo. It was the photo I'd shown her of me and Steve and Gary and Stella and Patrick, taken all those years ago at the Brick Shit-House show. But it wasn't the cutting I'd torn from the paper. It was a fresh print. 'We talked about this. They showed me, they told me - '

286

I was on my feet now with shock and anger and fear. That fresh print frightened me. Why did it frighten me? 'Did you tell them you were coming here? Do they know I'm here?'

'Listen, Will. Listen. Please.' She looked up at me, and her expression was so imploring, so tortured, that I fell silent. 'This one – here – this is you, right?' She pointed at one of the figures. 'This is the one you told me, isn't it?' I glanced quickly at the face she was indicated, and nodded. My mouth was dry. My heart was thumping. My lungs were being squeezed by panic, my guts were being twisted with fear. Why? What was I afraid of? What did I think she was going to tell me?

'Yes. That's you, Will. I can see that. You've changed, but not that much. Hair much longer. Beard. A bit of grey, premature perhaps, but still…' She laughed lightly, affectionately. 'More distinguished now, I suppose.' She nodded. 'The man I love. Years before I met him. You look so young. Not much more than a boy. Amazing.' Then she was serious again. 'But that isn't Harry Jutting. Is it?' Her voice was shaking, and her face was trembling as she looked up at me. She pointed at another figure. 'This one. This one is Jutting. Isn't it?'

I looked down at the photo. She was pointing at the man in the middle of the group now. He was leaning out from it, flicking a v-sign up at the camera. I looked at the face, leering, arrogant, drunken. Fair hair, damp and sweaty, plastered across his brow. The t-shirt, its obscene graphic and message blurred by movement and by dark patches of spilled beer or perspiration, stretched tight over a powerful torso. Strong chest, strong shoulders, strong arms. The huge fist like a weapon, brandishing a bottle of beer, a cigarette protruding from thick, stubby fingers. I looked at the big, handsome, bullying, bastard of an egomaniac and felt pure hatred. Poisonous, violent hatred.

'This one.' Helen pointed back at the first figure. Slight, pale, nervous-looking, somewhat withdrawn, but on this occasion happy enough, smiling almost with surprise, as if he can't quite believe that he's actually here, among friends, enjoying himself. 'That's you. We've agreed that's you, haven't we? But it isn't Harry Jutting. Is it? It's Patrick Joyce. Isn't it?'

I stared at her. There was a roaring in my ears, the deafening smash and crash and rumble of an ancient high-towered city collapsing under a barrage of artillery.

'Look, the names are here on the bottom of the photo. You aren't Harry Jutting, are you? You're Patrick Joyce.'

*

I was still standing up. I was shaking from head to toe. I felt faint, and had to put my hands out on the table for support.

'They told me all about you. How you had a breakdown, and thought you were Harry Jutting – because Jutting passed off your work as his, and if Jutting's work was your work, then you must be Jutting - and had to go to hospital. You were in hospital for years. But you got better, and came out, and put everything behind you, and started a whole new life - '

'Who? Who told you? Who have you been talking to?'

'They only want to help you, Will. We all do. That's all we want. Oh Will – I can't call you anything else, you're my Will, you - ' Her voice shook. She looked at me imploringly. She was trying hard not to cry, trying to be brave.

'Who knows I'm here? Did you tell anyone you were coming here to meet me? Did any of them follow you?' I looked past her to the window looking out onto the street. I couldn't see anyone waiting for me out there, but any trap they might have set for me would be hidden, wouldn't it? The road and the pavement looked pretty deserted. No traffic, no pedestrians. The world looked amazingly calm and quiet, as if unaware of the massive earthquake just taking place. I expected running, screaming, panicked crowds...

'Dr Allen spoke to me. We had a long talk. He's very hopeful, Will. He's still certain that you really were cured when they let you out of the hospital all those years ago, before we met. You're having another breakdown, some kind of relapse, but he says there's no reason why you shouldn't get better again. If you let us help you. Another breakdown, he says that was always a possibility, especially if anything happened to take you back, to trigger the old problems. And that has happened, hasn't it? That film, Art Crash Express, and the exhibition, Montezuma's Revenge, they've brought everything back, haven't they? But we'll help you. You were unwell, and then you got better; you're unwell again, but you'll get better again - '

'What have you done, Helen?' I stared at her in disbelief. 'Have you betrayed me?'

'I just want to help you. That's all.' Her face was white and strained. She looked very frightened, but very determined. She looked up past me, towards the back of the café, and gave some sort of nod. It was a signal, a pre-arranged signal, to someone standing behind me...

I whirled round. Someone was coming into the back of the café from the door out to the toilets and kitchen. A middle-aged man, tall and athletic, lean and tanned and completely bald. Gold-rimmed spectacles, ice-blue all-seeing eyes. Immaculate grey suite, white shirt, claret-coloured silk tie. The café's strip-lighting gleamed on his bald, tanned, polished head, on his polished black leather shoes, on his spectacles, on his eyes. He smiled at me, and held out his hand as he approached, friendly and relaxed.

'Hello, Patrick,' he said in that authoritative but strangely high-pitched voice. 'Good to see you again.' He took my hand and shook it, even though I had no recollection of offering it. His grip was warm and strong. 'Remember me? Dr Allen? Of course you do. It's been years, but we haven't forgotten each other, have we?' He smiled at Helen, and she managed to return a wan smile. 'Hello, Helen. Shall we all sit down? Is there still some tea in that pot?'

I turned on Helen. 'You've betrayed me, Helen! How... how could you! I trusted you and you betrayed me! This is a trap!'

Helen blinked and swallowed. There were tears in her eyes. She was trembling. But Dr Allen was still smiling. He waved his hand dismissively and sat down, reaching for the tea-pot. 'Oh, stop shouting, Patrick. Sit down and have some tea. It's still warm. Sit down and tell me you're not Harry Jutting and we can get this all sorted out. You know you're not Harry Jutting, don't you? Harry Jutting's dead and buried, he killed himself years ago. But right now your wife and children need you, Patrick. And you need them. Don't you?'

'How could you do this to me, Helen?' I was angry and frightened. My heart was pounding, I could hardly breathe, I trembled and shook as panic poured a hundred volts of electricity through me. Dr Allen was looking up at me, his eyebrows raised, his eyes sparking as they peered right through me. 'I didn't kill James Hobson!' I shouted. 'I didn't! I didn't kill him!'

'Who's saying you did?' Dr Allen said mildly, and shrugged. But he glanced up at Helen, and for a second they looked at each other, grim-faced and serious and frowning. It was only for a second – a moment later he was smiling and shaking his head and pouring tea and

Helen was reaching for her cup in an effort to avoid my eye – but it was enough.

'Where are the police? They're here, aren't they? They're waiting for me! Where are they hiding?'

Dr Allen was still smiling and shaking his head. 'This tea-pot dribbles. Look, it's spilt all over the table. Bad work. Your pots never dribble, do they, Patrick?'

I ran for the door. Away from Helen and Dr Allen. As fast as I could, weaving between the tables, stumbling and staggering as chair legs, table legs, human legs, tried to trip me up. There were shouts, and a figure loomed up in front of me, blocking the door. But no one was going to stand in my way, not with panic pumping a million volts through me. I thrust them aside and burst out through the door and onto the pavement. I turned to my left, and there in front of me, a few yards along the road, parked just out of sight of anyone in the café, was a police-car. Doors open. The crackle of a police radio. Uniformed policemen on the pavement, all ready to give chase. I turned, but there, just beyond the café in the other direction, was another police-car. Policemen on the pavement, more getting out of the back of the car. Shouts, gestures, the sound of running feet.

I couldn't go back into the café. I couldn't go up the road, I couldn't go down the road. I ran straight across the street and in through the first door I came to. A betting shop. I'd never been in there before. It was deserted. Television sets flashed images of racing horses and punching boxers and colliding footballers at the empty glassed-in counters, and yelled a garbled and excited commentary into the void. I ran towards a door at the back, my feet sliding on the drifts of abandoned betting-slips littering the floor. I crashed through the door, into a dim hallway, an open door onto a brightly-lit office on my left, a closed door on my right, a stairway going up ahead.

Hide! Quick! Hide! Without thinking I seized the handle of the door on my right, turned it and pushed. The door opened. It wasn't locked! Quick, quick! I slipped inside and slammed the door shut behind me.

PART IV

'…And much of Madness, and more of Sin,
And Horror the soul of the plot.'

Edgar Allan Poe, *The Conqueror Worm*

'Thou shalt break them with a rod of iron; thou shalt dash
them in pieces like a potter's vessel.'

Psalm 2

Chapter Fourteen

The room was lit by a single unshaded bulb hanging from the low ceiling. It was long and thin and had no windows. It was more like a short corridor than a room. It was stuffed with boxes of stationery and piles of old office machinery and stacks of furniture. Some kind of storage space. I peered around at the jumble of desks and chairs, old printers and computer screens, broken photocopiers, shredders, mountains of box-files and lever-arch files and plastic crates full of computer-disks. The light was harsh but inadequate – the junk immediately below the bulb was dazzlingly spot-lit, the rest lurked half-hidden in shadows. The air was thick with dust.

I wasn't alone. Someone was standing at the far end, his back to me. A thin and stooping figure. There was another door there. He had a big bunch of keys in one hand, and he was about to lock or unlock it.

He whipped round in surprise as I came in. An old man, short, grey-skinned, grey-haired, balding. A cloud of cigarette smoke and whisky fumes hung around him. An unlit roll-up, shedding tobacco, dangled from his lower lip. Brown corduroy trousers, a grey collarless shirt, braces, threadbare carpet slippers. He looked at me, then he looked at the door I'd just slammed shut behind me. Then he pushed past me, selected a key from the bunch in his hand, slid it into the door, and locked it.

He'd moved quickly for an old man. But it was only just in time. Seconds later there were muffled sounds from the hallway outside. Urgent shouts and the heavy pounding of running boots. Then someone tried to open the door. The handle rattled, the door shook. Then the noises passed quickly and soon faded to silence.

The old man laughed softly. I looked at him. A grubby, scruffy character. Face like a benevolent weasel. He winked at me, grinning. 'You the one they're after? The big boys out there?'

I nodded, too shocked and stunned to do anything else.

'I saw them. Throwing their weight around. Closing the street down, scaring our customers away. What poor bastard are they after now, I asked myself?' His voice had a trace of an Irish accent. He shook his head. 'There might be a deli next door selling seven different types of bread and ten different types of olive oil, but this is still the East End and we still don't much like the Old Bill round here.' He shuffled off down the narrow passage between the tottering mountains of stored goods. He unlocked the door at the far end, then turned and crooked a finger at me. 'I don't know what you've done, matey, and I don't care. But you're safe enough here.'

The door led into a bigger room. It was even more dimly-lit. The single light shone on a big table in the middle of the floor. Half a dozen men sat around the table, playing cards. Waves of tension and concentration came off them, but they were far from silent. They laughed and swore, shouted at each other, exchanged wise-cracks, threw down cards and money as noisily as they could. The air was wreathed with tobacco smoke and sharp with the smell of spirits.

'Make yourself at home,' my rescuer whispered. 'Clear off whenever you like, but I wouldn't budge for a good hour or two if I were you. We'll be here all night, so there's no rush.' He began to check the bottles on the table, removing empty ones and replacing them with new ones he took from a counter in the shadows at the far end of the room. He was so busy with corkscrew and bottle opener that he seemed to forget all about me. None of the men at the table paid us any attention. None of them so much as looked up from their game.

There was a leather sofa in one dim corner. It felt like the most comfortable sofa I'd ever sat on. My heart-beat and my breathing were beginning to return to normal, my nerves were no longer screaming at me. Panic was slowly receding. But exhaustion was creeping up to take its place. It was dark enough to sleep in that corner. There were black-out blinds all around that bare room, not a window in sight. I lay back on the sofa. I put my feet up. I closed my eyes.

Immediately, I could see those police-cars again. I heard the shouts of the policemen and the crackle of the radios. They'd been armed, some of those policemen. They'd had rifles – big, complicated, science-fiction looking weapons in mat-black metal – and they'd been wearing black military-style uniforms. Big boots, peaked caps. Shit. I felt a fresh wave of fear. I sat up. Shit. They could have shot me. They were ready to shoot me if necessary. Why? What were they afraid of? What were they worried about? What did they think they were up against?

'Come on, Hymie, place your bet, you chicken-livered, rabbit-hearted, gin-drinking old woman, you!' Fresh gales of laughter and shouting from the poker table. 'Place your bet, you bloody trembling young virgin!'

I could feel things shifting in my head. I could almost hear the click-click and the clack-clack as they snapped and tumbled and shuffled and fell into place. It felt good. It was as if my thoughts had suddenly found a smooth, straight, open road to run along; as if my eyes had found a clear, open window to look through. It felt good, but at the same time the things I saw through that window and the directions that road took were alarming, even frightening.

What did the police think they were up against? Of course, it was obvious. They thought they were up against a dangerous lunatic. Someone who had a record of running wild with a handgun, who had been charged with firearms offences and threatening behaviour, who had been sectioned under the mental health act, who was suspected no doubt of issuing anonymous death threats, of breaking and entering, of criminal damage. Of murder. No wonder the police had been armed. They'd probably been even more frightened than I'd been.

Well, they hadn't caught me. They must be really pissed off, letting me slip through their fingers like that. Would they blame Helen and Dr Allen for it? No doubt they'd both begged the police to let them try talking to me first. Would they be in trouble? Helen. She had betrayed me. I had told her not to tell anyone where she was going, not to tell anyone she was going to see me. And she had led the police straight to me. How could she have done that? Why did she do it? A sudden storm of anger burst over me. Yes, I thought, I hope she is in trouble, it would serve her right! But the storm of vengeful rage passed in seconds, and the anger gave way to anxiety and pain and a great sadness, and I didn't want to think about Helen any more. I thought about Dr Allen. I certainly didn't want him to get into trouble. I'd always liked him. I'd always felt safe with him. He'd understood me. He'd helped me.

*

High Beech. That's what they'd called the place. It was just outside London, on the other side of Epping Forrest, where the flatlands of Essex begin. There'd been a psychiatric hospital there for over a hundred years. Little remained of the nineteenth-century estate it had once been except the names of its two blocks. Fair Mead and Leopard's Hill Lodge.

Leopard's Hill Lodge was the secure unit, where the dangerous patients were kept under lock and key and close supervision. High metal fences, CCTV, barred windows, every door controlled by codes and push-button key-pads. It was a terrible place. Horrible and frightening. Full of fear and anger and hatred and suspicion. The atmosphere was explosive. And only the ever-present threat of physical coercion and the continual dosage of heavy medication kept the lid on it.

Fair Mead was the open unit. It was relaxed and leisurely, most of the time. Patients were free to wander its corridors and sitting-rooms unsupervised. They could even leave the building to walk in the grounds. There were twelve acres of lawns and gardens, and the patients were encouraged to help the gardeners in their work.

Most of the patients in Leopard's Hill Lodge were long term. Many of those in Fair Mead were short term. Very few patients made it from Leopard's Hill Lodge to Fair Mead. Of those that did, hardly any were released from High Beech back into the big wide world. But Dr Allen got me out of Leopard's Hill Lodge. He realised almost straight away that I didn't belong there. He got me out pretty quickly. And in Fair Mead he worked with me slowly and patiently, and eventually he got me out of there too. I was the only one of Dr Allen's patients who managed it, all the way in and all the way out again. I could remember him shaking my hand, all those years ago, as I was about to leave the hospital, a free man, a cured man. The last time I'd seen him.

'Congratulations, Patrick,' he'd said. 'Well done. I'm very proud of you. We're all very proud of you.'

I remembered shaking my head. 'The congratulations are yours, doctor. I haven't done anything. I didn't fight my illness, you did. I was just the battlefield.'

'Nonsense.' He'd taken my arm and was walking me down the drive towards the main gate where a taxi was waiting for me. It had been a cold day, and he'd been wearing a deer-stalker hat to keep his bald head warm. He was the only person I've ever seen wearing a deer-stalker. I could never decide whether he wore it as a joke or as a serious psychological ploy, a symbol to trigger trust and respect in his patients, identifying him with fiction's greatest solver of mysteries and righter of wrongs. 'We can only help a patient who chooses to let us help him and decides to work with us. The patient isn't always consciously aware of choosing and deciding, but nevertheless he is responsible for doing so and can take credit for it.'

'Well.' I'd shrugged. 'You can take all the credit as far as I'm concerned.' I wasn't sure exactly what he'd done or how he'd done it, but he had cured me, of that I'd been certain. I fully understood what had happened to me, and why it had happened, and to understand it was to overcome it. The stress of my work – the stress on my nerves, emotions, intellect and imagination – the loneliness of it, the disappointment at its lack of recognition, the frustration of seeing Jutting appropriate my ideas and work and find fame and fortune with them – and the most crass and least worthy of my ideas at that – it had all taken me right up to the edge and tipped me over it, so that the crazy logic of the equation 'Harry Jutting's work is my work, therefore I must be Harry Jutting' hadn't seemed crazy at all but a plain and overpowering reality.

That morning, the morning of my release, Dr Allen had opened my file up to me. He'd shown me transcripts of interviews, and the manuscript of the account I'd written down on my arrival at High Beech, the full record of my delusions. What a document it proved to be! A hundred pages, thirty thousand words, so vivid, so convincing, so coherent! It took me most of the morning to read it, from 'Number forty-seven, Navarino Row…' all the way through to '…friendship just isn't something that Harry Jutting ever did.' I took a photocopy of it, when Dr Allen left me reading on my own for an hour to attend a meeting. I could almost have believed that it was indeed Harry Jutting himself telling our story, correct as it was in almost all of its details, the events more or less as they had really happened. Yes, it was in fact a fair account of everything that had occurred between us. A reliable narrative. The narrator might not be who he claimed to be, but he was more or less reliable; the only evident fiction was the faked death. You could practically hear Harry's voice dictating it. And yet the hand-writing was my own, was Patrick Joyce's!

No, I was not Harry Jutting. I'd had no doubt about that as I sat and read, Dr Allen standing beside me, his hand on my shoulder. Harry Jutting had not faked his own death. Harry Jutting was dead and buried, resting in peace whether he deserved to or not. 'So it really was suicide. He really did blow his own brains out.'

'Indeed,' Dr Allen had said. 'Sad. Regrettable. But understandable. The things he'd done, they must have weighed heavily on his conscience after all, the weight of guilt must have been too heavy for him to bear. He may have been a monster, but to end up like that…' He'd shaken his head. 'Surely you feel some sympathy for him?'

'Sympathy? I don't know.' I'd shrugged. 'But a conscience? A sense of guilt? I'm amazed Jutting knew what they were, let alone possessed them. So perhaps he was human. Perhaps I misjudged him. But I don't think I can ever feel sorry for him.' I read every word in that file,

301

but I'd closed it with relief once I'd finished it. The extent of my delusions had been terrifying, but they were dead and buried now, like Harry Jutting. They had been dispersed, like clouds of fog and mist, and I could see clearly at last. And Dr Allen had been the fresh wind that had swept them away. 'I don't know how to thank you,' I'd stuttered. 'There aren't words for it... I'm so grateful...'

And Dr Allen had just laughed and shaken his head, as if it had been nothing, putting my sanity back together again, quite apart from the long hard battle for my freedom. The reports and the appeals, the court hearings and the committee briefings, the prolonged and draining warfare against entrenched admin and bureaucracy. I didn't know the details, but I could imagine it. I had a feeling I'd been shielded from it deliberately – no doubt that process was a threat to anyone's sanity, let alone someone in my position. 'Talking of gratitude, Mary asked me to thank you for that tea set,' he'd said as he'd punched the code into the panel beside the main gate. The gate had opened slowly. A muddy taxi was waiting outside, a tinny pop tune from its radio trickling out through the driver's open window. 'I don't know what it is, but a brew from your pot always tastes better than from any other. It's a kind of magic. I thought she'd splashed out on a really top-class Darjeeling. But no, same old char, just a magic new pot and cups.'

'Well, you can take credit for that, too.' They went in for art therapy in a big way at High Beech, but luckily Dr Allan had realised right away that painting was the last thing I needed. They could have forced me to participate, but he knew it would have undermined all his other work. So he set up a ceramics class, quite separate from the painting and drawing, and encouraged me to take part. I took to it immediately. Here was a creative pursuit which didn't break the third commandment and produced something useful and practical, of real benefit to others. And which might even provide me with a livelihood outside the sheltered refuge of High Beech.

He'd waved his deer-stalker in the air as the taxi pulled away, and he'd still been waving it when a turn in the road and a tall hedge had removed him from view.

He had no nervous ticks. I'd never seen him tug at his shirt collar. I'd made that up, a mean and trivial act of rebellion perhaps, but understandable. A child might have to rebel against even the best of parents – feared and respected as well as loved – if he is to strive for independence.

And I did strive for independence. Independence from Dr Allen, from High Beach, and from everything and everyone that had set me on the terrible road to that place. I didn't go back to London. I avoided it like a painful memory or a bad dream. I was determined to make a fresh start in a new place. A new life with a new name. I drifted down into rural Kent, living almost like a tramp among the fields and orchards. There was enough work to keep me fed and clothed. Seasonal, casual, unskilled agricultural labour – fruit-picking, potato-harvesting, hedging, ditching. I lived in tents and mobile-homes and pre-fabs and dormitories among migrant labourers from Eastern Europe. I was alone, isolated, alienated even. But I didn't mind that. I relished it. I signed up for a ceramics course run by an adult education college in Canterbury. I made pots and jugs and cups and mugs, and they began to sell. Slowly but surely my new life had gradually eclipsed my old one.

I had been cured. Hadn't I? Yes. I sat back on that deep sofa in that dark corner of that strange room and felt like someone coming awake again from an afternoon nap, emerging from recurring nightmares into day-lit reality.

That afternoon's shock of Helen's words and Dr Allen's appearance had worked like an alarm-clock, like a brutal but efficient sergeant-major bawling in a dozing recruit's ear, waking him from a dangerous nap. I was Patrick Joyce. Harry Jutting was dead and buried. I was as sure of that now as I had been when I'd been released from High Beech, as I had been ever since my release, as I had been until…

Until I had napped. I had been asleep for months. Or perhaps even longer. That was the thing. The delusions had returned, and for a while I had been completely in thrall to them. Why had they returned? Well, Helen had put her finger on it. Art Crash Express, and Montezuma's Revenge…

But was that all? Wasn't there something else? Couldn't I feel something else still there, just out of sight, darting back round the corner, ducking down into the shadows? Something I didn't want to confront, something I wasn't quite ready to shine a light on, not just yet? But which I was slowly and steadily approaching, nevertheless, nervously and uncertainly but with one hand groping for the torch in my pocket and the other preparing to tear the mask off whatever the torch's beam revealed?

And what had happened since the delusions' return? What had I done?

I began to shake again. I could feel cold sweat breaking out, running down my back and brow and ribs. Yes. That was the question. What had I done? I felt that Russian thug's handgun in my right fist again. What had I done with it? Where was it now? I could hear the explosion of a single shot, smell the cordite, see its smoke, feel it choking on the back of my throat. There was a body at my feet, face down in a spreading pool of blood, fair hair turning dark and matted. A young man, dead, at my feet, a brightly lit interior, dark night somewhere outside. A vivid image.

Too vivid to be merely my imagination? Too horrible to be a memory, that was for sure.

I dozed on that sofa for hours on end. Every now and then, random bubbles of fear and panic brought me up to the surface, burst, and then let me sink back down into the depths again. The card-players' cries and laughter hardly disturbed me.

'See you? See you? See your dick on a butcher's slab! See your wife run off with Abe here! See you mortgage your pig-sty by the time I've finished with you!'

*

At three o'clock in the morning I woke up. I was too cold and hungry to go back to sleep. There were only three players left in the game, and they were playing with a silent intensity now. None of them looked up as my weasel-faced rescuer let me out of a rear door. It was only a short walk through the dark streets back to the Ellerby. I didn't know whether it would be safe to go back there, but there was nowhere else to go. I walked swiftly and openly, not trying to avoid the street-lights, but vigilant, my nerves stretched tight. I wasn't alone, even at that time of night. There was a knot of youngsters outside the underground station (what time did that close?), a shivering queue of them waiting to go into some night-spot, and a laughing and steaming group spilling out of it. Cars came and went. No police cars. No one awake and watchful in the cars parked along the road.

I had a key to the Ellerby. I let myself in and locked the door behind me. It was very dark in there. The shutters were down and I didn't know where the light-switches were. I had to grope my way through the bar-area and out into the corridor and staircase beyond. I had one foot on the first step when I heard movement in the dark bar behind me. A chair scraping back. Someone standing up. Someone had been sitting there in the darkness, silent and invisible, waiting for me to come in, to go past. And now they were behind me, between me and the exit. They had me trapped, and now they were coming to get me.

I ran up the stairs. I wasn't thinking, I was just running away from the invisible stranger, running for my room, as if that could offer any kind of safety. I came out onto the landing. There was the door to my room. But it was ajar. And the light was on in there. I stopped for a moment, panting, leaning on the banisters. Who was in there? How many of them were there? The sound of footsteps from the hall below made me glance back down the stairs. A big human shape emerged from the shadows and began to climb up after me. One behind me, at least one ahead of me. Who were they? What was I to do?

The lighted doorway seemed the lesser of two evils. I forced my way along the passage – footsteps behind me growing louder and closer – and opened the door wide.

There was a body on my bed. Big, male, fully-dressed. Black leather jacket, jeans. Short-cropped hair, stubbly beard. The man who had whacked me in the gut the night before. He was lying on his side. Corpse-still. But he wasn't a corpse. He was only sleeping. Once inside the room, I could see that his eyes were shut and that he was breathing. My arrival must have disturbed him because he rolled onto his back and his mouth fell open and he began to snore. He'd taken his boots off and one big toe showed through a hole in his grey socks.

'Now's your chance to get him back,' a voice whispered in my ear. I whirled round. The man who'd been waiting in the dark bar, who'd followed me upstairs. It was the other thug from the night before, the smaller, younger one. He chuckled. 'Go on. Stick the boot in. In the balls.

In the kidneys. In the nut. Take your pick. He needs waking up anyway.'

'What is this?' I tried to keep my voice steady but it still shook. 'What do you want?'

'I want you to wake this lazy bastard up.' He pushed past me into the room. 'Go on. Take a piss on him. Slap him round the face.' I didn't move. 'No? Last chance? Oh well.' He leaned forwards and took the naked big toe between his finger and thumb and shook it gently. 'Wake up, dear,' he urged in a comically high-pitched, maternal voice. 'You're late for school.'

The snoring stopped. The mouth snapped shut. The eyes snapped open. They stared at nothing for a moment, then they stared at his companion, then they stared at me. 'Shit!' He sat up suddenly. 'Shit!' He groaned and rubbed his hands over his face. 'Two nights in a row. I can't take it. It ain't fair.'

'I like working nights,' his companion said. 'Safer. Freer. Not so many people around to see what you're up to.'

'Well, you can sleep during the day, you ain't got no young kids screaming at you all afternoon.' The big man pulled on his boots, grumbling, then stood up. He turned to me. He looked upset and annoyed, as if I'd let him down. 'Where have you been? We've been waiting hours!'

I stared at him. 'Did we have an appointment?'

He took me by the arm and marched me back along the corridor. 'Away we go,' he said. 'We need you. You got to do us a favour.' Down the stairs we went. I heard the other one on his mobile behind me. 'Yeah, we got him. Right now. Outside. Ten seconds.'

We stepped out of the Ellerby and onto the pavement and a car pulled up right beside us. The smaller man opened a back door and got in and the other one shoved me in after him and squeezed in after me. 'Sorry about this,' his companion said with exaggerated courtesy. 'I know it's no way to treat someone doing us a favour, but you don't want to see where we're going. I'm sure you understand.' A black woollen hood suddenly descended over my head. I couldn't see anything. The shock made me breathe in sharply and the wool clung to my nose and mouth. It felt like I was suffocating. I breathed out and in again quickly, the air immediately getting heavier and damper. The car pulled away and we were off.

*

I had no idea where we were going. No, I didn't try counting the right turns and the left turns. Or mentally noting the ascents and descents and the changes in the sound of the traffic around us. Or counting slowly to estimate times and distances. I was too busy trying not to throw up. I was frightened. I felt sick and dizzy. I could hardly breathe with that hood over my head. It was hot and clammy and airless, and so disorienting I could hardly tell up from down let alone left from right. I couldn't see anything but flashes of light in the darkness, and I could hardly hear anything either, the cloth was that thick and heavy. What did these characters want? They were Steve Smith's men. What could he want from me?

The journey seemed to last forever. But we stopped eventually. I was bundled out of the car and pushed and pulled this way and that. I stumbled and staggered, blindly following their rough lead as best I could. It was like some sort of macabre party game. At one point I tripped and would have fallen headlong but for the grip they had on my collar and elbows. At another I cracked my head on a low obstacle of some sort. Then we came to a halt and the hood was whipped off my head.

We were in the changing-rooms of what must have been a gymnasium or sports hall. Lockers and benches, tiled floor and walls, no windows, strip lighting. The sudden light seemed very bright and harsh and painful after the darkness, the noise in there – what sounded like the track of a sci-fi action adventure movie - very loud. But it was a relief to be free of the hood. I breathed in deeply and eagerly. But the place had a strange, unpleasant smell. After a few lungfuls of it, I wasn't sure that it was an improvement.

The place looked old-fashioned, as if it was attached to a gym which trained professional boxers rather than a sports club which trimmed the fat off the middle-class and middle-aged. A handful of young men were sitting around an open lap-top. A sci-fi movie was indeed flashing explosions and clashes of mighty machinery across its screen, epic sound-effects booming out at full volume. A crate of beer stood on the floor, and the young men swigged from open bottles as they swore and jeered at the on-screen action. But I could tell they were bored and impatient, just passing the time while they were waiting for something else. Waiting for us.

They were wearing all-in-one hooded suits in some kind of white synthetic anti-contamination material, over jeans and t-shirts. They looked like they were ready for work in a high-tech lab or nuclear power-station. Or for bio-chemical warfare.

They stood up as soon as we came in. They were grinning and nodding, relieved, the boring wait over, now back down to business at last, the movie instantly forgotten.

'That him?'

'Yeah.'

'Took you long enough. Using Google Earth, were you?'

'Fuck off.'

'All right then. Let the pit-bull see the bunny, eh?'

Someone turned the computer off. The sound of intergalactic warfare died away, and in its place I could hear muffled groans and yells. They were coming from beyond the changing rooms, from the shower cubicles I could see through an open doorway at the far end. A couple of the young men lead the way towards it. My two companions pushed me after them. The unpleasant smell grew stronger.

The showers were a narrow, tiled, harshly-lit corridor. A line of nozzles projected from each wall. Two male figures were leaning or rather suspended against the walls. They were naked, which I suppose wasn't surprising considering where they were. But they had hoods over their heads and their wrists were handcuffed. Their arms were stretched up above their heads because each set of handcuffs was wrapped around a shower-nozzle. They were dangling there, hanging limply but awkwardly, as if there was no strength left in their legs. One was big and pale and fat, the other was small and dark and lean.

Their hoods were just like the one I'd been wearing. I felt a blast of terror even more powerful than the futuristic arsenals the antagonists of that sci-fi movie had been letting loose on each other. So this is what they're going to do to me. They've taken the hood off me so I can see, now they're going to put it back on and cuff me and strip me and hang me up beside this pair, and then…

There was blood and vomit and piss and shit all over the shower walls and floor and all over the naked skin of the two hooded men.

I'd managed to stop myself throwing up in the car, but the stink and the sight and the horror of all this was surely too much. I felt the bile rising up my throat and tasted it in my mouth. I felt my legs beginning to give way. My two

310

guardians still had me by the collar and elbows. I felt their grips tighten as they held me upright. They shook me roughly as if to keep me awake. One of the young men who'd been waiting for us turned to me. He had long hair and a tattoo of a parrot on the side of his neck. His protective white over-alls were splashed with wet, dark patches. He looked at me uncertainly. 'You the one who was with Gary Hughes the other night?' he said.

I stared at him. My mind was too stunned with shock and terror to take in what he was saying.

'Gary Hughes. You know? Lamb's Conduit Street. Three nights ago.'

Yes. Yes, I was with Gary Hughes. Should I admit it? Shit, yes, they'll only beat it out of me if I don't. I nodded emphatically.

'He said you left the pub with him, saw what happened. Right?'

I nodded again. My memory replayed it all in a flash - the crack and thud and smack of the blows, Gary in the gutter, the fist and the boots and the club. Violence after dark. Did this happen every night, a bad dream playing for real somewhere in the sleeping city's dim subconscious?

'You saw the geezers what put him in hospital, right?'

I nodded once more. Two geezers… I saw them again, their hoods slipping as they got stuck into Gary, light from a street-lamp falling on their faces. One of them grinning all over his fat, fair face as he stepped out of the shadows into Gary's path and Gary ran into him. His mouth tightening as he swung one fist into Gary's gut, another onto his chin. The other geezer, thinner, darker, brandishing the club at me, shaking his head, warning me, threatening me, stay out of this. I was happy to stay out of it, but somehow it had caught up with me again and was pulling me back in.

'Get a good look? Know them again, would you?'

I nodded. Yes… I was still fighting my churning stomach. The stench in there was getting worse if anything. I didn't want to open my mouth, even to speak.

The long-haired thug looked relieved. He signalled to his mates. Two of them stepped forwards and took the hoods off their captives. One of the naked men – the big, pale one - immediately started shouting - swearing and cursing. The other just hung there, his head down, chin on his chest. The long-haired thug took something from a mate – a long metal rod of some sort – and thrust one end against the shouting man's chest. The rod seemed to light up. There was a sizzling and crackling of electricity. The man screamed. His body arched backwards, rigid and strained. The shower cubicles filled with the acrid smell of burnt flesh. The long-haired thug took the rod away. The light faded. The sizzling and crackling stopped. The screaming man fell silent. His body relaxed, shaking and trembling, the handcuffs and shower-nozzle rattling and creaking as they took its weight.

'Know them now, do you? Go on, take a good look.'

Heavy hands pushed me along the shower cubicle towards the two naked men. Other hands grabbed fistfuls of matted hair and pulled the slumped heads up and back so I could see the faces. One was thin and dark, the other fat and fair. Yes, I recognised them, even though the thin dark one – which had been warning and threatening me the one and only time I'd seen it before – was now shaking with fear and pain; even though the fat fair one was no longer grinning with brutal pleasure but was now spitting with anger and defiance.

'What are you going to do to them?'

'This them? What did Gary the other night?'

'Yes. But - '

'You sure?'

'It's them. Listen - '

'All right. You can clear off now.' The long-haired thug turned away. He and his mates started pulling on rubber gloves. They were no longer interested in me. They had work to do. They were focused and serious.

'Come on.' The two characters who had brought me there pushed me out of the shower cubicles and back into the dressing-room.

'What are they going to do?' Behind me, the shouting started again. Shouts of fear and alarm and defiance, rising to screams. Then the screams were abruptly choked off to moans and groans, as if they'd been gagged. Then I heard the hissing of water, as if the showers had been turned on. 'Those two... what'll happen to them?'

'You don't want to know.'

Suddenly the hood was back over my head. This time I was grateful for it. The sights, the smells, the sounds – I was glad to escape them all.

The return journey didn't seem to take as long as the journey out. No one spoke. Some words of Gary's ran round and round in my head as we drove in silence. 'Family Smith has been good to me,' Gary had said. 'They know how to reward loyalty.' So was that why Family Smith was sorting out the men who had attacked him?

No one spoke until they'd pulled up outside the Ellerby and dumped me on the dark pavement. 'Your old mate Gary's in UCH. Ward 19, Gower Wing,' one of the thugs said as he whipped off the hood. 'Go and see him tomorrow. He wants to tell you something. And you can tell him not to be such a fucking idiot in future. OK?'

*

I didn't want to see Gary Hughes again. I didn't want anything else to do with him and the violent nightmares he seemed to be dragging me into. I just wanted to stay in that dingy room – tiny and shabby though it was – curled up in bed with the light on, safe and comfortable, and never have to go outside again. Outside, where the police were hunting for me with nuclear-powered weapons. Outside, where even Dr Allen was waiting to get me back into Leopard's Hill Lodge. I didn't want to go back there, I really didn't.

But I couldn't stay in that room forever. I had to get out. I was no closer to solving the mysteries which had brought me here, and I wouldn't find any answers by staring at the peeling wall-paper. I had to get out and search for them. Gary had something to tell me. I had to find out what it was. I had to know who had killed James Hobson, and why. I had to know who had set the police onto me, and why. I had to hope that whatever Gary wanted to tell me would shed light on both those questions. There were no other leads. It was all I had. Yet it wasn't a desperate hope. The other night he had suggested that he knew all about James Hobson's death, hadn't he? What else could he want to talk to me about? The more I thought about it, the more hopeful and even excited I became. Could Gary indeed have all the answers? Yes, he could.

I lay low the next day until it was dark. I was exhausted, but I slept only fitfully. I was half-expecting the police to break the door down. And my dreams were vivid and alarming. I dreamed about Helen betraying me. I dreamed about Dr Allen, guiltily, as if I'd let him down. I dreamed about the policemen waiting outside the café for me with their terrifying sc-fi weaponry and black para-military uniforms. I dreamed about the two naked men handcuffed and hooded in the showers. What had happened to them? My dreams tried to answer that question, as if punishing me for identifying them. It was my fault. I was responsible. If I hadn't identified them… But my dreams did their best to show me what might have happened to me if I hadn't, and that was worse. So was it my fault? But what else could I have done?

I got up when it was dark and had a shower and changed my clothes. I didn't go to the Underground. I didn't want to walk past that café and the bookies or go to the station in case the police were watching out for me there. Instead I cut south through side-streets and got on a bus a good mile away.

I almost turned back at the hospital entrance. Wards, nurses, tiled corridors, doctors, pills, the smell of disinfectant. It was bringing it all back to me, High Beach, Fair Meadow, Leopard's Hill Lodge. But I forced myself in, forced myself to ask directions, forced myself along corridors, up stairs, through swing-doors.

Gary had a private room all to himself. I guessed he hadn't been making himself popular by the tight expressions on the nurses' faces when I asked for him. He was stabbing furiously at a button on a panel beside his bed when I came into his room.

'Where are those bitches?' he said. His brow was furrowed with anger. 'Can't they hear? Is this pile of shit broken or something? I've been ringing for them for hours.'

'Perhaps they're busy.'

He looked at me, puzzled and still angry, as if they couldn't possibly be busy when he wanted them.

'Life or death situation perhaps? This is a hospital, isn't it?'

'But this is a private room! I'm paying for this!'

'You're paying?'

'Well.' He grinned, and chuckled. 'Friends are paying.'

'The same friends who dragged me away from my bed in the middle of the night?'

'Oh, good! They found you, did they? And they found those two bastards? And you fingered them all right? You saw what they did, outside the pub, you saw them and identified them?'

'I did. I wish I hadn't.'

'You what?

'Do you know what happened to them?'

'Eye for an eye, mate, tooth for a tooth. Serves them right. Bastards. No one can push the beautiful Gary Hughes around like that, not when he's got friends like Family Smith. I told you they looked after me.'

Gary Hughes wasn't looking so beautiful today. He had a black-eye. His lips were swollen and bruised. There were butterfly-plasters on his brow. And his skin was beyond orange – it was a tired, sickly yellow. The make-up around his eyes was smudgy and runny, and his closely-cropped blond hair was sticking up so dark roots were visible. The off-white hospital gown didn't do him any favours. He looked small, his skin puffy and lined, his body slack, even plump. He saw me looking at him. 'You still look like shit,' he said.

'So do you now.'

'Yeah, but I'm in hospital. What's your excuse?'

My excuse? I looked at the big window on the other side of his bed. The blinds hadn't been closed. It was black outside, but bright and harshly lit inside. The glass was a dark mirror. A solitary figure was reflected in it. A thin and care-worn figure, obscure and isolated, peering out from the shadows. My reflection. I was on the run from the police for a murder I wasn't sure I hadn't committed. And if they caught me they'd send me back to a high-security hell of barred windows and CCTV cameras and mind-numbing medication. That was my excuse. I looked away. 'What's the damage?'

'A couple of broken ribs. Cuts and bruises. They took a brain-scan. Looks ok, but they're keeping me in for a day or two just to make sure.' He put a hand to his face, feeling the creases on his brow. 'Do you think I could get a spot of Bottox on the NHS as part of the treatment? If I pleaded mental distress, and all that? I mean, I am a tax-payer, and I'm saving them a packet, going private here. And I am suffering mental distress. I burst into tears when I looked in the mirror this morning.'

I looked at him. He wasn't joking. I wanted to give him a good slapping. The place was beginning to get to me. Panic wasn't far away. I didn't know how long I'd be able to stay calm and keep my temper. 'Those two men. Outside the Lamb and Flag. Why did they attack you?'

Gary laughed. 'Bet they're regretting it now, aren't they? Funny if they turned up here, in the next ward, eh? Give them a heart attack, finish them off all right.' He stopped laughing, and shook his head. 'They thought they could get the better of me, but they were wrong. I showed them. And I haven't finished with them, either. If they're not going to pay for my silence, I'm going to start shouting. I warned them.'

'You can start by telling me.'

'It's about James Hobson's death.' He reached for the bottle of water on his bedside table and took a mouthful from it. 'His murder.' He screwed the top back on it and pointed it at me. 'I know all about it. Everything. Every last detail.' Was he warning me? Was he threatening me? Or was he just boasting?

'You said he was shot.'

'He was. And I know who did it. Listen - '

The door opened. A nurse came in. She didn't look happy to be there. 'You were ringing?' she said coldly.

'Not now! Too late, you stupid cow! Clear off!'

She withdrew sharply and slammed the door behind her. Gary pulled a face at it. 'And some people have fantasies about women in nurses' uniforms. Can you believe it? I've taken the photos, I've sold the photos, but I still can't believe it.'

I wasn't listening. I was out on that backstreet in north London again, in the darkness, feeling the cold night air on my face, the Russian's handgun heavy and smooth in my right fist. I could see the row of lorries and trailers and coaches parked under the street-lamps at the kerb. I could feel the anger in my chest, the righteous anger...

'Patrick? You all right? What's up?' Gary was looking at me strangely. 'You were shaking – your eyes were half-closed – you're sweating like a fat bastard in a sauna!'

'I'm OK.' I shook my head to clear it. But I wasn't OK. I felt sick. My heart was thumping, I thought the suspense would make it burst, waiting for Gary to tell me about Hobson's death. I wanted him to tell me, I didn't want him to tell me. 'It's just the lack of sleep, the disturbed nights.'

'Listen, I'm going to tell you all about it. I'm going to tell the police, I'm going to tell everyone. The bastards.' He closed his eyes and lay back, looking suddenly tired and ill. He breathed in deeply, then out, then opened his eyes again. 'I saw everything. I've got photos to prove it. The bastards won't stand a chance.' He sat up in bed. 'I told you things were pretty wild on set, didn't I? All the cast were off their heads, all the time. Snorting, injecting, smoking, it was crazy, insane. Fun to start with – one big party – then it got rather nasty. It was all Hobson's fault – he was behind it, he encouraged it, he set the tone. And all the suppliers were his mates. They were all in his posse. They could come and go on set as they pleased, no one to stop them. Except each other. There were two groups of them. The first were those twats he made that crappy record with – what were they called, those rappers? The Zap Crew, that's it – or rather the bad-ass Jamaican gangstas they hung out with. The second were some local boys, cousins of his or something, family anyway, a new firm trying to move up from mugging and shop-lifting into something more organised, know what I mean? Anyway, these two groups of pushers were soon treading all over each other's toes, trying to elbow each other out, scare each other off. Hobson thought it was really funny. I reckon he was deliberately playing one lot off against the other, just for the laugh. And you can bet he was getting a cut from all of them, as well.'

He broke off to take another swig of water from the plastic bottle. Then he rummaged around in the drawer beside his bed. 'Can I smoke in here?' He pulled out a packet of cigarettes and a lighter. 'Fuck, course I can.' He lit up and inhaled deeply, exhaled slowly.

'Hobson had a trailer all to himself, where they were filming in north London. Why North, for fuck's sake? Islington? It was nothing like where it all happened for real, you know, Navarino Row, out east. Anyway, there they were, a big caravanserai of lorries and trailers and coaches and generators and caterer's vans, a mobile village parked in a backstreet off Essex Road. Anyway, Hobson's trailer. He crashed out in it almost every night when we were on location. He could have gone to a hotel, he could have gone back home to Essex, but it was convenient to stay put when the party was right there all the time. Why bother with a taxi-ride or a train-journey when you've got a bed and a room right where the action is? One night there was a load of us hanging out in his trailer, drinking and playing poker and stuff, and I passed out on his sofa, and when I was woken up by a loud banging on his door it was all dark and I was on my own. I had a really bad feeling about it. I was suddenly really sober and scared shitless. I was off that sofa and into the bathroom like a shot, even before Hobson was out of his bedroom to answer the door.

'I heard Hobson let his visitors in. I could tell by the tone of his voice that he knew them. I reckoned that there were two of them, two separate voices, both men. They weren't happy. They started rowing with Hobson straight away. I sat there on the bog, shivering with terror, looking for a way out, but there wasn't one. No window, nothing. Just the down-pipe on the bog, and I'd have been down that like a rat if I'd been any skinnier. The voices outside got louder, and I began to hear what they were saying, and gradually my curiosity got the better of my fear. I wanted to hear more, see more. You know, eavesdropping, peeping-Tomming, it isn't just my bread and butter, it's my vocation, it's in my DNA.

'I hadn't closed the door behind me. I eased it a little more open. The three of them were all shouting now, and I could clearly hear what they were saying. The visitors were from Hobson's cousins, and they were complaining about the competition from the Zap Crew's gangsta mates. They wanted him to get the Jamaicans kicked out, thrown off the set, run out of town. Blood was thicker than water, they were saying, family comes first and all that. Well, Hobson didn't like anyone telling him what to do. It was like a red flag to a bull. And they weren't just telling him, they were demanding, they were threatening him. This is going to get violent, I thought. I've got to see this. I've got to get some shots of this. I had my gear with me. Yes, I know, even though I'd been terrified, blind instinct had made me grab my bag in that mad rush for the bathroom. DNA, as I said. Vocation.

'I crept over to the crack in the door. I had a camera in my hand. I peered out. Yes, there were two of them. I recognised them from his posse. They were shouting at

Hobson, Hobson was shouting back, they were jabbing their fingers at each other, pushing and shoving. They were too angry to notice me, too loud to hear the clicking of my camera. Then there were punches thrown, the three of them completely lost it, they were rolling and bouncing around in that little space like kids in a play-house. The trailer was rocking from one end to the other like a trampoline. I thought it was funny at first. And then someone pulled a gun. One of the visitors. And everything seemed to freeze. All the action, one moment so violent and frenzied, it all seemed to run down and stop. The noise too.

'I got a good shot of that. The frozen scene. One visitor, his mouth bleeding, crouching off balance with the gun in one hand, the other visitor on the floor, Hobson kneeling on him with one fist raised but his head twisted round and back to look at the weapon the other one was aiming at him from just inches away. There was a shout – a single yell of warning or fear or defiance - I don't know who from. Then there was a shot. A sharp crack, not loud. Hobson collapsed. The two visitors stood over him, white-faced and shaking. The armed one seemed to be struck dumb, but the other one was swearing, the same word over and over again.

'Then there was a sound from the bedroom. A moan, someone stifling a scream. There was a girl in there. Of course there was, that was Hobson's bedroom. Whoever it was, she couldn't have seen anything, he'd closed the door behind him. But she must have heard more than enough.

'The two visitors looked at each other. Their eyes were wild with fear and panic. What were they going to do? Go in there and sort her out? How? Threaten her into silence? Bribe her into silence? Kill her too? No. They weren't up to any of that. They panicked and they ran. A mad scramble to the door – the two of them were fighting each other to get out of there, like characters in a bloody cartoon – and then they were gone.

'Stupid bastards. Bloody amateurs. They knew they'd stuffed up. They had no idea, none of them. No idea how to play the game, how to run the kind of business they were trying to break into. They were a joke. Bloody useless.

'I could hear the girl sobbing and moaning in the bedroom, feel the floor of the trailer bouncing around as she got dressed in a mad hurry. Then the door of the bedroom burst open and she came out of there like a greyhound out of a trap. She was through that sitting-room and out through the door the two visitors had left swinging open onto the night in seconds. Her hands were sort of over her eyes – she didn't want to see anything – she certainly didn't pause to find out what might have happened to the man she had presumably been fucking only a few hours before. I don't know who she was. I guess she just went home and put her head in the sand, too terrified to go to the police or anything. Understandable, I suppose. But pathetically un-enterprising.

'Me, I'm enterprising. I knew what I'd seen and recorded that night was worth a small fortune. I took some last shots of Hobson lying there dead – he was dead, all right, there was no point in calling for an ambulance – then I shut the door and turned off the lights and forced myself to wait there for a good half-hour – long enough to be sure that the coast was clear. It was cold and creepy – alone in there with a dead body and all that blood - but I didn't want to be caught if that pair of jokers was still lurking in the area. Then I buggered off.

'There was no way I was going to the police, of course. I know how to behave myself. But at the same time I knew that I deserved a big reward for behaving myself. I contacted Hobson's cousins or uncles or whatever they were, and suggested as much. A reward for remaining silent, and a reward for handing over the photographic evidence. Only just and proper, wouldn't you say? Particularly as I'd just lost my job, a really sweet number at that, the movie now being as dead as Hobson himself. I expected gratitude, fair-play, good faith. What did I get? Threats and intimidation. And then outright violence, as you witnessed. Those two we ran into outside the Lamb and Flag. Another pair of jokers sent out to do business for Hobson's cousins with only half a brain between them.

'Well, no one treats Gary Hughes like that and gets away with it. What were they thinking of? I'd told Hobson's lot straight off that I was a friend of Family Smith, eager as I was to be honest and above board with them. Didn't they believe me? Or are they just stupid? One phone call, as soon as I arrived here. That's all it took. And Family Smith aren't going to stop there, with tonight's little lesson. They've known all about Hobson's presumptuous cousins and their ridiculous pretensions for some time now. Hobson's lot seem to think of themselves as up and coming rivals, as competition, and the Smiths don't appreciate that. The Smiths have been biding their time, looking for the opportunity to hit them hard and roll them up and dump them in the rubbish bin. Well, this is it. Hobson's lot don't stand a chance. The Smiths know how to do things properly, Hobson's lot couldn't organise an orgy in a knocking-shop.

'Family Smith want me to go to the police with everything. The Law will hit Hobson's lot from one side, and the Smiths will hit them from the other. By the end of the month, there won't be a single one of them left outside the courthouse, the prison, the hospital or the cemetery. They'll be finished, good and proper. And it will serve them right, the stupid bastards.'

Chapter Fifteen

I did not kill James Hobson! I didn't kill him! It wasn't me! There was a witness, there was evidence!

I could barely control myself. I was sobbing with relief. I was laughing and crying, slumped forward in the armchair beside his bed, my head in my hands.

'Here, steady on, Patrick, mate,' Gary urged. He was puzzled and alarmed. 'Any doctors round here see you in that state, they'll drag you back to your loony bin!'

'And you're going to the police? You're going to tell them everything? Show them those photos?'

'Yeah. I know, mad, isn't it?' he said, mistaking my euphoria for incredulity. 'It's worth a fortune, and what am I getting out of it in the end? Bugger all. Except revenge, of course. And more goodwill from Family Smith. That's worth a fortune in itself, I suppose, but still…' He sighed. 'Wonder if I could sell those photos to some schlocky mag? Dramatic murder of a budding movie star. Strong stuff. Bit too strong, perhaps. Certainly for the UK. Italy? Some scummy rag might go for it over there…'

I shook my head and wiped my eyes. 'You're brilliant, Gary. You deserve that fortune.' I stood up. 'I'll come and see you again tomorrow. What can I bring you?'

'Vodka. And don't let those bitches see you bring it in.' He suddenly realised I was about to go. 'Hey, I almost forgot. There's something I wanted to tell you…'

'What?' I stopped at the door and turned back to him. 'You mean, Hobson's death wasn't it?'

'Nah, nah. There's something else. Nothing really, I suppose. Interesting coincidence, though.'

I waited, my heart in my mouth. What else was there? What could it be?

'Some journalist was asking about you, a week or two ago. She hunted me down and wanted to know all about you. She had two or three photos of you – old ones, press cuttings from years ago, Brick Shit-House and all that – wanted to see any I might have taken of you at that time, too. And she had her own shot of you – a really sneaky pap-shot on her mobile, looks like it was taken in a kitchen? On the sly, when you weren't looking? Not much of a shot, to be honest, she wouldn't hack it in this trade. Wanted me to confirm it was you. I wasn't sure it was, to be honest, awkward angle, big beard, long hair. But I can see it now. It was you, all right. You were making coffee or something.'

I stared at him. I could feel the gears of my mind slipping as it groped for a name, scanned a memory, struggled to make a connection.

Gary laughed. 'Really hot bitch. Young. Tasty. Wouldn't mind if she was on my tail. I'd grind her coffee, any day.'

What was her name? Betty? No, no… 'Becky? Becky something?' What had I done with her card?

'Can't remember.' He was scrabbling around in the drawer again. 'But she gave me this.' He found his wallet and opened it to slide out a business card. 'Here. I wouldn't have kept it, but she was hot. And journalists, magazines, I need them on my side.'

Yes. The name was Becky. Becky Short. I recognised the card, the orange swirls, the typography. I remembered her pulling it out of her own wallet just before I chucked her and her boyfriend out of the house. What was the name of the magazine she worked for? There it was, and its address. 'Forwards Backwards' I read. 'What sort of magazine is that? Do you know it?'

'Yeah, I've flicked through it once or twice.' He made a dismissive gesture. 'Pretentious arty wank. Know what I

325

mean? Intellectuals with PhDs in French Critical Theory slumming it in the fashion world. Showing how hip and with-it they are by engaging with pop music and movies and football as well as fine art and design. Photographers so busy trying to be cutting-edge and avant-garde that they take sexy, glamorous models and make them look ugly. Can't have anything so common and low-brow as a hard-on, can we, darlings?' He snorted. 'The usual Shoreditch shite. From typical Shoreditch tossers. Been there lately? Shoreditch? Changed a bit since we were there, eh? Forty-seven Navarino Row, must be worth getting on for a million quid these days, a property like that. Incredible.'

I waved the card at him. 'Can I keep this? Just for a day or two?'

He shrugged. 'Sure. But don't forget the vodka. Finnish. Aardvaarc. All right?'

I stopped at the door again. 'What was he like? James Hobson?'

Gary shrugged, and pulled a disdainful expression. 'Oh, he was just like Harry Jutting. You know. A right shitty bastard. I reckon he had it coming to him, one way or another.' He nodded. 'He was well-cast, all right. Looked like Jutting too. It was uncanny. But he was dead stupid. Really thick. Not like Jutting. Jutting wasn't stupid. He was clever enough, even if he was no genius.' He looked up at me and grinned, a big smile on his bruised and battered face, splitting the smeared make-up on his lips and eyes. 'You were the genius, Patrick. Weren't you?' He gave me the thumbs up. 'He used us all, didn't he, the bastard? Well, he's dead and done for, isn't he, no more or less than he deserved. And we're still here. Prison didn't finish me off, and the loony bin didn't finish you off, eh? So here's to you and me, Patrick, we've survived, and when I get out of here we'll both go and piss on Jutting's grave!'

Becky Short. I remembered her. And I'd thought she'd been sweet and innocent, even if she'd looked like a call-girl. And I'd felt bad about losing my temper and throwing her out of the house. I should never have let her in in the first place.

'Forwards Backwards' was published from an office just off Shoreditch High Street. There was no receptionist, no reception area, just a big open-plan space right there where you stepped in off the street. A horizontal organisation. Nothing so hierarchical as desks, let alone separate offices. In fact, it looked just like one of the bars or cafes lining the High Street: industrial-chic décor of bare brick walls, stripped wooden floors, undecorated iron-work; leather arm-chairs and sofas, low coffee-tables, rickety wooden tables and benches that could have come from an authentic east-end pub; bicycles propped up against any vertical surface; and smug, seriously on-trend youngsters lounging around peering at lap-tops and tablets, tapping at key-boards, chatting over big mugs of latte. They looked up – three or four of them – as I came in. Indie-rock whined and whimpered softly in the background. None of them was the girl I remembered.

'Becky in?' I asked. 'Becky Short?'

They peered at me. One of them looked blank. One looked confused. One looked challenging and confrontational. 'Do you have an appointment?'

I laughed. 'She's been after an appointment with me for weeks.'

She frowned at me. Her hair was dyed purple and green. Matching eye-shadow. She was wearing a grey singlet. She was very skinny and her arms were covered in tattoos. She was too cool to smile. 'She's in,' she admitted grudgingly. 'But…' She turned to glance towards the back of the office, just as a door there opened and Becky came bustling back into the room. Fair-haired, pretty, cheerful. She looked at her colleagues, and something in their expressions made her halt. She frowned, puzzled. Then she saw me and her confusion turned to surprise and terror. Eyes wide, mouth open. She gave a loud moan of fear and shock. Then she was gone, backing hurriedly away into the shadows beyond the office.

I ran after her. The cries of her colleagues – alarmed, angry, frightened – flew after me. A short corridor – Becky banging through a door at the end – I banged in after her – wash-basins, tiled walls, mirrors, another door leading no doubt to a toilet cubicle. Becky was trying to open the door. She was gasping and groaning with fear. But the door was locked. The cubicle was occupied. There was no escape from me there.

'All right, all right. Hang on there, I'll be done in a minute,' a harassed female voice exclaimed.

'Let me in!' Becky shouted. She was banging on the door. 'Let me in!'

'There's only room for one in here, babes! You'll have to wait!'

'Becky,' I said. 'Becky Short.'

She turned. She looked at me. She was shaking with fear. Her lips and her eyelids trembled. She pressed herself back against the door, trying to get away from me. 'What do you want?' Her voice was high and sharp, almost a shriek. 'What are you going to do? Have you got a gun? Don't kill me! Don't kill me, please!' She was wearing a loose white singlet. Fishnet tights. Tight, short, denim shorts. High heels. An amber necklace which I recognised. She started to cry. 'Don't kill me!' she wailed. 'Don't hurt me! Please!'

'Who's that?' the voice behind the door demanded. 'What's going on?'

'Call the police!' Becky shrieked. 'Have you got your mobile? Call the police! Now!'

I frowned. I was puzzled. 'Hurt you? Kill you? Why would I want to..?' Then I understood. I was the dangerous, gun-waving lunatic she'd been investigating for the last month. She'd tracked me down, uncovered my secret, identified me as the number one suspect in Hobson's murder, and told the police. It had been her – not Gary, not Stella, not Steve Smith! It had been this girl who had put the police onto me! And now here I was - a murder suspect, a sectioned lunatic, a convicted fire-arms offender, an issuer of death threats - hunting her down, after my revenge. So she thought. Was it any wonder she was terrified? I laughed. I had been so wrong. I had been so blind. 'Becky, there's nothing… I don't want…'

She started to scream. I backed away. I felt terrible. She was so pretty – round cheeks, tiny nose, sweet mouth, fair complexion, and yet here she was, scared out of her wits, her make-up running, her face distorted, and it was my fault. I had reduced her to this ugliness. I felt like a monster, the beast to her beauty.

'Right, right,' the voice behind the cubicle shook with panic. 'Phone – right – police – right – oh shit!' There the sound of fumbling and then a loud splash. 'Shit, I've dropped it in the toilet, and I've just done a shit!'

Becky was still screaming, her hands up to her face.

'Becky, please, I'm sorry, I'm not going to hurt you…' I held my hands out to her, empty, imploring. 'I just want to talk, I just want to know…'

There were running footsteps in the corridor behind me. I turned as a young man burst into the toilets. He was wearing very tight red jeans and a baggy grey sweater. He had a fluffy beard and hair short at the back and sides but floppy on top. He looked at Becky and then he looked at me. He was white-faced and trembling.

I took a step towards him. 'Do you mind? Can't you see this is the Ladies?'

He gave a wail of fear and turned and ran.

Becky had stopped screaming. She was staring at me, gasping for breath, her eyes still huge with terror.

'Becky,' I said. 'It was you, wasn't it? You realised who I was, after you came to my house?' I spoke as gently and calmly as I could. 'And you guessed it was me sending those letters to Hobson, warning him off the movie? You recognised the style, the ideas, from what I said to you in my house, when I lost my temper and threw you out? That had to make me a suspect, when Hobson was killed, so you told the police about me?'

Becky was slowly regaining her self-control. Her sobbing subsided. She nodded and shot me a calculating glance. Professional pride and curiosity were beginning to displace fear.

'But how did you do it? How did you put two and two together? What made you realise William Brin was Patrick Joyce?'

She turned away from me and went over to the mirrors. She looked at her reflection. She gulped and sighed and shook her head. Her shaking hands started to pat and tease her hair back into shape. 'I thought you looked familiar, as soon as I saw you. I thought I'd met you somewhere or seen you somewhere before, somewhere recently. But I couldn't place you at first.' She tore a paper towel from the dispenser and began to dab at her ruined make-up. 'Your work, those ceramics – brilliant, wonderful, beautiful, unusual – I knew that whoever made them wasn't just some sort of home-grown potter, sprung up from the back-end of nowhere and happy to stay there. I knew there had to be more to him than that. That was why I was so curious to meet William Brin. And when I met him, it just confirmed what I thought, that there was

330

some sort of mystery there, particularly as I was sure I recognised him from somewhere.' She ran some water into the basin and started bathing her face. 'And then it hit me, just after I got back to London. I'd written a piece about Harry Jutting for the magazine two months before, about his life and his work and the crowd he hung around with. There's been a huge resurgence of interest in him recently, what with that movie about him and the exhibition at the Tate, so it wasn't exactly a coincidence. I'd been going through files and books about him, looking at press-cuttings and photos. The early photos of Harry and his mates, always the same faces. That's where I'd seen you before. I came across one of them when I was tidying things up, and there you were, looking out at me. Patrick Joyce. The spitting image of William Brin, give or take ten years. Bingo.'

She dried her face and then reached into her handbag for mascara and lip-stick. She glanced aside at me before she started to apply the make-up. 'So it *was* you who sent those death-threats to Hobson? And it *is* you who's been waging guerrilla warfare against Jutting's work?'

I stared at her. 'You worked that one out as well?'

She laughed, grinning at me, lip-stick poised. I was no longer the beast, she was once again the beauty. 'Yes, all those random attacks, reported separately in different places around the country, I was the first one to put them together, to realise they were all part of a single campaign. Iconoclasm. And I guessed you were behind it, as well. Couldn't put your name in print, though. Not before you'd been arrested and charged. Didn't want to risk being sued.'

'I salute you.' I shook my head. I was having trouble taking it all in. It was this girl who had put the police onto me. Not Steve, not Stella, not Gary. It was this girl who had driven me away from Helen and Liz and Richard, who had precipitated me into this hellish mystery-quest through this nightmarish city. And yet I felt no animosity towards her. She had only been doing her job. There had been no betrayal, there was to be no revenge. I felt no hatred. Only relief. The quest was over at last, the mystery was solved. 'You're a brilliant journalist.'

The cubicle door opened, and a girl with long hair and a short skirt came out. She looked flushed and embarrassed. She was holding a mobile phone at arm's length between a finger and a thumb. She grimaced as she dropped it into a basin and turned the tap on, running water over it. She squirted liquid soap into her hands and washed them vigorously. She looked at me, then she looked at Becky. 'All right, babes?'

Becky nodded and grunted, intent on her lipstick.

'I couldn't call the police,' the other girl said sheepishly. 'It doesn't work. Might work, once it's dried out... Sorry...'

'Doesn't matter.' Becky rolled her lips together, nodded at her reflection, and put the lip-stick away.

The other girl grabbed a handful of paper towels to dry her hands and her phone, and turned to go. But then she paused, and squinted at me. 'Here, haven't I seen you at the Ellerby? Coming and going all the time. You live there or something?'

I blinked, and looked quickly away, but looking away I caught Becky's eye, and she must have seen my alarm and panic. 'The Ellerby?' I said. 'What's that?'

'A bar, just up the road, up towards Hoxton. My boyfriend works there of an evening. He's a musician, but he pulls pints to make ends meet. I'm there all the time.' She peered closely at me. 'I'm sure I've seen you there.'

I shook my head. 'Must be someone else.'

She shrugged, unconvinced, then left.

Becky was staring at me. She folded her arms and leant back against the basin. 'Did you kill James Hobson?'

I shook my head. 'No. I didn't. And the police will know who did, soon enough.'

'But the police are still after you?'

I nodded.

'Well, if you don't want to be caught, you'd better clear off pretty quickly. Because someone in the office is bound to have called them, and they'll be here any moment.'

She was right. Shit, I had to get out of there. 'I'm sorry, Becky, I didn't mean to frighten you…'

'Go! Quickly! And don't go back to the Ellerby, if Steph was right. Because she's bound to tell the police about it.'

I left only just in time. A police car – lights flashing, siren screaming – came roaring past me just as I came out onto Shoreditch High Street.

*

I took a bus from Shoreditch to Islington. I got off at the Green and walked up the Essex Road until I found the side-street I was after. The side-street where the Art Crash Express caravanserai had been parked on the night of James Hobson's death.

It looked so different. I hardly recognised it. There was the kids' playground on one side, and the office-block on the other, and further down the low terrace of little brick-built houses opposite the high-rise concrete council estate. But in the daylight it could have been a different street altogether. I had to check the name to make sure I'd got the right one. There were a few cars parked there, but it seemed strangely empty without that long row of lorries and coaches and caravans stretching its whole length. It was still a very quiet street – there was no traffic, and the pavement was bare apart from a woman walking a dog, some schoolchildren ambling home and a couple of hoodies on bicycles hanging around the playground gates. But what little sounds there were – kids calling from the swings and roundabouts, the woman urging the dog along, the hoodies mumbling obscenities at each other – overwhelmed the memory of that night's silence.

This was where James Hobson had died. He had been murdered right here, but there was nothing about this normal, ordinary, quiet London backstreet to suggest that anything so dramatic, sordid, terrible and tragic had ever occurred here. It had happened so recently, too; but already all traces of it had completely disappeared. No detectives peering at the gutter though magnifying glasses searching for clues, no scene-of-crime police tape fluttering from lamp-posts. Wait... what was that? There was a pile of what I had thought was garbage waiting for the dustmen at the side of the road just where it passed the playground and came up to the terrace of houses. But as I approached I could see that it was in fact a heap of offerings to the dead heart-throb. Mostly flowers in cellophane wrapping, already wilting and decayed; but also, bizarrely, teddy-bears, dolls and many photos of Hobson cut out of magazines and stuck on home-made heart-shaped cardboard mounts. There were cards with messages on them, too. I bent down to read them. Most of them were illegible, the ink running, the paper curled and torn and soggy. All were written in curly, feminine, adolescent scripts. I managed to decipher a few of them. 'Luv u Jamie.' 'My hart is broke Jamie see u in hevan.' 'Why? Who did this hartless scum I hate them they will rot in hell.' 'Good bye Jamie God bless you were great.' 'Come back Jamie I can't live without you.'

I stood up. I walked on, past the little terrace which I supposed had been standing in for Navarino Row in the movie. They were ordinary, typical, brick-built, flat-fronted, nineteenth-century London houses, like Navarino Row. But this wasn't Navarino Row. Once again I was struck by the pathetic absurdity, the silliness, of the business Hobson represented. Make-believe. That's all it was. A child's game. And yet grown-ups were prepared to invest so much time and effort and expense in it. It was absurd. They had filled this street with buses to take the cast and film crew to and fro, catering vans to feed them, trailers to pamper them, lorries stacked with tools and equipment, mobile generators to power them. The pavements had been thick with a milling host of runners and assistants, actors and extras, camera-men and directors, make-up artists and costume people. All in the service of some sort of fantasy. And now it was all gone, a mobile village which had disappeared into thin air as if it too had been a fantasy.

I walked past the terrace, looking keenly around. I'd hoped that going back there would trigger more memories, bring back up to the surface things that I'd forgotten or was subconsciously reluctant to remember. What had I done here that night? What had I seen? What had changed my mind? How had I disposed of the Russian's handgun? But there was nothing. In fact, the opposite seemed to be happening; those memories which I had been able to recall – the street-lighting, the long line of parked vehicles, the hum of the generators – seemed to be fading, until I wasn't sure that they were memories at all, rather than just tricks of the imagination. Was I mistaken about the whole thing? Had I even been there at all that night? Was it all just a delusion?

I turned and walked slowly back up the street. Concentrate, I told myself. Think. Remember. Had I seen Hobson's two visitors arriving? Had I seen them fleeing in panic? Had I seen the girl's hurried departure? Had I seen

335

Gary creeping away? Had I heard voices raised in anger? The cries and crashes of violent struggle? A gunshot? I stopped, and leaned against a lamp-post, and closed my eyes. I could see all those things, I could hear them, I could imagine them all so clearly and vividly. But that wasn't to say they were memories. No, it was just my imagination.

I opened my eyes. I sighed and walked on, back towards the Essex Road. I shook my head. It didn't matter. None of it mattered. Whatever I had done that night, I hadn't killed James Hobson. However much I might have wanted to kill him, whatever had made me change my mind, it was all irrelevant. I didn't do it. I hadn't killed him.

It was over. I knew who had killed James Hobson. And I knew who had put the police onto me. I had done what I had come back to London to do. There was no need to hide from the police any more. I could give myself up. They would know that I hadn't killed Hobson. I could go home. I could go back to Helen and Elizabeth and Richard.

But could I? I had written those letters to Hobson – death threats – surely I could be arrested and tried for that? And the attacks on Jutting's work – breaking and entering, criminal damage. I would go to prison for that.

I stopped and stared at the traffic thundering up and down the Essex Road. Would I be on the run from the police forever? Would I never be able to go back to that cottage under the hill? Would I never be a husband to Helen again, a father to Elizabeth and Richard?

The buses and cars and motorbikes rushing to and fro tore at my sight. The exhaust and diesel fumes made me feel sick. The roar of the traffic hammered at my ears. I knew I couldn't go on like this. I had to give myself up. I would surrender to the police, I would stand trial, I would go to prison, but some day, in a year's time, or five years, or ten years, I would be free. I would return to Helen and Richard and Elizabeth and it would all be over.

Helen. Who now knew everything about me. Everything I'd been hiding from her for years. Whose trust and respect and affection I must have lost forever. How could she trust me now, knowing that I had been deceiving her ever since we'd met? How could she respect me now, knowing who and what I really was? How could she love me now? No wonder she had betrayed me to the police, to Dr Allen. She wanted me locked up, she wanted me out of the way. It wasn't a betrayal. It was simply the right, the sensible thing to do. It was what I deserved. She didn't want me back. I knew then that there would be no return to the cottage. Helen, Liz, Richard, I had lost them all.

I started to cry. The euphoria of finding out that I hadn't killed James Hobson, that my friends hadn't set the police on me, that my nightmare quest was over, disappeared in an instant. What did any of it matter, if it had cost me everything that had made life worthwhile? I could hear someone laughing at me. I turned round, but I was alone in that quiet street, in the late afternoon, with the light fading. Then I recognised that laughter, and knew it was a just memory. It was the memory of Harry Jutting laughing at me, laughing at me for crying when I'd broken down in front of him once in that shared studio by the canal. Harry Jutting. Would he never be done with me? He had destroyed my life once already. I had rebuilt it, only to have him reach out from the grave and destroy it once again. Suddenly, anger and hatred choked my tears off and I wasn't crying any more. No, we hadn't finished with each other yet. He was laughing now, but if I could remain at liberty for one more day then I would have the last laugh.

I would finish it, once and for all. I felt a cold, hard determination. I knew what I had to do.

I came out onto the Essex Road again, past the corner by the boarded-up shop where I'd left my motorbike that night. Parked in the dark shadows against the wall where the pavement widened. The night had seemed very quiet when I'd cut off the engine.

I stopped, my mind whirling. I'd had no recollection of where or when I'd left my bike until that moment. At last, a fresh memory, an authentic memory!

I stared at that spot on the pavement. Yes. I could remember pulling it back onto its stand, dismounting, walking away with the Russian's revolver cold and heavy in my right hand. Shivering with the chill of the night and the excitement, the anticipation… And what else? What else could I remember? Nothing. Except returning to the bike who knows how many minutes or hours later? Yes. It was still dark, still cold, and I was still shivering. But only with the cold now. No excitement, no adrenalin, nothing. Just a tired dullness, a sense of disappointment, anti-climax, even of relief. The revolver was still in my hand – unused, I was sure of that – I'd been glad to dump the thing back into the pannier on the bike's rear wheel, so cold and heavy was it that it was painful to hold. Yes, I remembered that. I'd dropped it into the left-hand pannier.

The gun… the pannier… Was that where it was? Had it been there all this time? Was it still there?

My heart was pounding. I had to get back to the Ellerby. The bike was in the little car-park behind the pub. I had to get back and see if the weapon was still there. Would the police be there? Almost certainly. But I wasn't going to give myself up. Not yet. There was one more thing to do while I was still here and still free. One more thing, one more day, and then it wouldn't matter what happened to me.

I hadn't used my bike since arriving in London. I'd left it in the car park behind the Ellerby and travelled everywhere by tube or bus. There were CCTV cameras on every street in central London, and I didn't want them picking up my bike's registration number and tracking me wherever I went. The police would have grabbed me before I'd even had the chance to find a parking meter.

Were the police now waiting for me at the Ellerby? I had to believe they were; that girl at 'Forwards Backwards' must have made sure of that. They'd have a car outside, watching the street. And someone inside, in the bar, checking out everyone who came in. Perhaps even someone in my room itself, waiting for me there. But were they also watching my bike outside? Did they even know it was there?

There were two ways to the little car park: down the alleyway at the side of the pub, off Navarino Row; or through the pub and out of its back door. I wasn't going to go into the pub; that would be playing straight into their hands. So it would have to be down the alley.

I wasn't going to approach along the High Street, from the bus stops and the underground station; that was too obvious, it was what they must be expecting. So I got off the bus half a mile early, and cut down to the canal, along the towpath, then up through the playing fields and past the high-rise council estate to the bottom of Navarino Row.

I stopped half-way up the street and forced myself to take a dozen or so deep breaths, trying to calm myself down. I took the bike keys out of my pocket. My helmet and leathers were in my room, so there was no chance of just jumping on the bike and roaring away. If I only had my helmet… Was it worth trying to get into my room to collect it? No. No way. Besides, I didn't need my bike, just what was in its pannier. What I thought, what I hoped, was in the pannier. Just get in there as fast as you can, take them by surprise if they're waiting for you, unlock the pannier, grab what's inside, get out as fast as you can.

Not much of a plan.

It was getting dark. That was good. I tried to keep out of the street-lighting as I approached the pub on the corner. Sure enough there was a car parked opposite it, just off the high street. It was an ordinary dark blue or black hatchback. Two men sitting in the front seats. Inconspicuous enough, though it was parked on a double-yellow line. Well, nothing I can do about them.

I kept my head down and quickened my pace as I approached the alley. I was almost running by the time I came up to it. I heard the engine of the waiting car start up. Then I was into the alley and sprinting its short length. The echo of my footsteps rang out urgently between the high, blank brick walls of the pub on one hand and of the first house in Navarino Row on the other. Even before I'd reached the end I heard the car and saw the beam of its headlights sweep past and light up the tall wooden fence ahead. The car was turning into the alley, behind me, cutting me off.

The alley turned a corner into the little courtyard car-park behind the pub. The bike was still there! I ran up to it and crouched down to the rear wheel, the keys in my hand. I tried to get the key into the lock of the left pannier, but my hand was shaking too much. I heard the back door of the pub open. Someone came rushing out. Then the car-park was flooded by car headlamps as the hatchback turned the corner and came to a halt only a yard or two away. The sound of its motor filled the yard, its choking exhaust filled my throat.

'Stop! Police! Don't move!'

I glanced up at the man who had just come out of the pub. Tough-looking character. Not tall, but bulky. Solid. Scruffy jeans, leather jacket, dark beard. His face was distorted with the stress of excitement and fear and aggression. His mouth was still open from shouting, his brows were creased and his eyes were narrowed. One hand was reaching out to me, the other was reaching inside his jacket.

I turned back to the lock. My breath was rattling in and out between my teeth, my heart was pounding, but my hand was now steady. It slid the key into the lock. The key turned. The pannier fell open.

'Hands up! Stand up slowly!'

I ignored the order. Inside the pannier was a brown hessian shopping bag. Bag for life. Frayed and battered but still in service. Faded black lettering printed on its side which I couldn't read but knew what it said. Forrester's Farm Shop. I reached out and picket it up. It was heavy, inert, reluctant to shift, stretching under the weight of its contents then shifting and twisting with a clinking metallic rattle as I swung it up and out of the pannier. I stood up.

The bearded man hadn't moved. He stood with his feet wide apart, blocking the way through to the pub. His left hand was still stretched out towards me, his right was still inside his jacket. He was blinking rapidly. He took a deep breath, a sergeant-major on the parade ground about to bellow orders. 'Drop the bag! Put your hands up!'

I turned and looked behind me. The car head-lights were dazzling, I couldn't see much. The car was blocking the other exit, its doors open. Its motor was still running.

'Drop the bag!'

They knew they had me trapped. They were in front of me and behind me. On my left was the brick wall of the pub, on my right was a tall and rickety wooden fence,

341

hung with plant pots and at least twelve feet high. They knew I had to do what they ordered. They weren't going to rush me. They had the initiative. Time was on their side.

I didn't drop the bag. I didn't put my hands up. Without thinking, without making a decision, I sprang up that rickety wooden fence. I was as surprised as they were. It must have been over twice my height, but in seconds I was up it and astride it. I've no idea how I did it. I remember a dustbin crashing over, a big plastic rainwater butt rocking and glugging, plant pots flying. A frantic, scrambling, scrabbling vertical take-off, the wooden posts and planks swaying and creaking and groaning under my weight. A glimpse of stunned, upturned faces below me – three policemen now, strangely foreshortened, gathered around my abandoned bike, glaring up at me with expressions of shock and anger and alarm, deep shadows and harsh car headlights casting the whole scene in dramatic chiaroscuro – then I was over on the other side, tumbling down into the darkness of the neighbouring backyard.

I landed awkwardly, off-balance. One foot, then an elbow, then a shoulder hitting a hard surface. I rolled over on gritty paving-stones and stood up. Amazingly I still had the bag-for-life and its freight-for-death in my hand. I could hear the policemen shouting and yelling, the rumble of their car's engine, the wooden fence banging as it shuddered to and fro in my wake. I glanced around. A neat patio, a table and chairs, steps leading up to a rear door. Someone was standing in the doorway, the light behind them. A young man. White shirt, red tie, smoking. He was staring at me, frozen, mouth open, cigarette arrested half way to his lips. I ran to the steps, up the steps. The man shrank away, his mouth open but nothing coming out. I pushed past him and sprinted down the short passage beyond. I burst through a doorway and out

342

into a brightly-lit office. Of course, the estate agents next to the pub. I could see the street through the big windows on the other side of the office, a couple out there on the pavement peering in at the displayed details. The street door… I made for it as fast as I could. I passed a young man sitting at a table in shirt-sleeves and tie looking up at me in dumb amazement. A girl in a neat white blouse at another table called out something wordless and indignant and half-rose to her feet. Then I had the door open and I was out on the street.

I ran as fast as I could. Blind, panic-stricken, out of control. There were only two imperatives – get away, and don't let go of the bag. I had the heavy bundle gripped tight in my right hand, tucked under my elbow like a rugby ball, pressed hard to my ribs. I was like a three-quarter charging for the try-line. Bodies on the pavement lurched into view. I dodged some, I crashed into others. There were shouts of protest, curses, grabbing hands which I managed to shrug off, pushing hands which I managed to slip past. 'Bus!' I gasped. I'm not on the run, I'm not a fugitive, the police aren't chasing me, I just want to catch that bus… 'Bus!' I pleaded. And lo and behold there was a bus, just ahead, towering big and red above the slow traffic, lumbering towards a stop a mere hundred yards away.

I ran faster. The bus made the stop. It pulled in, disgorged passengers, began to swallow others. Faster. Only three waiting to get on now. Only two. Only one. Then the last one was aboard, and the doors…were they closing? But one last spurt and I was there, leaping on board just as the doors hissed and began to close.

The bus pulled away from the pavement. I stood there in the aisle, lungs heaving, gasping for breath, hot sweat turning cold as it ran down my face and chest and back and soaked into my shirt. I was shaking and trembling, I

343

felt sick from the exertion, but frozen with amazement and disbelief. Had I got away? Was I clear and free? I moved along the aisle towards the rear of the bus, bending down to peer out of the window, scanning the pavement and road behind for signs of pursuit. But there weren't any. No screaming sirens, flashing lights, racing cars, screaming tyres. No sprinting figures, angry shouts or urgent gestures. Just an ordinary, relatively calm, moderately busy London high street. I had left the police behind. I had escaped.

*

I got off the bus at Old Street. I went down into the underground station, walked right through it and came back up to the surface on the south side of the roundabout. Crowds were streaming up from the City, heading home after another day in the office. I could lose myself in them for the next two or three hours, and then the City would become the ghost town it was every night, just the place to hide out in and wait for tomorrow.

Down past Moorgate I walked. It was like passing through some great heaving ocean. The roads were full of taxis and couriers' vans, the pavements were packed with the secretaries and bankers and lawyers and analysts hurrying to or from meetings or simply heading for buses and underground and main-line stations to take them home at the end of the day. All around, massive steel and glass buildings were being torn down or put up by armies in hard hats and yellow jackets riding herds of roaring machines. I turned west along Cheapside and headed for St Paul's. I stopped when I came to the Millennium footbridge and looked south across the river at the great black fortress of Tate Modern, its dark tower thrusting up into the sky like a challenge at the far end of the bridge.

I went into a café by Saint Paul's. I headed for the gent's toilets and found a free cubicle and locked the door and sat down on the toilet seat. I lifted the hessian bag onto my lap. I opened it and peered inside. There it was, the Russian's handgun. Its dull metal caught the light. It glittered and winked at me, coming to life in the shadows at the bottom of the bag like a snake or reptile warmed by stray sun-beams.

So it had been there all this time, wrapped in the bag and lying in the bottom of the motorcycle pannier, ever since that night when I had destroyed Dirty Flirt and James Hobson had been killed.

I reached into the bag and took hold of it. I lifted it out of the bag and stared at it. I checked the ammunition. The magazine was full. It had not been fired, after all, not since that thug had loaded it and crept downstairs to confront me with it. I put it back into the bag, stood up, unlocked the door and walked out of the gents, the bag heavy in my left hand.

I sat in the café and drank cup after cup of tea, the Hessian bag on the floor between my feet. My hands were stinging. The scramble over the wooden fence had left them full of splinters, and the drop down into the next yard had grazed the skin off them. My left shoulder and elbow and knee were beginning to ache. I must have landed on them. They felt bruised and cut. There was a hole torn in one sleeve of my jacket, another in one leg of my jeans. But these aches and pains were nothing compared to the realisation that Helen… The idea that I'd lost her, it was a cold, dull, unbearable agony. I had to talk to her, even if we never saw each other again. I had to say sorry, apologise for everything. To say that I forgave her for betraying me, that she hadn't really betrayed me at all. I had to tell her that I understood that she was only doing what she felt she had to do, what she felt was right.

Whatever happened tomorrow, I had to speak to her tonight, before it was too late.

There was a pay-phone at the back of the café. I pumped coins into it and rang the number of the cottage. I listened to the dialling tone and imagined the phone ringing from room to room, perhaps even sending a tinny echo to pierce the darkness in the lane outside and disturb the cows grazing in the moonlight on the marsh at the back. It rang and rang. Helen wasn't there. Nobody was there. The place was empty.

She must still be in town, with Dr Allen and the police, trying to find me. But where were the children? Who was looking after them? Don't panic. Think clearly. What would Helen have arranged for them? Yes. Of course. They must be with Frank and Mary, in the farm at the end of the lane. Phone them. Phone the farm.

I hesitated. Would Frank and Mary talk to me? Would they let me talk to Liz and Richard? How much did they know? They had to know I was on the run from the police, at least, even if they didn't know any more than that. What had the police said to them? What had Helen told them? Had they been given instructions? How would they react to my call? Would they refuse to take it?

I thought about Liz and Richard with Fred and Mary's children. Andrew and Kylie, so sullen, so bored, their aggression and hostility fed and encouraged by the make-believe of television and computers and make-up and gangster music. A world I had been protecting Liz and Richard from. A world Liz and Richard were now sharing with them.

I rang the farm's number. I was prepared to wait, expecting the dialling tone to ring and ring, unanswered in another empty house. But it was answered almost straight away.

'Hello?' It was Mary. 'Hello?'

I hesitated. I couldn't speak. I felt as if I'd been taken by surprise, as if I was being forced into something I wasn't ready for. 'Mary' I managed. 'Mary, it's me… Will…'

She gasped. 'Will!'

'Are the children with you, Mary? Liz and Richard? How are they? Are they… are they all right?'

'They're fine, Will. But you… are you OK?'

'Listen, Mary, is Liz still awake? Could I speak to her?'

'Right. I'll go and get her. She's just brushing her teeth.'

I waited. Then there was the rattle of the receiver being picked up again and changing from hand to hand.

'Daddy!' It was Lizzie. The surprise and delight in her voice squeezed the breath from my lungs, brought tears to my eyes. I thought I was going to cry again.

'Hello, Lizzy.'

'Where are you?'

'I'm in town, Lizzie. In London.'

'Are you with mummy?'

'No, not at the moment.'

'When are you coming home?'

I paused, swallowing. What could I say? 'Soon, Lizzie. But listen, how are you? Are you looking after Richard? Are you both being good for Mary and Frank?'

'Of course we are, Daddy. Sometimes Richard cries a lot, but nobody seems to mind. He's fast asleep now, he's just had his bottle. I gave it to him.'

'Well done, Lizzie. How are you getting on with Kylie and Andy?'

'Ok. But they watch television all the time.'

'Don't you watch television with them?'

'No. It's noisy and boring. I help Mrs Mary with the chickens, and Mr Frank with the cows. He's showing me how to do the milking. It's really fun, all wet and squirty, and the cows try and stand on your feet and kick the

347

bucket over. But I think they like it. I'm sure they like it better than the machine. And the chickens are really silly, they run all over the place, squawking and fussing, even if you're not chasing them.'

'Perhaps they want you to chase them. Perhaps they think it's a game.'

'No, Daddy, they're just silly and frightened.' She sounded a bit sad for a moment. 'I don't think the chickens like me.'

I closed my eyes. My daughter. My serious daughter. Too serious, just like her father. I wished Helen was there. I wished we were all talking together. What would Helen say? She'd make a joke, she'd make Liz laugh. 'That's because they can see your foxy ears, sticking up all big and red and furry. You'd better wear a hat when you feed them, cover your ears up.'

'I'm not a fox, daddy! You're the fox! You are!' She was laughing and excited now. I felt a bit guilty and sorry for Mary, getting Liz worked up just before she was trying to get her to bed.

'Ok, Lizzy. Are you ready for bed?'

'Yes. I've got my pyjamas on. The ones with the stars. Mrs Mary says she's going to read me a story.'

'All right, Lizzie. It's been lovely talking to you, but you sleep tight now, sweetheart.'

'Night night, Daddy. I can't wait for you and mummy to come home.'

'Sweet dreams, Lizzie. Give Richard a kiss from me.'

There was silence, and then Mary was on the line again. 'Will? You look after yourself now, Will.' She sounded anxious and concerned. 'Do you hear? You be careful now. We're all thinking about you. We're all praying for you.'

'Thanks, Mary. And thank you for looking after Richard and Liz. She sounds very well, very happy. Thank you.'

'It's nothing, they're a pleasure to look after. And we're only too glad to do what we can for you and Helen, you two have always been ready to help us whenever we've needed it. Oh, here's Frank. I think he wants a word, too.'

The phone changed hands again. 'Will, Will, can you hear me?' It was Frank. His voice shook. He sounded awkward but determined. He never said much, but there was clearly something he wanted to say now. 'Don't let the buggers grind you down, Will. Do you hear me?'

'Yes, Frank. Thanks.'

'Don't let them get to you, Will. You stay in there, Will. We trust you, mate. We know you're a good man. I don't know what's going on, but we trust you. All right?'

I swallowed hard. 'Thanks, Frank. I appreciate it.'

'All right. You look after yourself, now. And don't worry about the kids. They're fine. Mary's taking good care of them.'

'Ok, Frank.'

'Good bye, Will. God bless.'

When the café closed, I walked along to Cannon Street and found a fast-food joint and sat down with a baked potato. I tried to gather heat for the night ahead like some sort of flesh-and-blood storage heater. I sat there drinking coffee until the place closed, and then I walked east along the river and cut up a narrow alleyway just before the Tower came in sight. I turned into the entrance to the ruins of St Dunstan in the East. The metal gate was locked for the night, but I climbed over it easily enough. The ruins were deserted. I went into the garden within the roofless medieval shell and sat down on a bench beneath Wren's indestructible tower.

349

It was a quiet and secluded place. I could feel the City emptying around me. The darkness thickened, the distant roar of crowds and traffic gradually faded. The towering office blocks were shutting down for the night. The building sites were coming to a halt, diggers and cranes and hard-hats abandoned for the next twelve hours. Shops closing, cafes closing, pubs draining the last dregs of life and energy in off the streets. I lay back on the bench, the bag clasped to my stomach. I was tired, I wanted to sleep but knew I wouldn't be able to, cold and uncomfortable as the night was sure to be. But it didn't matter. I didn't have to sleep. I just had to get through the night, stay free for the next twelve hours. And then I would do what I had to do.

Something – that something, whatever it was, the final mystery, the last monster waiting to be unmasked, which since yesterday I had sensed hiding round the corner, lurking in the shadows – I could now feel it shifting, getting ready to move, preparing to come out into plain sight, to come out from behind the corner, from beneath the shadows. And I was ready to confront it, I was marching towards it, the torch was in my hands, its powerful beam was about to be switched on, I was about to shine it into the dark heart of the matter. And then there'd be no hiding place left for it anywhere in the whole world.

Chapter Sixteen

I was waiting outside a chemist's in Cheapside when it opened at eight-thirty the next morning.

I bought a pair of scissors, some shaving cream, a razor and a bar of soap. I was so cold and tired I could hardly move. My hands were shaking so much I knew I wouldn't be able to hold the scissors or the razor, let alone use them. I had to get warm, fuel myself up, gather strength for the task ahead.

I went to a café a few doors away and had a breakfast of coffee and porridge and toast. The Gents in the café was down some stairs at the back, in the basement. I stood in front of the cracked mirror, beneath the flickering strip-lighting, and hacked at my long hair with the new scissors. My hands were still shaking with the cold, but now I could at least hold the scissors and use them. I cut and cut until it was cropped so short that I could see my scalp through it. Then I took the scissors to my beard and trimmed it as close to my cheeks and chin and jaws as I could. I made a plug from a wad of toilet paper and filled a basin with warm water and washed my face and rubbed shaving cream into the stubble and shaved thoroughly and carefully. I was planning to shave my head as well, but my hands weren't steady enough. A man with a bleeding scalp would attract the kind of attention I was trying to avoid.

They would be on the look-out for a man with a beard and long hair. But I was no longer a man with a beard and long hair.

I looked at myself in the mirror. I barely recognised the man I saw there. I'd had a beard for ten years. I couldn't remember the last time I'd had a haircut. The shape of my head was like a new discovery. My face - its angles, the size and dimension of its features – seemed utterly changed, transformed rather than simply revealed. It was a wild-looking face. Thin and lined with stress and exhaustion and the cold. Completely naked but for the patchy, tufty crew-cut. The man in the mirror could have been an escaped convict from a nineteenth-century prison-hulk.

There wasn't much else I could do to transform my appearance. I didn't have a change of clothes. The hessian bag-for-life – I could get rid of that. I took the weapon out – it was colder and heavier than ever - and put it in the plastic bag from the pharmacy. I threw the hessian bag into the rubbish bin along with the scissors, soap, shaving cream and razor.

The City streets were at their busiest. The pavements were packed with crowds swarming in for another day in the office. I pushed my way through them down to Saint Paul's. I went round its east end and crossed the road to the steps leading down to the Millennium Bridge.

I looked out across the bridge. It was crowded with pedestrians. Smartly-dressed City workers, urgent and purposeful, all moving in the same direction, all hurrying towards me, a multitude flowing away from the south bank where the dark tower of Tate Modern loomed up from the horizon behind them. It was like some sort of apocalyptic vision, crowds fleeing the site of a terrible and epic disaster, desperate to make the safety of Saint Paul's and the north bank. A disaster which had taken place in the vicinity of that brooding, black building; a disaster over which the building itself presided.

And I was having to go in the opposite direction, away from safety, towards the disaster, into its very heart. Alone.

Was I ready for this? Was I up to it? I felt cold and tired and hungry. I had not slept all night. Day had broken, but the dark hours' chill was still frozen inside me like ice in my bones. The café breakfast had done little to

352

shift my exhaustion. I felt strange. Light-headed and heavy-bodied. My thoughts and my vision were like crystal, sharp and clear, but fragile, easily broken. They were threatening to break way from my body, trying to rush ahead over the river, trying to drag my slow, dull limbs along behind them.

Could I do it? Yes. It had to be done. And it had to be done today.

I walked down the steps and onto the bridge. The crowd flowed around me, past me, and I had to push against it and through it. It was like fighting against a powerful tide. The sky overhead was heavy and overcast, white cloud shading to grey shading to an ominous black. The river underneath was high and fast-moving, the water dark and troubled, the waves high-crested and deep-troughed. The sound of many feet trampling the bridge rang out like hammers striking a giant alarm bell. The blank black walls of Tate Modern rose bigger and higher as I approached. The bridge was channelling me straight towards it like some sort of sacred processional avenue.

The police were sure to be waiting for me there. In the whole of this vast city, that was the one place where they knew I would be found, sooner or later. I could imagine them there, hiding behind the scenes in their black para-military uniforms with their terrifying science-fiction weaponry at the ready. Were Helen and Dr Allen there with them? I was sure they were. I could imagine them all there, not just the psychiatrist and my wife, but also Gary and Stella, Becky and even Steve Smith, ready and waiting for me somewhere inside that windowless building ahead, like an audience in a dark theatre waiting for the performance to start. Yes, and Harry Jutting was there too, even him; that dark and sinister figure in the glass case in the middle of that white-washed room, that body which was dead but also alive, that is Harry Jutting, obstinately

353

and ostentatiously displaying his exhumed remains, refusing to go back into the dark earth where he belongs. An egomaniac and exhibitionist even in death. If everyone else is in the audience, he is on stage, centre-stage, waiting for me to come out of the wings and confront him with my opening lines.

I felt a moment of fear. Harry Jutting was much bigger than me, much stronger than me. And how could I fight someone who was already dead but who refused to die? Then I felt the plastic bag hanging heavy in my right hand, and I felt brave and reassured. I was going to finish Harry Jutting off once and for all. I was going to put him in his grave and this time he wasn't going to come back.

*

I hadn't felt any fear that night ten years ago. I'd waited hours in the darkness, my heart so full of hatred that there'd been no room for fear. No – there had been fear – I'd been afraid that I wouldn't catch him, that he wouldn't come home that night.

It had been easy enough to escape from the hospital. After all, it wasn't a prison or a police cell. Just a psychiatric unit supposedly made secure by a twenty-four hour police presence, a few extra CCTV cameras and a week's training course for the nursing staff. There were no insurmountable obstacles for someone of reasonable intelligence and great determination. Going mad doesn't mean you become stupid.

It was only a week after I'd been arrested for shooting at Jutting in the gallery. I'd spent a few nights in a police cell, then they'd transferred me to the hospital pending my trial. The days were busy with psychiatric tests and assessments, but the nights were quiet. Lights out at ten o'clock, and after midnight you could never find a nurse on the ward. They'd all be huddled together in their office, giggling and gossiping and drinking coffee and flirting with the hunky policemen who were supposed to be guarding the place. Somewhere no doubt there were security guards scanning CCTV images, but those men weren't machines and I guessed they couldn't watch all of the screens all of the time. Besides, such cameras aren't really there to prevent things from happening, but to record them so that there are clues and evidence for the investigation after the event. Chances are they wouldn't spot me sneaking out, and they wouldn't search the footage later to see if I had indeed sneaked out unless my absence was noted, and as long as I got back in time there was little chance of that.

I knew I had to seize my chance while I could. They could send me to prison on remand once the tests and assessments were completed; they would certainly send me to prison or to a proper secure psychiatric institution once they'd tried me and found me guilty.

So that night, at five minutes past midnight, I'd got out of bed and put on my dressing gown and slippers. I'd put two spare pillows under my quilt to look like a sleeping body. I'd walked out of the ward and across the corridor to the toilets. I'd seen no-one, but I could hear a low buzz of laughter and chatter coming from the sister's office along the corridor. I'd waited a moment or two in the toilets to gather my courage and calm my racing heart-beat and wild breathing. Then I'd walked out. Out of the toilets, along the corridor, down the stairs. Out of the hospital.

It had been easy. I'd walked calmly and unhurriedly – but purposefully – along the quiet passages and through the near-empty hallways of that labyrinthine institution, hands in pockets, nodding a confident 'goodnight' to the few cleaners and nurses and receptionists I'd passed. No one had challenged me. No one had tried to stop me. The only real obstacle had been the door between the corridor outside my ward and the staircase. You could unlock it only by punching a security code into the panel of buttons beside it. But the nurses who took me to and from the ward for meetings with psychiatrists and policemen were careless. Their attempts to hide the panel from me while they keyed in the code were usually pretty hopeless. The code changed every day – my one worry had been that it changed at midnight, but the previous day's code got me through OK, so it must have changed when duties started again each morning.

The hospital was in central London. It had taken me less than an hour to walk back east to the squat. In my pyjamas and slippers and dressing-gown. On the streets at half-past midnight. And no-one had batted an eye-lid at me. What a city.

I got into the squat through the window in my room. None of the sashes in the house were ever locked, even the one or two that had functioning locks on them. Why should they be? It was a squat! I grabbed what I needed, pulled a pair of jeans on over my pyjama bottoms, a sweater over my pyjama top, put the dressing-gown back on like an overcoat – it had been very cold in the early hours – and climbed back out through the window. Then I'd got on my bike and cycled south through the darkness, over Tower Bridge and along the river to the converted waterfront warehouse where Harry Jutting lived. Or rather, the impostor who called himself Harry Jutting lived, as my delusions insisted. And that was the time when my delusions were at their strongest. I was Harry Jutting, of course, and I couldn't understand why nobody believed me, but I had a good idea it was all the impostor's fault. After all, everything else was. Gary's imprisonment. Stella's suicide attempt. The disappearance of my sketchbooks. The hi-jacking of my work. The strange things that were going on in my head. Things that I wasn't aware of most of the time. And even when I was aware of them I had no idea what they were.

I hated him. He was a bastard, and at last he was going to pay for it all.

I got there just after one-thirty. He wasn't in. I buzzed up to his apartment two or three times, but there was no answer. I hadn't really expected him to be in, I knew the way he lived. I would just have to wait for his return. But first I had to get into the building. I buzzed a number at random. No answer. I buzzed another number. Hello? Hello? Who's there? The voice on the intercom sounded distant and tinny, it could have been coming from a spaceship on the other side of the universe. 'Oh, hello, I'm really sorry to bother you. It's me, John, from flat 37. I've lost my fob. Could you buzz the door open for me, please?' No way. Nothing doing. But I persevered, and another three attempts found someone careless enough to buzz me in.

I crossed the lobby to the lift. Out of bounds – security fob needed. But beside the lift were some fire-doors, and through the fire-doors was a stair-well. Up I went, step by step, one flight after another, ever closer to my goal. By the time I reached the top I was light-headed and dizzy with the exertion and the excitement and the anticipation. I staggered across the landing and pushed through another set of fire-doors into a small lobby. There were the lift doors, and there, opposite them, was Harry Jutting's front door.

I withdrew to the landing at the top of the stairs and settled down to wait. The lights flickered off – they were movement-sensitive – and left me in darkness. I sat on the floor with my back against the wall separating the lift-shaft from the stair-well. I couldn't see the lobby through the glass panels in the top half of the fire-doors. But I'd know when Jutting was on his way. I'd feel and hear the lift rising as he approached, and I'd see the lights flicker on in the lobby when he arrived.

Two o'clock came and went. Three o'clock. What if he was going to be out all night? How long could I afford to wait? I reckoned I had to be back in my hospital bed by six o'clock if my absence wasn't to be discovered. So I had to be out of there by five at the latest, come what may. What if he wasn't alone when he returned? What if he had a girl with him, or a crowd of mates?

It was just before four o'clock when I heard the whining and grinding of the rising lift and felt the shuddering vibrations of its ascent. My heart was suddenly in my mouth. Was it going to stop on the first floor? The second? The third? No. It was coming all the way up. I heard it come to a clanking halt on the other side of the wall. I heard the doors slide open. I saw the lights come on in the lobby as someone stepped out of the lift. I stood up slowly. I peered into the lobby through the glass panels in the fire-doors.

It was Harry Jutting. And he was on his own.

He had his back towards me. He was heading for his front door, his characteristic swagger unmistakeable even though it was modified by a stumbling and staggering which suggested tiredness or intoxication. He looked huge, even bigger than ever. He seemed to fill the whole of that little lobby. He was wearing a baseball cap, and fumbling in the pockets of his jeans and battered leather jacket for his keys. He came to his door, leaned lazily against it, pulled out his keys and slid them into the lock.

I waited behind the fire-doors, tense and ready. As soon as I saw his door opening, I threw myself through the swinging fire-doors and across the lobby. I was right behind him as he stepped into his flat; but I couldn't stop myself; the momentum of my rush threw me against him and the two of us tumbled across his threshold together.

'What the f - ?' He thrust me off, somehow managing to stay on his feet. He peered at me, angry and startled. His eyes blazed with aggression and alarm but he seemed to have difficulty focusing them. Then he recognised me, and he laughed, jeering and dismissive. 'What the fuck do you want?'

'What do you think, Harry?'

'God knows what you want, Patrick, bloody lunatic like you.' He slammed the door shut and took his baseball cap off and sent it skimming through the big open-plan space of his apartment without caring where it fell. There he was, Harry Jutting, a big blond gorilla, gross and coarse, strong and fearless, arrogant and careless. In his paint-splashed jeans and his battered leather jacket and his grubby t-shirt, he looked even more like a scaffolder or builder than ever. He started turning on the lights with his big hands, his thick stubby fingers. That absurd apartment sprang up around us, as ridiculous and unreal as a movie-set or an advert or a spread in a life-style magazine. What was he doing in this millionaire's pad, this estate-agent's wet-dream, its wide open spaces so subtly zoned and so dramatically lit, furnished and decorated with such understated elegance by some genius interior designer? He looked more like the guy who had come to fix the plumbing or paint the ceiling than some slim, suave, effete, Italian-suited sophisticate who should have been living there.

He went straight to the fridge in the kitchen area and took out a bottle of beer. He didn't offer me one. He cracked it open and poured half of it down his throat. 'So what is this, Patrick?' He looked me up and down, and laughed again. 'A bloody pyjama party? And what's that in the bag? Present for me? Looks like a bottle. Bring-a-bottle pyjama party? You've got the wrong venue, mate. You've misread the invitation. So you can bugger off. Leave the bottle if it's worth drinking. But bugger off, will you? Because I could do with some kip, I've just been to a real party.'

'Yes,' I said, feeling the weight of the bag in my right hand. 'It is something for you. But it isn't a bottle.' It wasn't a hessian bag for life. It wasn't a chemist's bag. But it was a plastic bag, from a supermarket. Sainsbury's, or Budgens, or something like that.

He yawned. 'I'm not interested, Patrick. Just clear off, will you?' He took another gulp of beer. 'I thought you were locked up in some loony bin somewhere?' He snorted. 'Bloody should be.' He looked at his watch. 'I'll give you thirty seconds to get out of my flat, a minute to get out of the building, then I'm going to call the police. If I don't decide to beat the fucking shit out of you first.'

He was trying to play it cool, but I could tell he was tense and alert, watching me like a hawk. After all, I'd waved a gun at him the last time we'd been face to face, little more than a week ago. I'd threatened his life, I'd shot at him. He was pretending to be chilled and laid-back, but I could see the wariness in his eyes. He wasn't afraid, but he was aware of the danger I represented.

I didn't say anything. I stood there, between the kitchen area and the sitting area, and licked my dry lips.

He reached into his back pocket and pulled out his mobile. 'You're boring me, Patrick. You're annoying me. I thought lunatics were supposed to be entertaining. You know, in the old days, before TV and movies and all that shit, you'd go down to Bedlam and pay a penny to have a good laugh at the loonies? Well, if you're not going to piss off, at least do something funny while we're waiting. Go on, you mad fucker. Give us a laugh. What about a crazy jig? A mad caper? A bit of hilarious gurning? Can you jibber? Can you howl? Come on, Patrick. Call yourself a lunatic? You're letting the side down.'

I didn't move. I glanced around the flat, and my eyes fell on the big unmade bed in the corner beyond the bookcases. 'Is that where you did it to Stella?' The place suddenly felt very hot, as if the heating had been turned full up, and the recessed lighting overhead was suddenly bright and dazzling.

His eyes followed my glance. He shrugged. 'Stella? Yeah. Suppose so.' He scratched his head, an absent-minded ape shifting fleas. 'Just the once, if I remember right.' He didn't sound bothered. He sounded bored, uninterested.

I felt something coming to the boil inside me. 'You promised, remember? In the studio that day, in the summer! You promised me you wouldn't touch her! You promised!'

'Did I?' He frowned at me, puzzled. 'Perhaps I did. But so what? I can screw whoever I want, can't I?'

'Not if they end up in hospital, you can't! Not if you drive them to suicide!'

He laughed, groaning. 'Is it my fault if the stupid bitch gets hysterical? Besides, she didn't kill herself, did she? She's still alive, isn't she? I'm not going to let some drama queen manipulate me into a massive guilt-trip just because I don't want to spend the rest of my life fucking her!' He squinted at me. 'Ah, yes, I remember now. You're in love with her, aren't you? Well, you should thank me for dropping her. For standing aside for you. Why don't you go and hold her hand in hospital and she might fall in love with you, too? Then you could get married and live happily ever after.' He chuckled. 'I could be your best man!'

'You don't feel any guilt at all?'

'Guilt?' He grinned. 'What's that?'

'Guilt! Remorse!'

'No. You've lost me. Don't know what you're talking about.'

'Gary is in prison because you wouldn't lend him any money. You sponge off him for years, and then when he needs your help and you can easily afford to give it to him, you turn your back on him!'

He groaned again. 'Gary? That twat? That loser? He's in prison because he was stupid enough to break the law and get caught! That's nothing to do with me!'

'But he worshipped you! You were his hero! He thought you were god!'

He shrugged, grinning with conceit. 'So do thousands of others, these days.'

'Where are my sketch-books, Harry?' I was shaking. I could feel the weight of the plastic bag jiggling about it my right fist. It was very bright in there, and very dark outside, out in the night beyond those big windows. 'Where are they?'

'Bugger off, Patrick. Your thirty seconds are long gone.'

'How dare you steal them?' The lights out there were flashing at me, the lights of the offices Harry's high windows looked down on. On and off, on and off, some kind of message, urgent, insistent. 'How dare you use them? How dare you!'

'Get out of here, you fucking lunatic.'

'Stella tries to kill herself and ends up in hospital, and you couldn't care less. Gary goes to prison because you wouldn't lend him the money he needed, and you couldn't care less. And me... I... I...'

'Yes, you end up in a loony bin. And no, you're right, I couldn't care less.'

I opened the plastic bag and looked inside. There it was, oiled and gleaming. The handgun, loaded and ready.

When the police caught Gary with that gun in his laptop case, it wasn't the first time he'd run that kind of errand for the Smith Family. He wouldn't have been caught at all if he hadn't been grassed by rivals. He was efficient and reliable, and the Smiths used him whenever they had a weapon to dispose off. Once or twice he brought a gun back to the house to show off, posing as the macho outlaw who knew all about shooters. One of them he even kept for himself, so carefully hidden in the squat that even the police couldn't find it when they searched the place after his arrest. But I knew where it was hidden, and thanks to him showing off I knew how to use it. Strip it, clean it, oil it, reassemble it, load it. Fire it.

I reached into the bag and grasped the piece by its hard, metallic butt. That's when Harry should have moved. That's when anyone with the humility to be afraid would have moved. But Harry was too confident of his own strength and courage, too complacent, too arrogant, too contemptuous of other people to believe that they could ever be any real danger to him. He'd laughed at me when I'd brandished the gun at him before, at the gallery, he'd laughed and jeered. He hadn't run, he hadn't fallen to his knees, he hadn't begged for his life. He'd challenged me to do my worst, he'd called my bluff, and he'd lived to prove himself right. I couldn't possibly be any sort of threat to him. The experience hadn't left any mark on him whatsoever, physically or psychologically. But it was going to be different this time.

I tightened my grip on the gun and lifted it out of the bag.

*

I walked faster and faster across the bridge until I was almost running. I felt an over-powering sense of urgency, as if the dark building ahead was about to close for the day. I could feel the structure wobbling under my feet, I could see the people streaming past me wobbling with it, but I knew that couldn't be right. The thing hadn't wobbled for years, not since it had first opened, and they'd fixed it almost straight away. I felt strange, I could feel the cold wind cutting along the river, feel its chilly breath on my weirdly naked face and unprotected scalp, but I was over-heating, the sweat was pouring down my ribs and I was panting like a thirsty dog.

I came to the end of the bridge and the screen of silver birches. I'd always liked them. They were beautiful and natural, like nothing else that hollow temple had to offer. Then I realised my bag would be checked at the security desk inside the door. I had to hide it. I bundled it tight around its hard, heavy cargo and thrust the whole thing under my jacket, sliding it round my back and shoving it down into the waist-band of my jeans.

There was a small crowd outside the main entrance, a patient and slow-moving mass of foreign tourists bundled up in ski-jackets or furs and families on day-trips to London. I joined them, shuffled forwards with them, fighting the urge to push and shove my way to the front and dash inside. Hoping that my contraband wouldn't fall clattering to the floor, hoping that there wasn't a conspicuous and suspicious bulge under my jacket.

I could have turned and walked away at that point; it was my last chance to change my mind, to call the whole thing off. But the thought didn't occur to me. As far as I was concerned, I had already passed the point of no return. I knew what I had to do, and I had no reason to back down now. I had nothing to lose. Not now that Helen knew who and what I was. A criminally dangerous and mentally unstable failure. I was sure that I would never see Helen or Elizabeth or Richard again. I was sure I would never return to that cottage below the hill, looking out over the marsh, listening to the crash and rumble of the unseen waves beyond the sea-wall. I had lost them forever. But I couldn't think about that now. The horror of it, the sorrow of it, would break me, drain me of life and strength. And I couldn't let that happen right now. So I had nothing to fear, and only one thing to live for. The one thing I was about to do. Nothing would matter after that.

The security guard waved me through impatiently, his eyes already on the shopping-bags and hand-bags clutched by the people behind me. Suddenly I was through. I was inside that strangely gloomy and echoing space. I stood still and looked around as others streamed past me to the lifts and the stairs and the gift-shops. There were plenty of security cameras, but I could see no policemen. Keep moving. Move fast. Don't let them spot you, wherever they are. Don't let them catch you. Not until it's too late for them. You know where you're going. Get there fast.

Up the stairs I went, following the crowds, followed by crowds. Out onto the third floor we flowed, and there my heart sank to see the long queue half-way across that vast landing from the doorway into the little room where Montezuma's Revenge was on show. There were four uniformed attendants in the doorway – two girls sitting, two men standing – and they were letting only a few people through at a time. I joined the end of the queue. Stay calm, I told myself. Be patient. The queue is moving. It's slow, but it is moving. You will get there. Stay calm…

'What's the problem?' A young man in a parka was complaining to his companion in front of me. 'Why are they being so slow?'

'It's packed in there. I told you. Pete and Marcus were queuing all afternoon yesterday, and in the end they didn't even get in. But we'll be all right. We're here early enough.'

'Oh yeah? Even if we get in, it'll be too crowded to see anything. Let's clear off. No point in wasting our time.'

'No, no, you've got to see this. It's fantastic. Wonderful. You'll never forget it.'

The first man grunted, unconvinced. 'But look at them. It's like airport security. Anyone would think they were after a terrorist. Why four of them? Haven't they got anything better to do? And look at the way they're peering at everyone. Perhaps we should have brought our passports. And look, here are two policemen! Are we going to be frisked?'

Two policemen – and a policewoman – were strolling up and down the queue. They were trying hard to look casual and unhurried – nodding and smiling at anyone who caught their eye – but there was no hiding their vigilance. They were looking for someone, searching every face in the queue. Closer and closer they came. Run for it. Run to the head of the queue, push your way into the room, draw your weapon, shout, shoot if you have to! Run for it!

No. I stood firm, hands in pockets, shuffling slowly forwards in the queue. The first policeman was almost level with me. The young man in the parka giggled as the policeman's gaze swept him. Then that gaze was on me. Blue eyes, impersonal, expressionless, boring through me. I looked away, shaking, sweating. They're looking for a bearded man. A long-haired man. I am not bearded or long-haired. Nobody knows what I look like now. Nobody knows what I've looked like for the last ten years. But still I was expecting violent movement, a grasping hand, a shouting voice, the sudden urgent crackle of police intercoms.

Nothing happened. I looked away, out of the wide window, down onto the river, and shuffled slowly forwards. The second policeman was patrolling that side of the queue, but he too passed by, though I didn't have the courage to meet his eye this time. I was nearly at the front now. The policewoman had stopped there, beside the uniformed attendants. The attendants were smiling at the visitors as they let them through – hello, good morning, thank you for your patience, sorry for the delay – but the policewoman was aloof and wary. I could feel her eyes on me as I came to the head of the queue – good morning, thank you, sorry – and I looked up at her as I stepped forwards to the doors. She was peering at me. She frowned. She looked uncertain and troubled. Then I looked away. I pushed my way through the swing doors. I was inside.

The little room was packed. It was hot and stuffy and brightly-lit. There was hardly room to move. No one was looking at the exhibits on the walls. Everyone was shuffling round the central exhibit, eyes raised, gazing up at the figure looming over them in the big glass box. There were occasional whispers and occasional gasps, but apart from that everyone was silent.

Now. Now! Move! Do it!

I pushed forwards. There were protests and exclamations, angry and indignant. I shouldered and elbowed my way towards the big glass case. I felt toes under my feet, ribs against my elbows, bodies pushed aside by my shoulders. I tried to apologise, but there was no point, no time. At last I was in front of the big glass case. I reached behind me, under my jacket, and seized hold of the bundle stuffed down the seat of my jeans and tugged it free. I held the plastic bag in my left hand and reached into it with my right. And looked up at the still figure towering over me.

What I saw was a shock, a surprise. It was no longer the dark, sinister effigy I remembered from a week ago. It had been transformed. It was covered with flowers.

Hundreds, thousands of flowers. Its body bloomed with every colour, every shade imaginable. Reds and yellows, greens and blues. White and black, orange and pink, purple and violet. Shining bright or glowing dark. Deep and powerful or pale and delicate. It seemed to flood that little white room with light and colour. It seemed to cast dazzling rainbows all over the bleached walls and the gasping, smiling crowd.

It was beautiful. It was alive.

I froze. My right hand was gripping the gun but wouldn't draw it from the plastic bag. I was suddenly back at the flat Jutting had rented in Islington when he left the squat, back at that party when we'd first had the idea of Montezuma's Revenge. We'd all been there, Jutting and Garry and Stella and myself, we'd all been happy together, laughing and joking, excited by the idea, by the creation we were all to be involved in. It had been the last time we'd all been together, and here was that moment's monument. It was a monument to the four of us. It was the four of us, quite literally; our blood, mixed together, giving birth to this amazing creature.

Suddenly the gallery was empty. There was just me and the flower-man, face to face. No one else. I began to draw the gun out of the plastic bag. Then I was no longer alone. There was someone beside me. No, two people beside me. Stella and Gary.

'What are you doing, you mad bastard?' Gary was saying. 'Put the gun down! Put it down!'

'Patrick, please...' Stella was saying. 'Don't! Please don't! It's beautiful! Patrick! Can't you see it's beautiful?'

But it wasn't Gary and Stella, it was Dr Allen and Helen. And Dr Allen wasn't saying anything. He was just smiling at me, sadly, and shaking his head. And Helen, her hand stretched out to me, seemed to be fading further and further away. 'Come back, Will,' she was saying. 'Please, come back! Will, please..!'

'But I've got to do it!' I shouted. 'I've got to!'

Suddenly I was back in the crowded gallery. The crowd was no longer silent. A troubled murmur was rumbling through it. There were some stifled giggles. It was no longer pushing up against me; in fact, it was trying to edge away from me. The crowd's faces were turning from the glass case to look at me – I was surrounded by them, curious faces, puzzled faces, amused faces, annoyed faces.

'I've got to do it!' I shouted again.

Someone in the crowd was laughing. It was Harry Jutting. But he wasn't in the crowd, he was in the glass case, he was the flowering man. No, the flowering man had gone, and there was Harry Jutting in his place, Harry Jutting as I'd seen him in the Pyramid gallery when I'd tried to shoot him all those years ago, laughing and jeering and calling my bluff as he'd backed away from the weapon trembling in my fist, backed away across the gallery floor and out of the rear doors and into the garden.

'Go ahead!' he laughed, as he'd laughed all those years ago. 'Shoot! Go on, pull the trigger!' He'd opened his arms wide, offering himself as a target as I'd come out into the garden after him. 'Go on, you mad bastard!' He was laughing as if the weapon aiming at him was the funniest thing he'd seen in years. 'You're not going to do it, are you? You don't have the guts for it, do you? You don't have the bottle! You can't do it, can you!'

He'd been so sure, so certain. And he'd been right. His certainty, his confidence, had overwhelmed me. It had frightened me, it had drained my resolve. In the garden of the gallery, ten years ago, I had fired, twice, but both shots had gone wide. I hadn't been able to bring myself to aim at that big, spread-armed, willing, taunting target. I had

369

deliberately aimed wide. It had been the best I could manage. And then I had fled.

His jeering laughter had followed me – 'I told you! I knew you wouldn't do it! I knew it!' – and haunted me for days afterwards, as it haunted me now. But it didn't frighten me now, it wasn't going to overwhelm me, it couldn't drain my resolve. It strengthened it. I looked up into the glass case, and where Jutting had been a moment ago, and the flower-man a moment before that, I now saw the grizzly effigy I'd seen a week ago, a figure of clotted, frozen blood and matted, entwined organic fibre. Human remains, exhumed and exhibited, rotting and putrefying as they were, refusing to go back into the grave where they belonged. A dead body refusing to die. Well, I was going to kill it once and for all. I was going to put it back into the dark earth where it belonged.

I tugged the heavy handgun free of the plastic bag. I held it up. I aimed straight at the figure in the glass case.

Someone screamed. Someone shouted. The crowd surged away from me. It boiled and seethed with panic and fear. Everyone was scrambling for the door, but there were too many people in the little room, they were packed too tight, they were all jammed up against each other. Their screams and shouts thrashed round and round through the air like a flock of trapped birds.

I stood there unmoved, my teeth gritted, the heavy gun steady in my hand. I wasn't going to miss this time. I squeezed the trigger.

*

Harry had realised I was serious as soon as I'd pulled the gun out of the bag that night in his apartment. He saw the weapon steady in my hand, he saw the look in my eye, and he knew I was going to do it this time.

370

He moved fast, but it was already too late. He tightened his grip on the bottle of beer, smashed it against the fridge, and leapt at me. I'd barely had time to raise the gun and take aim. I crouched down, thrusting the weapon almost blindly at him, and fired.

The noise, the smoke, the smell, the blood, it was like being in a car crash. The explosion had thrown him away from me. He was lying on his back, blood soaking his hair, spreading a dark stain across the Persian rug, puddling the stripped-wood floor. There wasn't much of his head left. His arms and legs stirred for a few moments. Then he lay still. He was dead.

It had been a lucky shot. He'd done me a favour by leaping on me like that. The barrel had caught him under the chin, and the bullet had gone right up through his skull and come out of the top of his head. A suicide's shot. He was making it easy for me.

I stood over him, careful not to tread in the spreading pool of blood. I looked down at Harry Jutting's corpse, relishing the moment. I was breathing heavily, but I felt calm, perfectly in control. And I felt very alert. Every sense – hearing, sight, taste, smell, touch – was tingling and alive. I felt like a radar turned up to full strength. I stood still and waited, expecting to hear a hammering at the door, a clamour of angry shouts, the scream of police sirens, see flashing lights break the darkness outside. But there was nothing. I went over to the big glass windows. The blinds were never closed. Could we have been overlooked? No. We were too high up to be seen from the road or the river. The other buildings were too far away. I could see lights on in distant windows, but nothing more. It was easy to imagine telescopes and binoculars out there, but I knew it was unlikely.

I looked at my watch. It was just after four o'clock. Amazing. It was only a few minutes since I'd been waiting for him out in the darkened stairwell. Plenty of time to finish off here and then sneak back to the hospital.

I slipped the gun into the pocket of my dressing gown. My left hand was still clutching the plastic bag. There was a pair of woollen gloves in there. I pulled them out and put them on, bundling the bag up and stuffing it into the other pocket. I took the gun out again and gave it a good rub-over with the tails of the dressing-gown. When I was sure there couldn't be any prints left on it, I took Harry's right hand – still warm – and put the gun in it. I wrapped his palm and fingers round it, put his index finger through the trigger. Then I dropped it on the floor at the corpse's feet.

There were dark, wet stains splashed up the wall in front of me. I looked up. The stains were smeared over the ceiling as well. My face felt hot and wet, and I was suddenly convinced that Harry's blood and brains were all over me too. I resisted the temptation to wipe my face with my gloved hands. I went into the bathroom and looked in the big mirror. No. Nothing. Not a mark. I stared at my reflection, somehow amazed that my appearance hadn't changed, that I was still exactly the same person.

I left the bathroom. There was broken glass from the smashed beer bottle all over the floor. They didn't look particularly out-of-place – Harry lived like a pig in a sty. But a broken bottle suggested a violent confrontation, a fight. I found a dustpan and brush in a cupboard just outside the kitchen, swept up the shards and dumped them in the bin.

What else? There was a lap-top open on a table in the sitting-area. I could see that it was plugged in. Had he left it switched on? The screen was blank, but a little blue light blinked on the side of the keyboard. I crouched over it. I reached out to stroke the mouse-panel, but stopped myself just in time. I was wearing gloves, which meant that I wouldn't leave any prints, but it also meant that I would wipe Harry's prints from the keys, which might make any investigator suspicious. I got a knife from the kitchen and tapped the panel with its point. The screen sprang into life. Harry had left himself logged into some sort of porn site. How predictable. Tapping the keys lightly with the knife, I got into a word-processing program and pulled up a blank sheet and wrote out Harry Jutting's suicide note for him.

'It's all shit and bollocks and I've had enough of it. I'm going to piss off now. If any of you bastards try to follow me, I'll come back and haunt your kids for the rest of their lives.'

I was back at the hospital by five o'clock that morning. Getting in was no more difficult than getting out. Hospitals are open all night, and as far as the dozing receptionist was concerned I was just an insomniac patient who had nipped out for a crafty fag. I climbed into bed and lay awake in the darkness, reviewing the precautions I'd taken. I'd thrown the plastic bag and the gloves away in a rubbish bin a good mile from Jutting's flat. I'd dumped my old bicycle only a few streets away from the hospital, but it wouldn't stay there for long. I'd left it unlocked, propped up against a skip on a street corner. Someone would find it and use it to get to work that morning or home from the pub that evening, or just ride it round London all day then dump it in the Thames for fun. They were welcome to it. I wouldn't be needing it again. My pyjamas and dressing-gown - the gunshot must have left forensic give-aways all over them. I had to get rid of them somehow. I had to get rid of them innocently. They couldn't just disappear – that would be too suspicious. And my hands, my hair, my skin… would the police be

373

able to find anything on them, with their sci-fi scans and microscopes and chemical tests?

When the nurses roused me the next morning, I went out into the bathroom and took a dump and a piss without taking off my pyjamas or dressing gown or slippers. They were bagged up as organic waste and carted off to the hospital's incinerator. They made me spend the next few hours in the shower and the bath, scrubbing myself cleaner than a surgeon's tool-kit. It was one of the many things that convinced them of my insanity. Which is amusing, because it was one of the most sane and clear-headed things I've ever done.

*

The sound of the gun-shot from the Russian's big weapon was even louder than I'd expected. It roared around that little exhibition room like a thunderbolt, its amplified echo crashing from wall to wall. I was shaking and gasping. I could see a hole punched in the glass case, cracks spreading out from it, but the figure was still standing, unmoved. I tightened my grip on the weapon and fired again. Another hole. More cracks spreading out, seeking each other. A creaking, splintering sound joined the echo of the gunshot. The figure had moved slightly, wasn't standing quite so upright. I fired again. Smashed glass, flying shards, the figure leaning backwards and to the side at an odd angle, crystal blades embedded in its head and chest. Flower petals falling slowly – red and blue and white - like drifting spring blossom.

A storm of screams and shouts roared in my ears. My nose was full of the stink of oiled gunmetal and the sharp, bitter smoke of high explosives. My eyes seemed to be full of mist – the seething crowd was just a dim mass heaving and pushing towards the doorways – surely just three shots from a modern handgun didn't give off this much smoke? An elbow or shoulder caught the cracked glass and a big sheet of it fell crashing to the ground. Someone tripped over the pedestal and set the whole thing wobbling. An alarm was ringing somewhere. An urgent and insistent clamour which seemed distant one moment, but right inside my head the next. Someone lost their balance in the jostling crowd and put out a hand to stop themselves falling and caught the flower-man himself a glancing blow on the hip. Clutching fingers – lucky to miss broken glass - came away full of crushed pink and yellow petals. But it set the flower-man rocking to and fro. Now the mist was dispersing and I could see everything sharp and clear. To and fro he went, in a strange, stiff wobble. To and fro like a pendulum. And then he began to topple. Over to one side he went, slow and stiff and unbending, until the jagged remains of the glass case cut him off at the knees. Then down he suddenly tumbled, out of the shattered case, off the pedestal, and hit the floor with a heavy thud.

He fell at my feet. I looked down at him. There were flower petals everywhere, drifting in the air, scattered over the floor. They looked like frightened, dying butterflies. Big bald patches had appeared on the figure, glistening with reddish-black slime. Puddles of watery brown liquid were spreading out over the floor. The flowers that now only partially covered him seemed to be wilting in front of my very eyes, fading and rotting away as if seconds were hours. A stink of decaying vegetation, of rotting flesh even, began to fill the room. If the flower man had been alive five minutes ago, he was certainly dying now. If he had been beautiful five minutes ago, he was ugly now – frighteningly, disgustingly ugly.

I was shaking and sobbing. What had I done? It was like looking down on Harry Jutting's corpse again, only now I was aghast with the horror of what I had done. I was back in his absurd penthouse, but outside myself, an invisible observer, like a camera in the ceiling. In shocked disbelief I watched myself calmly wiping my prints from the gun, covering it with Jutting's prints, depositing it on the floor at his feet. How could I be so calm, so untroubled, so in control? There I was, carefully checking myself in his bathroom mirror, efficiently sweeping up the broken beer-bottle from his floor, coldly writing the suicide note on his lap-top. Didn't I know what I had done? Didn't I realise what I had become?

I was a murderer. I hadn't killed James Hobson, but I had killed Harry Jutting. Yes, he was a bastard, perhaps he deserved to die, but that didn't change the fact that I had murdered another human being. Murder. The worst of crimes. The most evil of acts. By killing Jutting I had proved myself to be a worse man than even he had ever been.

That's what I'd been hiding from for ten years, that's why I'd run away from my own life, had tried to leave behind what I had been and what I had done, had tried to forget about it, to conceal it from the world and from myself. Well, there was no hiding from myself now. No more concealing, no more running away. I knew now what I was, what I'd done. I was a murderer. I had killed Harry Jutting.

The final mystery had emerged from the shadows at last, the monster had finally come out from its hiding place round the corner. I had caught it, frozen, in a powerful beam of torch-light and I had torn its mask off. The face that now squinted back at me through the dazzling light was my own, and it was the face of a murderer.

It took some moments for the frightened crowd to clear the doorways. Even then, the two policemen and the policewoman outside wouldn't come into the room to get me. The room was sealed off and the whole building was emptied. Specialist police marksmen and negotiators were summonsed. Helen and Dr Allen were with them. I wouldn't speak to any of them. It was hours before they came into the room to get me, but I was still on my knees beside the flower-man's stinking corpse, shaking and sobbing and wondering why I'd destroyed something which had been so beautiful. They found the gun lying where I'd dropped it among the shards of broken glass, the scattered drifts of fading petals and the puddles of congealing blood.

Chapter Seventeen

I spent two nights in a police cell. Then I was transferred to a prison, on remand.

'Don't waste your time applying for bail,' a solicitor advised me. 'There's no way they'll grant it. You'll have to undergo medical assessments and examinations instead. Then they'll probably send you to a psychiatric institution pending your trial.'

I didn't care. I didn't care what they did with me or where they sent me. My only hope was that they'd put me back on the medication I remembered from the last time I'd been locked up as a dangerous lunatic. A potion which had purged me of all thought and emotion and left me numb and empty. I'd hated it then, but I longed for it now.

The first psychiatrist to see me was more like a harassed social worker than a doctor. The session with her was just a form-filling exercise. But on the second day, after a long interview with a police officer in an over-heated interrogation room, I was taken to another cell and there was Dr Allen.

He did a double-take when he stood up to shake my hand, as if he didn't recognise me. 'You've lost that beard and moustache! Good!' He nodded in approval. Then he grimaced. 'But that's a bloody awful haircut!'

Dr Allen. I stared at him in dismay. It had been Dr Allen who had taken me off that medication the last time. If he was on the case, what chance did I have of oblivion now?

'Harry Jutting's having a second funeral tomorrow,' he said as we sat down. 'I've arranged for us to attend it, Patrick. You and me. Though we'll have to take a couple of prison guards with us, I'm afraid. I've told the authorities that it would be an invaluable contribution to our assessment of you, and a healing experience for you. An opportunity not to be missed, in other words. What do you think?'

I looked at him. There was a carefree grin on his kind, intelligent face. I didn't know what to make of it, any more than I knew what to make of his suggestion. Not that I cared about it one way or another.

'An informal event. Low key. I believe a vicar will be present, but there'll be no ceremony, as I understand it, no spiritual element. Of course, if you refuse, there'd be no point in forcing you.'

Still I didn't speak. So they were sticking Harry Jutting back underground. What was the point of going to see it happen? What was the point of anything? He was dead. Nothing else mattered now.

'I don't suppose there'll be crowds there. No one will be there, really. It's being kept pretty quiet. Though I understand Stella Foreman will be attending. And Gary Hughes.' He looked me square in the eyes. 'And Helen.'

I felt things stirring in distant corners of my being as he looked at me. Thoughts and feelings I didn't want to consider. I wanted that potion which would take them away forever. I looked away, but I could still feel his eyes on me. It made me uneasy. I reluctantly broke my silence. 'Helen? Why would Helen be going to Harry Jutting's funeral?'

Dr Allen was still smiling. 'Because I told her you'd be there.'

'Why should she want to see me?'

He raised his eyebrows at me, as if it was a stupid question.

'She must hate me. Despise me. I deceived her for so long. But now she knows what I am. I can't believe she ever wants to see me again. Which is just as well, because

I'd be too ashamed, too…' Too what? Too frightened. Frightened of her anger and disgust. Her pain and sadness.

'Don't you think there are questions she might want to ask you? Aren't there things you want to explain to her?'

He could see right inside me. He knew better than I did that I wanted to see Helen. He knew how much I wanted to see her in spite of what I might be telling myself or anyone else. And he was trying to help me. But he didn't know everything. If I was going to let him help me, I had to tell him what I hadn't told anyone else. The truth about Harry Jutting's death. I hadn't told the police. I had no intention of telling the police. Even though it was something I wasn't going to hide from myself any more, I was still going to hide it from the world. The world wouldn't understand, it wasn't the world's business, I was scared of what the world might do about it. But Dr Allen would understand. I could tell him. Yes. I had to tell him. Tell him now. I looked at him. Then I looked around the room. There were no policemen or prison wardens in there with us. We were on our own. 'Is this interview being recorded?'

'No.' He spread his hands. 'I'm not even taking notes. Listen, Patrick, I don't think you're insane. Not now. You have been, but, well, we all have our mad moments, don't we? Even though yours have been more intense than most. So I won't have you sectioned. And there'll be no mitigating circumstances at your trial, either. No 'while the balance of his mind etc etc'. You'll have to stick it out in a real prison this time. But I can't tell anyone that just yet, or they won't let you come out to Walthamstow with me tomorrow. Which would be a shame, because I do think that would be good for you.'

'Listen, Dr Allen…' I felt hot and tense, almost panic-stricken. I found the words tumbling out really quickly, as if they were desperate to escape before I could change my mind. 'About Harry Jutting – his death - '

'Woah!' He held up his hand to stop me. 'Let me warn you, Patrick. I'm not a priest. There are no secrets of the confessional in here. If you're going to tell me anything that the police would be interested in, I'd have no option but to pass the information on to them.' He spoke firmly, but his voice was kind and gentle, and there was a sparkle in his eyes, as if he was pleased, even amused.

'You know! You've guessed!'

He laughed. 'When you left High Beeches, I really thought you'd been cured. So when I heard that your delusion had returned, I was very puzzled. Why had it persisted? Why did you once again believe that you were Harry Jutting? Or rather, why did you still believe? Clearly, in your subconscious, the delusion had persisted for the last ten years. Why, when I thought it had gone forever? What had I missed?'

'I should have told you back then. I'm sorry. I'm so sorry. You were trying so hard to help me, to cure me, and I didn't tell you…'

'No, no, you mustn't tell me, even now. Not unless you want to go to prison for the rest of your life. No, I should have guessed, I should have understood. As it is, it only came to me when I heard that they were digging up Jutting's remains. The truth is, your delusion was a mask for something you couldn't face up to, a way of hiding from something too terrible to admit to.' He leaned forwards, his eyebrows raised, his finger pointing at me to emphasise his words. 'If you were Harry Jutting, then Harry Jutting was still alive. And if he was still alive, then you couldn't have killed him!'

That was it. That was it precisely. It was terrifying to hear it put so clearly and bluntly. It was almost cruel, almost brutal of him. I was trembling in my seat. I'd always been frightened of Dr Allen. Now I was more frightened than ever. He knew. He knew why I had persisted in hiding behind the mask of Harry Jutting. I had been hiding from what I had done to Jutting. It was a way of convincing myself that he wasn't dead, that he hadn't been killed, that I hadn't killed him.

Dr Allen knew I was a murderer. He held my fate in the palm his hand. He had complete power over me. But I had always trusted him as well. I believed in him, in his word and in his judgement. I had to, now more than ever. I had no alternative. 'How do you know that the delusion has gone at last? That I'm no longer hiding from… what I did to Harry Jutting?'

'Because you were about to confess! Weren't you? You were about to tell me everything!' He laughed triumphantly, and shook his head. 'Patrick, I wish I could let you tell me! It would be the most satisfying moment of my professional life! But I can't, for your sake! Nevertheless, you must tell someone, if your cure is to be complete. You have confessed to yourself, now you must confess to someone else, or the delusion will only be partially banished. Once you have fully committed to acknowledging the truth of what you have done, once you have admitted it irrevocably to another human being, then there will be no possibility of denying it ever again. Do you understand?'

I nodded. I understood. 'But who can I talk to?' I asked stupidly.

'Isn't there someone you should tell? Who deserves to be told? Who deserves to know everything about you? Who you have been keeping secrets from for far too long?'

I nodded again.

'Tell her. Confess to her. Put yourself in her hands. Then you will know whether you have any chance of a life together. Isn't that what you want?'

'Yes. It's what I want. But is it what I deserve?'

He shook his head. 'Patrick, why do you think I'm helping you?'

So that was why he wanted me to go to Jutting's funeral. Why he wanted Helen to go to the funeral. So I would have a chance to tell her, in safety and confidence, in a way I would never be free to tell her when she visited me behind bars. 'Why are you doing this for us, doctor?' It came out as little more than a whisper. I was so moved I could hardly speak.

'Because I'm a doctor, not a policeman or a judge. It isn't my job to punish, it's my job to cure. And because I don't believe you deserve to spend the rest of your life in prison. Helen doesn't deserve to spend the rest of her life without you. Elizabeth and Richard don't deserve to lose their father.'

I was amazed, almost horrified. 'But doctor, you're risking... just for me...'

'I'm risking nothing, Patrick. I'm withholding nothing from the police. No evidence, no privileged knowledge. If I talked to them, what could they do? Just shrug their shoulders. Mere suspicion is no use to them. They need evidence and information. I have neither. I'm not standing in their way. They do their work, I do mine.'

'But doctor, murder...'

'Murder? A man commits suicide, a man who nobody misses, who did nothing but harm, who many believe deserved to die. Of course, nobody deserves to die, no life is worthless, death is always sad. But it would be tragic if other lives were destroyed as well.' He sighed. 'You will go to prison, Patrick. The charges against you – criminal damage, breaking and entering, illegal possession of a

383

firearm, public affray, death threats - '. He paused, scratching his head. 'You know, Patrick, I've seen those letters you sent to Hobson. With hindsight, they do indeed read like warnings rather than threats. As if you were trying to help him, trying to lead him away from the dangers he was bringing down on himself. Almost prophetic, really. If he'd heeded you, then perhaps...' He sighed, and shrugged. 'Nevertheless, you will get anything between five and ten years. If you plead guilty, which you would be wise to do. But that's nothing compared to what you would have got if... if you had indeed killed James Hobson, for instance. And you'll probably serve less than five years. If you spend your time wisely. The kind of prison you'll go to, Patrick, there will be facilities, you will be able to work...'

'Work?'

'You have destroyed property which belonged to other people. You can make restitution, reparations, over the next few years. You can create new work, to make up for what you have destroyed.'

'New work?'

'The world doesn't deserve to lose your gift, Patrick.'

I shook my head and laughed bitterly. 'My gift? My curse...'

'You are brilliantly gifted, Patrick. I know you've rejected your vocation, but let me tell you, God or whoever the great creator is has given you your gifts for a purpose, so you had better use them or He will be mightily pissed off with you. That purpose is to celebrate His creation, to praise and glorify it, to explore it, to explain it and open it up to the rest of us who are not lucky enough to be as talented as you, who are relying on you to do it for us.'

I remembered that last glimpse of Montezuma's Revenge, the beauty of it, the joy in its suggestion that life and the world could be, and indeed are, wonderful and mysterious. And I had destroyed it. I remembered the horror of its death. It was meant to die, all things had to die, but in their own time. I had cut its life short. I had murdered it. There was joy in creation, misery in destruction...

'God made the world, He took pleasure in its creation, and don't you think He wants to share that pleasure with us?' Dr Allen urged gently. As ever, he appeared to be reading my thoughts. 'Why else would He have given us the instinct to create and the ability to enjoy it? Doesn't He love us? Why would He give us a power He didn't want us to use? Why would He give us a pleasure He didn't want us to enjoy?' He leaned back in his chair, put his hands behind his head and closed his eyes. 'If you give a lump of clay to a child, any child, your daughter Liz, for instance, that child will immediately try to make something out of it, a dog or a cat or a mouse or something, if you give the child a pencil and a sheet of paper she will automatically try to draw a picture, of her mother and father, perhaps, of the family home. And she will take great pleasure in it. And she doesn't do it because she wants to compete with the creator of the real dog or cat or mouse, but because she sees that real dogs and cats and mice are wonderful and miraculous and wants to enjoy and understand and appreciate and salute their existence! An act of love, if you like. Prompted by a natural instinct, built into us by whoever or whatever made us. So, in that sense, a sacred instinct.'

He leaned forwards over his desk again. He opened his leather briefcase and took out a bubble-wrapped package. 'Helen brought this to London for you. But you were rude enough to clear off out of the café before she had a chance to hand it over.' He unwrapped it and stood it on his desk.

It was a porcelain cylinder about six inches in height and an inch in diameter. I peered at it. It looked incredibly thin and delicate - light seemed to pass right through it - but also strong and durable. Its shape was slightly irregular, which made it look dynamic, somehow alive. If it had been a perfectly symmetrical cylinder it would have looked inert and lifeless. Its colours were subtle – pale green shading into pale blue. But it wasn't cold. It glowed, as if it was lighting up and warming up the air around it with those colours.

It was very beautiful. I could see that it was a small vase, but that didn't seem to be its point. It didn't need a flower in it. Just standing on the desk there, a simple piece of sculpture, was enough. Enough to transform that cold, drab and depressing room, to relax and reassure and at the same time stimulate any human beings sharing that room with it. To warm their hearts.

'She thought you might want to see how that last firing turned out. You asked her to empty the kiln for you, remember? Thoughtful of her, don't you think?' He picked the piece up, and examined it, smiling. 'I'm sure she recognises it for what it is. A thing of beauty, a work of art.' He looked up at me. 'It's a curious fact that the all-male religions have produced no religious imagery – in most cases have positively forbidden it. Kenneth Clark said that. The great religious art of the world is deeply involved in the female principle. Why is that, do you think? Something to do with child-birth being the ultimate creative act, perhaps? The one that brings humanity closest to the divine? I only mention it as a way of saying that I think Helen would understand if you returned to your vocation.' He put the piece back on the desk. He sighed, and shook his head. 'Religion only has a problem with art because religion's enemies – the older superstitions - had appropriated art as a branch of their magic. Cave-paintings, for instance. Spells to ensure success in the hunt. And the Ancient Egyptians. What we think of as art was for them literally a form of magic. And Van Eyck, in the fifteenth century – his work was so life-like that people accused him of witchcraft.' He laughed and shook his head again. 'But the world's moved on from such ignorance and superstition, hasn't it?' He was still looking at the vase. Suddenly he sat up straight and snatched it up again. He peered closely at it, frowning. 'That's odd. Those cracks – I could have sworn they weren't there when I looked at it the other day...'

He held it out to me, puzzled. I took it from him and examined it carefully. The whole piece was indeed covered in an intricate spider's web of very fine cracks. I grimaced. 'Crackle. That's what potters call it. It's a fault in the firing. The glaze cracks up if it expands and contracts at a different rate to the clay body.' I shrugged. 'It happens from time to time. A number of things could have caused it. Firing isn't an entirely predictable business. Pots can crack, blister, warp. Sometimes there's a reason for it, sometimes there isn't. Hardly surprising, considering the very, very high temperatures you get in the kiln. The huge stresses and strains of it. All kind of strange and mysterious transformations take place.'

'But... but... I'm sure those cracks weren't there yesterday...'

'Perhaps not. Crackle usually shows up when you empty the kiln, but it can take days or weeks or even months to come out.'

'It's funny, when I unwrapped it just now, the first thing I thought was, wow, it's even more beautiful than I remember it, even more striking. Unconsciously, I must have registered the change, and you know, it does seem to add something, it's a definite enhancement...'

'Well, some studio potters see it as a form of decoration. They deliberately encourage it. They welcome it when it happens by accident. But in industrially-produced pots, it's definitely a fault; those cracks, they could make the pot porous, they could make it unhygienic, a health-hazard.'

'And you?'

'My pots, I make them to be used. That's their whole point.' I shrugged again. 'Chuck them away and hope for better luck next time. No point in crying about it.'

'This pot?'

I looked at it carefully. Dr Allen was right. The cracks added to its beauty, its individuality. They were part of the irregularity which made the piece dynamic, which gave it life. They were the element which added warmth to the otherwise cold colours, which somehow made them glow. This was something I could work on in the future. I could experiment with different methods, see what effect different degrees of crackle had on a pot's appearance. And the crackle itself – I could highlight it – rub an iron oxide glaze into the cracks and re-fire it... This pot – what the hell - no one was going to eat out of it, there was no need to put water in it. 'No,' I said. 'I'm not going to chuck it out.'

'Ah. Well.' Dr Allen coughed awkwardly. 'Listen, Patrick...' He was embarrassed. He was actually blushing. 'I wonder... could I... would you...'

I laughed. 'Doctor, I would like you to have this pot. An unworthy gift. You deserve much more.' I handed it back to him.

'Thank you! I'll treasure it.' He began to put it back in its bubble-wrapping, then stopped and took one last look at it. 'You're like this pot, Patrick. You've been through the fire. Not once, but twice. Biscuit-fired, then glaze-fired. You talk about the stresses and strains inside the kiln, the immense heat, the strange transformations. I guess you should know.'

'Damaged or enhanced?'

'That depends on whether you see yourself as a studio-produced pot or an industrially-produced pot.' He looked at me, waiting for an answer, but I was silent. He shook his head. 'Dammit, Patrick, this is a studio pot! All of us human beings, we're all studio-pots! We're none of us factory-made, utilitarian, identical! We're all one-offs!'

He held the vase up to the light. I could see the pleasure it gave him. So a pot can have other uses than to eat out of or drink out of, or to put flowers in, or to keep loose change together or keys where you won't forget them. Uses equal to or even more valuable than the merely utilitarian. I've been wrong all these years. So wrong. I shivered with horror and sadness. I had surrendered to fear, superstition and stupidity. And where had it lead me? To criminal destruction. To deceit. To putting Helen and Liz and Richard in danger. To abandoning, abusing, insulting the talent I had been given. I felt ashamed. It was as if I had rejected a wonderful and valuable gift carefully chosen just for me by kind and loving parents. I had been an ungrateful, mean-spirited, self-important child.

Was it too late to accept that gift? To try and make the most of it? No! It was still there, I was sure, waiting for me to take it up again. In my mind's eye I could see the flower man standing there in all his glory, and I had an idea... A vague idea, but I could feel it taking shape... Yes, I could do that, it might work, it would work if I... My hand ached for a pencil or pen or paint-brush, my eye and my mind ached for a sheet of paper to project themselves onto. My heart quickened with the excitement of it, the anticipation. 'Those people whose property I destroyed, are they likely to accept work by Patrick Joyce as adequate compensation?'

'Very soon everyone will know that Harry Jutting cast a big shadow only because he was standing on Patrick Joyce's shoulders. I guess that won't do much for the value of his work. But it will do wonders for your work, Patrick. After all this, there'll be a huge demand for it. You'll come into your own, believe me.' He put the vase back into its bubble-wrap, and put it in his case. 'Have faith, Patrick.' He smiled. 'You've been blessed with a great talent, and a great wife. You must have faith in them both.' He stood up, then he pressed a button on the desk. It must have rung a bell outside, announcing the end of our interview, because the door opened and a policeman and a warden came in almost straight away. 'Goodbye then,' he said, shaking my hand. 'I'll see you tomorrow morning. We'll collect you at nine o'clock.'

*

It rained heavily that night. It had stopped by the time we arrived at the cemetery the next morning, but the place was awash with mud and puddles. Harry's emptied grave was covered with plastic tarpaulins weighed down with bricks and planks of wood. It looked more like a building site than a graveyard. An abandoned digger sat at an awkward angle on top of a heap of spoil beside the path. Workmen in dirty overalls and hard hats and fluorescent waterproof jackets stood around with cigarettes or spades in their hands. There were no undertakers and I couldn't see a priest anywhere.

There was a chapel in the middle of the cemetery. A small group of people was waiting in the shelter of its porch. Gary and Stella, some policemen, the cemetery foreman with a coffin on what looked like a wheel-barrow. But not Helen. Where was Helen?

Stella looked sombre and white-faced, but Gary was laughing. 'We'll see the bastard underground this time, won't we, eh?' he said, embracing me clumsily. He was looking well. The cuts and bruises had gone. He was as tanned and over-groomed as ever. But there was something manic about him. He was eager and over-excited. His laughter was too loud, and he was bouncing up and down on his toes and nodding and blinking rapidly. 'We missed it last time, but we're here now, aren't we? What did I say to you? We're still here, and Jutting's as dead as he deserves to be. And now it's time to piss on his grave. Can't wait!'

'Good to see you're out of the hospital, Gary.'

'You still owe me a bottle of vodka, Pat,' he said. 'But never mind, I've got something here.' He pulled a bottle from his pocket. A colourless liquid in a clear bottle with a very colourful label. He uncorked it and the tang of strong spirits stung the air. 'Fancy a drop? No? All right then.' He took a drink from it himself. 'But I'm really going to do it. I am. I'm going to piss all over him!'

Stella and I embraced. 'Patrick…' she said uncertainly.

'Yes,' I reassured her. 'I am Patrick. Not Harry.'

She nodded, and smiled with relief. 'I guess this is going to be pretty traumatic for all of us. We'd better stick together.'

There was something at the back of my mind, something I wanted to ask her. What was it? Ah, yes. That man who had come into the café while we were talking… she'd been upset, she'd left in a hurry… Then it suddenly hit me. Of course. It wasn't the man that had upset her. It was nothing to do with him, whoever he was. She didn't know him, she probably hadn't even noticed him. She had been upset by what I had just said. We'd been talking about Art Crash Express, about the actors playing our parts, and I'd said that James Hobson had been cast as me.

391

That was it. That was the moment Stella had realised that I still thought I was Harry Jutting. That was what had upset her. That was what had hit her so hard.

I took her hand. 'I'm all right,' I said. 'And you?'

She nodded, trying to smile. She took Gary's hand, and the three of us followed the man with the big wheelbarrow as he pushed it out of the shelter of the porch and steered it along the pathway to the muddy patch where the workmen were clearing the plastic sheeting from a hole in the ground.

'Yeah! Yeah!' Gary was saying with increasing excitement. 'Let's stick him where he belongs!' He cackled like a mad witch. 'You big bastard, we're doing for you now!'

Where was Helen? I looked round but she wasn't in the small group splashing along the puddled pathway behind us. There was Dr Allen, talking in hushed tones to a police officer at his side. There were the two prison wardens who had come with us, their expressionless eyes levelled at me like rifle-sights. Was she late? Was she lost? Had I been tricked in some way I didn't understand? I tried to catch Dr Allen's eye, but he was too deep in conversation to notice.

I hadn't slept much the night before. I'd been too excited and too frightened by the idea of seeing Helen, by what I had to tell her. I longed for it, yet I dreaded it at the same time. How would she greet me? Would she be glad to see me? Or would she be hostile and angry? Or cold and indifferent? Would I have the courage to tell her everything? That I had committed the very worst of crimes. Murder. Yes, I had to, I was sure of that. What would she do, what would she say? That was the question. Would she embrace me, try to comfort me, support me? Would she turn her back on me? Would she walk away from me? Would she tell the police? Would she insist that

I told the police? I would, if that was her wish. There was no doubt about that. It would all be in her hands. It was all up to her. Whether I spent three or four years in jail, or a lifetime. Whether I remained her husband. Whether I remained Elizabeth and Richard's father. Or whether I was to be cast into outer darkness for evermore.

Harry's grave was some twenty yards away from the path. The wheelbarrow bumped over the wet grass and we followed, our feet slipping and squelching on the muddy turf. We arranged ourselves silently around the gaping hole and watched the workmen lower the coffin into the depths. I felt Stella's hand tighten its grasp on mine. Gary was standing on her far side, holding her other hand. 'Yeah!' I heard him mutter and chuckle quietly. 'Yeah! Good riddance, bastard!' Then the only sound was the thud and rattle of earth falling on wood. I reminded myself that Harry Jutting's remains were in that box, I tried to imagine them in there, that big body lying still with half its head blown away by the bullet I'd sent smashing through it. But my imagination shrugged the task off. Those remains were ten years old. What would be left of Harry Jutting after all that time? Not much. He was stone cold dead, and what we did with what little remained of him really made no difference one way or another to anything, neither to the damage he had done while he was alive, nor to the guilty horror that had aggravated that damage after his death. We could just as well be burying the remains of Montezuma's Revenge. That I could imagine, and the idea that we were returning the flower-man to the earth was somehow comforting, reassuring.

Then it was very quiet once more. It was all done.

'Harry…' Gary's gasp was little more than a whisper, but I heard it clearly in the silence. Then I heard him sob. 'Harry!' Then he started to cry. 'Harry!' Suddenly he was weeping openly and heart-breakingly, great gulps of pure sorrow exploding from the depths of his being. I looked at him. Tears as bleak and wild and relentless as winter rain were bursting over his face, a face ravaged by grief and shock and disbelief, twisted and lined, mottled red and white. He suddenly looked like a little, old, ugly man. Stella put her arms round him and he clung to her as if she was his mother.

I felt a hand on my arm. 'Patrick,' Dr Allen said softly. He was standing at my shoulder. 'Helen's here. She's waiting for you in the chapel.'

I looked into his clear blue eyes. They were serious, but calm and kind. I looked past him to the chapel. Its steep roof rose sharply against the cloudy sky, its slates dark with the rain. My heart missed a beat, seemed to stop altogether for some seconds, than it started again, thumping with such violence and speed that I thought I was having some kind of attack.

'Go on,' he urged gently. 'The two wardens will follow you, but they'll wait outside the door. You can talk in privacy.'

I walked back to the path. I felt dizzy and breathless. Sounds came and went strangely, the sound of Garry crying, the sound of my feet in the wet grass, the sound of the wind in the trees overhead. I could walk only with the greatest of effort, I was having to push myself forward. I've got to tell her, I told myself. I've got to tell her. But I was frightened. I was terrified. I made it to the path, but I could go no further. I was too scared. I couldn't look at the chapel ahead of me. I looked back, towards the grave. Everyone in the little group had their backs towards me. Except Dr Allen. He was watching me. He nodded and waved at me, smiling encouragingly. He mouthed something, and I understood his words, I kind of heard them, almost as if he'd raised his voice and called out to me.

But the voice I heard was Helen's, or rather just an echo of her voice, and they were her words, the words she'd spoken to me the last time I'd seen her. 'They only want to help you, Will,' she'd said. 'We all do. That's all we want.' But will she feel the same once she knows I'm a murderer?

I took a deep breath and turned back to the path. I began to walk towards the chapel. I could see the two prison guards ahead of me, waiting at the doorway. I tried to imagine Helen inside, a little, skinny, lively girl in the cold shadows. Flame-haired, sharp-featured, in jeans and a suede jacket. Was she standing, frozen in anticipation? Was she restlessly pacing to and fro? Was she sitting calmly? Was she kneeling in prayer? Everything around me seemed to freeze and stop as I walked forwards, the whole world seemed to pause and wait. I could imagine the court-room I would have to face before too long, the judge and barristers unmoving as they waited for me to find Helen and tell her what I had to tell her, waiting for her reaction. I could imagine the prison-cell waiting for me, the rough blankets on the thin mattress, the worn but laundered uniform ironed and folded ready for me. I could imagine Elizabeth and Richard with Mary and Fred on the path across the marshy meadow to the sea, right now, Elizabeth running ahead in her red wellington boots and her little yellow oil-skin, Richard being carried on Fred's shoulders, waving and gurgling at his sister, relishing her speed, her movement, somehow knowing that the time will come when he will be able to share them with her.

The chapel door was closed. Its handle - a big metal ring – hung stiff and cold and heavy. I grasped the ring, turned it and pushed the door open.

Helen was standing with her back to the door, ten yards away in the aisle, her hair bright in the semi-darkness. I saw her jump at the sound of the door creaking open.

Suddenly Elizabeth stops in her tracks. Richard is still and silent. They are both listening and waiting, waiting for their mother to turn and face their father. Waiting for him to tell her what he should have told her years ago. Waiting for her answer. The gulls cry overhead. The waves beat on the shingled shore beyond the sea-wall. The grazing cows watch Elizabeth and Richard. They raise their heads from the lush pasture, their jaws still, their mouths stuffed with unchewed grass, as if they too are waiting to see what the children's mother will do.

Helen turned and looked at me. She was pale and trembling, but she was smiling.

'Have faith' Dr Allen had said, also smiling. 'You must have faith.'

I suddenly realised what his smile had meant. He knows, I thought. He knows that Helen will understand. He knows that she won't condemn me to a lifetime in prison. After all, he understands. He doesn't want me to spend the rest of my life behind bars. That's why he wouldn't let me confess to him. Why would he be sending me to confess to Helen, unless he felt that she too would understand, that she too wouldn't want me to spend the rest of my life in prison?

It was more than I deserved. But Helen had always been more than I deserved. Yes, I thought, I have faith. I took a deep breath and stepped into the chapel.

She came running towards me, laughing. She was crying too. She couldn't speak, but the way she threw her arms round me said it all. "Whatever you have to tell me, I don't care. I know who you are. I know what you are. I know you're a good man. Tell me whatever you have to tell me, but it won't make any difference. It doesn't matter. We still love you."

I was going to tell her everything. And everything was going to be all right.

THE END

25560723R00240

Printed in Poland
by Amazon Fulfillment
Poland Sp. z o.o., Wrocław